Sincerely
Yours...

Sincerely Yours...

Written by Liyah Mai Leoni

First Edition: 2016
First Published Edition: 2019
Cover Photographer Kerian J Daniels
Creative Directors: Sophie Jagne & Davina J Rodriques
Printed in the United Kingdom, England. U.K

www.lmleoni.com

FOCUS

"I've always had this heightened sense of smell. There's nothing better than the person you love and trust having a beautiful scent to them. And I'm not just talking about perfumes or added fragrances we use on a daily basis to enhance it. I'm talking about that natural warmth and essence coming from your skin that lingers on my lips just by kissing you. And how, when you leave an item of clothing with me, I catch glimpses of you racing across my mind just by closing my eyes... and recognising '*you*' trapped in the looms of the woven fabric.

I could find you in a crowded room with my eyes shut tight... It's crazy how I remember the fragrances of them all. Taking me back in time to a moment I can revisit and smile.

It doesn't matter if you broke my heart or not. I still feel you here when I catch a breeze of you in my memory.

If I knew you were going to leave, I would have bottled it up in a never-ending trinket, then placed it on the end of a necklace like a charm; wearing it, keeping it close to my heart. So that every now and then, when I'm missing you the most, I can inhale you... deeply.

Do you remember those nights where I would lay on your chest? Your arms wrapped round my body, my face pressed against your neck, smelling you softly as you drifted off to sleep. I would stay awake with the tip of my nose caressing your soft skin, trying to separate each and every individual scent of you smelling beautifully hypnotic- yes *you*! That husky like sandalwood, amber musk, cedar, mahogany kind of... I can't explain it but then there was this ginger, reminding me of violets. Almost like a purple haze for some reason. Strong like a cactus but warm like sage and so, so sweet. I can't forget the pineapple, berry, lavender and lemon all sitting in your skin, nestled deep in your neck.

But the one thing you smelled like the most... was "*home*", I was home, I was safe... I could have easily stayed there for forever and a day...

Who knew that forever had an end? I should have stayed... *you* should have stayed... we should have stayed *us*.

It's crazy, out of every scent I've come into contact with, yours is the one I miss the most."

- *Liyah Mai Leoni, Confessions of Her.*
//20.04.16

Prologue.

Dear Aaliyah,

Where in the hell did we go wrong? We had simple problems, you not being able to talk to me and avoiding me.

You also have this thing with not trusting me or losing trust in me, but we were happy.
We were okay, right?

I meant it when I said, "I love you." I wanted to believe you meant what you said in return, but I knew you were only telling me what I wanted to hear. I don't really know if you feel the same but that's okay. I can wait for you to feel for me. To be open to me, to maybe one day, love me.

But back to the question at hand, where in the hell did we go wrong?

To be honest with you, you do things to protect yourself from getting hurt. You build up these walls and barriers, and it's starting to pull us further apart, we're going backwards from the beautiful shit we once had.

You have this attitude; I try to talk to you and all you have to say is; *"I don't care." "I can't be bothered." "go away."* *"I don't want to talk about it."* and *"whatever."*
Whatever happens between us, your heart will never get broken because you refuse to use it, you're just protecting it.

As far as myself, I have begun to magnify all your faults and fear you are starting to feel as if you want to maybe move on or you're getting bored of us.
I find it irritating the way you pull yourself away from me. Why do you do this all the time?

I know you won't be able to love me fully. But I cannot let you go. I don't want to ever let you go.

I'm sorry for everything I have done, and for everything I've put you through. For hurting you, I'm so sorry. I mean it when I say I will never call you out of your name again, I will never put my hands on you ever again.

No matter how angry you make me, I promise that this time is the last time I will ever raise my fists to you and I will never ever hit or beat on you again.

I am so sorry baby. Believe me.

I love you, forever and always.
Kisses
Delilah

I can hear her shouting through the house, ranting and raging on about another thing that I haven't done right. Slamming doors for no real reason, until the front door was slammed last.

My eyes full with tears, turning my reflection into a blur. But once I wiped the tears away, I couldn't do it. I couldn't even look at myself... well not directly in the eyes anyway.

Sat at my dressing table taking a look in the mirror past the reflection of who I used to be, onto photos of how it used to be, tucked into the corners of my golden framed vintage rococo mirror. In one of the photos, Delilah's arm was wrapped over me, while kissing me softly. She had to stretch her arm all the way out to get us both in the photo. As big as my smile was that day, it could have easily stretched onto two photos.

Another photo of us, sat on a wall by the River Thames. I was sat in-between Delilah's legs. leaning back into her chest, her big strong arms around me again. I was holding onto her so tightly. It was freezing that day, so windy. I remember it because my hair was blowing in every direction you could think of. I didn't have a jacket and Delilah had given me her massive oversized jumper. It was so soft and smelled of her "everything" along with that wooden, husky men's cologne she always wore. The skin under her neck, right where I rest my face whilst I lay on her at night, smelt like it too.

We had walked up and down the River Thames South Bank most of that day... just us. The sun was starting to set, and we were sitting on this short wall, watching as the city lights began to take over the darkening city sky. Barely talking just adoring the comfort and silence of each other's company. When suddenly, she jumped up and asked a man passing by to take a photo of us. It's such a simple photo. Looking at it, you would have never known how cold we really were, two women sat shivering and holding onto each other. She was protecting me from the cold. She made me feel so safe. So secure, it was perfect.

Now look at us... look at me! A mixture of a colour palette Delilah has painted on my face with her fists: Blue and purple blotches on my skin. Green and yellow from my previous bruises healing, with a drop of red blood falling from my bottom lip. Busted open from my teeth being forced against it too hard and too fast- again.

I should've seen her fist coming, but I never do. I never seem to miss her connection, even though in the back of my mind, I know when it's coming.

I place her letter into a box hidden at the back of the left-hand side top drawer of my dressing table, along with many others she had written to me, all of them arranged in date order. The one I read the most, was dated 13th of May 2005. This day was the first time she raised a dominating hand to me, about a week before my birthday party. Which I had to cancel because my mind couldn't decide on what lie to tell when answering the questions my many guests would have asked me. Like, how I got butterfly stitches by my eye and a broken wrist?

That was three years ago. I don't remember what I did. But I remember the feeling of being thrown across the room, landing on my arm and... hearing that snap of my hand going in the wrong direction.

I like to read the letters to try and remember how it got to this point. But I don't remember much of anything anymore, only how I got this scar or that one really... but I guess three and a half years of constantly getting punched in the head is bound to do that to you. You know, to have some kind of effect on your memory.

But still I sit. Still I stay with the ugly truth of my life plastered all over my face, and after all these years of fist after foot, after fist, after heavy objects about the house she grabs randomly and throws at me- I still have yet to master the simple art of "the dodge."

So, what do I do now? Do I walk out and start again...? (Scared) No. (Weakness) I simply close the drawer, tuck the letters away and attempt to make sense of what I call "The Mess" another wonderful master piece that Delilah has created on my face with her fists. My body covered in unexplainable scars, I hide with my choice of never revealing clothes but I know they are there, reminding me of my life when I can't 'bare' to look at my face. Opening the drawer on the top right-hand side of the dressing table, taking out one of my many bottles of Dettol disinfectant and some cotton padded wipes, I wipe over the split skin and the blood.

I don't flinch from the sting of the antiseptic anymore, I was used to it, practically painless and numb from everything. I couldn't feel much of anything anymore. My makeup that I wear has become heavier than my usual; needs to be thicker layers of foundation, concealer to conceal; the hidden cuts and bruises, brighter lipstick to take the attention away. Smoky blended shades of eye shadow, my new trick to hiding black eyes. Topped off with a darker shade of blusher and contour to shape. Now that I'm done hiding the lies behind the layers of makeup, I can look at my reflection, but not for too long.

Holding my cheek, proud of my patch up, I smile but quickly. Although painless, I can feel my face throbbing. But it's okay, I can smile internally because I know. I know she loves me... she tells me she loves me all the time. I know I make her angry most of the time... I say things that I shouldn't. She's right... it is my fault... I make her behave the way she does. She says, the things that I do make her act this way. Well... that's what she tells me so it must be true... right?

I just can't figure out or know what I do, so I can prevent it or at least calm her down before it happens.

Delilah was gone for now, she'd left out for whatever reason. But my feet are telling me not to move, to stay seated but my brain is telling me to look back at the mirror, really look this time. So I did. And here I am. Or there I was...

Sitting here looking in the mirror trying to recognize myself because I don't look like the girl I used to be and I used to be so happy. And now I'm going through three bottles of foundation a week to keep this cracked picture from breaking into a thousand shattered pieces. But I can feel it all slipping away. I need to fix this with more than an extra coat of make-up to mask over my reality. Look at what I have become, and this life that has become me.

What was left of me? Nothing? (Empty)

Nothing much but empty spaces in my mind from shit I just can't remember or seem to place. Things that my head just couldn't add up, can't add up. I don't know. I just don't know, but shit needs to change. How?

I've always said I would never become the woman my mother is. She's like those women, who always make excuses for every single time an abusive pig of a partner put their hands on them. Blaming it on everyone else, praying they'll change. Praying it was all a dream, but in the morning seeing the latest bruise forming on your skin and trying to think of ways to hide the pain because you love them. Drinking yourself into a numbness so strong because facing your reality hurts way too much.

I thought I was stronger than this! I thought I would never take a beating from anyone and the day my partner so much as attempted to raise their voice to me let alone their hand, would be out of my life before I can say, "what's love got to do with it?"

I'm so tired, battered, drained and lost... I can't keep replaying each day of my life like this something has to change. She's never going to change. I've got to change this! I need to break away from this. I have to do it... today, right now! It's now or never!

Where do I start? What do I take? Where do I go?

My legs spring up and in one clean sweeping movement, brushing my arm along my dressing table my makeup falls into its box. I shoot over to the wardrobe grabbing clothes off the rails, most with the hangers still attached, scratching my hands and forearms stuffing them quickly into the bag that I had hidden between the crack of the wardrobes. For the moment, I found the courage to leave this life and Delilah behind.

Telling myself to move faster, quicker! Quick, quick grab anything. Whatever I can grab, just grab it and go! Grab it and get out! (Bravery)

Where is my purse? I can't remember where I put it? Now is not the time to have a mental memory block of where I put it- shit!

Stop... think for a second, think.

Not in the bedside table drawers, not in my jacket pockets, not on any of the sides and surfaces in the bedroom, shit! Shit!

Where is it? Handbag- no not in there, check my coat pockets again, check my back pockets, where is it? Where?

"*You going somewhere Aaliyah?*" (Power)

SHIT! Shit! Shit...

My feet froze. My body backed up. My heart skipping beats, I can't breathe.

I turn... slowly, cautiously, not moving my hands from my sides. Delilah leant against the door frame of our bedroom; her arms crossed clutching my purse firmly in her hand.

Think before you speak, think before you speak...

"*No... I...was, erm... going to give some of my stuff away to charity, I fancied a change. I, erm thought I would-*"

"*The fuck do you need money for?*"

Cutting into my lie, she steps into the room towards me. I slowly take a left step back. My eyes darting over her trying to find an exit, but she's blocking it. Trying to calculate her next move, but I never get it right.

She said nothing else, she didn't need to because her face said it all, she doesn't believe me.

I didn't believe myself. I mean, my nervous stutter and pauses didn't help my lie, not one bit.

"*I... I thought, I'd go for a haircut or something and b-buy some new things, feel good about myself you know?*"

"*No.*" (Control) *that devious smile she does started to form in the corners of her mouth, now standing over me. I watch my purse disappear into the back pocket of her baggy jeans.*

Although she appears calm, I know this too well; this was just the calm before the storm.

"*No?*" *why did I question the silence? Idiot!* (Stupid).

"*You're not going anywhere!*" *her hand raised.*

"*De, wait- no- uh*", *I had no time to scream, no time to move, no time to run. No time to let any air out.*

The laminate wood flooring suddenly went from under my feet to under my face, hearing my body hit the floor with a collapsing **thud!** *It all happened so fast and slow all at the same time, but there was nothing I could've done. I try to curl my body into a ball, but it was too late. Before I could even think to bring my legs to my chest, I hear the next two thumps;*

Thump! One- her fist on my head.

Thump!! Two- her Timberland boot connecting with my stomach.

I watch the blurred upside-down vision of her Timberland boots walk out of the room and down the hall. Leaving me to find the little strength left in me, to pull myself up off of the blood-stained wooden floor.

Back up onto the stool, doubled over holding onto my ribs. My body pulsating, feeling like if I let go now, I will fall apart and have to pick the pieces of my body up off the floor. Staring at the blood as it seeps slowly into the grains of wood, joining the older darker dried up red stains. All I can think about are the colours that are going to appear all over my body in the morning. Lifting my head up from my lap, I move my hair away from my face...

My reflection more of a blur then before behind waves of tears sitting on my bottom eyelids, focusing my eyes, letting go of my side. I sit up straight, ignoring the aggressive throbs of pain shooting across my body, reminding me that I would be hurting for the next however long...

I start again...

Opening the drawer on the top right-hand side of the dressing table, taking out one of my many bottles of Dettol disinfectant and some cotton padded wipes, I wipe over the split skin and the blood.

I don't flinch from the sting of the antiseptic anymore, I was used to it, practically painless and numb from everything. I couldn't feel much of anything anymore. My makeup that I wear has become heavier than my usual; needs to be thicker layers of foundation, concealer to conceal; the hidden cuts and bruises, brighter lipstick to take the attention away. Smoky blended shades of eye shadow, my new trick to hiding black eyes. Topped off with a darker shade of blusher and contour to shape...

Temptation

/tɛm(p)ˈteɪʃ(ə)n/

noun

To entice (a person) to do something wrong or

unwise to **tempt fate**

Tempt, (fem) **Temptress**

Origin:/ **LATIN**

Temptare
handle, test, try

The desire to do something with or without the intent of hurt.

To take foolish and unnecessary risks.

To do something wrong or unwise.

To entice, lure, urge, seduce, invite, attract, desire, want, need, lust, betray, deceit, lie… cheat…

Temptation is that flickering light in the back of your mind. A flame fighting against the wind of deception, but once the flame has been blown out, the darkness of temptation, that desire and selfishness takes over and the former you is no more...

"You see this is my problem; always wanting shit that wasn't mine… it's not who I am…It's just what I do. And to be honest, I don't - give - a - fuck!"

- Aaliyah Monroe

1. The Cascading Chandelier

"What?! Noooo… I don't. We weren't thinking, it wasn't *that* big of a deal, come on! Seriously? Babe, I don't even like her like that; besides, it's not like we fucked or anything… come on now babe."

Lies. Slipping easily from my mouth and falling into Blue's feeble and fickle mind. You see, Blue rarely listened to anyone but herself anyway and this allowed my lies to move forward fluidly and very quickly.

"Just tell me. Honestly, do you like her?"

Grilling me about my actions the other night, asking me questions that I have no problem answering because I have, of course, pre-calculated all my answers in my head to her questioning me about the same thing- over, and over, and *ov-er* (roll my eyes) a-gain.

"I mean Blue, *really?* Why would I want *your* woman? She's so far from *my* type and has absolutely *nothing* I want. I need a woman who can bring something to the table *I* have provided. It was just like I told you; nothing more than a spontaneous, thoughtless moment… *(Pause for effect, softer tone for delivery, hang head down slightly)* I wasn't thinking babe *(look up, slight sad side head tilt with a bottom lip drop but don't overdo it)* I didn't mean to hurt you in anyway." *(Sorry, not sorry bitch!)*

Watching her twiddle her thumbs, she bites the inside of her mouth looking like she's got it all wrong, like she should have *never* even come at me with *these* accusations at all… she opens her mouth

"No babe… *I'm* sorry" (Jackpot) "I should have *never* questioned you it's, you see. I have this thing about trust and all that and I, erm. I didn't want to put it all on you, but I had to ask, you know? To clear things up?" And just like that, with minimal effort, I am back in control! Regardless of my immoral actions but hey, all is forgiven and I am in the clear so, leave me be.

I sat back, chilling on the small metal balcony of Blue's apartment share in West London. She continues to question me about my intentions.

You see what happened is, I lied to Blue about the other night - well I didn't technically lie but I decided to take… I had a night out with Blue's woman… *without* Blue. And to be honest, there was nothing really to it. It was minor, I mean I don't think it's really *that* big of a deal, I just wanted to have her *all* to *myself* - and!?

"You know, it's okay, right? You can tell me if you like her Aaliyah."

Although sorry for what she said, in her mind she still has room for doubt; asking me the same damn questions over and over like a broken record on repeat, skipping and starting to get on my fucking nerves! Can she put the 'shut' in the 'up' and move on, or? What does she want me to say? Yes? Yes! I like your woman and want her face between my legs?!

"Yes! I like her." I answer loud, her eyes pop out of her head, "but not like that. I don't like her like, *like her, like her,* I just like her like, like her, like her she's cool you know?"

Shrugging my shoulders explaining it to Blue in a way she would get what I meant but be *very* confused all at the same time; she's a little slow like that and I enjoy fucking with her mental, have her over thinking and panicked. She has the funniest little confused face. But if you're having trouble making out the sheer simplicity of the above statement, I'll wait here while you read it three times over until it makes sense to you… go on, go ahead- I'll wait.

You got it? Good! Moving forward.

Today being a hot sunny sexy summer day works perfectly to my advantage, allowing me to wear my blacked-out designer sunglasses; shielding me and my *lying* eyes. It had taken me a while to choose these sunglasses in the store because I had to make sure that number one, they were *completely* blacked out. And number two, that I looked on point in them. And for five hundred and fifty pounds they were *"fool"* proof. Allowing me to sit here; calm, cool, composed and collected, pulling on my menthol cigarette and enjoying the warm yet cool coating of minty smoke drift down my throat and relieve my lungs. Doing what I do best, which is not giving a fuck because I have zero fucks *to* give!

Blue continues talking bullshit, going on and on about being friends forever, about trust, about loyalty and honesty and blah, blah fucking blah!! I stopped listening to Blue's speech a good while back, blocking out her irritating 'trying to be somebody she isn't' type of voice. So, I entertained the conversation she was *clearly* having by herself. with the basic uninterested pretending to listen but yet agree with what she had to say sort of replies like, *"uh huh,"* *"sure,"* *"yeah,"* and *"of course,"* whenever she paused for me to approve whatever the fuck she was saying or when a response was due.

Me, my mind and my eyes are far too busy elsewhere. Observing past Blue and her bullshit, talking shit onto *Mali* through the bedroom window. Sitting on the bed with her back against the wall, listening to music and singing along. I can hear the music ever so slightly but feel the treble and bass vibrating through the metal balcony floor where Blue and I are sat. Blue said it was appropriate to shut the window on our *"private"* conversation out here. I know she's playing detective and will be asking Mali the same questions later, if she hasn't questioned her already. Either way I'm not bothered, as I had already pre-coached Mali on what to say and more importantly what _not_ to say.

Watching and following the words Mali's beautiful lips form, trying to figure out what song she is singing along to. She's zoning out to the music lost in her own vibe. I wish I could leave this stupid balcony, this dry toast solo conversation, climb through the window and get lost inside Mali instead.
Looking up at me, as if she senses me day dreaming in her direction; I smile at her... she smiles back, coyly but swiftly then diverts the attention of her eyes onto anything else other than me, before Blue could even notice our stolen seconds...

Although quick and small as her smile was, it's all I needed. The creases in the corners of her pretty little mouth, followed by her deep dimples in either cheek reassuring me our pages still remained aligned.

Her smile was the first thing I saw...

***

"Hey, I'm Mali!" I heard her voice next.

"Aaliyah." Smiling politely, watching her move as she took my hand to shake, introducing herself boldly.

Well damn! She's fucking hot!

Blocking out the music, I hear only the tone of her husky voice surge through my body like the feeling of the sub bass speakers filling the club with deep vibrations. Her smile stays on her face but coming from the side of her mouth with her pretty slight tom-boyish subtle swag; delicate brown skin, beautiful face and *that* smile I could not stop looking at.

"You alright, yeah?" so smooth giving nothing away, she asks. Engaging pleasantries of small talk.

"Yeah. I'm good." Not asking how she was doing or if she was alright because from what I could see... and from where I am standing, she was *all right!*

"I'll see you around yeah."

"Yeah... Maybe..." I said, with my own smug smile, sitting in the corner of my pout. Not taking my eyes off of her; she turns to her people and I turn towards mine after making a mental note of her body.

Watching the shape of a woman walk away is essential in seeing how she carries herself; highly, head up and confidently whilst she walks away into the crowded club scene.

"She's cute, innit!" My sister shouts in my ear, excited and over eager, extra and cutting into my unsolicited thoughts.

"Yeah she's okay-ish!" I shouted back in her ear with a different look on my face. Scrunching my nose up and waving my hand like Mali was nothing special at all.

Diverting my attention to the rest of the girls in the club that was *rudely* named *Heaven*. Trust me, there's *never* anything "heavenly" up in here to entertain. *Well,* apart from me, that is. The only cute, borderline sexy women - *if* any, were always hard to find or glued to the side and on the arms of them *really* butch bitches. You know, your prototype dick dykes; them not too attractive man looking creations. The ones that make society question the whole lesbian woman to woman love ethic:

> *"If you're attracted to a girl that looks like a man…*
> *Then why aren't you with a man, man!?"*

The ones, if you squint your eyes real tight and real quick, you'd think was a dude. You know, the ones that you have to do a double take on or nudge your friend in the side with your elbow to get their attention on the sly, so that they can confirm that it *is* a chick. But you're still confused because he, I mean *she* is talking with a *really* deep tone or on some next sort of hype acting like "man's not hot"; Walking around with a lean and bop like she's *actually* got a dick and two balls swinging in-between her thick thighs. You *know* what I'm talking about, those *"man dem"* women that are trying *so* fucking hard to prove their *"male dominance"* they've forgotten they've got body, breasts and a pussy that they bleed from monthly just like the rest of us *females*. Which after my first *"woman"* is a road I will *never* take a stroll down on a dark night- *EVER* again!? Trust me! Tomboyish and pretty with hints of femininity, yes. Borderline man looking and hench, not so much.

To this day they puzzle me. I mean, isn't the whole point of being a lesbian the fact that you are two *women*? That within the dynamics of your relationship there isn't the whole *"male vs. female"* who wears the trousers bag of egotistical bullshit going on? What? You thought just because you wear a fitted hat and Timberland boots, you think you're entitled with the rights to "act" as the dominant one in the relationship?

22

Uh, uh honey! Since *when* has dominance been down to dress sense? When did wearing a certain aesthetic of clothing enable you to take control? Dominance is a state of mind; an inner trait and ability to influence and control (dominate) a situation, moment, place, or person with an air of power.

It is most definitely not referring to oneself and fellow female associates as 'man like Rachel' or 'man dem'. Putting on an act, pretending you don't like to be forced down onto the bed and given some head so good, your Bambi legs can't even get up because your clit is still throbbing, body is still shaking. No, you want to play:

"Lay down and take this plastic D!"

Huh?? Sorry, you what mate? No, Young M.A, no one will be deep throating your plastic penis. No plastic sausage allowed around here. Thank you and goodnight!

But it's like there's this 'unwritten rule of lesbian initiation'. That you have to look a certain way, act or be a certain way, like you either have to be a stud or be with a stud. Who the hell carved out the commandments of lesbianism?

Stud *noun*

A lesbian woman who identifies with an external appearance of a dominate male role. An attitude and swag and does not conform to the social standards of a feminine woman. They are more masculine and dominate within a relationship. Normally seen wearing men's clothing which aids to their "act" and "look" of intimidation.

Other names: Butch, Butch –Broad, Dyke, Doms, Tommy, Daddy, Zaddy.

Ladies, please, if you find yourself attracted to these types of women, you should *staaaaaap* baby girl! Stop and go running like 'run forest, run' back to men. Because that's clearly what you're attracted to. Chances are you're probably a pillow princess, doing absolutely nothing in bed but laying on your back! Yes, you! I'm talking to you! The woman who lies back talking shit about:

"My baby gets pleasure from pleasing me."

Oh girl! Bye!! Stop talking shit! Shut the fuck up and start licking something! As much as I don't understand or get the overly stud/butch lesbian women, *these* so-called 'pillow princesses' aka 'lazy lesbians' aka 'don't want to touch nothing' ones are far fucking worse! They make me itch! Like, what are you here for? To be pretty?!

Don't get me wrong, I do have my lazy nights, when all I want to do is relax, get fucked and leave without returning the favour. But my point is, there is a whole lot that even I- yes me, a whole lesbian, question about lesbians in general and I'm sure you do to. But just because I am a Lesbian myself, does not mean that *I* am a walking manual for 'Lesbianism Handbook 101' or that I agree with everything they/we say or do.

For starters why are lesbians the only sexuality with subcategories? They all sound like character preferences rather than real sexualities. I scroll through these dating apps for the fuck of it (literally) and I see so many damn orientations: Lesbian, Bi, Stud, Stemme, Femme, Butch, Fluid, Tomboy, Pansexual, Blahsexual, Queer, Androgynous. It's all too much; all I want to know is do you like pussy or nah bitch? Maybe I should make my own app because I don't have time.

My type of woman, is *any* woman 'type of woman' (look at me just expressing my 'hoe is life' ways) Don't get it twisted, she needs to be a beautiful, pretty, bad ass, boss bitch (not a worker bitch) And if I like you… then I *like* y. o. u. the question is, can you handle me?

Any-way, the point is, it's always fun taking those pretty ones off of their stud and showing them what a *real* woman is all about. But only for the night, never much else really. I am not about that commitment life, I'm more of a… *hoe*-how do I put this, hmm? I'm a get up and go kind of woman. Literally the kind that will 'get up and go' once I get mine- ciao! The kind you *don't* want to bring home to your mama or get too attached to. The woman you hate to love, but like many, cannot help the fall. And once there, allowing me, my ways and my bloody shoes to take a walk up, down and *all - over - you.*

So, let the night be what it is, just don't expect me to be there in the morning. Because honey, I do not do breakfast, lunch or dinner... I only do dessert! And trust me when I tell you, as sweet as it tastes, you'll be calling me, begging me for more. Unfortunately for you, I won't answer or I haven't even given you my number. Why you ask? Come on, if I give out my phone number to every female I come into contact with, I'd have to hire a little Asian call centre of my own to take all the calls because unlike Drake, I *know* when that hotline bling's, it's most definitely means *more* than one thing and I am not here for any of it!

I do not need twenty voicemail, ninety-nine missed calls, fifty-two texts and twelve paragraphs telling me I'm a horrible person or a bitch because you *knew* that the day we met. Now you're doing all of that turning up to houses unannounced and uninvited, crying over fingers. Calling from private withheld numbers a million times and not saying nothing when I answer, that desperate shit is not attractive! Get the point it's done, I'm officially done with you. Thanks for the experience, now - let - it - the - fuck - go! (imagine the dashes are clapping hand emoji for the effect ladies)

The only women that are *privileged* enough to call my hotline are the ones that intrigue me from day dot or who give me that really good, *goood* sex. I *know*, *you know* what I'm talking about! That get the sheets fucking *drenched*, light a damn cigarette and have me wanting more and more 'type of sex.' The type of sex that will have the neighbours knowing your name, email address and national insurance number! The type of sex that will make you so fucking hungry after you cum and buss so hard that all you want to do is turn to the person beside you in the bed or whatever surface you've finished on from round to round, win, lose or draw fuck session and whisper sweetly in their ear:

"Go make me a sandwich bitch!"

***

Bored of my sister trying to shout a pointless conversation in my ear over the club base banging music. I cut her off mid-sentence with a dismissal flick of my hand and headed to the toilet to check myself out in the mirror one last time. I have to make sure I'm looking on point and that I stay slaying- which I always did and always do but still, it never hurts to double check that you're looking like a snack.

Beautiful brown, cocoa, soft, highly melanated, arc-android orchestrated skin. Long black wavy hair and yes, before you ask *(roll my damn eyes)* yes, I wear weave. What girl doesn't these days? Even you pretty little white girls, I see you out here baby girl; trying to culturally appropriate *another* thing from the culture of black beautiful women. The same white girls who had something to say about our big lips in school are now the same girls filling their "no lips" getting operated on to get hips and injecting their booty. When back in the day if that same *'omg does my butt look big in this?'* Becky would refuse to eat for weeks. Now here's Becky; tanned and bodied by the surgeon Dr Miami, looking *rather ethnic* with her "box braids" and two mixed race kids- okay, let me not, not today. Let me get back to <u>me</u>. This is after all, why you're here right?

My hair (weave) falls over my shoulders onto my tattooed arms and back. Tattoos cover a lot of my body but don't you worry, I'll tell you more about those later when the layers of my clothes come off of my skin and hit the floor.

5ft.5, with brown eyes. I'm always in heels so I appear taller with my little sexy self. Dressed in black skinny high waist jeans and a white vest top two sizes too small, complimenting my waist and my double D borderline, E cup breasts. Topped off with minimal gold accessories and a watch sitting pretty on my dainty wrist. Oh, and not forgetting the just in case, naughty *fuck me* thongs sitting on my ass and another to change into in the morning tucked away in the zip compartment of my oversized clutch bag. Listen, you never know whose bed the night will put you in. A woman needs to stay ready, so always carry that 'Just in Case Kit' baby!

Just in Case Kit *noun*

A small sized bag easy to hold, conceal or place in your car consisting of various essential items you will need "just in case" you do not go home. Each bag is different, catering to individual person's needs that allows the so-called *"walk of shame"* to look absolutely fucking flawless! Am I right? Of course, I am!

Mine, for example purposes consists of: A fresh pair of thongs, toothbrush, packet of makeup wipes, mascara, foundation, a brush, a hair band to tie up my hair from whatever state the previous night left it in, mini perfume, deodorant, moisturiser *and* sometimes a change of clothes. All concealed and tucked away in the boot of my car because I do *not* wake up like this. All of this takes effort, art and time.

Not conceited to say that I'm beautiful or sexy or stunning but I'll tell you anyway I am beautiful, sexy, stunning and fucking bang-ing! Confidence runs through me! I *do* love me some *me*. Besides, I got the sauce! Know that I am saucy!

The Sauce *noun*

Used to describe a characteristic of someone who is right in every way.

Someone who has a sense of 'greatness' to them in their air, presence and approach. Who beams a certain confidence, self-assurance, attraction and aura like no other - unique. Everyone wants to know or get to know them.

Sauce cannot be purchased. It is an element of yourself that no one has. So amazing, you could get lost in the sauce.

"If a woman does not have the sauce, then she is lost. But the same woman can get lost in the sauce she has"
- Gucci Mane

Lesson being, don't get lost in it.

The sauce is *so* good I got my ex and *her* ex stalking me daily! Watching my Instagram feed closely. Trust me, if I wasn't me then girl, I'd be fucking with me! Hard! In every position! Shit, I'd fall in love with me the first day I met me. #*Justsaying* #ineedmeame and I appreciate the body and skin that I'm in. You only get one life, one body, one mind and one soul. Sis, you *have* to love yourself, because no one can love you like you can. (Especially, if you know where your spot is, ouuu girl!) So, always take the time to appreciate who you are! Go on, take a minute to reflect on yourself and how much of a bad ass, boss ass bitch you really are and repeat after me:

> *"I love you bitch, you are fucking beautiful bitch!*
> *Keep doing you boo boo!"*

Follow it up with *"yaaassss bitch!"* a flick of your hair, your weave or your lace front wig over your shoulder. And if your hair is short, flick your earring or run your hand down the side of your neck and really *feel* yourself bitch! Feels great, doesn't it?

Okay, enough about you, let's get back to *me*! This is *not* some self-help "new year, new me, who dis?" bullshit 'secret' change your life type of book. I mean, it may help in some way but it will be done *my* way... The Aaliyah Monroe Way. So, feel free to grab a note pad, pen or highlighter and take notes at any point you feel inspired. This is your book, you paid for it so go crazy girl! Highlight the shit out of it!

(No refunds though sis- please see terms and conditions. Every purchase is final- LOL!)

Applying my diva deep dark rouge lipstick, I caught the reflection of Mali looking *my way*. I decide to ignore her. You know, pretend not to see her attractive self and continue my touch up, along with the many women here for the bathroom break/mirror session. Knowing she *is all the way* watching my every single move! Her eyes don't stray from my body, leaning into the mirror... all slow... and suggestive. Arching my back just a little while finishing my touch-up, keeping an eye on her trying to take her eyes off of me. #mezzed #gotcha

Mali has an ever so slightly tomboyish look, but it was this attractive, soft, pretty girl swag about her, something rare that you don't really get these days. She's got on fresh white trainers, boyfriend fit ripped jeans that bagged only a little in the right places but held onto her thick thighs tightly. White t-shirt tight-fitted perfectly to her very feminine deceiving frame. Tiny waist, curvy hips and nice round big booty. She has a slim beautiful frame, with the curvy indentations on her body that I like and peeped from the mental note I took earlier. Her long jet-black thick hair lay smoothly pulled back and tied in a ponytail. Falling over her left shoulder, past her breasts and hitting her waistline. Mascara on her very long full eyelashes, complementing her beautiful big but gentle very light brown, almost hazel eyes. The eyes that lighten with the summer days and darken in the fall; you could get lost looking in them. Kissable lips with a pale nude pink almost clear gloss on them. She reminded me of a young Sanaa Lathan from her Love and Basketball days. Striking feminine features that pop through this foreign skin tone of a golden sun kissed mixed race but fair brown kind of tinted caramel brown and- I don't know really but everything about her is different and *nothing* like anything I've seen before… hard to describe but stunning to look at… I like it, umm.

Mali knew she looked good but I didn't need her knowing that I thought she did too. So, I kept my eyes drifting onto her and other things, purposely catching her eye, making her wonder if I was looking at her or not at all. I like that I have the ability to make people question themselves through my actions. A natural ability you attain when you embody 'the sauce'.

"Yo Aaliyah! What's good babes?" For fuck sake-eerrr!!

My concentration on Mali, broken by an insignificant bunch of loud ass associates walking into the toilets shouting out my name like they know me, but they don't *know* me. Urgh! An-noy-ying girls, you see, (and try to avoid) in the club on a regular basis that *think* they know you on a personal level. I call them *"insignificants"*.

Insignificants *noun*

Definition: Level one basic bitches. Girls/women that just are not in your lane and never going to be on your level. Whose sole purpose will be to adore you, appreciate you and want to claim that they know you. (roll eyes)

Other names: Beg friends/Groupies/Fans/Followers/Supporters/Dem girls der.

Well, here they are surrounding me, like we laugh and kiki together. Usually telling me shit like I give a fuck about their opinions or approval of me:

"How you been?" "You look sooo dope." "Love the tattoos." "You're too much babe, you gotta style me." "How'd you get your hair like that though?"

I'm not going to lie to you, although they are *irritating* as fuck! I *love* the attention of the insignificants. The way I see it is this- Oh, remember when I said, feel free to take notes at any point? Here's your moment, get your highlighter ready.

[start highlight here] There's nothing wrong with having a gang of cheerleaders routing for you. Because you're going to get insignificants/groupies like these lot over here and you're going to get the haters somewhere way, *way* over there. So, keep your *groupies* happy and let the haters *hate* to wonder *why* you have so many fucking groupies! [end highlight here]

I always pacify my adoring fans and the public crowd of appreciation with a fake smile, a tilted head movement, slightly scrunched shoulders and a fake:

"Aww thanks. Yeah, I'm good. Have a goodnight, yeah."

Keep it simple, look entertained, be gracious, accept the compliments and do not, I repeat **DO NOT** return *any* compliments at all! Chances are they'll probably never look as good as you or are wearing something that is completely inappropriate for their body mass index. Walking around looking like they don't give a fuck about how they look, which is cool. But you can have all that confidence and wear whatever you want but... just not next to me. My girl, tuck in your belly over there somewhere please and thanks.

Even, if the insignificants *do* look good, still, do not compliment them. Because it's a trap and *will* open a conversation you have no interest in and make them think that they are your equals- lol no, *no*! *We* do not socialise with basic bitches that are beneath us and not in our lane. Keep it moving along swiftly, but sweetly.

Turning back to the mirror, a quick whip of my hair, a "yaasss bitch" said in my head and glance over my shoulder at my booty. I say my goodbyes and walk through the group of insignificants, straight towards Mali. *Purposely*, engaging my eyes in her direction and brushing my soft skin against her, right as she attempts to get me in conversation but I pass her and turn away. She squeezes my arm lightly, attempting to get my attention but I act like I didn't feel anything or notice her at all and continue with my gracious exit. But I *know* she's watching me leave. You'd be fucking crazy not to watch all of *this,* walk away baby! And that's a fact!

Note: *Attention*

To get the attention of someone you want, don't give them any *attention* (sounds tricky but keep following.) You're in a social setting; a club, a house party, bar, shoobs, motive or whatever it is- you are there. You see a woman or man (listen, I do not have time to appeal to all, so please insert 'his', 'him' and 'he' where appropriate, thanks.) You like what you're seeing, you want her and you're wondering… what she would be like between your sheets or her sheet or her legs or yours. Follow these next very simple steps to get what you want:

Step One: *Brief encounter*

Go over and initiate a *brief* moment of light conversation- it *has* to be small. I'm talking two minutes tops. Smile and give her all the signs that you're interested. Now you've entered her space, she is "expecting" you to request her phone number, Instagram, snapchat, some kind of social connect or contact details.

Step Two: *Don't You Dare!*

Don't ask for any, not a single one! End the convo abruptly and walk your pretty self away. Sounds a little harsh but, trust me, she is all the way thrown off! She's thinking why *wouldn't* you have asked for her number? Why did you go over there in the first place? Now she's stuck thinking about you.

Step Three: **_Ignore her ass_**

For the rest of the night- ignore the shit out of her. Give your attention to the other women, laugh at shit jokes, kiki and blush. Because _the woman whose attention you want is watching you_ closely! Trust me, you have her full attention! She is trying not to but can't help her eyes wandering in your direction. It's only a matter of time until she walks on over to your space – Bonne appétit baby!

Back to the club; packed from wall to wall and popping off like it's usual Wednesday night settings; full to the brim with people from _all_ walks of life and out for a lit night.

Heaven has countless of different rooms and areas with music catering to the extensive lesbian, gay, bi, pansexual, transsexual, and transgender folk.

The androgynous, insatiable, open, fluid, fruity, eager, keen, kinky and everything in between that London has to offer.

Stepping in this club is almost like falling down the white rabbits' hole into a wonderland (wonder-_lust_ if you will) of all sorts of people.

Once you step down the steep stairs into the low red lit club entrance, past the tall, stocky and big for no good reason drag queen of all queens that always stood there in some deep bondage, latex, bright fluorescent and fluffy face mask, big hair and ridiculously high heels that I cannot imagine any woman walking in. Tread through the fluttering gay fairies full of sparkle and glitter. In their crop tops, doing death drops in short shorts and endless pouted, glossed and fully loaded pumped lips. Holding loosely onto their glasses with pinkie fingers extended, while using their other hand to explain things _so the-atric-cally_. Dragging out their words making sentences sound sooooo many seconds longer than what they needed to be:

"like ooooh myyy god baaabe! Honeeestly right, I could noooot be-liiieve it."

Past the fresh out of the office had way, way, _waaaay_ too much to drink at the pub, now 'how the hell did we end up here it's only Wednesday?' Feeling all kinds of fruity, straight as a ruler work associates, who will have one too many stories and blanks to fill in at the office over the morning coffee pot with blushing faces and whispers about what the boss *"didn't do last night"*.

Past the bar where couples stuck to each other's faces, lost in the lust and the public display of affection that a new relationship brings. Holding tight onto hips that barely move to the rhythm of any beat but hands hold them anyway.

Through the main dance floor where the *'oh la la'* look at me 'I'm *sooo* gay' ambassador kind of gays and lesbians swing from poles, dancing with their hands in the air, high off their faces from *who* knows what sort of drugs.

You know the kind I'm talking about, the ones that taste the rainbow, shit the rainbow, proud to be a part of the rainbow, have the rainbow flag emoji in their bio or name on Instagram, hashtag every post #LGBTQ. Hoping to bring likes and follows from their fellow gay brethren across the globe who hang a rainbow flag from their windows or around their necks at gay pride and talk all god damn day about the fucking rainbow and answer when asked:

"So, tell me something interesting about yourself..."
. *"Well, I'm a lesbian..." [or whatever sexuality they are]*

Really bitch? *Really*?? That's the *only* thing interesting about your entire existence? That you like the same sex? Well, If I could insert an upside-down face emoji in right <u>here</u> I would! Please, get the fuck out of here with that bullshit answer!! Your sexuality is not *who* you are its' a - you know what... never mind because I'm going off subject- again, so let me not even and focus. Otherwise I'll be here all day telling you how much I <u>cannot</u> with *these* kind of people.

Anywaaaaays- in the club, you go through the double doors at the back where the transgender, cross dressers, transitioning and transitioned roam freely proud among themselves, gallivanting and grabbing any piece of ass that walks past- *but* will most likely, if not always end the night with each other because... well... how can I put this without sounding like- fuck it, they've just got the spare bits, pieces and parts that each other need, right? (Think about it, take a second… *ting*) Penny dropped yet!?

My crew of people and I always place ourselves under the radar in the "urban" room as *they* call it, because *they* don't want to say "black" or "black-ish". Located on the top floor of the club where they played the kind of music that I live for. It doesn't matter if you are slow dancing with the person you're fucking with, getting lit with your people, dancing on your own moving your waist and feeling the bass run through your body, there is always a vibe!

So, I'm here right- dancing slowly along with Nova my club *heux.*

Club Heux (hoe) *noun*
Definition: Not a friend or someone you kick it with on a regular basis or depend on for anything at all, but a girl that can go hard & knows how to party hard. Where the 'turn ups' is at. She is the connect, the social link, socialite or plug to the events you *need* to be at. No invite or guest list required because she is getting in regardless and she always has a good fucking time. Phone calls usually consist of:

> *"Hey girl what you doing tonight? You coming to*
> [insert club name or motive here]? *It's gonna be fucking lit bitch!"*

Nova holds onto me, using my body like a stripper pole- as you do. We're always so provocative together. I'm standing with my arms up and running through my hair whilst she twirls that ass around me. Dancing, bending over and looking back at me, watching me watching her twerk- God *Dayum*!

Nova has this way of looking at you or touching your body that makes you -let me not, I can't focus. She's soo so fucking sexual and seductive. She has this thing about her femininity that makes me want to grab her and fuck – *buuuut,* I would never go there because she's also is my *untouchable* and I am hers.

Untouchable *noun*
Definition: That one bad ass fucking bitch you roll with.

You both want to fuck each other because you know it would be fucking a-maz-zing but would *never* dare to. Because you're both a pair of two *completely* complicated unemotional sexual driven, sexy, bad and boujie bitches.

Other names: Homie. Lover. Friend. Aka *Boss Ass Bitch and My Down Ass Bitch.*

Tipsy and getting lit with the rest of my Club Heuxs and my -wait for it … Wait… are you ready? I don't think you're ready because I wasn't ready. Okay let me start again below.

Tipsy, partying and getting lit with the rest of my Club Heuxs; my recently out for the moment trying to emulate me, some kind of gay sister

Samantha!

Cue the trumpets, Cue the horns. Cue the mother fucking bullshit!

Samantha and I were born only thirteen months apart by different dads- yeah, I know my mum's a hoe.

Me and Samantha could *not* be more different if we tried. Believe me, we tried time and time again and continue to fail to have some kind of *"sister-ship"* but it never lasts. Deep down, we really don't like each other – well, I know I don't like her on most days.

We spent the majority of our childhood ignoring each other, kicking the shit out of each other or plotting to kill each other. I couldn't stand her and I *may* have attempted to smother her with a pillow in her sleep, after being forced to share a room with her for three weeks as punishment. One more week and I *would* have killed her, facts! Oh, don't be shocked, it was exactly how I said it was, <u>we</u> (yes, her and I) attempted (multiple times) to kill *each other* growing up.

There was this one time, she put a glass tumbler on the floor at the foot off the bed which I jumped off of, landed directly on top of and it practically took my toes off! Luckily for me, all five little piggies made it but I *still* have the fucking scars on the ball of my foot from the doctors and nurses pinning me down and stitching my foot back together again - evil little bitch!

She hated everything I said or did, I couldn't tell you why?? But she always had and continues to have something smart to say about the way I do *anything*. Now look, here she is up in the club trying to look like… a slightly older version of me? Who knows? I'm trying to figure it all out because next week she'll probably be off changing her name by deed poll, wearing a headscarf, dressed from head to toe in a burka and praying to the skies. Or prancing around like a fool offering herself to the sun and sea as a free wisdom, spirited away, holistic vegan who loves everything- bullshit!

Samantha has too much time on her hands! She's out here experimentally changing her identity and picking up hobbies- along with men.

Samantha hasn't worked since who knows when. No job, no education, five kids and four-hundred-pound designer shoes on her feet that mine and your taxes pay for. Shout out to the U.K Benefit System. Yes, my sister is *that* "benefit mum." The one that has no control over their children, that you see them pushing a tangent buggy with too many damn babies. Whilst the eldest kid is running loose down the road, ignoring her, laughing and telling her to 'fuck off'. While she's trying to catch up to him screaming, he's a little shit and involving people in her discipline. Why the hell do useless parents do that? Use strangers as a threat to their children?

"That lady is going to tell you off?"

The fuck I am? I will kick your kid, you better move and leave me alone.

My sister has absolutely nothing going for her at all; my bet is she'll be pushing forty, pushing out her eighth baby and still pushing in the queue at the benefits office and signing on for another week.

I prefer not to tell people I have family, let alone siblings to claim and she's *here* telling everyone in the club she comes into conversational contact with her that I'm her sister. They stare at us, wondering how the hell can a light skin borderline Caucasian looking chick be sisters with a brown skin melanin popping queen like myself. Oh, come on, like it's the weirdest thing out here?

No, what the weirdest thing out here is an Eastern European blonde white woman transitioning herself into becoming a *black woman* through chemical injections and body modification. Like you can just pop to the supermarket and *buy* melanin in a jar off the shelf!? They are injecting her with melanin?! Whose melanin is she getting?? What black person do you know who will *willingly* give up their melanin?? Well, apart from Vybz Kartel & Spice but that's beside the point- they are a different kind of exception that no one is claiming. The point is, this woman seems to be spending a lot of time in Africa with under privileged communities though? Just saying, this is obviously where all that melanin could be coming from. Have you seen 'it' (her)?

Well if you haven't, take a moment, pull out you phone and Google the name 'Martina Big'. What the fuck is that all about?

Let's get back to *my* night.

Singing away, lost in the music agreeing with Trey Songz because *I* know I only came here for two reasons. I came for the *ladies* and the *drinks!!* And I'll take them in that order… or in reverse or at the same time.

        "Having fun?"

That voice, entering my ear once again sending way, *way* too many tingles to my toes. Mali stood beside me, smiling that perfect bright Colgate white smile; looking so fucking sexy!!

Everything about her makes me wonder… what does she taste like? I bet she's sweet. Biting and licking the inside of my lip, imagining the smallest drop of her right there on it. Ummm! I can imagine the taste already. But I better answer her question before she thinks I'm crazy as fuck, standing here not taking me eyes off of her, giving her that I want to fuck, "come here girl, sit on my face" face.

        [**Side note:** Oh, remember what I said earlier about getting *attention.* Well, it works. She's in front of me giving me her *full* attention. Stay with me, there's so much more to learn.]

"Yeah, I guess I am!" Letting go of my lip, my mouth finally decides to answer her. The music switched to a slower beat; Ciara's Body Party fills the club. I. Fucking *love* this song!

"Come here."

Without hesitation she pulls me towards her, embracing my waist while our bodies move, matching rhythms perfectly. Her hands syncing with my curves whilst I move my body from left to right, I follow the beat of the music and she follows me. Her palms hold tighter, her fingertips dip, gripping me not letting go, not missing a single move I made. She can't keep her hands off me. Strobe lights and other coloured lights flash across her beautiful face as it gets closer to mine. I can't lie, I won't lie; she's amazing and I can see temptation rising in her eyes while her body is calling me, she shouldn't fight it. Moving closer, dancing on me; we're in a zone, she's got me so excited- it's me on her and her on me. (see what I did there? Played with the lyrics of the song? I'm not just a pretty face)

Her lips so close to mine, drawing me in closer and closer. She smells like a tropical fusion of cocoa butter, sweet mangos, diced pineapples and hot smooth chocolate. Fuck me, she smells so damn good!

I have always had this strong sense of smell, heightened by my desire, lust and attraction. I cannot resist a woman who smells amazing! I remember *every single* perfume and skin scent of my ex's, y's- as in *why* did I go there, we all have those, don't judge.

Picking up each individual scent of Mali smelling too damn fucking good. I'm not talking about her perfume or cream. No, I'm talking about the warmth of her natural skin scent taking my thoughts to higher heights. I turn my body, back against her front; swinging my hips, pushing against her body frame. She follows my rhythm daring not to touch too much but touching just enough. I can feel myself melting for this woman, pussy fluttering and pulsing for this woman.

It could be the nine, maybe ten drinks I had in my system but my mind is doing the most! Somersault thoughts thinking about the damage I could do to this woman and what she could do to me. Thinking about us… one night, two girls lost in a bed for hours and hours, twisted in the sheets or on the floor, or the staircase, or in the shower, or against the walls even up on the fucking ceiling! Shit! Anywhere, anytime and *any* surface, body to body, don't tell nobody! Fingers and tongue inside and all around my dripping wet pussy! Fuck yes!

"Where's Blue?" Come again, say what?
That's when it hit me! Like a double decker night bus full of strays, drunks and nutters at dirty o'clock in the morning. Trying to get back home from whatever they've done, did and sniffed during the previous night of shameful madness in Central London. Fuck, fuck, fuck!!! My dirty, filthy, racy mindless thoughts of Mali on top of me twisted in sheets fucking the night away till morning, halted. This *whole* time I was picturing Mali doing whatever she wanted to do to me, I had *forgotten*. Forgotten that she's my *friend's* woman… my *longest friend's* woman!!

[**Side Note:** Just so you know the words '*best*' and '*friend*' are compound words that sound like child's play to me. Beside you can't be my *best* friend when I'm clearly the best, so…]

My body stiffened, frozen against the music. Removing her hands, that held onto my waist comfortably, like she was *single* and out here to be taken, like she wants to know my body. I step out of her grasp and attempt to push all my dirty reckless and naughty thoughts to the back of my filthy dirty nasty brain. But I want her *sooo* bad, I can taste her! Fuck!!
Trying hard to conceal my attitude, however, my face is a snitch and by the way she is looking back at me, my face is telling her I'm not impressed. The alcohol is making me to struggle to answer her question with my usual quick petty snap back or clap back capabilities. I can feel my attitude creeping slowly up my throat and out my very big 'no filter' mouth- it's too late. My 'zero fucks given' had long taken over my body, way back when she decided to come over here and interrupt me with her "Having fun?" self.

"She's your woman, you should know, shouldn't you? *Ooorr* do you not have your shit on lock like that? I mean..." Me, standing in some ghetto stance waiting for her to respond to me, hands on my hips and raised eyebrows like I even do that. Head tilted to the side. What am I doing? Is my name Felicia or Shanaynay Keisha to be acting like this? No, it's not. It's Aaliyah Monroe, so get your shit together, take your hand off your hip and at act like the boujie bitch you know you are!

"She's your friend Miss Aaliyah, you should know."

She tilts her head mirroring mine, attitude all over her face with her neck stretched forward. She's not serious, come on, say something!? Don't just stand here, she *clearly* doesn't know who the fuck you are- you better tell her! Go on, tell her!! Looking over my shoulder, trying to figure out who the fuck she's talking to because it could never be me!? I am not the one, no one talks back to me?

One hand still sat on my hip, like I didn't just tell myself to take it off. The other hand swaying in the air, waiting for my 'shouldn't have had all those drinks' alcoholic tongue to form a response. I waited... she waited... I opened my mouth we waited... and

"Well I guess den, wear, we are, booth fucked!! You're a shit ghoul friend, I'm a shiat fence."

That's it...? That's *all* my brain could deliver. *Really?* What kind of confusion of back chat, bullshit gibberish talk was that? Oh, you thought that was a typo? Nah! Go back read it again but this time, I'm going to need you to see the tipsy words, talking shit with a tiny hiccup at the end for the perfect delivery and maybe you'll get what the fuck my drunk ass was *trying* to fucking say! I'm a mess, I know. I apologise.

For those of you who don't read alcoholic, the correct Aaliyah Dictionary translation is available below and continuous on next page depending how the printing of this book went:

Translation: *(What I was trying to say and thought I said when in reality I said the above mess)*

"Well then I guess we're both fucked! You're a shit woman, seeing as though you don't know the current location of your woman and we can both see that I don't give a fuck either because I've fucked you in my mind and wouldn't mind doing round two right here, in the middle of the club! In front of everyone! Because obviously, I think I'm Trey Songz out here, acting like I'm about to dive in and be Mrs Steal Your Girl!"

She chuckles at my honesty and attitude *(let's be shit together)* biting my tongue trying *not* to say a-noth-er word. Not another stupid drunk fucking word!

So where does the conversation go from here? She looks around and over her shoulders, I looked over mine to see my people watching me closely, shaking their heads with that *"Aaliyah, what are you doing?"* look all over their faces. But I'm not *doing* anything wrong, right?? All I'm doing is talking to the woman, who happens to be my friend's woman... so? What, Blue's not here *and* I am not doing anything to interrupt 'couple's paradise' because we -are- just- *talking,* relax! Seriously- I don't know who I'm trying to convince, myself or you. Because we both know my intentions are to fuck, lol!

"Ima buy you a drink?" Alright T-pain, although I am secretly hoping that her next thing she said is *"then Ima take you home with me-ee?"* Like I need another drink in my system but let's be honest, I practically bleed tequila so in theory, another drink won't *technically* hurt.

"Sure, *but* it better have two ice cubes, a little bit of apple juice, don't bother coming back if it's not a double!" My hands busy emphasising the size of the drink I wanted. Then I wiggle two fingers in her face making sure she got the double measurement I am expecting.

"I'll be right back." Winking at me, she disappears deep into the darkness and crowded people towards the bar.

***

"You know Mali… it's really *me* you should be thanking for having your woman, in your life"

Composing myself, trying to make the borderline drunk me disappear by applying what I believe to be a very good sober poker face. Although my speech is currently clear, the alcohol units in my body are floating around in my stomach, have taken control and were not allowing me to shut the fuck up and find my filter.

You know that one friend you can't take anywhere; the one who doesn't think before she speaks, has a big mouth and says it like it is. You know that friend, you *always* have to apologise for because she labels her 'no behaviour' as honesty…? Well, I am that friend! But don't go apologising on my behalf because I'm not sorry for the shit that I say- I said, what I said!

"You were thinking about that one for a while now, huh Miss Aaliyah?" She laughs at my trying to concentrate, mouth to the side face.

"Well yeah… be-*cause* it's the truth! I'm being honest." I said after a long uninterrupted pause.

"Is it now? Tell me how, I'm curious."

"Yes! It-is *now!*"

Nudging her in her side with my elbow, mocking the way she spoke. She's unfazed by everything I've said so far during this conversation of me saying shit that I have no business saying and should *not* be saying but… I'm going to say it anyway. She leans into me, interested in what I would shout out next over the music and in the direction of her ear.

We have been sat in this small arch of the club, on a ledge step type thing that's about three or so foot high off of the floor along the walls of the club. *Which* Mali had to give me a boost onto because, along with my words, alcohol also decided it was a bit of banter to fuck with my ability to balance. Nevertheless, I am not complaining, having felt Mali's strength hold and lift my body up on to the ledge. Which sparked a very creative sex position in my mind… that I am obviously *not* going to do! (You know I will) But for now, I'll keep it deposited in my bank of dirty thoughts that is currently over flowing. [insert river reference here] – because I can't think of one.

"Go on then, tell me, I wanna know…" she nudged me, the same way I nudged her, encouraging me to keep talking.

"If your woman wasn't trying to be me so damn bad, she wouldn't even know about the existence of your pussy, baby girl!" How's that for honesty? Too much? Yup! Oh well.

"Seriously?" She practically choked on her drink not expecting me to say that at *all*.

"As serious as a multiple orgasm babe. And *they* are *very* fucking serious! So, if your inexperienced woman hasn't given you one yet… I'd be more than happy to assist." Mali's mouth dropped open with a slight smirk of shock while I kept that serious resting 'fuck around and find out' face on.

Wait? Did I really say that… out loud? Whelp, I'm obviously waved so, I might as well keep talking. If you're going to be wrong, be *wrong* and *strong*. No point in back tracking on your words and trying to take it back. I said, what I said and its fucking facts!

Blue is yet another one of these straight girls and women who jump in the *"Pussy Wagon"* take it for a ride one long weekend and hand the keys back. Grateful for the experience, like it's a car rental customer service survey that needs to be filled from one to ten, for satisfactory. This is happening now more than ever and my sister is another example of this type of confused female. Like all the girls on social media out there kissing on girls for likes, follows and identity crisis reasons. Walking around caught up in the *'I want to be a lesbian'* media faze, hash tags all over the fucking place:

#Ieatpussy #lgbt #lesbianf4life #ilikegirls #girlsonly #babygirl #girlslikegirls #queer #teamnodick

What's wrong with these women? Lesbianism is **not** a faze or a fashion accessory! No honey, you cannot pick it up and drop it whenever you fucking like! This ain't no fucking clutch bag that goes with your outfit today, this is life! It's like they've watched one too many episodes of Orange Is the New Black and decided they're about this life. Nah, I'm sorry but you're either a lesbian or you're not. Don't be sitting here asking me questions like:

"So, how do lesbians have sex?"

Ladies, please! Before asking me a question, ask yourself if it's worth my time? Can you Google it? And is it my job to educate you? Keep asking your questions hoping to get my attention. You're about to fuck around and find out! Because I'll show you, using *your* body as a diagram for what and how I touch. But you *won't* see me in the *morning* and you'll be feeling some different type of way when I don't call you back! And now, you're questioning yourself about *"yourself"* and your own sexuality. Some women are *so* fucking desperate for any lesbian attention slash sexual experience, so they can run back and tell their little friends on Snapchat. Bragging about it all, starting sentences like *all* girls on social media, arms stretched out for a great lighting angle while talking to their phone, hand on the record button for fifteen or so seconds.

"Sooo, guys…"

Annoying, right? Soon enough she'll be back sucking on dick like it's her favourite flavour lollipop, talking about:

"I missed the touch of a man"

Urgh! Go a-way! Go sleep in the hallway or go sit in the corner and think about your damn self! Oh, and don't you *dare* start me on bisexual women, who claim to be straight when with a man, then a lesbian with a woman labelling it a new sexuality called fluid; going with the flow or whatever. You are not a lake you hoe! Fluid? Don't piss me off please; please I do not have the time. I seriously don't get women who go from one thing to the next, then back again! Are you a baton in a relay to me passed from one hand to the next? If you're bisexual, then *be* bi, boo boo. It doesn't matter that you're greedy; the world knows who you are because you've told them. But do not go claiming to be a *lesbian* because you're currently with a woman, meanwhile eyeing up the guy past her, trying to see how far down his dick sits in his grey sweat pants. We both know you'd rather be elsewhere with that same hard dick inside of *any* of your holes. Just be real, no one's judging you... well, apart from me. Listen! Women are what *I* do and believe me when I tell you I have been doing them *very - fucking – well*, and that's facts. Rant over, for now, until the next time I am proving my point or telling something relatively irrelevant and losing focus; because my story telling has no concept of time and the "other day" can mean *any* day between yesterday and my birth! Going back and forth and fitting in other stories in the one story I have been trying to tell you because I lose focus really quickly- where were we...? Shit!

"Continue." She took a sip of her drink.

"Blue is always trying to keep up, for as long as I can remember. It's like she's in this imaginary competition with me. I get something, she wants it or imitates it. I stopped telling her about the shit I wanted *however,* I got into women and she got into... she's fucking you - how the fuck *that* happens, I don't know?!" Raising my eyebrows, mocking the whole idea of them two together, I backed the remains of my drink. Speaking quietly into my glass with the alcohol sitting close by my lip, "bet she ain't fucking you right though." I swallowed my drink before Mali had time to hear or notice what I said.

"What was that?" she didn't hear me clear enough.

"I *said* I bet she can't fuck you... like I can! I bet she lays back not doing anything because she doesn't know shit. I bet she's too busy trying to be me and not pleasing your body in the right way. But if it *was* me fucking you, shit... I'd make sure I was fucking you right! And I wouldn't stop until your legs were weak... shaking. Screaming my name and scratching the shit out my back trying to escape... but I'd make sure you didn't go *nowhere* until you got yours and you're dripping all over me, out of breath wanting more."

- Is what I *really* wanted to say, when in reality I said:

"I bet she's a pillow princess, I bet she doesn't do anything right."

Watching my mouth, not stepping over the line but testing the line. Laughing out loud thinking about what I *really* wanted to say.

The thought of Blue lost with Mali's body played out in my mind, like a comedy cut off sketch from Family Guy. An animated Blue trying to find her way to Mali's clit with a map in one hand and a compass in the other, like

"Where's the orgasm baby, I can't seem to find the clit?"

While Mali laid impatiently, legs open on the bed trying to guide her, had me cracking up to myself. Mali didn't ask what I found so funny, instead she laughed along me. Whether it was with me or at me I don't care, I think I am fucking hilarious.

"Something like that." She said after her laughter ended.

"Next time you're fucking her, try *not* to think of me..." I finished my amusement, looking at Mali with her brow raised and her lips turned up. Her facial expression saying '*is it*? – intrigued by me, obviously.

"Think of you how??"

"Wait, what?" I said that out loud? Whoops, oh well; remember what I said, be wrong and strong! I shrugged and slumped onto her shoulder and gave up on talking altogether.

"I know what you meant lady… it's cool." She nudges me once more in my side, erasing any awkwardness.

"Good, then." I nudged her back, she didn't totally get what I *didn't* mean to say out loud about her and hers.

"But I'm not making any promises." I glance up at her, she flashes a cheeky grin at me then looks away.

"Promises? What promises?"

"That I won't be thinking about you." She looks back at me with that smile she had on her face and a sudden seriousness of lust overcoming those gorgeous big eyes. She switched from this sweet, shy and playful to dark and provoking, *real* quick. God… *damn*!

"Some promises aren't easy to keep. So I've heard." I return the unspoken feelings floating in the air between and around us. Lost in each other's gaze; I wonder if she saw our bodies intertwined in her mind like I did?

"Aaliyah, c'mon we're going!"
Nova stood beside me, breaking my concentration of undressing Mali slowly with my eyes. I forgot I came to the club with *people*- well, shit then!
Nova held onto me, supporting me as I make my way off of the little ledge and into her arms.

"Oi!" I pointed back at Mali shouting over the music one last time "Tell your female *I* said hi, when *you* find her!"

"Tell your friend, I said hi when *you* find her… see you later Miss Aaliyah."

"Yeah… maybe." Not looking back at her, I know she is watching my every move.
I threw my deuces up and walked out the club, waving goodbye to my bitches, groupies, insignificants, fans, haters and hoes and all the other people that make up the gay congregation of this place called Heaven.

***

Back at home and lying down fully clothed without a woman to entertain, fuck me right at her place and then I leave; disappearing into the morning without a trace, before she opens her eyes. Because I spent my night in the club talking to Mali instead of locating a little hottie to play with. So, I returned to my apartment with my 'fuck me thong' still on my booty and the 'just in case kit' remains unused in my car.

Flat on my back in my low-lit bedroom, watching the cascading chandelier dance in the breeze, bouncing streams of light onto the walls and the four posters of my king size bed. My drunkenness began to fade and my ears start to recognise the sounds creeping out from the numbed silence. I held my wrist up, looking at my watch, listening closely to it as it ticked and tocked the seconds away.

My brain ticking over thoughts, thinking about her smile, her humbleness and her laughing at the stupid shit I said. The way she would shy from compliments, like she's never heard the sentence *"you're stunning!"* before. The way the dimples would appear in her cheeks every time she smiled. The way her baby finger held onto the glass in her hand a little looser than the other fingers and extended up. She has these stray baby hairs on one side of her head that sit over her ear in a tight little balled curl, which she curled a lot between her finger and thumb during our conversation. A form of comfort or habit, maybe? Either way, I could curl it softly between my fingers, while she lay on top of me with her face pressed on my chest. Breathing slowly into my neck, exhausted after a night of fucking differently. Bodies locked until we fall asleep, dripping wet from sweat and other things. Woah!! Cut! Wait a minute! Stop!

What the hell is wrong with me? I can't close my eyes without seeing Mali's stupid *beautiful* face. Urgh! Get out of my head! No wait... don't leave. Laughing at myself again, laying here a hot mess, unmoved by my brains inability to get the hell out of *"Mali-Ville"*. The only thing I have managed to do is drag and kick my bottoms off in the most unattractive, fish out of water, floppy chicken legs, drunken mermaid trying to walk on her first day of land shuffle kind of movement *ever*!! I mean, I could have used my hands but whatever.

Sinking into my king-sized fluffy duvet covers, eight pillows and endless amounts of scattered cushions. They really don't seem like a good idea now that I am all the way drunk and all I want to do is get under them and sleep. So, instead I give up on life and sprawl out, spread eagle on top of them all instead. Tossing and flipping like a pancake trying to get comfortable, like I haven't got to go to work in few fucking hours!

Gazing up at the ceiling trying to get this *female* out of my head. But it's *not* happening- dammit!! For fuck sake! Every thought keeps shifting into seeing her face in everything. This is bull-shit!!

I want her! I have to have her! But, how can I? I've known Blue for as long as I can remember; but they've not been together *that* long and Blue doesn't even *really* like girls like that anyway. But I *dooo*, I like them!!

I want Mali! Hearing my own voice in my head *whining* like a little bitch. Urrrgh! Shut up! The things we could do... she has no idea! I'll just have to wait until they break it off, it's not going to last long anyway. But I am not having Blue's remains, **I** refuse. What is this? What do I look like, a Nando's doggy bag to be getting someone's leftovers? Do you know who I am; I **don't** want any leftovers. I'll just steal a cheeky taste. You know, a flick of my wrist and a slip of my finger. I'm obviously crossing a line that I shouldn't. But why should I **care!** I'm me! And I'm sure Mali won't mind having a *real* woman for a change. Come on, look at me. Well- not at this exact moment, I couldn't even tell you what I look like right about now, flapping about my bed like a pancake, trying to stop these thoughts and the voice in my head telling me to fuck with this woman. I think I've gone crazy! My mum always said these women would turn me crazy, maybe the witch is right? What kind of sorcery is this?

I've never had something so forbidden, so dangerously tempting right there; *right* in front of me. I can't be tempted, I have to behave, **I'm** trying but I *can't* behave - I don't know how to behave, even if I wanted to, *which I don't.* I have no behaviour, you've known me for like forty or fifty something pages.

- Did you just go check on the bottom right corner of page count whilst I'm in a crisis? Don't you dare! I'm going to need you to get back to reading, okay. I can't do *nothing* at all whilst Mali parades all that sexiness around me. Who says this is wrong, when it is **going to** feel so good. I always get what I want! **Fuck**, it doesn't matter who's in my way. I don't see why I can't simply take what I want, which is obviously **her,** come on, no one has to know, and no one needs to know. Just you... and well you're not exactly going to say anything, are you? It's not like you can jump into this book and start talking shit. You've read the way she looks at me. I've *seen* the way she looks at me. If you could see it, you'd probably want her too but she's mine... maybe... maybe I'll give her a little bit of me, like a sample- yeah, that sounds legit.

A sample, *An Aaliyah Monroe Exclusive* and then *her* actions after that won't be anything to do with me. Because if she comes to m... then I'm not in the wrong, am I? It won't be *my* fault.

You know, *you* could have some kind of input here. You're just sitting there reading this damn book like this isn't my life that I'm talking about. Help me out sis!?

But seeing as though you insist on keeping your silence, go back slightly and read the **bold** font only, go on.

You done?

See, I told you I'm funny…

2. The Careless Shuffle

"Yah Yah!" Blue screams down my phone.

Pissed off, aggravated and woken up by her noise in my ear on my day off – rude! Seriously, what the fuck does she want!? Why did I answer the phone in the first place?

One eye open looking at the time on my watch; 5:53am, my other eye refused to open. Seriously, this bitch cannot be for real? She's no okay, who the hell calls someone at this time in the fucking morning?

"Blue, there's only three kinds of people that are up at this hour on a Sunday. Jesus, prostitutes and immigrants. What *the fuck* do you want!?" I said roughly.

Blue, like most days is unfazed and used to the way I spoke and put things so bluntly. So, she keeps on talking shit in my ear, like usual with her usual self.

"Well I haven't slept yet *aaand* I've moved into this *amaaaazing* flat share, you should come over and check it out. I've been up all- *shush!*" She brushes off my morning aggression, informing me of her latest achievement, bragging like I give a fuck. Like I wasn't already winning in this competition she played in her head with me called:

"I have to do better than Aaliyah"
-but never comes close

Blue is insecure to say the least. And insecure people seemed to like to be around me, to make themselves feel better by having someone as *incredible* as me in their lives. How me looking good and doing good, makes *them* feel good, I don't know? I guess one look at me is enough to brighten up anyone's dull day.

Blue is beginning to bang on every single one of my nerves! How are you going to call my phone and then have me listen to all the bullshit and foolishness in *your* background? Giggling in my ear, I don't want to hear all this shit. Girl bye!

"Blue if that's all you called to tell me, I'm gone! I'm not trying to hear you chatting shit to whoever is there."

"No wait -Shush *baaabe!*" the person in her background needs to shut the fuck up!

"You gonna come over?"

"Look at the time and ask me again..." Now I'm getting pissed!

"Not now! Later today, obviously." Her energy this early is irritating! It's too much.

"I don't know, the journey down to those sides is long and then to have to drive back?"

"Come on don't be silly, what the hell is a car for? *Mali* is here?" She practically sang her name all loud and proud down the phone to prove a point. Whatever! However, the registration of Mali's name entices my other eye to gain interest in the conversation and open.

"Yeah, *my* baby is staying with me. She said she saw you in the club the other night, thinks you're lovely! We can all have a little drink, a little smoke. C'mon don't be a boring bitch, pleeease."

Screwing up my face; I don't know why she sounds so fucking smug but she needs to reel it in real quick. *But...* The idea of Mali being there does make the mission of driving all the way to West London, that little bit more desirable but... can I *really* be fucked to go though? For someone who has a car, I really don't like driving to unnecessary destinations- for why? I am not that friend who is willing to pick you up and drop you off anywhere or for you to call in for a favour. Listen, if you're not going the way I'm going then you better have Uber on your phone or have your Oyster Card in your back pocket, ready to tap that ass all the way home because my car does not run on friendship! I'm not about this 'drop me off here, pick me up here please' life.

"How you doing Miss Aaliyah?" Pause... I know that voice... hold on

53

The sound of *her* voice ringing through my head, reminding me of the tingles I felt the other night. They attempted to form over my body again but I'm not allowing them to. Laying here keeping my cool telling myself to be *calm* it. Relax, Aaliyah chill.

"Who's this?" Convincing attitude on my tone of voice, knowing full damn well who it is in my ear. I *do not* need her knowing that I know, remember or have had any thoughts of her.

"It's Mali, wow you forgotten me already yeah? Okay, say no more."

Note: Swerve and dismiss *(now pay close attention)*
As much as it is a playground and very childish move to "pretend" *not* to have an interest in a person you want. You'd be surprised how delicate egos actually are. Your actions or words have so much power and you don't even know it. Especially if that person *thinks* ("thinks" being the operative word) that they have had or have an effect on you.
I knew for me to respond pleased to talk to her again would affect her ego. So, I chose to withhold that small information. Which will now make her wonder if I *thought* about her or if she ever had an effect on me. Now her mind in ticking over thoughts of me…

"Oh, it's you… hey, yeah, I'm good thanks."
(Effective silence, deflective pauses, nonchalant tone and not bothering to ask her how she was doing- causing an awkward silence whilst she thinks about my reaction to her along with the next thing to say)

"You coming over yeah...? *(She pauses, thrown off).* It was cool talking the other night. *(She gently reminds me about the night, other than that moment we have nothing else to converse about- I don't know her like that),* we can smoke a little something, chill and talk again" supressing her excitement of talking to me in front of her woman.

"Baby girl, I don't do that shit! So, won't be smoking anything… I might pass by. Put Blue back on."

I've already made up my mind, of course I'm going! I'm already planning my outfit in my head; what goes with what, what looks hotter on my body and deciding on what's revealing but not *too* revealing, the *second* Blue said Mali was there. Invited or not, I would have drove by to say 'hey' or found a reason to get my ass over there, looking cute as fuck!

"Sorry Yah Yah. Mali took the phone off of me."

"Well don't make that shit a habit! I don't know her like that Blue, you know I don't like people!" Hearing the static echo surrounding my voice, I knew they placed the call on speaker phone. So I purposely piped up, intending to throw Mali off of the path of closeness we shared the other night at the club.

"Anyway, I love that she met you and my two favourite people get along." Blue smooths over my attitude and finishes her sentence with what sounded like a kiss on Mali's lips. *Urgh*! Really?

"Whatever. I might be about after I drop Raee'n to St Pancras"

"Oh shit, you're in bed with *Raee'n*! Sorry for interrupting." Blue whispers, now knowing I had company.

"Yes, and I'd rather be fucking her then having this dry conversation- you talk too much, goodbye!"

Hanging up with the biggest grin slash devious pout on my lips, I bet *that* got Mali's attention. Yes, sweetie I am single but don't you dare think I'm over here all caught up thinking about *you* while you're stuck to your *one* girlfriend thinking about me. Lol, no. What do you think this is? Obviiiiiiously, I'm not in bed alone, in fact... I'm not in bed at all! I'm actually on the floor of a five-star hotel suite, wrapped in the sheets, in the finishing position of last night's knock out rounds with Raee'n.

Pronounced *Rain* not Rianne, or Rene. She is most definitely a trophy of accomplishment, on the list of things (women) I label as 'mine'.

She lay facing me, fast asleep. I lift the sheet and take a moment to admire her physique and take a moment to appreciate her body right before I leave. Trailing my hand all along the smooth skin on her curvy, slim thick with her cute ass frame.

Finished with the body appreciation session, I pull the sheet off of me and move away from her, getting up slow as fuck. Sitting up and looking around the room, mapping out the quickest and easiest escape route out the door with my eyes- but where the hell is my dress?

I don't remember? It be like that sometimes, *especially* after two bottles of prosecco because that right there, is one drink that always turns me on something differently and -wait... I don't remember anything from last night, except the last glass touching my lips, Raee'n dragging my dress off but the rest is history. Call it drunk as fuck or selective memory, who knows?

"You know the rules, *I'm not done!*"

Snapped out of my lost thoughts of nothing, looking over my shoulder at Raee'n; wide awake. Her hand over mine, not wanting me to go anywhere just yet. She sits up and the sheet falls effortlessly from her skin to the floor perfectly, like something out of a movie scene. She holds my shoulders, placing kisses on my body then lightly wiping them away no sooner than she placed them there. Knowing full well I do not do mornings, let alone morning kisses or morning anything really, well... apart from *one* thing. Besides, you heard the lady, 'rules are rules' and her southern soft American accent is so sexy and it makes me melt, the way she- I don't have a clue what she's saying half the time but that tone of voice though! Damn!

Saying nothing else, she forces me onto my back roughly- just the way I like it. Wearing nothing but her sex face, letting me know that the next moments were for me only, like I am her number one and she is mine. However, this is far from the reality and this moment between us is a fantasy... her fantasy because we know the deal.

We have an understanding on what *this* is and what this *isn't*.

Parting my thighs with her leg, she leans her body into mine, I don't need to touch her to know her pussy is still wet and dripping. Excited for what she is about to do to me. Unravelling the thoughts in her mind, while she is on top of me. I know she wants to hear me moan for her loud enough to forget that she's a *married* woman. I never gave any fucks or thoughts to whoever, whatever or where ever *he* is or was as long as I kept getting mine!

Raee'n with her dark soft caramel Pocahontas complexion, straight long black soft and silky hair that she always had parted in the middle; it falls right down her back and shines perfectly. Reminding me of the black women you see on a box of hair relaxer with the perfect, jet black, beautiful thick shiny hair. Her body and her curves are something else, she's so fucking sexy and she fucking knows it!

Confidence looks sooo good on a woman, better than any dress or outfit ever could! The way she switches her hips with each step she takes in her stilettos, the way she moves- I can't explain it in words enough for it to make sense but it's this way she speaks; so calmly and assertive. How she tucks her hair behind her ears and smiles at me from across the room of a private award ceremony, I was told to unexpectedly attend.

Invited to join the festivity, held for her husband and peers to applaud his countless achievements during the many years of his service in the American Military.

She was able to slip away from the lime light of the crowds surrounding herself and husband. Letting go of his arm she held *so* proudly, adoring him the way a devoted and loving wife should, in the moments of his celebrated glory.

But… she excused herself in a very lady like manner; from conversations she had absolutely no interest in and followed *me* distantly up the grand marble staircase- but not too close or too quickly, she needed to make sure no one was watching her. She found me by following the scent of the favourite fragrant perfume she enjoys on my skin the most, into an empty room. Then past the blowing curtains and out the doors of an open balcony. Lifting up the black gown that she bought for me and had couriered to me along with my invitation and instructions to fuck each other on the edge of the city night sky. As the breeze dances around our bodies, between our legs and blew her ball gown up around her waist. My fingers deep inside of her, the other hand was over her mouth- keeping her quiet whilst her husband continued to converse with his guests, commending himself highly on his *vigilance* to detail and not missing a *single* thing right on the balcony below us. Well… he seemed to of missed all of that, vigilant my ass!!

Raee'ns sex appeal is on one hundred, she's my Nicki Minaj look-a-like with her entire juicy hour glass figure, without the all the fucking crazy *everything* else and those voices she does. You know, Nicki before the horse carriage booty surgery days? I'm talking about the back in the day 'five-star chick' video days. Yes! That Nicki was fucking hot! Not this foolish one, prancing around Prague talking about 'bitches can't spell Prague' when she can't spell 'natural'. Booty so fake and big, she's been entering the room since last Tuesday! See you next Tuesday!

Then again, no one has a natural figure these days, do they? Quick snip here and there, Brazilian butt lift (BBL) then stunt on the gram that they got it from, they mamma! When the only thing they got from their mamma is the ability to tell lies, mislead and trap men!

But not my Raee'n, she is naturally stunning! Her appearance so misleading, you would never know by looking into her *honest* and adorning eyes that she's got a little secret like me hidden away. The outer appearance of a humble, classy high-profile wife with the inner persona of a dominant, bad bitch in bed. She'll have you in positions you didn't even know your body could go!

No one needs to know that she uses the same lips to kiss her husband goodbye in the morning, making sure he starts his day off right, are the same lips she kisses *my* perfect pussy hello with, every time she sneaks out of their "happy home" to come and see me.

There have been *plenty* occasions where her 'hair appointments' have been held back. Or she's had to run out to get '*something*' from the store or she's gone to '*meet some friends for lunch*' or had a weekend spa break with the girls. When little does he know and will never know… she's with me, *just* like she is right now! On top of me, her fingertips inside me a little, she takes them out slowly. Raee'n is forever teasing me, she loves having my body anticipating her touch. Eyes locked whilst licking and tasting drops of me from between her fingers sucking on the tips, enjoying the taste of me on her tongue. She smiles looking down at me where her fingers came from, wanting more.

I don't see why we should let the commitment of her holy matrimony slash marriage get in the way of her enjoying me like this. Kissing my body in all the right places? Like, from the side of my neck right by my ear making me tremble, as she bites me hard, wanting to leave marks of her territory on me. Trailing her kisses and her tongue all the way down my body. She bites me again, this time harder, right at my hip. I know that's going to leave a bruise or a mark on my skin later on. But I like that shit! Nothing better than finding a bruise on your brown skin and having flashbacks flood your mind thinking about how it got there, or in my case, *who* put it there? Kind of like playing a game of Cluedo on my body.

She sucks and twirls her tongue around my nipples making the cold metal of my piercings heat like wildfire. She continues her kisses down low, right in-between my thighs so close... but so far from my pussy. She *knows* it drives me crazy! Kissing up and down my inner thigh teasing the spot that makes me lose control. Making my heart race and my back arch, I can feel myself dripping everywhere, aching for her to fuck me- now! Back arched, wanting her to touch me, to feel her inside of me. Grabbing her by her hair I put her face right where I want it to be. Fuck waiting, I'm here to take control! She loves taking my commands.

Fin-nal-ly, she reintroduces her lips to mine, pushing her tongue slowly around my throbbing clit then stops - she always does this, getting another taste of me, grabbing my body, telling me constantly,

"I can't stop thinking about you! I'm in love with the way you taste baby!" Not looking at me, she spoke directly to my pretty pussy, which I completely take pride in and ownership of.

Note: Pussy Power *(You better take note!)*

As a woman, it's very important to take pride in your pussy. Don't be afraid to say 'pussy'. Make sure 'she' (your pussy) is always ready. Name her, claim her, take care of her, pat her, stroke her and every now and then hold on to her. Let her know that she is appreciated. Men should not be the only ones who are allowed to hold onto their genitalia. So, ladies you better hold your pussy power with pride! That's your pussy! Don't break it, you only get on and no one wants a broken pussy. Know you're walking around with a bomb ass pussy that grabs back- but only if she wants to, especially if you're like me and your pelvic floor muscles are on point, grab back!

Now go back and count how many times I said pussy in that note.

.

Pussy count total: _____

Raee'n rotates her tongue, running it around and around my clit. Umm yes, sucking it then pushing inside of me, making me lose my breath. Hand holding onto the back of her head, moving her hair out of the way, wrapping it around my hand, pulling it! Looking down at her taking my commands and watching her tongue move. She always kisses my clit like it was going to be her kiss goodbye. After all, who knows when she might.

Dominating and controlling as I am, in both life and sex. I need a woman who can flip it on me and hold it down! A woman who can lock my thighs open and not let me go. Telling me to stay the fuck still and not move, as I'm clawing her neck and back because I can't take the constant orgasms she's giving me. One hand around my throat, I tell her not to stop to push harder to fuck harder, to not stop- don't stop- don't fucking stop!

"Want me to stop baby?" She teases, with a grin on her face.

"Don't you dare!"

Pushing harder in and out of me, her tongue back on my clit, taking me to higher heights until I peek but I hold on… I'm not climaxing yet, not that easy, she's still got work to do.

"You little bitch, I almost had you!" She laughs, slapping me on my ass.

"Fuck!" big smile on my face, "almost baby." Giggling turning my body to the side, Catching my breath.

Raee'n sat up pleased with herself, looking at me sideways with her eyes lost in our sex and that sexy pout on her lips.

"You taste *so fucking* good! I'm not done with you yet though…"

"Oh, I fucking know, bitch!"

Throwing herself beside me she pointed to her mouth.

"Sit on my face!"

Four words *every* woman loves to fucking hear!! Urgh! I love it!

This is an official announcement on behalf of the sisters of womanhood:

If you're a woman that does not like sitting on faces, are you even really a woman?? I mean, what other uses does a face actually have besides from looking pretty enough to sit on?

Crawling over her body seductively and slow, placing kisses on her belly, between her breast, her neck and her lips. I suck on her tongue tasting myself. Oh, and you're *definitely* not a woman, if you do not kiss and taste your sex off of the lips of your significant other, whatever or whoever!

"Oh, okay is that what I do for you, yeah?" My fingers literally gliding past her wet pussy- she's so fucking wet! The insides of her thighs covered with it all, she couldn't stop flowing from all that excitement of being inside of me. My body on top of hers and our bodies together in *any* position, connected.

"Always, now hurry up and come sit on my face!"

She demands, maintaining her calm tone of voice. Taking my hand away, she holds my waist and shifts my position, encouraging me to move up and over her body frame. Onto my knees, on top of her just above her face.

She smiles waiting, watching and wanting! I lower myself slowly over her face. Looking down passed my breast at her; thirsty enough to lick up every single drop of me. I decide to move as slow as I can, she holds her tongue between her teeth waiting for me to drop *it*. But I decide to keep tormenting her, moving my body up... and down... and up... and down... and-

"Come here!" frustrated, Raee'n grabs me by the hips pulling me on top of her and she places her tongue back inside of me. Pushing her fingers in behind her tongue, working her wrist while I pushed back on her fingers. Back and forth and back and forth and around working my waist. This shit felt so fucking good! My head back loving every moment of this, rolling my hips with her tongue.

Feeling like we've been at this shit forever and a day. Damn, she knows my body too fucking well and knows how to make it *rain* all over her, telling me to

"Cum for me..."

She loves it when I trail all over her and her chest glistens with it all. Raee'n forever predicting showers like an English summer forecast. I don't want anything else from her, I don't care about her marriage or how *he* would feel if he ever found out his wife is fucking around with a woman. I am more than happy with the time I get and then she can go back to living whatever life with him and call me whenever she wants more of me.

I have always had this desire and need to want shit that isn't mine to take. Playing with fire and tempting fate. Raee'n is *definitely* one of them at the top of the list of things 'not to do' but it's what *I* do and I am not even sorry!

Although our time together is short, it couldn't get any sweeter. So sweet, I always leave her wanting more... needing more and craving more of me inside of her or her inside of me.

Put it this way I am her drug, her addiction, her habit, her dirty little secret!

We met some time ago at my sisters' house, I couldn't tell you when but Raee'n and her people were over there at Samantha's. Getting ready and having their pre-club drinks and pre-party bullshit. You know, because my sister is all *gay* and what not and knows *everyone* – big mistake!

Note: No New Friends *(No, no, new)*

Always... no, *never* have a large circle of people who know you! Keep it min-ni-mal! You LGBTQ-RSTUVLMNOP people talk too damn much, trust me! The biggest gay social mistake ever is to have more than a handful of close friends; everyone you talk to doesn't need to be your friend, associate or acquaintance. If people start to know you or of you, then *their* people's people and their people's, people know you and *now,* too many fucking people know your name! Alicia Keys said it best, 'you don't know my name'- let's keep it that way! So, keep your circle small and tight like your pussy- and just like your pussy, not everyone needs to be up in it!

We were all heading out to Bootylicious; the monthly urban scene gay club. Down somewhere in one of the many clubs that made the arches of Vauxhall. Another playground for all the gays in London town. Somewhere along the ever-changing clubs and past the red painted gay tavern pub on the corner. Where all the renascence gay men reside, in their bootcut Levi 501 jeans, leather jackets with far too many buckles on them. All stood outside with their, mullets, moustaches and shiny bald heads. Smoking a 'fag' and chugging on a pint of lager. Inside the tavern, Martha Maria La Boom Bum La'trice, the queen of drag queens, lip syncs her Friday night, headline secret career away. Unbeknown to *his* wife and kids, who are at home waiting for him to come back from the same excuse of:

"Sorry darling, I have to work late tonight."

Bootylicious was the place you had to be! Everyone who was *anyone* on the scene would be showing up to show out, in their best and doing the most.

Samantha invited me over to hers to meet her people, not that I had any interest in any of them but I remember walking into the house expecting a bunch of goofy, funny looking misfits that Samantha usually chills with. So, you can imagine, I was *completely* thrown off guard by *this woman...* standing in the hallway. Fixing her eye shadow in the mirror; gently patting and blending the dusty golden glitter onto her eyelids. Pouting with her head tilted to one side. She turned to my direction, hearing my heels step into the house and clip down the tiled hallway…

"Hey Ma…"

She spoke with this silky smooth, southern American accent, I was not expecting to come out of her pretty mouth. We stood, looking each other up and down for the longest seconds. She wore this camouflage print outfit, looking like the baddest boujie military officer! She had on a flat cap and a tight cropped midriff jacket; that fit tightly just over her breasts. With her small waist, curvy hips and long legs that went on and on for days, she had my full attention- sir yes sir! She was also caught up; unable to take her eyes off of me, forgetting she is a married woman. Busy thinking to herself that she definitely does not have better at home. Come on! Why else would she be rolling with the "gays" to the gay club, unless she had intentions of trying something new and in female form?

At the club we were inseparable but very careful of the people around. She needed to be very discreet. There is nothing worse than people all up in your business, dictating what you shouldn't be doing, telling you what's right or wrong- shut up! People in glass houses should not throw stones… or bricks in some cases. Dancing body to body; her hand somehow slyly finding its way in my jeans and moving her fingers with the rhythm of my body, circling my clit to the beat of the music.

Later, when the night was over and done, I agreed to stay over at my sisters, which is a very rare occurrence because I love my bed; It's the only place where I can get a good night's peaceful sleep. I mean, I'm not exactly "sleeping" when I lay down in other beds, now am I?

Anyway, there wasn't anywhere left to sleep as my sister's people walked into the house off their faces and dropped where ever they landed. So, I aimlessly walked the hallway, attempting to walk off my own wave, so I could drive my ass home.

... Raee'n stood in the doorway of the spare room, blushing and holding out her hand, saying nothing. Taking her hand, I followed her to the bed and we lay wrapped in each other while I whisper all that she wanted to hear in her ear. About men being trash and women being so fucking sexy, to the point where the only three thoughts entering her mind were

"fuck it!" "fuck him!" and "fuck me!!"

Disregarding her marriage and the big diamond rock she wore on her finger. She wanted me to do whatever I wanted to do, to her. From the moment I stepped into the house and we locked eyes... and I did! Fuck me, her kisses were so... damn! They make me weak thinking about them. Hot and heavy, like fire and in sync. Before her, I had never kissed anyone that made my body pulse that way. Kissing, for me, was always far too intimate, I never used to let anyone kiss me. Before her, no one under any circumstances kisses me above my waist. But she... has these kisses that have me feeling some type of way. Like someone lit a match, set me on fire and my body rushes with bursts of flames!

Raee'n and I have been doing "us" for some time now. There are no strings attached- absolutely nadda!! Well apart from all the great fucking sex!!!"

***

"Aww, that's sooo *cute*."

Blue scrunches her face, reacting to my story about Raee'n, like I was telling her about unicorns and fluffy fucking rainbow candy floss! I told you she doesn't fucking *listen*! She's lives in her own little dream world, overlooking the reality she's faced with, which is a hot *mess*!

So delusional and old enough to know better and still making fatal dumb bullshit choices!

Listen to this: she chose to blow an *en-ti-re* inheritance cheque... no, not half... or some or even a little bit but ALL of eleven and a half grand on fixing up an ex-boyfriend's house- oh, I'm sorry, let me correct myself *"the love of her life's"* house with *everything*! I'm talking all mod cons and the latest technology. Like a smart fridge- *who* in the fuck needs a smart fridge?? Why the *hell* is a fridge talking and trying to tell me my weeks agenda? Like I need another damn device giving me notifications from Facebook, informing me it's another person's birthday that I don't give a fuck about!?

She also got him expensive pure Egyptian cotton bed sheets, that you would have thought were woven by the Egyptian Gods and Goddesses themselves with the price she paid for them! Obviously, she *thought* she would be resting her pretty little head on them for forever. However, forever didn't last long and ended shortly after her money ran out. He changed the locks, his number and blocked her from every social network you can think of. She *finally* realised he *was* the using fuck boy that *every-one* had been telling her he was! Well, that and the fact that her bank account was, of course, eleven and a half grand lighter- with nothing left but receipts of purchases for him.

Too fucking stupid to see he was bleeding her dry because and I quote (whiney pathetic pitch voice)

"I love him and he loves me. He would never do that" – Love? Pah!!

Here Blue is, not long after her visit to The Heartbreak hotel, sad love songs and ballads all night long. Eating ice cream and crying into the one hoody she took from him- because that's all a fuck boy has to offer; an oversized hoody and lies!!

Well she's back to her *regular* self in a (feel free to read the below with the most sarcastic tone- ready… here we go.)

"LeSBiaN rElaTiONsHip!!"

I know right! She has this tendency to annoy me very fucking quickly and without trying. She is a friend I can only take in small bursts. Hang out with her for a day or two. Let her fill me in all the shit that she needs to about her life, her dramas and whatever else then I'm gooooood! For, say… the next two months, maybe six, maybe even twelve! The less I see her, the better it is for my mental health.

Blue is mixed race and has all the features and appearance of a white girl. You couldn't tell she was mixed until she *braaagged* to you where her parents were originated from. I can hear her now, all annoying and:

"My mum is from Zimbabwe and my dad is from Mauritius"

I don't know *how* many times I've heard that damn sentence?? Every time I hear it. It's like fingernails on a chalkboard to my ears. Please, ask this woman the colours on both damn flags or where the hell they are located on a global map and she will quickly go off subject, slyly slide out of the convo or shut the fuck up!

Tall and busty, she has long brown fine European hair that she recently cut into this awful bobbed 60's Iggy Pop Art looking style.

"I'm going for a Brick Lane, vintage, edgy Shoreditchy kind of thing. I think it looks amazing, don't you?" She said trying to justify her style of fashion confusion, looking like about twenty different statement trends at once!

"Nope, I don't." Do not ask me stupid questions please because I don't have time. No, I fucking don't fucking think it's *amazing*!

Blue is an odd thing, with a name to match. Originally birthed as Leslie McKenzie, she decided a few months ago that she wanted more of a- and I quote:

"Earthy name."

If I keep rolling my eyes like this, I'm going to have no eyes left. Apparently, 'Blue' made 'Leslie' feel, you know… all *earthy* and what not. Leslie, felt at one with peace, nature and herself?? Because she came up with Blue… that's it no last name nothing, nope nadda, zip, zilch just Blue!?

Honestly, I constantly question our friendship. Although it hurts my head, she's been around for so long now, that I might as well keep her around. She's like one of those useless items you have around the house, that you don't use anymore. You spend your 'clear out day' convincing yourself not to throw it away. Because one day you *know* you will find a use for it. Besides she'd be lost without me. Without me, she would have no one to worship, admire and imitate.

Anyway, we – Blue, Mali I, are all here sitting on this 'practically on the floor, should be on the floor' bed. In Blue's Moulin Rouge red decorated and smelling like a tin of fresh paint bedroom. Containing nothing but this bed, a mirrored wardrobe, a speaker and a flat screen television, Blue's interpretation of *"fabulous"*- she' delusional!

She's annoyingly clinging onto Mali, like a bra you've had on all day and all you want to get it off and give your tits the *juiciest* scratch and let them bad boys loose into gravity. Her arms are wrapped around Mali's neck; smothering and smug. It's obvious she's insecure and feeling a type of way about me being over here and sitting not too far from *her* woman but *she* invited me, so why is *she* on edge? Besides, I can see from where I am sat that the dynamics of their relationship are off. Anyone could figure it out just by looking at them; the way Blue is clinging and Mali is chill, very nonchalant and not reacting to her woman's constant push for affection. Her attention is focused out the window, not listening to anything either of us had to say. Uninterested like she was trying to plan a way out of Blue's tight clutches.

"What's the sex like?"

Mali snapped her gaze away from the window and her deep thoughts. Glancing directly at me with a bold look all over face. Her lips scowled slightly, eyes bright and intrigued.

"Mali!" Shocked at her woman's sudden interest and questioning, Blue roughly elbowed her in the side. Me, however, I am not shocked; caught off guard, maybe, shocked, never! Because of the way she's looking at me, confidently waiting for an answer, almost like she's trying to say:

"I bet she can't fuck like me?"

"Did I say something wrong?" laughing it off and turning her attention back to Blue. Placing a kiss on her lips to console her insecurities and unsettledness towards the question.

"You can't ask Aaliyah that- ignore her." Blue attempting to brush aside the sudden interest Mali has taken on me and my sex life.

"*What*? I'm trying to get in with the girl talk..." Mali's focus on me, she takes a deep pull from her spliff. Tilting her head back, the smoke leaves her mouth; slowly, inhaling back through her nose then releasing it, talking as she blows out "...so, talk- *girl*!" Just the sound of her voice all husky, while the thick weed smoke drifted out of her throat- she is sexy as fuck!

"It's cool Blue, I have no problem answering the question... if you're okay with it?" Asking to make sure I come across somewhat of a decent, caring individual. Although, I'm going to answer her regardless.

"Why would I have a problem?" Blue takes the spliff from Mali's hand, in an attempt to act as laid back as the two other people in the room. She shrugs her shoulders, acting like it's nothing. Slumping against the wall in imitation of the relaxed vibe and energy in the room but looking uncomfortable and uptight.

My aim now is not only to answer the question but to grasp Mali's interest to the point she *wished* she was Raee'n in this next story I'm about to tell them and *you* of course.

I close my eyes before answering, pausing… taking my time… I bite the inside of my lip slightly. Tilt my head back *just* a little… I open my mouth and smile as a quick flash of Raee'n inside of me races across my mind, moaning to myself quietly. So quietly that Mali tilts her head, questioning herself if she heard me make a noise. But stumbling on her thoughts because she's too intrigued to ask Blue if she heard the same thing.

Feeling my pussy tighten and flutter, imagining Raee'n here between my thighs. Zoning out and feeling her all over my body on replay in my mind.

Do you ever get that *'thing'* happen to you? You're chilling or busy with your day… then all of a sudden, out of *nowhere* that certain 'someone' flashes across your mind. You remember that good, *good* sex you had with them or that one thing they did right and your body reacts and tenses. Your thighs twitch and you feel yourself smiling to yourself at the glimpse of them in your memory. So vivid but it's always for that split second when you close your eyes and all you want to do is send them 'that' text… you know what I'm talking about;

"Hey big head" or *"You up?"* or my favourite *"Hey stranger"*

Note: *Late night/You up text*
A not so clever ploy, used to gage whether someone is awake, active and horny.
I myself, am a receiver of texts of this nature. And I take them as a compliment- majority of you don't. You get all uptight, offended, hostile and boujie. In your feelings for the wrong reasons. You scoff at their name on your screen *'why does she* [insert the *'he'* when necessary] *think it's okay to message me?'*. Asking your friends if you should respond. Fuck that!

Girl, take it as a compliment! It means your sex is f-i-r-e!!!! And they want you! So, put on something that can be taken off easily and respond!!

Right- where was I?

"Ummm. Two words" opening my eyes, I hold my deuces up.

"Go on…" Mali, leaning forward a little, eagerly awaiting my answer.

[Side note: See how I've got her hooked already and I've barely said a thing?! Sometimes; pause, take your time to answer and let your body and lack of words do the talking for you.]

"Fucking Fire!"

"What? From the get-go?" Mali's curiosity of question, leading her onto another. Eagerly waiting to know more- eyes wide and intrigued.

"Alright Mali, relax!" Blue said, regaining Mali's attention by placing a hand on the inside of Mali's thigh and giving it a little squeeze. Reminding her that she *is* sitting here too.

"Yeah, I *knew* what she wanted. There was no time for any formalities, all she needed to do was take off her clothes. We are two grown women who understand that all we ever need to do is 'fuck' and get it over with." No more pauses necessary; instead a corrupted use of words to make her mind wander off her path and into mine. Taking a sip of my drink, I use my glass to peak at Mali. Her eyes drifted to mine, for only a second… a very important second, feeling like a minute and defining the mutual wave, we both want to ride.

"Tell *us* a sex story then?" Blue interrupts, asking a question she has no real interest in but she wants to be involved.

Ladies hold on to your knickers, thongs, boxers! Whatever you put on!

"My boss has these hotel suites scattered across London that she has no use for. So, I decided to occupy one of them the with our bodies for a weekend. Raee'n told her husband she was off to a spa girl's trip or whatever. I told her to give him *all*

71

the hotel details, in case he decided to check it out for himself. So, if he did call to check it out- which he did. What man is going to think something dodgy is going on between two *women* sharing a hotel room? It's all about the details."

Note: *(uh and another one)* Details/Your movements.

Don't give your partner/spouse a reason to go snooping around your phone and socials or whatever. Tell all the *necessary* details but don't overdo it. If you're going "away" or "staying out late" be real with it. Point your spouse in the direction of *where* you're going but not what you are doing. I call it the **'Two Truths & One lie"**

Example: Give *location/contact*, *name* and *activity*. (one of those will be a lie)

"I'm going to a spa weekend with the **girls**. Here's the number in case you need me."

Don't act shady, the minute you start to withhold info and leave questions unanswered is when suspicions begins.

Another quick note: Make sure, if you're going to fuck around, have fun with it! That you're being treated like the fucking lady you are! And if you're the entrapment, be sure she/he has a sensational time! After all, when was the last time the significant other treated them to a five-star hotel? - But only for the weekend.

- Now you know what is expected and accepted, let's get back into my story.

Raee'n walked through that door and dropped her bags. Grabbing me by the waist kissing me, hands all over me but I pushed her off of me,

"Why?" Mali asked interrupting.

"I'm getting to it, hold on!"

I wanted her to wait just a little bit longer. To be so excited that she would be dripping wet, drenched right through so I could slide my fingers into her so effortlessly. So excited, her pussy would be gripping onto my fingers and not wanting to let them go.

I stripped to nothing in front of her and walked towards the spiral staircase with her following close behind me...

"No... sit down over there and don't move until I tell you to." I pointed to the sofa. She didn't take her eyes off of me. Disorientated by my demand for her to move away from my naked body but she did what she was told. I love a woman who takes direction and lets' me take control.

So... I'm there, stood at the bottom of the staircase staring right at her. Running my hands from the back of my neck, down between my breast squeezing them, not taking my eyes off of her. I sit on the stairs, feeling myself; down my stomach and opening my legs wide, trailing my fingertips along my thighs. Legs open, one hand, fingertips parting my lips... and well, slowly pushing my fingers inside me, tilting my head back, letting out deep breaths and saying her name so quietly that her face questioned what she was hearing come out of my mouth. But she didn't say a word. She didn't want to interrupt me.

Her face lit up - I watch her, watching me touch my body, imagining it was her hand instead of my own. Knowing exactly where to push inside of me to make myself cum like 'rain'. I stop suddenly, her jaw drops looking at the mess I made on the wooden step. Standing up slowly, I feel the trail down the inside of my leg, I turn around switching my naked hips up the spiral staircase.

"I didn't say move," I heard her attempt to get up. She obeys me once more and stays seated. "Good girl..."

Leaving her there, I ran a full to the brim bubble bath and lit candles all around. Playing my Slow Jams sex playlist from the surrounding ceiling speakers. I call her phone, she answers... listening to me let out a broken deep gasp of air down the phone. She asked me what was I doing? The anticipation had her thinking but I wasn't doing anything but making her mind work over time. Nothing wrong with a good old-fashioned tease!

"...come find me..." I said and hang up

As soon as I did, I hear her high heels race up the stairs and speed down the hallway. Following the music, she opens the bathroom door; I'm there in this huge bathtub in the middle of the bathroom that was lit by the candles and the night lights of the city coming through the ceiling to floor windows.

I held a glass of cold champagne; placing myself in behind the bubbles for her to see the steam coming from the water and off of my brown tattooed skin. Her mouth hit the floor once more. The only thing left to say was,

"Details now!!" Both Mali *and* Blue were sat leaning, listening closer, not wanting to miss a single detail. Eagerly, waiting for me to keep talking…

"…get in!"

Turning her back to me, moving slowly unzipping her pencil skirt… it drops to the floor. She undresses, revealing more and more skin as each layer of clothing hits the floor.

"Nu-uh you better keep them on!"

Stopping her as she bent over to take her feet out of her red-soled heels. I don't care if they got ruined, I wanted her to keep them on!

She walks over to me, seductively following the beat of the music with each step. Her hair falling over her body, her 'everything' looking good enough to lick 'anything' off of. Lifting her leg up and over, she steps into the bubbles. Leaning softly on my shoulder, she sits on the edge of the bath, her legs wide open just waiting on me to taste it. I kneeled up towards her, kissing her, holding onto her tight. Moving her hair over her shoulders, handing her a glass of champagne I told her:

"Do not fucking let it go!"

She tightens her grip on the champagne glass. And watches me pour what remained in my glass, all across her chest. She gasps, arching her back. I watch the liquid run down her body, falling into the exact places I was about to lick it off of. My tongue on her body, following the trail of champagne trickling, licking

74

every drop off of her skin. Running my hand along her thighs, I quickly slide my fingers inside of her, I was done playing. She gripped onto my fingers so tight, exactly the way I wanted it to be. Stroking my fingers in circular, hard motions, moving my body with hers, locked with her legs around me. Causing the water to splash over us and the edge of the bath. Loving the sound of her moaning my name over and over and over again. I could barely hear the music over the splashes of water and the sound of her telling me how she wants to be fucked. Catering to my ego, heavy breathing in my ear.

I hear the faint sound of the glass I told her not to let go of, hit the bathroom floor with a smash. She gripped onto my back and her nails dig in as she clawed away at it. Working her hips with me, allowing me to go harder and faster inside of her until feeling the warmth of her squirting onto my wrist but I kept going and going, getting her to squirt again and again and again. She was all like

       "Don't fucking stop!" and I couldn't decide what was hotter though; looking at my fingers fucking her, the sound of my fingers fucking her or looking at both of us in the mirror on the bathroom wall.

Standing her up, so I can see her full body in the reflection and watch her legs tremble and shake trying to keep herself up. One leg over my shoulder with those fucking sexy heels on her feet. She holds onto this towel stand that was by the bath, luckily it was screwed into the floor. The other hand on the back of my neck, my face between her thighs, while I sucked on her clit.

Then… out of nowhere she flips the script on me! To this day, I don't know how it happened? But she somehow had me laid back in the bath, holding onto the taps, working my waist as her tongue followed my clits every move. She held me above the water by the small of my back, pushing her long tongue in, out and all around me. Fuck me, it felt soo good! Champagne on the tip of her tongue- so cold! Lifting me out of the hot water completely, she stayed on her knees and I wrapped my legs around her neck pushed up against the cold bar towel stand. I fucking love a woman that can show her dominating power during a good fuck! I couldn't help watching us in the mirror, thinking I should have had a camera up on a tripod recording from that angle because I wanted to watch that shit back. Water every fucking where! Bathroom looking like a tsunami just rolled through it and back again, I was fucking worked, my hair was drenched-

"-and you know, my hair doesn't get wet for no one!"

"Wow!" Mali didn't know where to look. At me, her woman or to check between her legs real quick, to see how wet she is... how are you holding up there? Feel free to check yourself. I don't mind waiting...
You good? You sure? - You want a moment?

"We went from the bathroom, to the window, to the hallway, the bed, floor, balcony, stairs, sofa, kitchen tops and the fucking walls! There wasn't a surface our bodies did not touch! Days later I was *still* finding bruises on my body. It was a battle of who fucks who to sleep but no one was sleeping, no one was backing down!" I topped up my glass, taking a sip to keep my slight wave going.

"Was it the best sex you've *ever* had?" Blue, also taken in and mesmerised or trying to appear as though she was because she didn't expect all of that in one answer. Mali stares at me waiting for me answer Blue's question.

"Honestly..." [time to pause again and answer in your own time.] taking another sip, I look at my glass and shrug "... I've had better."

"Yaas bitch! That's what I'm talking about!" Blue holds her hand up waiting for a high five, like she's experienced women longer than this 'four-week phase' she's got going on here, to know what the fuck *I'm talking* about? Girl, goodbye! Go sit in the corner and shush! I said it before and I'll say it again, *women* are what I do and *have* been doing! Blue needs to stay in whatever lane with her commentary of approval I didn't ask for.
Mali stays silent, maybe she's trying to stop herself from imagining me in-between her legs... so returned her gaze back out of the window and onto whatever thoughts she was having before joining the so-called 'girl talk'.

Waiting for Mali to look back at me but she won't and that's okay. I'll leave her with her thoughts in the darkness. I know what she's thinking; she's thinking, she definitely deserves to experience a *real* woman... to tie her up and show her who's running shit. Let me stop myself right there and focus. Sorry, my mind has no control over the inappropriate expectancies that I have. I'm telling you, self-control is a mother fucker!

"...she's married yeah?" Finally, Mali broke her moment of silence and spoke, wanting to know more. Asking me another question but her gaze remained out the window; as if she could see more than the street lights shining through the darkness. I know she is watching me in the faint reflection of the glass.
She's not as eager as before, she's back to her cool, calm and nonchalant self. However, I can see right through her stance and calm exterior... her *interior* is dripping... wet.

[Kids, gather round, listen and learn as I bring her *full* attention back to me with a few simple but very clever *choice* of words. Delivering them with the correct tone of voice whilst looking around the room blushing in my thoughts, exaggerating and looking down at myself.]

"Yeah, it is what it is. I don't mind that *she has someone else. I always get mine.* I go over to their place when he's *not around* or away on business trips. [*Pause; looking up at her, I widen my eyes and move my hair away from my face, so she sees me clearly.*] I don't know, it's just such a *turn on for me...* when you're doing shit that you *know* you *shouldn't be doing.* I don't think anything comes close to that feeling, it's dangerously sexy... *you should try it sometime.*"

And just like that, with all those sly hints to her mental, she's now evoked the thoughts of what *we* could be getting up to. She turns to me without hesitation, unable to take her eyes off of me and I can see it... the thoughts building up in her mind... that familiar spark of enticement in her eyes. I've seen it *sooo* many times before on the faces of my many other desired women. Ouuu, Miss Temptation is doing her thing again. Penetrating her mind and starting to pump throughout her veins. A whole new urge she knows is wrong but it feels good. I don't know how much longer she can fight it but, I'm more than happy to plant more corrupt thoughts to help aid the process.

Eventually, she'll find herself drawn to me. She's making this far too easy for me, her eyes are calling out my name along with hers and it sounds so sweet to my ears: *Aaliyah and Mali*, umm what do you think? How does it sound to you? Go on say it out loud... *Aaliyah and Mali*, sounds sexy right?

"Errm, okay?!" Blue interrupted my thoughts about her woman- It's just rude really! Disturbing people's thoughts and what not, so selfish. Lol

"*You two* should try it- is what I'm saying babe," I said, playing on Blue's inability to read between the lines. I point between the two of them, "you and Mali should act it out; pretend that you're having an affair. Fuck like... someone *is* going to catch you both inside of each other!" Playfully winking at Blue, she blushes a slight blush at her woman with flirtatious giggles. *My* idea has clearly turned something on in her feeble mind.

Isn't it crazy how words can just spark people off? Maybe it's the way I say things or maybe it's my clever choice of words, either way *I* am a sexual genius! Goddess if you will. Excuse me while I drift off, into a daydream to receive my excellence award for Sexual Genius and Indecent Proposals:

"Thank you, thank you all! I'd like to thank my mum for showing me love is nothing but a myth and that as women, our bodies contain so much fucking power! But most of all I'd like to thank my main motive 'temptation', because they always give in!"
Crowd goes wild- Hercules, Hercules!! Sherman, Sherman, Sherman!!!

Okay, I'm done for now... where were we? Oh, right, that's it- I had given Blue this idea of sexual enhancement- blah blah blah, here we go-

"But not tonight bitches, I'm staying over and I don't want to see shit, I don't want to hear shit, in fact, I don't want to know shit!" We all laugh; a little tipsy and waved from the substantial amount of shared intoxication of alcohol, drugs and sex talk floating in the air-

Mali catches me looking her way one last time, for a quick second hidden amongst the group laughter

***

I can't sleep! Blue is in the middle of this poor excuse of a bed with me and Mali on either side of her. She's spread out like butter on a bagel *and* I'm against the wall, which I cannot fucking stand but Mali already called *"dibs"* on the outside edge of the bed. I had no choice in the matter, because *ap-par-rent-ly* people still call out 'dibs' in their flipping late-twenties- really!? What are we going to play next? The floor is lava?

My watch ticking onto 4:07am, eyes are wide open and for why? For who? Forget this, I'm out, I have my own bed! I only laid down to cool off the bottle I drunk with myself… by myself. Because I am the kind of person who brings a bottle for *myself* at these 'bring a bottle' festivities, parties, occasions and events. No, I am not sharing! You received the same invite I did, so follow the simple instructions. There were no fine lines about sharing 'the bottle you bring'. So, you better not bring your empty red cup this way begging for drink- nope, you got the wrong one! You better take your empty cup to the nearest Off License, holler at 'Boss Man' or be thirsty! No one told you bringing that dead bottle of Echo Falls certifies your bottle as admission to be reaching for everyone else's liquor.

Getting out the bed and climbing over two bodies that you did not participate in a threesome with, is long! I am lying! Girl, I am *way* too selfish to even attend a threesome let alone participate- watch one, of course… participate- nah I'm good.

It is way too flipping hot in this 'happy meal' box size room to be containing this amount of bodies and I'm still a little waved but that's beside the point... wait? what's the point again? ...? That's it, the point is, *how* are you supposed to get comfortable with two people in the same bed and *no one* is fucking or watching? Someone, tell me please.

Picking up my bag I head to the door and look back at the *"happy couple"* sound asleep. Blue being needy as fuck even in her sleep, clinging onto Mali. All the while, Mali is probably dreaming about a great escape plan with me by her side on some Bonnie and Clyde type vibe. Shaking my head, I chuckle quietly to myself and creep slowly out the door and down the stairs.

"Hey,"

The timid voice of Blues flatmate Amelia; petite framed female with a face like a porcelain doll. Dark brown golden beautiful skin tone, black Caribbean Island looking girl with dark hair that's wet and dripping over the top half of her 'might as well take it off, fresh out of the shower half-naked, come here girl' body!

She held the knot of her towel tight and close to her chest, gripping onto it tighter because my face isn't trying to hide the fact that I'm thinking about what she looks like without the towel. My facial expression does *not* keep anything to myself, looking at her some type of way, telling her to:

"Take it off."

"Okay." She places her hands by her sides, the towel lets go of her body and drops effortlessly to the floor.

"Damn!" Not taking my eyes off of her

"Excuse me?"

"Huh?"

Snapping out of my daydream, Amelia looking at me with a laugh of confusion and awkward blush. - I didn't mean to get you excited but I tend to do that sometimes- see a beautiful woman and drift off into my own world, my bad.

"Wait, why don't I know you yet?"

[sometimes a cheesy line, wins you charm points for a later encounter.]

Her warm wet arm brushes against me as she continues past me up the stairs. My eyes freely wondering up her legs with each step she took. I wonder what her body looks like without that fluffy pastel pink towel covering it up? Looking over her shoulder at me, she opens her bedroom door and she steps in.

"Maybe one day you will," she says quietly and coyly smiling back at me- well okay! I'm standing somewhere in the middle of the staircase, my head tilted to the side smiling, stretching my neck and watching her closely through the gap between the frame and the door she *purposely* left open. Watching her silhouette in the shadows of her dark room, as she takes off her towel. She steps towards the door and slides her slim wrist out between the gap, holding onto the fluffy pink towel. She lets it go and it hits the floor softly gathering into a pile.

"Goodnight." She says closing the door gently, I didn't see a thing! Fucking tease! Hmm, 'maybe one day *you* will'. We'll see but right now I have the better project of Mali on my mind- but saying that, having Little Miss Fluffy Pink Towel might come in use.

Downstairs is fucking cold! My toes curl from the coldness of the grey granite tiled kitchen floor. Pouring myself a glass of water, I step outside with my bare feet onto an even colder, rough concrete floor of what was trying to be a front garden. It's not much of a garden, with its no grass and lack of anything green at all. And it's not really "front" either but more like, to the side of the house with this rickety old tired falling apart, 'don't sit on it' bench. The only greenery is coming from the thick moss on the tall brick walled off area, which allowed a little privacy and entry through a wooden gate that is hanging on its last door hinge.

Shivering from the early morning breeze, my cigarette finally decided to light after five fucking attempts! It *probably* would have been easier, had I turned my back against the breeze but I guess my lack of sleep has finally kicked in. It would *also* be easier if I quit smoking altogether but what can I say? I'm an addict, stuck with a dirty habit and a grey box of twenties in my hand advertising death, still births and organ failure but... I still make the conscious decision and inhale these ten pound sterling sticks of death.

Anyway, my mind drifting off and into the nothingness of my surroundings, head tilted to the side, looking at the gate and the zigzag-shaped structure of wood that was holding it from falling apart. You know that feeling you get when you feel yourself zone all the way out? And you can't be bothered to zone back in, so you stay... drifted into the nothing of empty thoughts and let your mind do its own thing and keep drifting into the further while your eyes lose focus but your ears listen and take in all the sounds around you. It's a quiet morning, every so often I caught the whispers of cars on the main high road, flying pass. Speeding, taking advantage of the open roads that the early morning brings. Cars of people who are in the beginning stages of their day or returning home wanting the day to end.

Looking down at my feet, a bunch of leaves dance around in a careless shuffle over my toes, tickling them in the cold breeze.

"What you doing out here?"

Jumping at the sound of a voice, outside of my thoughts; zoning back in from the randomness of nothing floating in my head, forgetting that there are people inside the house and where I was for a moment.

I turn to see who has joined me out here in the cold of the early a.m... and sure enough, there she is- Mali... I should have known by the tone of her voice but she caught me by surprise. She stood, posted up on the doorway squinting at me, half asleep, moving her big hair out of her face. She's so pretty with all that hair out, flying about the breeze. I wish you could see her for yourself.

Have you ever met someone, from the moment you laid your eyes on them you just wondered... wondered about their *everything*, wondered about them being with you and wondered about the taste of their kiss... on both sets of lips? -Thought I was being sentimental and cute there for a second, didn't you? No, don't be silly. My mind is racing, over wondering, over wanting and over anticipating.

"I thought you were sleeping?" speaking quietly, blowing cigarette smoke out my mouth, trying to act like she didn't just scare the shit out of me. "What you doing out here?"

"You didn't exactly leave the room quietly." Welp, there goes my dreams of becoming a ninja assassin; I could have sworn I was quiet?! "You climbed over us like some military course. I came to see if you were still here." She dug her hands into her jogging bottoms but not in the pockets. She placed her hands past the waistband and rested them on the tops of her thighs then she stepped outside. Her toes, through her thick bright cartoon character socks took the same curled shape as mine.

"*Why?* You planning on coming with me?" I wink at her.

"Depends on where you're taking me?" She's giving me the *sexiest* look! But she blushed a little, attempting to keep up with me. She has no idea the places I can (and will) take her, our first stop will be ecstasy…

"Where am I running to in my pj's female?" Directing her eyes with my hands to my deliberate choice in lack of clothing

"Those are pj's? Rah, I thought that was an underwear set not, gonna lie?" She raised a brow of slight confusion and pleasure biting the inside of her lip discreetly. Eyes set on where they should *not* be… wondering.

But she's right. I mean, it *is* an underwear set and I'm not one for sleeping with anything on other than my perfume or music. But I done some Instagram girl stalking behaviour. We all do it, don't @ me or come for me. Every woman has that stalker instinct inside of her. Besides, it really doesn't take much to find someone; just a few tagged photos here, hashtags and locations there and done.

Anyway, I found out Mali liked illustrations and cartoons and so I bought this set from Victoria Secrets on the drive down here and all I had to do was pop the tags and put it on. A turquoise silk slip cami with black a lace trim that cut over my breast along with matching tight, tight short shorts with a few of her favourite Sponge Bob images scattered here and there. All enough for her to see my body shape and make her eyes stray away every now and then from her unwanted commitment- I mean, Blue. Which worked *very* fucking well and just as I expected it to. I caught Mali on several occasions, sneaking a peak in my direction. Now, here *we* are engaged and *alone* with each other and she's standing over there looking at me some type of way, refusing to take her eyes off of me;

"Of course, they are!" I said sarcastically. "You're out here wearing jogging bottoms and cartoon socks. Looking like you're about to sit down and watch cartoons on morning T.V. with a bowl of cereal, what do *you* possibly know about women and *silk* pj's?"

"I know when women are *cold,* in their *silk* pj's Miss Aa-liyah!?" Mocking me, responding quickly, holding her laughter behind her fist Mali points at me. I follow her point to my breasts, looking down at myself and yup! There *they* were or *here* they are; my nipples, trying to make a guest appearance out of my silk top to join the conversation. Mali let out a little burst of laughter, I quickly cross my arms over my chest and stuck my middle finger up at her and laughed a little too- for fuck sake! Only *I* would be out here being all sexy, bold and brave and my nipples are harder than most people's lives- Uckin' ell Julie!

"Whatever Mali." I giggle a little.

"Stop acting like you don't wanna be watching cartoons with me in a pair of matching socks? You won't be needing pj's, besides I've been told I make a good bowl of cereal, you know?"

"Oh really?"

"Yup, that's why you wore that for me."

"Did I now?"

"Why else? You're not slick."

I shake my head a little at her confident banter and quick thinking, the look in her eyes… It's telling me she's *so* serious thought, *so* daring- I fucking like it!

Silence fell between us; I continue to imagine the conundrum of our naked bodies together whilst she peers down at the leaves still dancing their careless shuffle about the concrete floor.

Her hands back in her bottoms like before, rested on the top of her thighs. Her shoulders stiff from the constant breeze, looking at me with my arms folded over my breast trying to hide my cold nipples and light another cigarette at the same time. She smiles sideways in my direction… daringly and takes a slight step towards me.

"Hey, Miss Aaliyah…" Her tone deepened, "let me- one sec..."

She's right in front of me, *how* the fuck did she get over here so quick? She holds my cheek softly in the palm of her hand, brushing her thumb passed the corners of my mouth. Staring at my lips… I'm staring at hers, wanting them on mine (do it- kiss me), so close I can feel the heat from them fighting through the thick cold air.

"Yeah…?" the word barely exits my mouth. Waiting for her next move, my bottom lip drifting slowly away from the top one.

"…you have a leaf in your hair." Again, holding her laughter in the corners of her mouth, she let out a loud cheeky chuckle. She's lucky she's fucking cute!

"What… where? For fuck sake!" Laughing with her trying to find the fucking bastard leaf trespassing in my hair! Does it *know* how much this hair costs, for it to be chilling in my hair like this isn't Brazilian bundles? I'm going to need it to get out!

"I got you, don't worry," moving my hand away gently, she took the leaf from out of my hair. Wiggling it in my face, she brushes it over my nose with a cute little giggle.

"Thanks… leaves these days just think they can just -"

Her smile drops. My words cut short and silenced. Watching her move, take hold of my wrist pulling my hand towards her face. Saying nothing, holding onto my wrist. What is she doing? The seconds going by, my cigarette burning out in the other hand, standing here, locked in this silence. Moving her hand from my wrist to interlocking her fingers with mine. Drawing me in, our bodies now pressed together looking up at her seconds away from…

She looks away from me catching herself, remembering that she *is* taken. That her woman *is* inside the house, a few stairs and a window away from where we are stood. Her hands on my waist contemplating *their* next moves, feeling like they wanted to let go but stay at the same time. Her eyes looking back at the entrance of the house. Her thoughts, dancing around her head like the careless shuffling leaves in the wind- going from her woman… to me… then back to her woman… then back to me. Wondering whether she should or shouldn't do what she *wants* to do. Would you risk it for a chocolate biscuit, better yet, a chocolate snack? Should she risk it? Is it worth the risk? Of course, it fucking is!! Encouraging her behaviour, wrapping my arms around her neck, tugging her with the smallest subtle unnoticeable force. So subtle, she may have easily mistaken it for the loss of her self-control and subconscious mind had taken over. The look on my face engaging, luring her in, tempting her- eyes wide.

"Kiss me… I know you wan-"

My sentence cut short, she kisses me, so suddenly, so intense. Her tongue lapping over mine, her hands feeling all over my body. Not fast or in a hurry but in control and passionately, like she didn't care *if* we got caught. Like if Blue was to walk out here, she wouldn't care to stop. I live for intensity like this!

My hands under her T-shirt scratching her back, encouraging her to keep going.

You see, Blue told me earlier during our *"girl talk"* that Mali *loves* all that back scratching, getting clawed up type of shit. Silly rabbit, *never* ever tell a wolf your hiding place, because the cunning wolf will always use it to *her* advantage. Blue should have known better and that some details, *especially* the sexual details about what drives your partner crazy sexually, should always be kept between you and yours. Not distributed out to all like free leafleted information or the Metro newspaper. It's none of *your* friend's business. It's none of *their* friend's business;

it's between the two of you. Otherwise you could end up with someone like me, wanting to know more and using all the information you provided to my own advantage points- game set!

Mali shoves me against the wall and I hit it with a thud. I feel my shoulders graze a little and my skin stings instantly from the raw brick scrapping it but I like that rough shit. We pause... noses touching, breathing heavy, out of breath with the intensity rising to the highest.

That. Kiss. Was. Every. Thing! The excitement has my heart beating over double time. I can feel it pounding in my chest so hard, it feels like it's in my throat. Holding onto my face, she gives me these quick small kisses, again and again and again. Leading to longer ones; adoring, passionate, extreme, smooth and hot. Taking her bottom lip between my teeth, I bite gently and I suck. Something I love to do to them *all*! A trademark, something so small but so significant, when they go home it makes their woman question if those lips have been kissing someone else. Which is the biggest clue when someone is cheating; their kiss pattern changes, they don't kiss you like they used to because their lips have been kissed by different lips and learning new tongue tricks and ways to kiss- which Mali will do too...

"You're so fucking sexy, you know I want you! Why are you doing this to me?" She whispers, caught up on me. I say nothing holding onto her back, nails waiting, digging in a little whilst she keeps kissing on the side of my neck. I could answer with a shy 'who me?' but I own my shit! I know exactly what I am doing and I need her to know who runs this!

"Because I know you want me and I enjoy fucking with that!"

"You're going to be a fucking problem!" She says through her kisses.

Not responding, bored of all this talking. Moving my hand down her back slowly, slipping it underneath the elastic waistband of her jogging bottoms that sat loosely on her hips. She didn't stop me bringing my hand around to her front, right above her pussy, grabbing it a little. Moving my hand down past her underwear, pushing to one side I parted her lips with my two fingers... I know.... I *know* but I want to feel her. I have to know if she has a pretty pussy to match her beautiful face *and* what effect I caused on her body. Just like I thought... she is sooo fucking wet! Oooh I love it! Feeling how wet she is passing my fingers over her clit ever so softly just enough to make her tense her body little, all the while keeping that eye contact on lock.

Note: Eye Contact *(it's just so fucking sexy)*
I know I've mentioned *"eyes locked"* or *"eye contact"* because it's a very fucking dangerous thing. It's intimate but still dangerous. If I lock eyes with you and you can hold the stare... *know* that we are about to fuck because I don't attempt to lock eyes with everyone. Shit, I don't even look in the direction of people because I don't like people and I don't have time. But when I *do* look your way baby girl, it's just a matter of time until I get you right where *I* want *you*!

She doesn't attempt to stop me or my hand moving in circular motions, teasing, feeling on her clit. Moving slowly enough to make her lose her breath a little and be expecting more at the same time – keep them wanting more, don't give it to them all at once.

Looking down at my hand hidden underneath her clothes- I literally have her *in the palm of my hand*! Pulling her towards me, kissing her again, I slide inside of her so slowly. She's tighter than what I expected. She crosses me as one of those lesbians that takes dick, occasionally. You know, when these pretty young things she's tired of chasing give her frequent headaches. Don't be fooled, a fair few lesbians do this, you'd be surprised at how many of them call Tyrone looking like *Tyrone*.

"Sh-hit." She lets out quietly, trying not to make a sound. My ego rising, from the control of my fingers inside of her running circles, like the circles I've been running through her mind from the moment she met me. With a flick of my wrist, her legs weaken a little... her short panting breaths in my ear made it quick to locate the places she likes. Pressing the tips of my fingers against her, speaking into her ear slow, soft and seductively

"I already am a problem." Right as she starts pulsing and tightening her grip on my fingers, wanting more- I slowly take my dripping fingers out of her and let go

88

of her body completely. Before she got the chance to exhale the feeling of me touching the right places she's been wanting Blue to touch for however long they've been fucking around for.

Standing, one arm folded over the other circling my two dripping fingers with my thumbs inspecting. Obviously, it's making my body rush from head to toe but I keep it cool, not showing her a *thing*, poker face at its finest. Kissing her lips slowly again her mouth opens a little she waits for my tongue to meet hers... instead I move my lips away from hers and push my wet fingers into her mouth. She sucks on my finger slowly, running her tongue around it. Damn!

"Tell me how you taste..." I wait for her answer, taking my fingers out her mouth.

"Like *everything* you've ever wanted..." She says, with her stance calm, acting like she didn't get caught up a moment ago. The evidence is trailing between my fingers and on her own taste buds. Grabbing her face again, holding my tongue out a little, she follows me, allowing the tips of our tongues to touch one last time.

"I'll let you know *if* I agree... one day... maybe."

"Why are you like this?"

"Because I am!"

"You're not going to say anything are-"

"There's nothing to say, *nothing* happened!" I cut her off holding her face and making sure she understood her mouth stays the fuck closed!

"Cool."

"Now go upstairs, tuck your undies in your overnight bag, get back in the bed. Wake your girl up and fuck her! Keep your eyes closed and fuck me, through her." (I listen to The Weeknd *way* too much- honestly)

Her pupils grew bigger with every word I spoke, getting high off of the instructions she was given. She says nothing more, nothing more to be said. Stepping away from me, walking back into the house. She steps cautiously down the hall towards the staircase. She stops getting one last look at me then disappears up the stairs and out of sight.

Taking my phone that was tucked away by the side of my shorts, I scroll down through my contacts and hit 'call'. Waiting for the answer, phone pressed between my ear and my shoulder because who knows where my ear phones are? Grabbing my bag from the kitchen, I put my arms in the sleeves of my long black trench overcoat, put on my heels and leave.

"You up?" – I know right! "I'm on my way over… stay awake… so I can fuck you back to sleep."

What? You think I'm going to instruct *her* to go fuck and I'm going to run along home with *nothing* to satisfy me but my own fingers? And go to my bed with no pussy? Come on, you should know me better than that. I mean, are you paying attention to who I am or what?

3. The Relationship of Sisterhood

My possessions are and have always been my pride and joy. My trophies and things which I have worked hard for and bought for myself with my own money. They are mine; they belonged to me! I have always had expensive taste because I'm boujie as fuck! So, each purchase is as important as the last and the next. I don't expect anything from anyone, I buy my own shit. There's no one needs to buy me a single thing! I never want to hear anyone telling me:

"I want my shit back!"

That's too much noise for my liking. What's mine is mine and what's yours is yours and I don't want or need anything you have... unless it's your body on top of mine, then I'm cool with that. Do not go around buying me things expecting some kind of *claiming shit* to be going on because I have my own, I buy my own and get by on my own. All my possessions have been purchased by 'The Bank of Aaliyah Monroe' yours sincerely.

My things are not to be touched, I am *not* one of those friends you can ask to borrow things from because you have nothing to wear tonight. Nope, I don't care so don't ask because you already know the answer is no bitch. I'm a very particular person, not that you haven't already noticed; some people say I'm too fussy; I say... shut the fuck up, no one asked your opinion- *I'm par-tic-ular!*

There is nothing wrong with knowing what I like and what I *don't* like, it just so happens that the things I like are nicer and more expensive and tasteful than yours.

Anyone can see my taste for the finer things in life by looking at the interior of my beautiful apartment, which took me *for-ever* to find.

The building itself, is old and unattractive from the outside but the moment I stepped inside I knew it was *exactly* everything I wanted and more!

Open, spacious and full of things I love!

Everything has a perfect place and perfect position. It's a split-level warehouse apartment off of the Docklands Light Railway known to you fellow TFL underground users as the DLR. I'm not telling you exactly where it is because I am not WhatsApp for me to be sharing my location like that.

My ceilings are high, my walls are very tall and full of raw rust coloured brick or slightly bricked in places. It has this very urban un-established feeling to it. Big Georgian style windows allowing plenty of light in through them that bounces off of all corners of the apartment. There are *no* hidden spaces in my huge open plan living area and no hidden corners limiting my sight of one room from the other.

The ground level is decorated minimally but brightly. The lounge being the main focal point of the apartment has a huge dusty lilac fabric L shaped sofa that sat in the middle area on a massive shaggy grey rug that I love to bury the balls of my feet into. Scattered cushions *everywhere*, adding colour to the big open room with assorted fabrics, patterns.

My glass coffee table sat in front of the sofa which had a wide selection of cultural, tattoo, fashion magazines and books resting on top and underneath.

The TV is a projected onto the wall and however big I want it to be. My solitude and I love spending nights alone, half-naked and slouched on my sofa. Legs hanging off, feet dug into the rug, playing old school 1990's Mario on my SNES vintage console and drinking a can of cider from a champagne flute. Because *that* my friend, is how a classy lesbian drinks her cider!

Further down, away from the lounge a dining table sitting far over on the other side. Black chairs and a huge deep varnished black wooden oak table with the natural colour of the wood grains breaking through the brush strokes of dye. Holding a beautiful lay out for eight people to dine with gold and black plate setting that is never to be touched. I know I don't entertain people in my space, I don't like people over here, people ruin things and throw the energy of your home off. But I'm not going to let that stop me from having a beautiful dining table. It was so pretty when I saw it in the vintage shop, old and battered but perfect. I bought it and had delivered and set perfectly and in place. All it needed was a coat of dark wood varnish.

I remember sitting on the table, wearing an old white t-shirt varnishing it all night. It was a summer night I think and I had the balcony doors wide open and a bottle of red wine by my side. Now hidden along the table within the brush strokes, if you look close enough, you can see ring marks along the table as I moved further down the table until I was finished. By that time the bottle was empty, my knees, my hands and my t-shirt were covered in black varnish.

A colourful bouquet of flowers always centred the table. Eleni, my cleaner changes them regularly... every week or so, I think, I can never really remember- I'm not one for flowers or remembering important shit but it brings me small comfort knowing that she's been, cleaned and freshened up the place.

The kitchen is straight over to the right, up a few steps on a platform level; very sexy, sleek and black marble kitchen tops and purple LED lights under them, making the room feel warm along with heated tiled flooring.

Around the apartment, I've got various Buddha's. I have this little weird thing with placing geek glasses on all my Buddha's, I don't know why I do but their eyes are kind of squinting and they looked like they needed a pair.

My bedroom is up on the mezzanine level that over looked the *whole* apartment. Four poster king size bed pushed against another raw brick wall centred. One bedside table, I only slept on one side; had a stack of notebooks I like to buy but never really complete. Scattered notes of things I need to remember and stuff I have to do but never do. Someone told me it was always good to keep track of things and write them down, so I do... or I try? Don't know who told me that?

The mezzanine level was supposed to be used as some kind of other social area but the idea of it being a bedroom works way better for me. I need to be able to see *every* corner and admire my apartment from a height with great lighting. And everyone knows that great lighting leads to great half-naked or naked selfies- also known as nudes. [send nudes] But enough of the MTV Cribs Aaliyah special edition. I hope you now have a good visual image in your mind of my place- if not go read it again. I am in love with my space and love nothing more than coming home from whatever stress the day had, opening my front door and leaving the stress right there on the doorstep, like when my coat leaves my shoulders. I always make it a habit to greet my house with,

"Hello house" and a smile.

I want my space to know it's appreciated and today is no exception. I am all the way done with today and have reached my daily limit of human interaction. It's the time of day where I ignore the world, my phone and my hoes and dedicate time to value myself.

Kicking my heels off and placing them under a black chaise by the door that house a few pairs of my favourite shoes that I like to wear on a regular. And holler at my main bitch Alexia

"Alexia, play my 'Aaliyah and Chill' playlist on shuffle."

"Playing your Aaliyah and chill playlist." The surround sound speakers fill the whole apartment with music. Today's song of choice is Redbone by Child Gambino. Everyone has a song that makes them feel sexy as fuck! And this song makes me strip with every step I take into my sanctuary. Layer by layer of my clothes come off and hit floor. While my feet stay busy taking steps and feeling the surfaces underneath the balls of my feet change as I dance into the different areas of my apartment. Eyes closed, relaxed, trusting my instincts of knowing where everything is. Dancing on my tip toes, feeling the oak wood floor of the hallway change as I step onto the soft bouncy warm carpet in the lounge. Then to the massive shaggy grey rug, around it and up the four wooden steps, dancing around the kitchen island and feeling the heated tiled kitchen floor warm up my toes.

Opening my eyes watching my hips swaying in the mirror, observing the way I make my tattoos move with the beat of the music. My phoenix bird tattoo in a tribal design on the left side of my body, stomach and back moves with me whilst I sing - like I can even sing?

Why is that? Why do people who cannot sing, always want to sing the loudest? Trying to pass of riffs and tricks like their name is Jazmine Sullivan and they've perfected singing since they were eleven. When in reality they sound pitchy as fuck, like Mariah Carey trying so hard to hold her voice and her career. Which are trying to divorce her and get away like Nick Canon but the settlement claim is pending and she's praying her voice will come back like her tenth come back! Do doo doop dumb, just saying.

Or how about when you're at a concert, having paid big money to hear your favourite artist perform live and you've got one Doris singing over the music and the artist on stage. Err Doris, can you relax?! I did not pay to hear you 'try' to sing. Have you held a Grammy? No! Can you spell 'award' bitch?! Can't even hold a note if it was handed to her with instructions! Saying that, here's me stood singing my 'I can't sing' heart out, half-naked in my apartment- because I fucking can!

Pouring myself a large glass of wine and taking the bottle with me, obviously. Dancing my ass in circles eyes closed again. Perfect moments in my perfect sanctuary of solitude and solace, in my paradise! All I want to do is sit on my sofa, listen to my music and drink my drink. No interruptions, no one ruin my element of self, simplicity, peace and quiet. All alone with my wine, this is bliss…

"BUUUZZZ! BUZZ BUUUUZZZ!"

Ahh, come on! *Now?? Really?? What* the actual fuck, why? My door buzzer going off like crazy, this is *not* serious! Turning off my music, interrupted feet back flat on the floor, stomping like Godzilla all the way to the intercom on the wall that was buzzing non-stop. Alright! Shit!

"I'm coming!! Shit! WHAT! WHO IS IT!?" Shouting in the intercom!

"It's Sam babe!" Argh, shit my sister? What the *hell* is she doing here? What does she want for fuck sake? Urgh, pushing the button again I shouted back.

"I'm sorry, me NOT here!!" singing into the intercom with an accent.

"Stop messing about, buzz me in Aaliyah."

I didn't respond, hoping she goes away but I hear her saying *'thank you'*, the door opening and someone letting her in the building- ahhh shit! Fuck! Shit!

Pouting like a pre-teen throwing a tantrum. Didn't I just say I hate people over?! *Especially family* and with no warning. Stood by the door hearing her quick steps hurry down the building corridor, I hesitantly roll my eyes and open my door...

"You are not serious! Sam!? What the fuck, Samantha? No way!?"

My mouth wide open, I can't help myself I have to laugh. I need to laugh- loud and in her face! She's in my doorway covered head to toe in what looked like some kind of Arabian or Muslim type clothing- I called it! Haha! I knew it! She's *sooo* fucking predictable it's unreal! Did I not *tell* you she'd be into whatever the next trend going? Do you see what I have to put up with? It's *so* fucking typical of her. She goes whatever, which way the crowd is going. I'm telling you now, if the crowd were, let's say... I don't know, jumping off a cliff?? Well, Sam's dumb arse would be the next idiot in the fucking queue getting ready to shout 'Geronimo!'

"Hello Aaliyah."

She's acting normal, like nothing about her appearance has changed at all! As if she wasn't 'skin out' last week dancing up on *gyal dem sugar* up in the gay club and now she's here looking like she's hopped over the walls of Jasmine's palace and escaped the guards- oooookay then...

"Can we please discuss what that is on your head please?" tugging on the scarf she had around her head as she passed me at the door.

"It's a hijab." She steps past me with her wardrobe flowing in after her like a colourful flowing river of fabric- this is going to be fun!

She has *ruined* my peaceful mood, now *I* feel like *ruining hers*, annoying her and acting ignorant because I want her out of here as quick as she turned up, uninvited.

Note: Ignorance *(is really bliss)*
I often choose to purposely piss people off by acting like an actual *"dickhead"*.
This usually results in me not seeing them for a lengthy period of time. I tend to do this with family because I can tell everyone else to *"fuck off and leave me alone."* But my family are never easy to get rid of, they never take me seriously and they're used to me being well… 'me' really.
That being said, watch me work.

"I know what it is! Why are you wearing it? You look like Princess Jasmine escaped. Quick! The guards are coming!" Shouting and pointing at nothing behind her, she jumps and ducks like a doughnut.

"Shut up Aaliyah!"

She shoves me a little in my side and sits down on my sofa, adjusting the mistake she chose to wear on her head, whilst I dance around her humming the tune to Arabian Nights from Aladdin. She looks far from impressed with my reaction but I couldn't care less, I can tell I'm getting to her already. Give me five minutes and she'll be out of here fuming with me.

Throwing myself on the chaise end of my sofa I light a cigarette. I'm not normally one for smoking in my house *but* I know she is about to give me a banging headache, so might as well. Samantha moves further away from me and my fumes and sits opposite me on the single armchair shaking her colourful head at me.

"Are you going to put some clothes on or…?" Wagging her pointing finger of disapproval at me like she always does.

"Are you going to tell me why you're in my house or…?" mocking her uptight trying to be all brand-new self, whilst returning her stupid pointing finger motion.

"You know the rules, call me first so I can pretend *not* to be here, or be busy doing *any-thing* else"

"Ha ha! Very *funny* Aaliyah!" she pulls a face at me.

"There's nothing funny about it, I'm being dead serious!" She doesn't appreciate my honesty but then again, most people don't.

"I did call you Lili, you didn't answer."

"Don't call me that and no, you didn't call me." Picking up my phone so she can see the screen, which held no missed calls, no texts and not one notification. Because I *stay* ignoring this chick, place her contact on divert call or on the 'do not disturb' list of people that I don't want calling me after a certain time or at all.

"Actually, I did call. I called three times, on your *house* phone." She points at the house phone flashing its three missed calls and messages. Shit! I always forget about that one because *who* uses a house phone these days? The only purpose of owning a landline is to hook up your Wi-Fi and not as a form of vocal communication.

"If someone *doesn't* answer the house phone *Sam*, it means they're *not* home."

"Or it could mean they have a sister who ignores them. Even though *she* should be thankful that *someone* comes around to check if she's alive!" She tilts her head, sarcastically "You know I have to check in on you, make sure you're okay. We worry about you sometimes." She says concerned but I can't take her head-scarf seriously.

"I'm alive, I'm fine, I'm well, I'm okay now what do you want?" Rolling my eyes- again, waiting for her to answer.

"Well Lili…" Didn't I just tell her *not* to call me that?

"What?!" I snap at her frustrated with her being around me and in my space.

"I've officially changed my name to Imani." She smiles proudly sitting up straight like I am supposed to react to her foolishness. Does she want a badge? Because I am not Blue Peter to be handing them out!

Closing my eyes, holding the side of my head, hoping she'd fucked off with her bullshit by the time I open them. What is it, with people and changing their name these days? I can't fucking keep up! I'm going to have to get a Sharpie and write names on foreheads to fucking remember!

"I've converted to Islam and changed my name to Imani, it means faith and I thought it was the best fit, seeing as though I've found a new *faith*."

Opening my eyes- nope! She's still *flipping* here!! Sat upright and uptight, smiling like a clown talking shit, proudly. My face can't help but react to her *"news"*. It doesn't matter how hard I try not to, my face is the biggest snitch I know, especially when it comes to bullshit and uninteresting subjects, or *things* or person like my *sister*!

I'm still trying to figure out *why* she is here? She has friends? She knows people? Why couldn't she go tell them? My ears are highly sensitive to bullshit and all of this is giving me a headache I didn't ask for. Where's my drink? I need my drink.

"Oookay, *Imani*... so, why are you telling me, please?" taking a gulp from my glass, I set it back down on the table and pour myself a top up, waiting for her response, which I know is going to be a ridiculous pile of shit! Why I asked and why am I entertaining this, I don't know? Taking down another glass in one - she smiles, opens her mouth and I brace myself.

"I've come to convert you sis!" Excuse me?

It is taking every muscle in my body not to spit out my drink onto my beautiful rug, nope! No way, holding my hand over my mouth trying to get my throat and stomach muscles loosen so I can swallow- *she's trying to kill me*. She's trying to fucking kill me! This is it, this is how I'm *going* to die, this is how I'm going to meet Satan, I can see my headstone now:

"Aaliyah DEAD by bag of utter BULLSHIT!"

Wait, wait, what the hell did Princess Jasmine just say to me? She wants to convert who? *Me...*? ME of all the fucking people in her whole entire contact list... me? For why? For who?

No, wait, can I replay to make sure that's what she said because I am confused. Can I get a Craig David re-ee-wind, real quick;

"I've come to convert you sis!" Yup, that's what the fuck she said! But I needed to hear it again. Rewind it and take it back one time for my head top, for it to make sense and all now I'm waiting for my brain to respond. To say something... anything!   "The way you're living is wrong sis, it's bad... it's a ticket to hell. And I want all of my family to come with me, so we can be together to be in paradise, we have to live the good way, the right way." She's talking about *"we"* a lot   *oh*   she   speaks   French   also   now!? I literally don't know what to say, I'm actually stunned into silence, I can't speak, I cannot deal. I am done, I am *officially* done! This bitch is *crazy*! Someone, please come and claim her. She's your sister now, she's lost the plot! This has to be some planned out YouTube prank and any second now, she's going to point   out   all   the   hidden   cameras   scattered   across   the   place. My eyes are trying to refocus after rudely being blinded by that colourful layers of fabric she drifted into my apartment with. She's *still* talking, saying some shit about you can't turn the lamp on with two plug holes; that you need a plug to put in the hole and turn the light on... I have absolutely no idea where she's going with this. She's talking so much and I'm zoning in and out. This must be her 'parental guardian rated' interpretation of heterosexual sex vs lesbian sex. She's trying to tell me that being straight, is the *only* way. Oh, okay, I get it this is a 'stop eating pussy' lecture. She doesn't know who I am?? Does she not know that pussy is a five a day dietary requirement, for me? It is a daily essential that I have to have! Some people need juicy fruits or vegetables; however, I prefer a different fruit and the pretty taste of the sweet nectar between a woman's legs... ummm, what was I saying? Oh right... Samantha's not finished yet, reaching for her bag- oh shit! Oh Jesus! Oh Moses!!

Wait, Moses is the dude with the stick, who parted the ocean, right? I have those kinds of powers when it comes to parting women's legs- you can call me Moses.

"I bought a Quran for you, all you have to do is place it in the highest point of your room," whipping out a small green and red book with golden looking lettering all over it, she holds it up with this commercial smile stretched out on her face like it's some product placement selling. She places it on my coffee table, giving it a little proud pat and pushes it into my direction. Looking at it then back up at her while my cigarette is busy smoking itself away, because I am far too baffled to function. Stubbing out what was left out in the ashtray.

"I want you to find a good Muslim man, like I'm doing and live right sis, in the eyes of Allah, how we all should. Stop objectifying your beauty for this western culture and cover up your beauty. Keep it sacred for love." Is she *still* talking? She *is still talking*? It sounds like she is repeating a speech she prepared on the way over here. Like she revised it in her head over and over because she is flowing with words and I haven't got a word in, I cannot fucking speak!

She has rendered me speechless and she's misunderstanding my silence for acceptance, because her next move is walking around my place with this religious 'Lord of the Rings' book of mythology in her hands, looking for somewhere to put it *in my house*, with my *perfect* things!?

"Now then, where can we put this? Hmmm?"
Nope! I'm officially done listening to her; I can't take her shit anymore!!!

"WOAH! SAMANTHA NO!! STOP!" Shouting at her she practically jumped out of her head-scarf.

"What's wrong Lili...?" She looks at me confused, like she wasn't aware there was a problem.

"Don't. You. Dare! You are *not* leaving Winifred's book of spells in my house! NO! Nope, not happening!"

"My name is *Imani* and I bought it for *you*! To keep here…"

"Woman! If you leave that shit in my house, I'm telling you now it will be eight ninety-nine and a trip to WHSmith's wasted because it's going the fuck *in* the bin!"

"It was nine ninety-five actually. I'm only trying to help?"

Opening it, flicking through it with her thumb, she attempts to show me some pages of this holy book. I throw my arm over my eyes and put up my other hand moving my face away from it. I have it in my head that if I step into church, I'll melt like the Wicked Witch of the East. So, I can only imagine that if you try to show me anything religious, it will result in me spontaneously combusting- so, I'd rather not take the risk, thank you!

"Samantha, please! Start by helping yourself and look in fucking the mirror! No, really look at yourself. Are you hearing what you're saying? I don't need help? I never asked for your help or for you to come and chit chat this bag of bullshit to me!"

"Aaliyah I'm-"

"No, Sam! I'm fine, okay! I *love* my life. I LOVE women and I love pussy and… I love my hair far too much to be wearing *that* on my head, fuck that!"

"Hijab!"

"Whatever, it's obviously too fucking tight and compressing your common sense. I'm happy that you've found a new trend, hobby or whatever for this week. By all means you do you boo boo but you can't fucking go around *forcing* this shit onto people like this!"

"Aaliyah, calm down. You don't have to shout and swear." She's delusional! Nothing is sinking into that *thick* head-scarf of hers. Let me stand up and talk because she's not hearing me and she needs to understand the shit I am about to say. Deep breath in…

My therapist told me to count to ten and think of others before speaking my mind with no filter or regards to their feelings. However, that didn't work out *too* great for him- considering I didn't count to ten before telling him about his self with no filter or regards of his feelings and firing his arse!

"Alright now you little tree hugging, 'I kissed a girl and I liked it' weekend lesbian, confused Muslim, preaching without a god damn cause hippy!! Who in the *hell* do *you* think you are? Inviting yourself over to MY HOUSE dictating the way I live MY LIFE when you need to concern yourself with your own! Look at you! You've got a bucket full of fucking kids with how many different baby fathers and your 'ex' *in case you forgot* was a WOMAN! So, don't come up in here, telling me about the right life when yours is a fucking mess! Standing here looking like Jacob's Technicolor dream coat! You don't have a clue *and...*"

"It's Joseph's."

"What?" She threw me off. She - threw- me- off- mid- rant!

"It's Joseph's Technicolor dream coat. And Jacob's Crackers." Correcting me, a-gain with that smug smile on her face *and* I was mid rant! *Never* interrupt me mid rant!

UUUURRGHHHH-AAAAAAAAAAAAAARRRGGGHH!!
[Very fucking big internal scream.]

(Eucaifcmmnfdj fdfdsdkmsdl dpwoidcfeufcacuasiiflxkcvn lnvcl ncx; xc;c xc xckj clk nhisbedbj sd,bj,frhoohwfhilwif kfjrhfhrh;rhd jsdgjfsdjksdfjhsdf*) – This is me, punching the fuck out of the keyboard with my fresh full set of nails, frustrated like a mother fucker! Wait... that doesn't actually make sense because, "Liyah" is typing my story and I, "Aaliyah" am Narrating my story?? Look, I don't know, there was a lot of creative juice flowing aka wine.*
Anyway-

"So, what? You're an expert in Christian folktales too? You're actually *nuts*! I am done with you, all the way done; you've lost your mind!"

"I've lost *my* mind? You're not serious, you've got a cheek when you-"

"When I what? At least I know who I am"

"Yeah, just about."

"Erm says you? The weekend lesbian with a head-scarf! Every week you reinvent yourself, this week you're a Muslim. What's next week's plan? How to be a fucking tree? Get a fucking job you fool! You've got too much damn time on your hands to be reinventing yourself every other damn day!"

"I don't understand why you're shouting? I'm simply trying to do right, be right, live right and eat right..."

"Aaah, c'mon don't tell me... Pork's off your menu?" Mocking her, throwing my hands in the air, they smack back down loudly on my bare thighs.

"Do you know *how* dirty those animals are? Even after washing the meat *seven* times there is no guarantee it's free of filth! It's swine!" Her hands on her hips but I can't stop laughing, what else can I do?

"Please, Sam stop! For fuck sake! You've been eating bacon sandwiches your whole life! All those bacon baps, pork chops and crackling on a Sunday roast... you probably ate Peppa Pig's extended family babe!"

Urgh! My head. What's the point? I give up getting excited and talking loudly. She's frustrated every inch of me but this visit was no different from any other time spent with my sister. This is *us*. This is what we do. Me and *her*. Samantha and *me,* oh, no... it's now "Imani" and Me.

This is a real example of the relationship of our sisterhood. She continuously does dumb shit; I tell her openly she's a money grabbing, doll dossing, benefit system scamming, claiming to be a stay at home mother who hasn't worked a single job in thirty years plus change because she has undiagnosed leg problems, as well as anxiety and stress. Why are you stressed sis? Your life is paid for? Along with your bills and the money you spend on bullshit because your disability fund does. Then I ignore her until *she* ends up apologising for *her* behaviour- I am not Justin Bieber and yes, it is too late to say sorr- see, I can't even say the word.

This is just us on another Tuesday, feel free to tune into next week for another episode of:

"What Dumb Shit Will Samantha Say or Do This Week to Piss Off Aaliyah?"

Seven series strong now- lol

She's standing here acting as if everything she's doing and saying is normal; looking at me sideways like *I'm* crazy for raising *my* voice, when she can't hear herself!

Flopping back onto the sofa and sighing loud as fuck, I give up. Samantha is on her way to Shutter Island. Never mind heaven, she needs to be institutionalised with those white jackets... the ones with the sleeves that buckle up at the back? Yeah those! She's lost and too caught up to wake up but claiming to be 'woke' like everyone else.

"I'm only doing what sisters are supposed to do and look out for you?"

"Can't we just do what *normal* sisters are *supposed* to do and *not* like each other? I mean, I can't stand your face, so we're already halfway there. You've just got to commit to your half and BAM!" Smacking my hands together, using them as a diagram for Sam and me. She pauses in her thoughts and ignores me.

"Come with me to Mosque, I'm trying to find a husband, we can find you one too." What in the new reality TV show, 'Love & Hijab'? Dressing down and hunting for men in head-scarves and flipflops on holy ground, is going on here!?

There is no point in talking, my words aren't processing in her head. She thinks I am going to agree to her foolishness? What part of 'I like *women*' is she not getting? The breasts, the thighs, the waistline, the curves or the booty??

Rubbing my temples in circular motions. Getting rid of her has not been a success today, it never normally takes this long to get her out. I usually find her trigger and she's pissed off and out the door quicker than I can say 'hamdullah'.

"What, find a husband at your age with all your kids? Yeah, not exactly Muslim wife material, are you sis?" Crossing my arms, smug smile on my face, bringing up her *western culture baggage*, aka all her kids. She opens her mouth, attempting to find words, fiddling and faffing with the cuffs of her sleeves in her hands. That's it, I've fucking found her trigger! Her face changed completely, she bites on the inside of her lip. Awkward and uncomfortable.

"Well I'm... a..." looking around the room, not sure of what to say or where to go in her mission of saving me from *myself*, she's stuck for words, YES!

"A little *too old* for a young righteous Muslim man, no? I mean, I thought they married young but I'm sure you can find a husband. If you find a *Tyrone* who's on his 'dean' after deciding, he's not about that 'road man' life anymore. But then with *your* kids and him with *his* kids? I mean, you don't work, so you can actually do what you've been claiming to do during all this time of unemployment and actually raise your fucking kids!"

Now it's her turn to shut up and listen to me! She thinks in her silence and I lean forward, glowing, waiting for her to respond... she opens her mouth one more time and

"Oh, fuck off Aaliyah!" Yes!!!

"Well! That's not very 'Muslim' of you now is it, *Imani*? You don't want the gates of paradise close on your westernised ways." Putting on a deep voice, "no wife of mine shall speak like this; go cover your body and never leave the house unsupervised again!"

Walking away from me, she no longer wants to hear my childish shit and ignorant teasing but it is making her go exactly where I wanted her to go... to the door!

"Shut up Aaliyah!"

"Oh, look at me Sam, my phones ringing, maybe it's one of my plug hole hoes calling to lick my plug hole. We might not turn on a light but I know how to fuck up a current and make a woman buss a fuse *all* over me!"

"You're disgusting! Seriously, shut up!"

"You know what I'm talking about you part-time lesbian, you."

"Whatever!" She opened my door, ready to let herself out.

Pause.

Now, don't get me wrong I'm not against anything or anyone religious and I'm not trying to offend people, so don't bother getting excited talking about, *"oh my gosh I can't believe she said that"*- calm down, it's not that deep! I know my sister and I know this bitch is nowhere near serious. Give it a few days and she'll forget all of this faze and she will be onto the next thing trending on Twitter.

Please feel free to think of the next elaborate trend, thing, situation, idea or cult it may be.
Suggestions accepted below:

Right Here: (please suggest something you think my arse hole of a sister will be up to next, after the hashtag below.)

#...

"You're disgusting" She looks me up and down, lingering at my doorway.

"Whatever Sam, you were licking pussy a few days ago and you *loved* it like the non-halal double bacon cheeseburger from McDonald's you love so much."

"What the fuck *ever* Aaliyah, I'm gone!"

"Good, go ahead- don't let me stop you from getting the fuck out!"

Spotting her book of spells on my coffee table as she was about to leave "Oi Samantha! Don't forget your book!" I toss it lightly in the air, her face went into *straight panic*, watching it tumble turn through my apartment.

"NOOO!" She screams like I committed the un-holiest of all crimes known to a religious man, really? She's so dramatic.

Turning away and leaving her in her religious feelings, I answer my phone uninterested because I knew she'd catch it... and she did, without an issue. She's so extra; I can imagine she saw the whole thing twirling through the air in 'slow motion'.

Like in a movie, when they dive the 'dramatic dive' into the air to save the 'thing' they have been chasing and almost lose it but all is good, the movie ends blah, blah, blah, roll credits and exit cinema.

"Aaliyah's Electronics, Aaliyah speaking how can I help you light up your world?" Winking at my sister, stamping, huffing, puffing and slamming her way out.

If she continues to huff and puff, her clothes are going to take flight and she's going to end up in Oz, singing 'follow the yellow brick road', never mind heaven!

She's so annoying but she's my sister – unfortunately. And I *suppose* we all have to deal with things in life we *don't want*. Small annoying things that have no purpose, other than to irritate your life whilst they are there... kind of like thrush... no one wants it, it's annoying as fuck! Irritating and pointless but it happens, so what can you do? That definitely describes my sister to a capital 'T' ... for *Thrush*.

Sitting down, taking a much-needed gulp of wine and finishing the bottle. So much for a relaxed evening with me, myself and I. No, *she* had to come along and ruin my chill. Bothering my system on a Tuesday!!

"She's actually a joke!"

"Who's a joke B? Who you with?"

Oh shit! I completely forgot I answered my phone, sitting back down and ranting to myself about my sister. Thrown off, by a small voice coming from the phone in the palm of my hand, asking *me* questions? I didn't look to see who was calling when I answered. I was *way* too busy antagonising Sama- no, what was it? Amina, Imarna, Amnesia, Imani or whatever the hell she wants to call herself, I'm over it!

"Please, don't even ask." Responding to the voice, I pull the phone back from myself, to see who is talking in my ear- Tiana is on my line. "Anyway-*Tiana*, what are you doing asking me questions? Don't worry about who I'm with, what do you want baby girl?"

"It's my birthday today.... *remember*?"

"Of course, I did... *how* could *I* forget *my* baby girl's day?" She knows damn well I didn't remember, why would I?

"Don't lie bruv. Knowing you, you don't even know what day it is today." She *also* knows I don't remember shit either!

"I'm not lying, shut up you dick head, it's Tuesday?"

"Nope, It's Wednesday, you doughnut!"

"Really? I could have sworn it was Tuesday." Honestly, I did.

We both laugh, she knows what I'm like, she never expected more than what she *occasionally* gets from me but Tiana being Tiana, is audacious enough to challenge me on that by demanding more. Expressing her desire for me to *attend* and involving me in important things that happen in her life; such as birthdays, which I don't have any interest in but she persists anyway.

Tiana is not the usual *girl* I'd go for; she's a lot younger than me… somewhere in her very early or just turned twenties. Wait a minute, I didn't snatch her up young- in my defence, she was *already* snatched up by some other cradle snatching lesbian. And besides, her age left my mind from the start because she handled me better than some of the grown women that I have dealt with. So many women are out here talking so much shit! Bragging about their 'sex', telling you how they're going to leave you weak and out of breath…

Note: To the heterosexual women reading this

Even though I don't know who you are? You can most definitely relate. It's not just men that are out here talking a big dick game.

Fun fact about lesbians, is they share that *same* 'big dick, good sex' egotistical trait. I'm sure you can agree that having big dick does not automatically mean your sex is fire. And talking highly of your own sex also does not mean it is the best I've ever had and often, if not always leads to disappointment.

So instead of pretending to be satisfied and saving egos because I don't have time to be engaging in poorly executed sexual activities. I'll be reaching for my car keys and ready to leave. Expecting 'inhaler assistance' from all that breath I was *supposed* to be out of but I'm there unsatisfied, unimpressed and breathing… *fine!* Inhaling and exhaling at an extremely normal rate.

Tiana is cute as fuck with a personality to match! She's not the most knowledgeable person but 'youth' comes with lack of life's experience. Not having anything to worry about. Living life still sheltered, not having touched or caught sight of a single household bill. So, her outlook on life is this fun laid-back attitude.

She's taller and mixed with something, I don't know what, I couldn't tell you. And she's got big bouncy tight ringlet curls that surround her pretty face. Your typical light skinned chick, without the typical light skinned chick *'I think I'm too nice'* attitude. I am not about that whole team lighty "light skin attitude" thing- you can miss me with it. Tiana has these big brown eyes that have glimmers of mischievousness sparkling boldly throughout them. She pulls these comical expression-full faces that make me think of emoji's and memes. Having me laughing carelessly, when I am not trying to have laugh lines or any signs of ageing on my face.

She resembles one of those Westbrooks sisters; you know which ones I'm talking about. Or don't you? Not many people do? Google them if you don't know who they are. I don't pay attention to them because I think *we* as a nation of strong successful black women have *so much* more to offer to the world of media and entertainment than five girls trying *sooo* damn hard to do nothing but imitate the Kardashians- as if the world needs another fucking set of five talentless females allowing young girls to think that being nothing but a prosthetic body is *every*-thing and living life through 'sponsors', 'likes' and 'followers' is living. *However*, a couple of those Westbrooks are sexy as fuck!! I'm telling you now, that one covered in tattoos that rides those big boy bikes... well, she is a *problem* and would fucking get it differently! And she's not even a ten across the board, it's just her whole dominate attitude. Very feminine but she's on motorbikes and quad bikes popping wheelies like it's light work! Damn! I'm still amazed that the world has accepted the Kardashians, openly regardless of scandal and media propaganda. What is this world coming to? Is there no hope for the future of our kids? The next generation of women to come are fucked! Come on! Imagine, in forty to sixty years or so when the next generations after ours are left unsupervised. Looking back through the archives of historic female figures.

Gone are the days that women were strong, iconic and went down in history books as powerful leaders like Maya Angelou; who fucks shit up with her beautiful words of poetry and empowerment, making you feel like a phenomenal woman. Or when Disney movies had a story of morals, like Mulan posing as a man to fight in a war of men for what's right. The point I'm making is that your kids, kids, kids, kids will be looking back not knowing what an iconic woman or a single fairy tale is. They'll know nothing about the wonders of books or telling stories off the top of their heads like Jack and the Beanstalk (I'm getting to my point hang on, wait I know I'm waffling but there is definitely a point, it's coming.) So, Jack goes to sell the only cow, he fucks up, trades it for magic beans and grows a giant fucking beanstalk. Climbs up the fucker, steals golden eggs and the singing harp so his mother can eat and live her best life. No, no!! It's going to be:

Once upon a time there was a broke personal assistant named Kim Kardashian who sucked dick on camera and her mother leaked it to worldwide social media, put in a law claim and became stupidly famous and filthy rich and now is a female "figure" that girls all get surgery to become. She gives her mother fifteen to twenty percent of everything to fund her own 'should have left your face alone and aged gracefully' cosmetic surgery! Who was married to a man, that she *knew* – in fact, *everyone knew* he wanted to be a woman, who got awards for *womanhood* when there's still a "manhood" between his/her legs. And their youngest child has had more surgery than the whole family put together! But let's 'face' it, Kylie Jenner is yet another white woman who is culturally appropriating all things that signify beautiful black women as their own and is applauded for it. #transraciallivesmattertoo #fuckoff

Oh! *But!* If a black woman unintentionally speaks a certain way that people categorise as not being "black enough" even though it's the way she speaks. She's publicly shunned, called an "Oreo" or classed as a "Coconut" by her fellow black women…

Yes sis! The *same* black women paying homage to women like Kylie, Kim, Khloe and the rest of them! Why the fuck would I want to keep up with that when I have my very own, *very* dysfunctional family? I don't need to watch one on television, no thanks.

If I wanted to watch a dysfunctional family, I can pull up to my mum's house, pull up a chair and keep up with that kind of drama.

The Kardashians are and always will be a glorified white family, popping out mixed race babies with ridiculous names, raising them without any knowledge or interest of black history and culture. Why? For the gram of course, for the novelty, trend and social media attention! #mixedbabies #mixedbaby #mixedkids

And that kids of the future generation who won't know what a book is, is where the Kimoji's originated from kids

- The End.

Who knew things would be like this in big, big 2018? What do we really have to say for ourselves living in a big dysfunctional biosphere of illusion and lies? Where people actually wasted a vote that could have changed *everything* on a fucking dead gorilla!? Then again, I'm sure the gorilla would have wanted to build a giant wall too, to keep the humans out of his enclosure! 2016, let's not even go there shall we.

Americans + Trump = Keep your politics out of my vagina, thank you!!

I get it now! You know when old people sit and shake their heads in disapproval at the
ungrateful youth of today, I actually get it. Things weren't like this back in my day and
everyone born after the millennium, good luck to your wasted youth!
Any who, back to me and Tiana. You've got to learn to stop me when I go off on these
tangents otherwise we are never going to get anywhere! Let me take you back to how we started. She was a new pretty little face to the scene, in her tight circle of excited,

hyped up and fresh out the closet lesbian friends. Doing way too much to prove their right and place into the LGBTQ world! Things have changed, back in the day we used

to be scared of coming out or holding hands in public and now it's a coming of age celebration like a bar mitzvah. Soon they'll be throwing 'coming out and bad' parties

you heard it here first!

I clocked Tiana straight away! She was looking at me from across the way. We were inside of one of the gay night clubs in London. And she was taking a massive risk looking in my direction because her hands were tied by her very boisterous female she had selected for a girlfriend- newbies to the scene would almost always make this novice mistake, I mean, choice. They think they have to be with a masculine, butch looking 'stud' as initiation into the underground urban world of the gay scene. Choosing a less feminine woman to test the water. Unsure if they're ready to like women and only really dip a toe into lesbianism with a stud or woman with more of a masculine energy. I too, made that same fatal choice but like I said that's a whole different story. But don't get me wrong some of these studs are sexy as fuck and others are... well... just not my cup of tea really. Look there is someone out there for everyone and some (all) of them are not for me.

Anyway- *the same night a mutual insignificant associate introduced me to baby girl. And Tiana's cheeks instantly filled with this bright pink blush, as I gave her a subtle wink and held onto her handshake for a few too many seconds. Tiana's woman, pulled her back, tightening her grip and glared at me. I sensed her territorial "she's mine!" bullshit behaviour.*
She, (the woman), was intimidated by me- obviously! Have you seen me? She needed to be, I shouldn't be trusted around anyone's woman! Especially, if baby girl's fire! And not wearing a ring on her finger... not that, that's ever stopped me before.

So, later on, when Tiana was stood by the bar with her friends spectating as her woman proved her "manliness" in a fist fight.

[Typical testosterone fuelled lesbian 'stop looking at my girl' when no one was looking irrational beef]

I brushed past the back of Tiana's body so lightly, she didn't notice. I slipped my number swiftly into the back pocket of her tight jeans and gave her booty a nice firm tap. It jiggled a little, those pretty young things with those fit trimmed and toned for no reason bodies that are not clinging onto calories do that. Those slim bitches that can eat everything and their bodies are like "calories, who dis?!" Meanwhile, I look at a doughnut and put on weight! Calories cling to my body, unwanted like a lingering ex-girlfriend.

Before Tiana could look behind her to see who was all up on her, I was gone! Out of sight, leaving her lost, removing a small piece of folded paper from her back pocket. Looking behind and around her puzzled at who could have slipped it in there so smoothly.

Call me old school but I like to leave my number on folded pink scented paper sometimes. Think about it, I can't be out here with phones being held all out in the open, taking down or giving out numbers, it's too bait. These days you can't even drop your number in someone's ear without necks stretching in your direction. So, I figured leaving my number this way or handing it over on the sly during conversation is mysterious and intriguing. Like I said from the beginning, somewhere on page sixteen or seventeen; I don't go giving out my details to just anyone, so consider yourself very fucking lucky if you ever stumble across a small pink folded piece of paper with my details.

Tiana called me a little later that night, I knew she would. I knew her rising curiosity and over powering, controlling woman would lead her astray and into the direction of my open legs without me even saying or doing anything much at all.

"Hey it's... erm, Tiana." Her voice had this cute little nervous 'trying to stay confident' tremble. After all, she didn't know 'who' she was calling. It could have

been a trap for all she knew. These lesbians can do some crazy shit to try to catch their girls slipping on their loyalty. Setting little traps, playing games and doing erratic crazy things that make the bullshit on Jeremy Kyle seem remotely normal.

"I already know it's you baby girl, where are you?"
She exhales at the sound of my voice. Relieved it's not her woman's.
"I'm outside the club…"
"Where's your man?" I laughed, she knew exactly who I was talking about.
"I don't even know B. Probably inside using the men's toilets, tryna pee standing up, who fucking knows?" she laughed with me, less anxious and at ease.
I swung my car around at the next lights and before she knew it, I was pulling up in front of her. I let my blacked out tinted driver seat window down, just enough for her to see who I was then put it back up again real quick, before one of her friends started to stretch their necks to see who owned this sexy whip and was talking to Tiana.

"Get in!" I said, she looked over both shoulders then back at me.
"Ayo sis! Where you going?" One of her people hollered at her.
"Don't worry bout' me fam!" She stuck out her tongue and hopped in the car with the biggest smile on her face. "This is mad, how'd you know I'd call?"
"They always do."
"Say no more."
Driving through the city, in the early hours of the morning not saying anything at all. Letting my music do the talking. I love the slow, chilled, soulful, in a zone type vibe of songs. With a nice beat and banging bass that real undiscovered raw shit, not watered down commercial censored mainstream shit.
Tiana wasn't much of a talker, she wasn't too excited or over eager, she was cool and chill. Sitting back comfortably nodding along to the music. Whispering lyrics and tapping her hand along with the beat. Lost in her own vibe. I turned the music down low and spoke to her calmly.

"Understand this, your little friends don't need to know shit. You tell people your business, people will talk and talking will get you caught. No telling your best friend, so she can tell her best friend. Because by the look of your woman, your face is too pretty to be dealing with 'that' kind of drama. No one knows nothing! If you see me out, unless I approach you, do not approach me. It is what it is. Don't ask me any questions about what I'm doing, when I'm with you, I'm with you and it stays between us."

"Yeah, I hear you B." Keeping my eyes on the road, I could feel her listening intently to every single word.

"Good... and it's Aaliyah. But you can call me B, I like that." I placed my hand on her thigh and her cute cheeky blush reappears all over her face.

Telling her the deal was *absolutely* essential; no small talk. I'm not here for that. I couldn't have her thinking I was a way out of her girlfriends' probable abuse. She has to figure that one out on her own, that is her drama and not my problem! I don't do, the whole saving people from situationships

Situationship *noun*

The way in which two people are disconnected without the other persons awareness. Apart but not separated. A circumstance in which one finds oneself; a state of affairs. Could have started as a relationship, dating or beneficial sex but has now become a 'situation'. Not wanting to stay but not wanting to leave; hanging on for reasons either or are questioning. Used in a sentence: *"I'm in a siuationship"* or *"I like you, but I'm in a situationship"*

I don't do confidence boosts or the life coach thing either. Who has time for that? I know there are people out there that find themselves attracted to the *"ones that need fixing"* the basket cases, help the healing or broken hearted. But end up catching a case when the one who *needed* fixing- yes, that very same person who you gave *everything* to, who gave you *nothing* but continuous headaches. Ends up leaving you and being *everything* you tried to make them be for the next bitch they get with!

All that time invested for what? Because you loved them? And now they are out here pretending to be Mrs./Mr. Perfect? Stunting on social media time lines with the new boo thang. Hash tagging stupid hashtags and in-directly directing you like *you* were the one that fucked up? You got me fucked up! Nope, I'm not involved! I will physically hurt someone over that shit. Not me. What? You think you can go play *"the perfect partner"* to another bitch? Don't get me mad!

But sadly, we all know a story like this. Shit, it's probably happened to you or is happening to you right now! But take your time and do what you need to LET it the fuck GO!

Tiana knows exactly what I am about. She lives at home with her parents- and me not doing the whole;

> *"Hi mum hi dad, yoohoo family. I'm just here to fuck your daughter*
> *real quick and pretend I'm only her friend every time I come over."*

There's nothing worse than getting involved with a woman/girl who lives at home and hides her sexuality from her family, addressing you as her "friend".

Before you know it, when they *finally* find out what you've been doing, they want to attack you like *you* were the one who has been lying this whole time. Then you have a psychotic mother coming at you telling you to stay away from her precious child, that you are the devil blah, blah, blah another story for another day.

I took Tiana back to my apartment. And there was no time to say *any-thing* because as soon as my front door clicked onto its hinges and closed. She was on me like the perfume imbedded in my skin. Her age was nothing but a number, Tiana had me up, my jeans unbuttoned, unzipped, dragged down my legs and at my ankles. Aggressive and powerful, she picked me up, threw me on the sofa and introduced her tongue to my pretty pussy. The way she handled me- fuck! Her sex was fire! She must have been deprived from doing anything to her woman. You know, some studs and a good majority of tomboys are often like that. Don't want to be touched in certain places, getting completely naked or connecting skin to skin and say something like:

Deep, trying to be man-dem voice
"Nah don't touch me, I'm good. I get mine from hearing you."

Are you mad?? *We* are fucking till we get this shit right! No need for strap-on's they feel nothing other than some sense of male dominance. I find it hard to comprehend that *LESBIANS* have made a choice to not want dick BUT they are more than happy to strap up and give their women fake dick! I never understood that logic, ever? I'm going to need you to 'fuck' with what you have and participate with your fingers and tongue in the best way. Besides, studs aren't really as stud-*ish* as you think; it's all an act and part to play within the stereotypes of our sexuality. It's more of a way to dress, walk and talk. It's more of a stance and attitude because the moment you get hold of a stud, pin her down, open her legs and you're all over her clit while she's screaming *your* name and saying "Ohh baby!" like her name is Ashanti "Ouu baby!" legs shaking, can't take no more but doesn't want you to stop. Trust me! She'll forget *all* about her dominate ways and her fitted hats whilst she's up making you a sandwich, giggling. Legs still twitching from bussing that good, good nut.

Sex is way, *way* more than penetration. And I swear if you're one of these straight people reading this book and you've just asked yourself in your head:

"But how do lesbians have sex?"

It annoys my *life* when I get asked that question from anyone! Like shit! If you really want to know why don't you fuck around and find out!? I'll show you! Call me when you *really* want to know what's up, trust me you'll know the answer when I'm done! Then you'll be wanting to call Tyrone to tell him to come home and get his shit. So, you can show another female *exactly how we lesbians fuck*!

"Lie again! You're flipping annoying! I am done with you." Tiana laughs, finding herself hilarious.

"Don't you dare, behave yourself! You know you're not going anywhere!"

"Try me, I swear I will." She continues her banter.

"Whatever Tiana, it's not my job to remember. Birthday celebrations are for you and *her*. Not me baby."

"Oh okay, you had to go *there* huh? So, what's your job then Aaliyah?"

"To fuck you right! Have you cum all over me, scream my name until you can't even remember hers and then to... kick your arse at Mario Kart. Obviously!?"

"I miss you man, haven't seen you in ages. You coming tonight or what?" She whispers down the phone all soft and cute. Pausing, making her wait for an answer, playing along, I whisper back.

"...Is *she* going to be there?"

"Yeah *she's* rolling. Bringing all her strap-on wearing friends too... but there *is* gonna be a lot of people about." I can hear the smile of mischievousness through her tone of voice.

"You like playing with fire, don't you?"

"I haven't been burnt yet, besides it's only a little fire called Aaliyah... do you know her?"

Already accepting her challenge, I need to have some fun tonight especially after my sister decided to pass by with her shit. I could do with a very active and sexual form of stress relief.

"Yeah, I do. I heard she's *fucking stunning!*"

"She *is*, you know..." Tiana's whisper got lower, I know *her woman* is lingering around *my* baby girl somewhere.

"She there now?" I know the answer but I ask anyway.

"Yeah, she's about. She's so annoying bruv!" she sighs.

"Say... my... name..."

"You're such a doughnut, I swear," before she could get into any kind of conversation about how her woman is; I switch her attention back to me.

"Say my name… tell me what you want me to do to you tonight, *if* I decide to *come* that is." Encouraging her 'no behaviour'. She hesitates a little, waiting for the coast to be completely clear before speaking

"Whatever, you're *coming*."

"Say it!"

"Why are you like this?"

"Tell me."

"… Aaliyah … I want you to *come* to the club tonight and… I want you to…"

"If you don't say it I won't *cum*."

"Aaliyah, I want you to fuck me, the way I like it." she said low and muffled with her mouth pressed hard against the phone, heavy thinking thoughts of me inside of her already.

"Tell me how you like it?"

"Hard and heavy and slow. Then rough and fucking messy," her voice lower, sexy and discreet. "and not to stop."

"Until?"

"Don't stop until I cum."

"Okay beautiful, I'll do that for you… what's *she* doing?" I have this deliberate habit of reminding *them* about *theirs* and then switching the conversation pace and tone to casual and calm.

"She decided *she* wants to take me to the club. Show me off and show out," she sighs again and I'm sure she rolled her eyes with it.

"What did she get you?" I threw myself back on the sofa, laying on my back on the phone to baby girl. Playing with my hair, running my nails through the free partitions in my scalp. Best feeling ever, running your nails through the vacant parts in your scalp that aren't occupied by weave tracks and braids.

"Bruv... she got me a fitted fucking hat and some other bullshit, I didn't bother with because she doesn't pay attention." My legs up crossed over, feet in the air, listening to Tiana unimpressed with her woman's inability to get to know her.

"Like all your big curly hair can get into a damn hat?"

"I know this! She don't! I had to lie like *aaww thanks babes*- urgh"

"She bought that for herself." I confirmed with ease. It makes shit so much easier

for me to be 'me' when the significant other messes up all on their own. All I have to do is sit back, just like I am now and agree, without having to do the whole *'she ain't shit'* trash talk.

"I'm getting my real shit later so, she says."

"Not if *I* give it to you first. I'm *coming* tonight. I'll give you something you *really* want baby and by the time I'm done, you're *never* going to want what she's got for you *ever* again!"

"I never want what she's got. I only want yours. What time you coming?" She's all excited now, I can hear it in her voice.

"Don't worry your pretty little self. I'll get there when I get there. But there's one condition" I whisper my entrapment down the phone.

"I'm listening..."

"When your night is over and she takes you home and wants to fuck... you tell her no! Go lock yourself in the bathroom and fuck yourself! Imagine me inside of you and all over your body. Call me, wait for me to answer and let me hear you. Then wait for me to tell you when to cum and say my name over and over again."

"Oh, you know I will!"

Ending the call, on my sofa in a different position; my body on the edge of the seat with my left leg hanging off; circling the ball of my foot along the shaggy soft bristled texture of the shaggy rug, unable to sit still thinking about what to wear that looked good but has easy access to get naughty, that won't require me to get completely naked. Hmm, what do you think should I wear?

4. The Pink Silk Ribbon

Entering a lesbian dominated club in Soho, feeling the heads turn as per usual- all eyes on me. I *know* I look fucking good, blending in amongst the younger crowd. Dressed down and ready to fuck in a casual but tight little black dress. Tight enough to not get creased up from being pulled up. Tiana's woman could *never* compete with me. How can she? There is no competition- *shit*, I am the competition and let's face it, I'm winning all the time sis!

#winning #yourgirlwantsmemorethanyou #ohwell #shitthen

By now you should have some sort of unpleasant mental image of 'her' going on- good! Keep that in mind, I'm not wasting my time describing her. So, picture anything really with an unpleasant looking character reference- example: Troll, Dobby, Man like Shrek, Gremlin, Kylie Jenner before surgery, *any* of the Kardashians before surgery and Drake without a beard... any of those will do.

At the bar (come on, where else would I be?) I got myself a glass of brandy along with a Jeroboam sized bottle of champagne sitting on ice. For those of you who don't believe in pouring it up and ballin' out at the club. Jeroboam is basically a big ass bottle! I accompanied it with plenty of glasses and a strawberry in each one. Why all of that...? You'll see soon enough.

I sat facing the club looking out over the crowd and people who I want nothing to do with searching for Tiana. Which never takes long to spot her out in the crowded sea of not so attractive people when she's so stunning!

Watching close, observing the way she moves her body- every move so seductive. Even down to the way she moves her hands. Do you ever do that? It's crazy to think that some of us are blessed with two eyes to see beauty and two feet to walk, skip and dance. But we all take our hands for granted, don't we? Think about it; I have an ongoing habit and no one notices that I do it- I really enjoy watching the way people use their hands. And no, it's not because I am a lesbian! Hear me out; we all have two hands and we all move them with so much character. It's like a language, an accent of individuality so to speak almost, the way we speak. Everyone that I know has the same two hands: one right and one left and they move them so differently. The way they move them when they talk and turn their wrists and fingers a certain way to point or describe something they have seen. Just going along with the words they say, no thought to it but they flow in a particular way. No one seems to notice that we all move our hands in a completely different way. So different that no one can replicate the unique movements. But I've been paying close attention to hands around me for so long that I could probably imitate another's movement if I tried- I guess it's just the small things that I find mesmerizing about people- women in particular. Makes me wonder.

Tiana dances in the distance celebrating another year of her life with her people. She notices me across the way, she smiles a different smile. One just for me. She looks so fucking amazing! Her tight curls are straightened, reaching way down her back, highlighted with the many colours of her natural dark, light golden brown and blonde hair. She looks as if she's stepped out of a dance studio or off stage with her combination of big and baggy and small and tight in all the right places clothes. A red tartan baggy shirt wrapped around her hips making her body move perfectly to every beat. There is something about a pretty girl in baggy clothes that makes me melt. Moving her hands in only a way she can, she runs them through her hair and over her snatched body.

Shrek (her woman) is close by but Tiana is busy turning me on with every move she makes. Her friends eagerly encouraging her to keep dancing, they have *no idea* that I am the one on her mind and she is dancing for me. Dance for you by Beyoncé filling the club and baby girl is dropping it and popping for me. Dancing as if she's imagining a spotlight only on her body and it's only the two of us here. No one else but me and her matter as I sit back watch and picture her body on my body.

"You wanna dance beautiful?" A voice speaks sensually, close to me.

"No. I'm good." I answer quickly with no consideration or thought to look in the direction of the woman talking into my ear, asking me to dance. I have absolutely no intention of taking my eyes away from Tiana hypnotising me. Tiana chuckles discreetly watching the rejected stranger step to the left and walk away. She dances unphased, slowly rotating her waist to the music while she mouthed the lyrics to the song in my direction.

The DJ switches the music which instantly changes the tempo in the room. The surrounding couples that were caught up in a slow whine let go of one another. Tiana's people crowd around her, excited by her sexy solo. She keeps me in her eye sight throughout the hype; clapping my hands together subtly and silently from across the way. Signalling her over to here where I am, by twirling my hair around the finger of my left hand- a gesture/signal for:

"The coast is clear; bring your arse over here…now!"

Once the hype around her started to calm down and fade, her squad spread out, acting out over the beat drop on the introduction of the next song. Looking like a bunch of fools that don't know how to behave. I mean, we can all appreciate music but not the shit they play up in the clubs today. Bunch of gibberish, making no sense or showing any lyrical pen to paper/off of the dome talent. No, just a bunch of words with 'ya', 'skrr skrr' or 'rat tat tat tat' on the end. Which has people jumping up and down pushing, shoving and twerking to bullshit. Phones out recording each other like they're in a music video. Uploading it on Snapchat with the latest filter for all to see. Some days enjoy real music, stop acting like you're a music video producer with a dog filter on your fucking face and chill the fuck out!!

Tiana checks over her left shoulder then over her right for preeing eyes. She slips away from her people and switches her steps right in my direction with a beautiful ease of confidence all over her demeanour. I usually don't like to be seen out in public lesbian places with the women on my rotation but tonight is an exception:

Number one: It's a special occasion

Number two: She looks fucking fire!

Number three: (see number two!)

She leans on the bar, resting her arms and stands beside me. The natural scent of her skin blended with her perfume, sits under my nose and settles on my top lip. She's only a few inches away from me and already I can taste her. She peers in my direction, over me and squints to double check. Then she orders herself a drink; double vodka and cranberry as always. I place my card on the bar not engaging with her just yet. Instead we both analyse and study the people surrounding both of us.

Note: *Study your surroundings first!*

This note is important!! You *always* need to make sure no one is watching you too close, paying any attention to you or up in your business. Remember the scene is small- so, it is compulsory to check each other's back! Once the coast is clear then and only then can you proceed in light engagement.

"What the fuck took you so long? I've been waiting for you!" Tiana's eyes penetrate my body, with just one look. Making me pause and hold in my smile before answering.

"I know!" I stare right back.

I intentionally took my sweet time to arrive. I wanted to keep her on her toes, waiting in suspense for my arrival. To be stretching her neck above the crowd and checking the time on her phone anxiously every half hour or so, hoping for me to appear in the overcrowded venue. Winding herself up, to the point where she gave up on the thought of me coming at all... and then all of a sudden and out of nowhere, I appear. Trust me, I'm worth the wait.

She leans towards me, giving me a *friendly* kiss on the cheek. Only I notice Tiana's lips landing right at the side of mine and remaining there for a few hot seconds longer than they should. Examining each other, our faces saying what our mouths don't need to. Our minds are elsewhere, doing things to each other you cannot imagine.

"I didn't know you could move like that baby girl" I break the sexual tension.

"That's because I'm not a *baby* anymore, girl." She moves her hips slowly, distracting me from my words while and my eyes follow her once more. She takes a seductive sip of her drink, her tongue stuck out a little reaching for the straw not taking her eyes off of mine *(eye contact- she knows)*.

"I still get to call you baby girl though, right?"

"You and you only B." She wants the taste of my pussy on her tongue instead of that drink. Her eyes a little hazed from whatever narcotic wave she is on.

"Happy birthday to *my* grown, baby girl!" Raising our glasses, we toast to Tiana's night.

"Thank you, B!" she smiles sweetly "Wait, I don't drink champagne? Who's that for" She notices the bottle on ice beside me with several glasses.

"Her and them." I signal over at Tiana's girl pacing towards us. I don't flinch, I just smile at the predictable movement I knew she would make when seeing us over here.

"Ay yo! Tiana, who's this!" Her deep voice interrupting our time and sexual intent together. The girlfriend, slash manfriend, slash troll friend is standing by Tiana. Waiting for answers and looking at me like she has something to say. You already know the attitude on my face is daring her to say something to me, anything! Let her try me because she needs to back up and take several seats down!

"Hey babe, remember my... uh, old friend from college Aali, Na-Natalie?" Tiana almost slips up with my name and introduces me to her '*woman*' with some other bitches' name instead. This won't be the first time I have had to take on another identity to fool the significant other on my case, wondering who I am. Urgh! Look at her! I know *all* about females like her! Out here preying on young girls like predators.

Mind fucking them to stay around till they are nothing but a shell of a girl they used to   be...   so   empty.

You think men are the *only* emotionally manipulative gender out here? Oh no, try putting two women together and wait… let me stop myself and not go there, let me be reasonable, seeing as though the girlfriend does have a reason to be looking at me sideways and questioning *who* the fuck I am and why her woman is closer than she needed to be. She's probably familiarising herself with my scent; I know she's smelt me on her woman's skin or tasted my pussy on her lips. Maybe she knows, I am the one showing Tiana all that new shit she brings to their bedroom. Like how to squirt over and over again or to control her pelvic floor muscles tighter, to be able grip onto her fingers. Meanwhile, the only thing she is showing Tiana is how to lay down and take her plastic strap on. So, someone needs to show baby girl how to fuck because we all know looking, dressing and acting like a pre-pubescent teenage boy does not qualify you as a certified ten between the sheets! So, let her attempt to come at me, I will always cum on top. She's too busy feeling threatened and intimidated by me that she hasn't realised; I'm *not* one of Tiana's little college friends and she has actually seen me in brief passing encounters here and there. Because I stay hidden under the radar of baitness and social networking of the lesbians within LGBT- queer community. I keep my identity hidden like H.E.R with my shades on. Only those who know me, know who I am. I am not to be associated with The Scene!

The Scene *noun*

The Gay Scene, The Gay Crowd (the gay night club socialite scene).

Definition: The **Urban** gay scene in London. Not a largely populated group of people. In most cases a close net of inhabitants who know of (but do not know) each other: Almost *too* close. Aka drama.

Example: (pay very close attention) *A* is friends with *B*. *B's* girlfriend is *C*. *C* is friends with *D*, who's ex is *A*. Who knows *C* and is *D's* woman. But *E* used to see *F*. *F* used to also fuck with *D* on the side but now is with *G*. *G* is in a relationship with *H* who is friends with *I*. And *I* knows every damn body and, in some way, is linked to them all or have come into to contact with them all but doesn't know them, know them- she only knows of *them*.

There is a whole lot more letters to throw in there but it will start to get fucking ridiculous! Before you know it, we'll be throwing in numbers, multiplications, divisions and square roots! We'll end up with a massive wall chart, playing connect the hoes and dots of *"who's fucking who."* Which is why I keep a note of all the little important pretty faces I see now and then. So, I can successfully calculate my next moves within the scene. Oh, you think all this promiscuity is easy? Not at all, baby girl you need to keep note and track of all your 'no behaviour' and have it written down. You want to make sure that the women you're fucking with are not in close contact or association. And that is not easy to do, considering the sheer size of the black lesbians in London. We are the minority within the minority! Hoe is life, for real!

"Oh yeah, hey Natalie!" She puts an arm out and I decline, moving back a little responding with a nonchalant head nod and say
        "Hey…"
She looks at Tiana, confused like she's trying to figure out a mathematical equation.
        "Natalie doesn't do the whole hug thing." Tiana shrugs her shoulders and pulls a little side emoji like face.
        "I got something for you baby girl." I'm bored of our attention on Felicia and hand Tiana a Selfridge's shopping bag, I tucked away behind my bar stool.
        "It's nothing special. Just something I know you wanted for a while now."
        "Oh shit! You shouldn't of!" Her face is glowing in the dark club, lit with admiration for me.
        "Open it." Insisting she opens the shopping bag. Tiana pulls out a designer black leather tote back with gold detailing.
        "No fucking way! I've wanted this for like *ever*! Thank you!" Tiana screams, throwing her arms around my neck, excited like a kid at Christmas finally getting the toy they circled in the Argos catalogue and waited all year for.
The squad had come over with their fast selves to see what all the commotion and fuss was about. I'd like to point out that Tiana's arms are *still* wrapped around me

tightly. All I need now is something to say to inject the sweet taste of pettiness into this situation.

"I almost got you a fitted hat but remembered how much you *hate* those fucking things." A slight fake smile and my eye line directly at her woman. Tiana turns to me and then to the ground trying not to laugh out loud. She knows I don't give a fuck.

"Honestly, I can't believe this is perfect!" Her happiness is on a hundred!

"Why don't you *open* your *new* bag?" She tilts her head looking at me like, *"bitch no you didn't?"*

"Fuck off!! Babyyyy!!" Tiana squeals, seeing the matching purse sitting inside her new bag. Throwing her arms around me again. But this time her body leans into me, squeezing me tighter than tight *should* be. She's terrible and bad, biting the side of my neck *hard,* trying to make me react. Softly, subtle and quick she sucks my neck and kisses it twice over. No one knows what she's doing apart from me and the goose bumps rising on my tingling skin. She moves so smoothly, lifting her head off of me. Her flowing hair shielding her 'no behaviour' follows, leaving me with a pout on my lips. Holding onto my neck, feeling the traces of her kiss. Not giving anything away behind my poker face. Keeping cool and looking at Tiana unaffected and nonchalant, I smile discreetly because she's learned from the best.

In the corner of my eye, I can see her woman opening the shopping bag- her jaw drops at the total on the receipt, oh dear… I *must* have *forgotten* to take out of there… how forgetful of me- lol! *Please!* I left the receipt in there on purpose! I want her to see there are levels to this shit, she couldn't reach!

The standard that she should always be at when it comes to gifting her woman. She *better* be threatened and anxious by every second Tiana is spending beside me and every centimetre she gets closer to me or by the hand that Tiana has no reason, resting on my thigh.

Everyone doesn't need to 'know' a woman to know that *all* women love a handbag. Come on, what woman doesn't want a designer handbag resting on their forearm or shoulder? Obviously, she has a lot to learn. So, she better start by taking notes because she's gonna learn today.

"You're more than welcome baby girl." Sipping on my drink whilst Tiana shows off and styles her new bag to her people, shifting it from hand to hand, shoulder to shoulder. Modelling her bag in different poses, while they take photos of her acting all modelish and being a little pretty bitch.

"Get one with Natalie!" One of them shouted.

"I got a bottle for you guys, so grab a glass and pour it up!" Time to distract her people with free alcohol. I don't want my face in someone's phone or circling social media apps. They crowd around the big bottle at the bar on ice like a swarm of thirsty vultures. Phones out, ready to Snapchat it to their story and stunt for the timeline like it's the Bow Wow Challenge. "I'm going out for a cigarette, you coming with me birthday girl?"

"Course!" She answers without hesitation and I hop off the bar stool signalling Tiana to come with me. I didn't come here for entertainment, chit chat and exchange pleasantries, I came to fuck!

"I'll come too Ti." Urgh!! Go away-eeerr! Pulling on Tiana's arm with all her cute little insecurities on display.

"Actually babe, could you put my present in the car. My friend spent a *lot* of money and I don't want some dickhead thinking they can take them." Tiana bats her eyelashes at her woman, looking lost like the rejected member that never made the final cut into B2k. She needs to bump, bump, bump her ass along that way!

"Anything for you baby." She agrees to the request- *good girl/boy!*

"Thank you, babe." Tiana gives her woman a reassuring kiss and she trolls off with the bag and insecurity of the situation in her hands.

Tiana looks at me, she knows *exactly* what time it is. Taking her hand, we walk off in the *opposite* direction, towards the smoking area, passing the toilets on the way. We stop… pause. Mischievous, promiscuous and great minds think alike. Fuck it! Tugging on her hand, leading her in. The toilets are packed wall to wall with females fixing their hair, weave, frontals, wigs, makeup and brows in the toilet mirrors. Caught up in drunk conversations like they know each other. They aren't about to notice me, standing at the doorway of a vacant cubicle pulling on Tiana's arm. Attempting to get her to come in and play.

"Aaliyah! There's *way* too many people about." She says quietly, hesitating. Looking around her and trying to pull her arm back from my grip.

"Oh shit, my bad… sorry," letting go of her hand sarcastically, I back into the cubicle. "I thought you liked playing with fire? I *thought* you were grown now?"

"You just don't give a fuck, do you?" She knows she *has* to give in to the temptation. She *knows* she cannot resist all of this- no one can, facts!

"Do you want your present or what!? Because I *can* take myself home?" Pulling up my dress a little, enticing her to come join me. She takes one step, all it took was a little bit of thigh. One last look, over either of her shoulders at 'no one' paying us any form of attention. She rubs her hands together, smiling from ear to ear, ready to come and get it.

"Fuck it! It's *my* birthday, I want you! You better be quiet though I know how loud you get."

"Let them hear us, I came to fuck!"

Grabbing my waist, she pushes me into the side wall of the cubicle. Kicking the door shut with my foot, I stretch over her and lock the bolt. Kissing me like she was long overdue a dose of 'Aaliyah'.

"Only one person per cubicle!" The toilet attendant bangs on the door…

"Yeah, in a minute man!" Tiana shouts back at the attendant. Not letting my body go and rolling her eyes.

"Only one at a time!" The attendant bangs again, louder.

"For fuck sake! Here!" Tiana lets me go, swings open the door digging her hand into her back pocket and shoves a twenty-pound note into the attendant's hand. "Now please, fuck off!" Tiana's rugged and aggressive tone stuns the woman to silence. She closes the door, bolting it shut again "Now, show me my *other* fucking present!" Her tone back to the husky, sexy and demanding.

Using Tiana's shoulders for support, I stand on the closed toilet lid. Letting her stare at me with that sexy pout on her lips while I hold onto the bottom of my dress. Taking my time, watching her watching me and not knowing what is next. Remember to leave them guessing and anticipating.

"Ask for it... *nicely...*"

"Can I have my birthday present now... *please?*" A naughty grin on her face as her stance stays demanding.

"Happy birthday baby girl."

Pulling up my dress slowly, inch... by... inch, revealing the bright pink silk ribbon I had tied around me with great precision. So the bow sits perfectly, over me. Just enough for her to see glimpses of my pussy beside the silk. Told you, I am worth the wait!

"Fuck! Ummm!" She loves it!

I'm fucking proud of my last-minute birthday bow creation. Taking a step towards me, arms reaching and attempting to untie the bow. I smack her hand away and wave my finger at her telling her

"Not with your hands. Untie it with... your mouth!"

Instructions clear, she grabs the back of my thighs and kisses my lower stomach, my hips, my thighs and either side of me. With one last gaze up at me, she opens her mouth and starts to pull on the pink silk ribbon with her teeth.

Knowing her tongue is seconds away from my pussy is making my legs weak. She slowly slips her tongue past the ribbon and between my pussy lips, locating my perfectly neat clit that is dripping and throbbing.

"Hold my hair up." She says not looking at me, enjoying the view.

Tucking her hair behind her ears, I scoop her long hair tightly into the palm of my hand. She pulls my body closer, moving her tongue in and out of me kissing, sucking, licking and doing everything so right! Opening my legs wider, reaching up with my other hand, holding onto the top of the cubicle wall. Giving me enough to support to lift and wrap one leg over her shoulder. Tiana stands firm, her fingers pushing against my spot, In. Out. Hard and fast! Over and over again, her tongue not going anywhere. The sounds my body is making, I'm biting my lip trying not to make a sound but fuck, this girl is too much!

"Uhh uuh uu-" A little moan slips out of my mouth.

Letting go of the wall, falling into her arms. She holds me up, shoving my back on the side of the cubicle wall that rattles from the force of her body against mine Tiana smugly smiling, ego rising but she didn't stop her fingers from moving.

"Has anyone seen Tiana? I can't find her man?" FUCK!

We stop- Frozen! Freeze! Hearing the voice of her Tiana's women talking along with her group of friends entering the toilet. Tiana's mouth drops, she's shook! The thought of her woman being just a few inches away from us on the other side of the thin little cubicle door, we are pushed up against with her fingers firmly inside of me. It couldn't get any more fucked up than this... *wait*... Yes, yes it can! This intensity is what I live for! And I am *here* for this! This rush, this excitement of getting caught! My heart is beating so fast, I can't control it and I can't stop smiling and Tiana still can't- she won't move. It's as if she is on pause, not knowing what to do while my mind has already calculated *my* next move. Oh, I know exactly what I am about to do. With her attention and focus on the chatter of conversation surrounding us, I quickly, undo the top button and unzip her jeans and slide her thong to the side. Fuck!! She's dripping like never before, it could be me or it could be the risk she's taking with me but this is not the first time we have found ourselves in, almost getting   caught.

Parting her pussy lips with two fingers, inside of her, she looks at me. I know, regardless of the compromising position, she wasn't going to stop me, come on, I'm me! She's always down, she would rather be anywhere with me inside of her on her birthday- in fact, any day of the week! She pushes her jeans further down her legs, kissing me quietly. We have to be as quiet as possible and not make a single sound, which is not easy to do with me, trust me!

"Nah, I ain't seen her since that chick came through, you know?" One ear open and listening to these bitches, talking shit and getting comfy on the other side of the door, the other ear listening to Tiana's body.

"I ain't seen her in a while." Another one adds.

"I don't know about *that* girl you know" Excuse me? Like there is another me out there to be referring to me as *that girl*, rude!! First of all, I am a woman! Second of all I am *that* woman who is currently fucking your *girl*!

"She alright man, she got us that big boy bottle of champs." I seem to be favoured among the crew.

Tiana closes her eyes tight, biting her lips and trying not to scream, remains silent, wanting more. Moving her waist along with my fingers, I feel her tighten up at the same time she found my spot again- I got distracted by counting the times I made her body shudder and the sounds her body is making. I didn't notice her hand in between my thighs.

Meanwhile on the other side...

"Almost too nice bruv! I don't like the way she looks at me or *my* woman!"

"I think she's fucking stunning!"

"I don't trust the bitch. Did you see how much she spent on Tiana!?"

"We all did. Step up your game fam! Can you put change in the purse though?"

She stays silent during the light banter, unimpressed.

Moving Tiana's hand away from my body, I want all my focus on her. Fingers back pushing in and out of her, she knows I'm trying to make her scream- a little game we like to play called *shut the fuck up or get caught*! She loves the dangerous rush of temptation just as much as I do. I watch her intently, trying her hardest not to make a sound. Holding it all in, losing her breath and whispering in my ear that she's missed me. Mouth open, eyes back in her head, she almost let out a moan. Pressing her body back up against the cubicle door, reminding her to shut the fuck up! She closes her mouth, keeping her lips sealed tightly shut, agreeing quietly by nodding her head. Grabbing onto me squeezing and scratching me trying to contain the scream she wants to let out- I don't cover her mouth I want her to scream, I want her to let it all out!

Whilst on the other side of the door her woman continues to wonder where she could possibly be? Hmm, I wonder...

"That's your drama. I'm gonna ask Ti if she's seeing anyone?"

"Really, a bitch like that? You sure you want a bitch like *that* on your arm?" Tiana's troll of a woman busy being a hater. Bitch! *Everyone* wants a bitch like me on their arms!

"Maybe if you spent more money on your girl, she'd you'd actually be on your arm and not lost in the club on her birthday." I love when strangers defend me.

"*OH, SHIT!! BABY YES*! FUCK!"

Tiana couldn't contain herself anymore, letting out this loud fucking orgasmic outburst and bussing all over my palm. Forgetting where she was, opening her eyes she let out a little giggle- *they* over on the other side start to laugh too. We hear their attention cut from their conversation and turn on the cubicle that Tiana and I are wrapped around each-others bodies in. Oh Shit! We can't help but laugh, Tiana put her hand over her mouth so quick. Her laugh is far *too* recognisable. One of those signature laughs you can tell someone by in an instant. Big, loud and goofy for no reason but beautiful black girl happy laughs. I know I am not the only one who thinks that a black woman's laugh in particular, is so damn contagious! She doesn't care if the whole world hears her expression of happiness because she is free! A Laugh so loud and contagious, you're laughing too and you haven't even caught the joke or know what's going on but you can't help but smile and let out a little chuckle of your own.

Tiana needs to keep her mouth covered! One more sound and its game over, well... for her anyway. We're both standing here trying not to laugh out loud, fixing our hair and clothes quickly. Kissing in-between the pulling down, the pulling up, the zipping up, the fixing up and the buttons that need doing up. I hold her face, mouthing to her how *fucking* sexy she was tonight. Wanting to go for round two but she knows she can't. I place my hand on her pussy because I want her to know, although she is going back to her woman that this- *this is mine* and she fucking knows it!

The audience of people on the other side are busy talking and whispering amongst themselves, waiting to see *who* is going to exit and reveal themselves. I got ready to make my exit; I don't care about what any of those insignificants thought of me but Tiana puts her arm across the door blocking the latch and my exit.

"Aaliyah, no," she mouths. "Wait, they'll go away."
"Baby girl, I got this… see you around." Her excitement faded and turned into fear and panic. Assuring her with a distracting kiss goodbye, I unlock the door and step out of the cubicle swiftly but smoothly. Giving Tiana enough seconds and room to not be seen and shut the door right behind me with ease.

Standing by Tiana's Troll of a woman purposely. I wonder if she can smell her girlfriend's perfume all over me? Better still, I wonder if she can smell *her* pussy on the tips of my fingers? Washing my hands, looking in the mirror past the reflection of myself and watching the green 'vacant' sign on the cubicle door lock and turn to the red 'engaged'. Tiana is probably sweating and stressing, thinking about how she was going to get the fuck out but like I said, *I got this*. I don't care for the drama *if* she gets caught but there are far too many little girls up in here to be knowing *my* business, so I need to get Tiana out of there without being seen and there is nothing wrong with being a bitch about the whole situation. All eyes on me, I'm used to it, moving boujie and unfazed with the eyes staring me down. Waiting for me to notice them with human interaction, however, I act like they aren't even there.

"Having fun in there huh?" Urgh, how dare *she* speak to me?! But she's shook, not knowing what to say and not knowing *if* I heard her everything she had to say- talking shit. But I take my time to answer. I am in no rush; shaking my 'wet' hands out over the sink and reaching in her direction for a hand towel, all while looking directly at her. I open my mouth to speak, her shoulders tense, waiting... mind racing.

"Did it sound like I was?" Holding my stare, she doesn't know what to say or where to look. People who answer a question with a question often cause a long pause like this.

"Yeah I guess, I wasn't listening." She adds uncomfortable laughter.

"That's a shame." I turn to the mirror fixing my lips, a little messy from all the kisses. "You often miss things if you don't pay close attention. Michelle, right?" Turning back to her, I asked knowing damn well that *isn't* her name.

"It's Mini." She said with her chest all proud. Tilting my head, getting a good look at her. Now, I am not one to get at someone for being bigger than the average BMI... But! Let me tell you this! She is far from fucking mini!

"Mini?"

I raised my eye brow, repeating what could never be her name, I can *not,* are you joking? Looking at her reflection in the mirror than back at her, I wanted to see what she saw in the mirror because *I* don't think she's *seen* her *whole lot of* self in!? Mini? Is she sure? No, not... extra-large, three XL maybe? but Mini- never!

"You should stop worrying about what I'm doing and worry about where *your woman* is, because from what I heard- it sounds like you've *lost* her!"

"I'm looking for her!" Assuring herself, standing upright and saying it with her chest once more.

"I mean... if you say so? You're in here with your friends talking about *me* and Tiana is out *there* in the club alone... on her birthday. Walking in circles looking for you, doesn't seem very fair now does it...?"

"She's got a point fam, we should be looking for her." One of her minions added, the others "umm hummed" in agreement. Mini shot them a look that shut them up and made them all look in different directions, exiting from this conversation. I give them all a wink for assurance and they nod discreetly agreeing with me.

"Look *Mini*, Hun. I'd be worried too if a... now what were your words exactly...?" Tapping my chin, gazing up at the ceiling wasting time, "that's it, a *bitch like me* was hanging around your woman. I *mean,* you don't know me, do you? For all you know, Tiana and I were behind door number three... because I'm *that kind of bitch* - right!"

"Nah I -" I cut her off, sis you said what you said.

"Go ahead, go see who's behind door number three."

I laugh and she laughs along with me, uncomfortable and unsure of how to process all of what I said. Thinking I'm just saying all of that, in confrontation of blatantly hearing her opinion of me. When in actual fact, Tiana's cum in still fresh in my mind. Either way, the paranoia on her brain is unable to connect all the dots... after all common sense is not common.

The majority of people who are fucking around wouldn't *direct* you to the truth and give you all the details [see Page 67 note: details]

So, by addressing the situation and focusing on what was already spiralling around her head the minute I arrived. She would tell herself she's overthinking shit and that Tiana is not in the cubicle hiding in silence *and* that she's being stupid for thinking it in the first place! Because her 'baby' wouldn't do that... would she?

Chuckling to myself, Tiana's right there! And she has no idea! Overhearing everything, nervous as fuck, sweating and expecting Mini to knock on the door and play 'guess who?'. Mind games are so much fun to play, especially with simpletons who can never quite get it... you're getting it though, right? Good, keep up.

Note: Truth

People are blinded by the obvious truth. Caught somewhere between the feeling of disbelief, trust and intuition- always go with your gut feeling, it never fails! Trust yourself first and then others later and don't put anything past anyone. It's a dog eat dog world.

And if you're the one that's telling the lies... then keep lying because the truth hurts- them, not you. Lie! Take that shit to your grave! Hire and arrange a team of geologists to clear the fossils and bones of lies out of your closet, when you're long gone! Ha!

"Nah, I'm good," she wants to check but she won't. She should, she could and it will stay bugging her long after this, what if she would have? "so... have you *seen* Tiana?" her voice low, her words slow and unsure. Talking to the back of me, having turned to fix my hair in the mirror. She *knows* I have seen her, I was the last person inside of her- I mean with her- focus! Lol.

"Hmmm, let me think... no?" I shook my head "look Michelle-"

"Mini." She reminded me of her ridiculous name. I'm sorry but someone the size of a fridge cannot be called fucking *Mini*! It's an insult to all things small.

"Anyway Mins. I'm heading home, so you've got nothing to worry about. I gave Tiana her present and that's all I *came* to do. Tell her when you see her that I wish I could've *cum* too..." I could feel the devious bitch smile forming at the corners of my pretty mouth pouted mouth, I couldn't help myself.

"...you mean stayed?" She looks confused. It didn't take much, clearly, for fuck sake, honestly!

"I'm sorry? What?" Acting innocent, batting my big lashes.

"You said you wish you could've *come* too?" she's concerned with my choice of *words*. Expressionless, I stare letting her watch my nonchalant stance.

"Did I?" Pause for fake thoughts, "Oh, I'm sorry my mind is *clearly* still elsewhere." Gesturing to door number three once more. Her friends giggle along with me pulling a face and beating the imaginary booty in the air (not every day dark and dominate, some days goofy and playful)

"You know what I mean. Give her the message"

A queen's wave goodbye, towards the doorway of the crowded toilet feeling the hating eyes, of Biggie not so fucking Smalls watching me walk. I stop, noticing something lightly on my wrist. Looking down, the pink silk ribbon Tiana earlier untied from around my pussy with her mouth is wrapped around my wrist in a loose knot. How the fuck did it get there? Smiling to myself, Tiana probably attempted to tie my hands together, maybe tie them to the coat hook on the back of the door, who knows? I step one foot back into the toilet, I have one final thing to do and then I will leave.

"Oh Mins," Calling her over to me with an excited wave, she troops over. "I forgot to leave *this* with Tiana it was on her present." I showed her the ribbon.

"She's opened it already though?"

"Yeah, I know she did." I pause, thinking about being in-between Tiana's legs and her in-between mine. "It's a personal thing, she'll understand it. Can you do that for me, Mini?" I shove the bow in her hand.

"Sure…" She looks at the pink ribbon in her hand.

"You're a star" *now* I was ready to go, "Oh and Mins…" I click and point up then pat my finger on my lip. "I *was* with Tiana…"

"What!?" Her eyes popping open looking at the cubicle door.

"No! *Earlier* silly!" I burst out laughing. "Outside, we went for a cigarette but she did say something about heading back in for you lot. So, like I told you she's probably walking around the club looking for you."

I stare at her waiting for her and hers to scadoosh and move out of the toilets. I wait for them to leave, letting them all pass me at the door, watching them move and shuffle away back to the main room of the club, looking for baby girl and I head right towards the exit and text her:

Me: "Give it 5 and slip back into the club baby girl."
Tiana: "Ok B. Thnks 4 my bday present!! I fucking loved it. Best bday eva! xx"
Me: "I know, see u around baby girl. Kisses."

5. The Golden Door Handle

Sunlight crept through the venetian blinds, lighting up another bedroom that doesn't belong to me- fuck!! I don't remember how I ended up here? Or where fucking 'here' is?

The shadows that blocked out the outline of this *"happy home"* began to disappear and fade; framed photographs on the walls of the happy couple, displayed like trophies, sparkling in the early daylight.

Raee'n; *pure* in her *white* wedding dress smiling proud, stood hand in hand with her groom. On the day which she chose to forever carry his last name along with his everlasting love… clearly a very *big* inaccuracy

My head heavy as hell! Last night's mix of alcohol: vodka, brandy and everything else is not allowing me to lift my head off this fucking pillow. Nope! Not today, not right now.

I'm in Raee'ns bed, in her house for *fuck* sake! This has to stop, how am I slipping like this? I need to get out of here real quick but my head feels like a sack of big fucking sweet potatoes.

Why do I do this to myself? My head? My body? My everything? Damn! Do you think… if predicted text inserts the word "Tequila" when you type "T" & "E" does it make you a functioning alcoholic? Either that or Siri has some serious banter, little bitch!

Raee'ns side of the bed is empty, turned over and made up. However, his side of the bed, now *temporally* my side of the bed. I'm naked underneath the heavy duck feathered duvet all snug and comfortable. On my back, warm and wiggling my nakedness onto the thick cotton sheets- The Chronicles of a Side Bae – lol! His ties are hanging grimily over the wardrobe doors. Things here and there indicating that this *is* a man's home but occupied by husband and wife. Turning on my side to the rest of the room faced with *another* photo in a frame on *his* bedside table. Really? Come on, how many photos do you need? This time the happy couple kissing, all loved up in another moment of bliss, intimacy and closeness. Caught on camera and placed in a frame, displayed for him to turn and see every morning he wakes in this fairy tale love of his- aww, how sweet. Picking it up, taking a closer look at *him*, the man that owns *this* house, *this* bed, *those* ties and *this* frame… and Raee'n.

"Urrgh! Disgusting!" the sight of him. I cannot!

Letting go of the frame, it hits the floor with a satisfying *smash* that made me smirk with pleasure. "Oops my bad." I'll just tell her it fell. Laughing to myself stretching my nudity all up in *his* bed. Who told Raee'n to leave me alone and unsupervised?

Raee'n works nights and late shifts doing some sort of something. I couldn't tell you, I didn't pay too much attention to her when she was telling me. All I paid attention to is that she is in U.S Military and wore this banging uniform that made my pussy pulse. There's just this thing, you know, *something* about seeing her in that camouflage print; those baggy trousers with that fitted jacket, tight shirt buttoned up, holding her signs of military ranking and oh, she can keep her hat on!

Her uniform is a subtle reminder of her fuckery of a marriage. With her surname embroidered into it reminding her of her responsibilities as a wife, all the while being in between my thighs that makes this affair of ours so damn delicious! Just image getting caught, I can see a divorce or some kind of dramatic split/break-up happening. But being the pitiful, pathetic man, I'm assuming he is – most men are. He'd take her back and beg her to stay. On his knees, drowning in his tears of sorrow, singing 'please don't go' like Tank.

I just think it would be fucking funny to watch everything they built together fall apart.

Imagine, now picture this; a woman having to explain to *her* husband that *she* has been cheating on him with another *woman!?* How fucking emasculated would any man feel to hear that? To know that his 'big dick' sense of self ego, alpha male, silver back gorilla, banging on his chest bullshit was not enough to keep *her* at home. And that a woman has been hitting all the spots that *he* didn't even know existed inside of her!

I bet every time a man hears the confessions of his woman leaving him to be with another *woman*, he can literally feel his balls retract into his body one by one.

Let me break it down for you real quick; fellas, gentlemen, guys and my fellow man dem can't forget about the few intellectual ones that will actually pick up a book, let me holler at you right quick. If you're a man who… let's say, who isn't loyal to your "bae" and lack consistency and thoughtfulness and give your lady nothing but headaches. Keeping her busy wondering where your arse is and worrying constantly about other bitches running your dick down. Calling your phone and giving her stress with the non-stop baby mamma drama. You talk a lot of shit but don't do shit *or* you're constantly absent in her life. Never show up or show out and never there when she needs that special someone. Or you don't want to commit and she only knows your 'road name'. Why in the *hell* would she want another *man* to give her those same stresses!? Come on, times are changing and women are levitating at a rapid rate. Women like me are out here keeping shit running! Doing bad all by ourselves and making your woman's head turn the other way and think

"Ima get me a bad bitch!"

All of a sudden, she switches up on you. Stops the fighting, the fussing and the aggravated attention. You're convinced she's fucking around with another man, checking her phone when she's out of the room, looking in the wrong places. Maybe worry about her *new* "female friend"… you know, the *new* female friend she met through her "friend's, friend's, friend" The one she's *always* talking about, the one she goes *everywhere* with and the same one she goes to see *all* the time. Yes! The one whose house she stays at *frequently* and her weekend bag is packed, ready and at the door. Telling you not to wait up because she'll see you morning but then text's you saying she'll be back on Sunday. And when she gets back, she's walking around the house on her tiptoes just *glowing*- not mad at you for doing your dumb shit because she's busy reminiscing about her weekend with her new *bestie*. Umm hmm, all makes sense now huh? Yes! She's the one fucking your woman! And every time you fuck up, do something wrong or work her nerves she goes running to *her* and *she* gets it so 'fucking' right!

Think I don't know who I am talking about... have you forgotten who I am? Why don't you call her now and see where she is...

Oh, she's with *her*... say no more.

These thoughts give me the strength to get myself up because it is *way* overdue my time to leave.

Raee'n would have put me in bed because I was in no sober state to *walk,* let alone *drive* my pretty self out of here.

Sat naked at the end of *their* bed, facing the dressing table mirror, arms in the air, stretching out the sleep and last night's behaviour lingering in my body. Pulling my hair up into the best messy bun I could, my arms aren't cooperating in the best way, not yet fully revived from the dead weight of my body sleeping heavily on them.

I love admiring my body, the shape of me and the way my tattoos sit on my skin. Naked, staring at myself in the mirror, this would be a perfect time to tell you about my tattoos.

So, guys! (the intro to every selfie queen on social media, getting ready to tell you the tea and gossip) One of my favourite tattoos is the one that sits just below my left collar bone: a backwards tattoo. All people see is a squiggled line similar to heartbeat. But when reflected I see the words "strength" in the mirror, every day. It's for me and only me. My secret symbol of strength.

Majority of my tattoos are placed on the left-hand side of my body. I have a full sleeve on my left arm made up of oriental flowers, a koi carp fish, tattooed in an upwards direction facing me and almost kissing my favourite beauty spots on the top of my left shoulder. The bottom half has a peacock and his beautiful tail feathers flow and wrap around my arm and wrist. beside the words, *"I think I could fall in love with you, very easily"* because well, I am me and I hear it from women all the time. Reminds me that I am more than enough just the way I am.

To be honest, I've lost count of my tattoos, I started them not too long ago and like women, they are an addiction of mine. A therapeutic process that relaxes any tension within me. Majority of women go shopping for that 'retail therapy' and collect unnecessary materialistic items. But I, however, prefer collecting multiple orgasms from women or chilling on a tattooist chair whilst they create beautiful artwork on my beautiful highly melinated skin.

Tattoos cover the majority of my body and they all have a great meaning to my memories and my everyday life. They are a gentle and subtle reminder of a memory or thought I can never forget. A true representation of who I am.

Stepping out of the shower, naked walking back to their room wearing his bath robe. Clothes on again, I take my time getting ready, placing my dark red lipstick back on my devious lips. I peer over my shoulder, at his side of the bed where I have stuffed my red lace thong between the head of the bed and the mattress, leaving just enough red lace peeking out- left deliberately to be *found.*

I enjoy leaving little things here and there around, playing 'Aaliyah's Clues' to keep him on the edge, overthinking and wondering what the fuck is going on.

Raee'n wasn't entertained by my little game, she's running out of little white lies to tell her husband when he questions:

"Honey, who's thongs are these?"

I think it's fucking hilarious listening to Raee'n over the phone, telling me about the unconvincing lie she told her husband. As to why there's underwear in his bed or jewellery in his car or perfume and lipstick marks on his shirt that does *not* belong to his wife? I love it when she calls me after she's found whatever I had hidden or done before him.

Laughing, unapologetically:

"I don't know how they got there?" – Never, apologise.

Grabbing my coat from the banister, ready to get out of here. Turning the handle on the front door... wait a minute, it's not opening, what the fuck?? Trying again, pulling and rattling the door- why? Trying again and again and it's *not* budging, what! Why is it locked? Kicking the door from the inside, won't help it open but I *need* to try something. I can't get out, I *need* to get out. Throwing my bag to the floor reaching for the door frame. Running my fingers frantically down the right-hand side of the door peering closely in at the tiny gap between the door and the frame trying to figure out which bolts are locked.

"One... two...three..." counting three locks.
Who the *fuck* locks all three locks with someone *inside* the fucking house!! Why would you do that?
I am trying to hold down my internal panic but my hands are shaking and I can't... I can't stop them from shaking and I can feel a panic attack holding my breath and not wanting me to breathe. Hands keep fucking shaking! Calm down, for fuck sake!
I unlock my phone, scrolling to find Raee'ns contact on my call list because I can't fucking remember anyone's number off the top of my head, I don't even know my own! Her phone doesn't ring and goes straight to voicemail! Shit!! I don't understand why she's done this, why would she lock me inside?!
Deep breaths, control your breathing Aaliyah, in... and out. In ...and out. In and out... I'm going to wait and to leave a voicemail after the beep because I have lost all sense of calm at the door.

"Raee'n!! What the fuck? Why is your door locked!! Where the hell are you!! I *need* to get the fuck out of here! Now! I swear, if you're not back in four fucking minutes, I'm smashing my way out of your fucking house!"

So much for calm and rational... maybe I should have counted to ten. One... breathe, two... breathe... three- *his* silver golf clubs catches my eye, sitting in the corner by the front door in a big golf club bucket bag. I reach out and grab one- fuck, it's heavy but it will do. "Then you can explain it to your *husband* because you will *NEVER* see *me* again! I'm counting!"

Fucking fuming!! Locking doors, who the fuck locks doors? There's got to be spare keys *somewhere* in this house! Where though, where in this big fucking house, that is too damn big for two people would a set of keys be!?

"Arrrrgggh!!" screaming, stomping back upstairs, with his heaviest golf club in my hand dragging behind me and letting it hit each step with a loud *'doof, doof, doof'*. Standing with my legs apart, shoulders firm getting ready to aim and take a swing at my first targeted window.

Three minutes.

Fuck knows why I'm choosing a window upstairs and not downstairs, I don't know and I couldn't tell you? Trying to call her again and again and again! Fucking voicemail! Every time! She's. Taking. The. Fucking. Piss! She knows I'm here! Pacing up and down, aggravated and angry. Back downstairs- because breaking a window upstairs made no fucking sense! What's wrong with me??

Two minutes.

I am not fucking playing with this female! I am *not* waiting!

Pulling drawers open in the kitchen rummaging through them, digging and searching for any kind of key. Throwing all the shit from inside of the drawers behind me. Everything landing everywhere, smacking the floor with *'clinks'* and *'clanks'* I don't give a shit, I just want to *get* out this house! I *need* to get out this house! There has to be a spare key! Somewhere!

One minute.

Standing still- pausing, pounding panicking beats of my heart counting down the remaining seconds, my body shaking out of control- fuck this! I am done waiting! Raising my arm up, golf club tightly back in my grip ready to smash my way out of here.

Seconds away from swinging…

Twenty seconds.

I hear Raee'ns Range Rover outside, pulling up to the house. My heart has missed several beats. My ears emphasising every single sound as every single second passes. The tyres pulling up slowly over the gravelled driveway. The engine stops. The car door slams shut. The sound of her boots kicking up the gravelled stones that cover the front of the house grounds with each of her steps. The keys jingling in her hand at the door.

I watch frozen still as her silhouette appears through the glass panels of the door

Finally! The familiar sounds of each of the locks unlocking one after the other. As each one of the locks released, small reliefs of air escape my lungs and let me breathe easier. She places her key into the final lock… she door opens…

"Oh hey, morning beautiful I-"

She stops, barely stepping a foot into her house, eyes set on her mistress in distress. I'm a mess! Stood in the hallway with a heavy golf club in my shaking hands. The kitchen behind me trashed with the contents of every drawer all over the floor, wearing a look on my face that could kill someone or *has* killed someone.

"WHAT THE FUCK!?" Screaming at her, asking the question on her face.

"What's going on! Is someone here? Are you okay? The fuck babe, are you hurt?"

She steps further in the house, cautiously. Her eyes darting from left to right and all over me. Studying the settings, taking in details with vigilance. Her arms up and her palms open in alert, tactically getting ready to disarm the crazy bitch of the golf club.

"Don't. Lock. Doors. On. Me. Ever!" Dragging out each capital letter through my gritted teeth. Pointing the club in her direction. She doesn't speak, all I can hear is her boots on the laminate floor, delicately treading heel to toe towards me, one foot cautiously after the other. My heart pounding heavily over time missing beats- all over the place like a white girl trying to catch a beat on a song she has no business dancing too.

"Aaliyah, I don't know what the fuck is goin' on wit chu but you need to calm down, you heard me?" Her Southern American tongue strong, assertive and firm.

"Don't tell me what to do! Don't you *EVER* fucking lock me in, I don't want to stay! Whoever told you I was dick head lied! This isn't me, I don't want to be locked in here, I don't want to stay. You can't make me!"

My eyes are glassed over with tears that my eyelids hold hostage, refusing to let them fall onto my face. Still clutching the golf club that is now down by my side but I'm not letting it go. Trying to calm myself down, breathing slowly. But this is as calm as I can get.

Holding back this damn panic attack that is about to take over my entire body again, not allowing or wanting me to take another full deep breath out – again!

"Aaliyah, its' okay I'm here now…"

Before I could see her make the next move; in one swift swoop she knocks the golf club out of my hand and grabs me, asking no more questions embracing me in her arms. Her strong arms swallowing me, holding me tight. My face pressed against her chest, she attempts to calm me. Talking softly and gently in my ear, I don't know what she is saying because all I keep saying over and over is

"You can't keep me locked away- I'm not yours, I'm *not* yours."

My body won't stop shaking, my tears escaping my eyes, run down my face. I fucking hate crying and here I am bawling like a new born baby in her chest- she squeezes me tighter, constricting me like she's trying to stop me from completely falling apart.

"Aaliyah, I didn't even realise. I got caught up and locked it behind me like any other day, I wasn't thinking, I would *never* lock you away, you heard me. This is me you're talking about, *me*?"

"I come and go as I fucking please!"

And just like that. The quivering frail woman that was in her arms, all but a few seconds ago is gone! Taking a step back from her, pushing her arms away from me. She looks at me a type of way, confused. Having *never* seen me vulnerable like that, let alone crazy like this. Wondering what the fuck is going on. Thinking of what questions to ask me next.

"Did I say something wrong?" She pauses "What is going on Aaliyah? What happened to you… who hurt you?" Concerned asking me questions my mouth refuses to answer. My tongue remained silent and tucked away behind my grinding teeth and closed lips.

"Talk to me Aaliyah, you know you can tell me anything."

"Talk to your *husband!* I don't want to talk so, get the fuck out my way!" My effort full attempt to push past her didn't do shit against her military stance and firm shoulders, she didn't budge an inch or sway- she didn't move.

"No Aaliyah, talk to me!" She held the sides of my arms tight.

"GET THE FUCK OFF ME!"

Screaming dramatically like I'm being slaughtered at a murder mystery dinner party. Shutting me up, she holds my face to hers staring into my eyes. As if she's gazing behind them trying her hardest to figure me out and what the fuck she thinks is broken -I look away from her, I don't want to look at her.

"Who…" taking a soft breath and opens her mouth, "…who hurt you?"

Closing her eyes like she felt my pain I was not discussing. Her words quiet as a murmur, a whisper or mime rather than anything vocal and clear. I can barely even make them out.

"Raee'n, let me go. Please… let me go." Eyes closed, not wanting to answer, I can't answer. "ple-"

Stopping me from fighting her off with the little energy I had left. Flopping in her arms, she stops me from saying anything else. Lifting my chin gently, she kisses me. The kind of kiss that makes you weak at the knees and forget your sentences, your words and the whole damn conversation and any thoughts you were holing in your mind - time stops.

No more talking, fuck talking! Letting go and pushing the door shut but *not* locked. She picks me up effortlessly and places me on the staircase, leaning over me, kissing me and pushing her body weight onto me. I feel the pressure of the steps against my back. She bites my neck. Umm I love that shit! Pushing her away from me, I want to get a good look at her in that sexy camouflage uniform. I want her out of it all - now!

"Strip Stevens! Now!" Folding my arms, smiling through my sexual seriousness. Her face glowing from me calling out her last name ready to take orders from me playing the role of her superior. She knows I am in charge and I want to play and says nothing, taking her orders from me.

"Except the hat." Tilting my head to the side, speaking slowly and assertively- the way she likes it. Unbuttoning her shirt, she let it drop off her shoulders and fall to the floor landing by her ankles. Kicking off her loose boots, without taking her eyes away from mine, her trousers are next. Pushing them down her thick thighs and toned smooth legs. She steps out of them, arms crossed around her waist. Holding the bottom of her vest and raises her arms up, arching her back and rolling her hips, taking it off in one swift movement.

Sitting back, in love with the view of her body, revealed to me layer by layer. It's almost as if watching a gift unwrap itself, eager to see it all. Stood in a khaki green underwear set with her that flat camo hat still on, as instructed. Circling my wrist and my index finger at point - that body, that frame and that ass!

"Take off your bra."

Placing her hand onto her back she unhooks her bra with a single pinch, it falls to the floor. Then she places her arms back by her sides.

"Now get over here!"

"Yes baby!"

Stepping towards me on the balls of her feet, she crouches down in front of me and starts to take off my clothes without any hesitation. Our nudity opposite; my bra on and no thong because they're hidden somewhere on his side of the bed, remember? She brings her face to my lap, kissing my thighs. Leaving traces of her lipstick and goose bumps all over my skin. Opening my legs, she continues her kisses up and down my body. Lifting me slightly and placing my legs over her shoulders, she gets that little bit closer to my pussy then instantly changes her direction. Kissing all the way back down my thighs then licking slowly back up again. She looks up at me with a look of thirst deep in her eyes and then returns her face back in between my thighs, right where they need to be… fuck me!

My thighs have always been a problem, touch me, kiss me, tease me or even brush past anywhere remotely close to inner thigh and we are going to have a situation on our hands or more so you' re going to have a situation in your hands- my pussy to be exact.

***

Dressed and ready, sat at the top of the staircase waiting for Raee'n to finish getting ready. I never had a reason or felt the need to enter any other room in *their* house.

I only need to be in the bed, on the bed, on the floor by the bed or the wall by the bed. The rest of the house is completely irrelevant to my sexual needs. I do not come over here to chill on the sofa and watch movies and pop popcorn! Don't be ridiculous, I come here to get fucked!

But right now, I am irritated with the time Raee'n continues to take, to get ready. I hate waiting for anyone or anything. Yes! I'm that impatient bitch who will ask every three minutes if you're ready but don't get it twisted, I'm *also* the same person who will scream at you if you attempt to bother my life when I'm taking my time to get ready.

"Hurry the fuck up!"

Shouting at her while digging my heels repeatedly into the carpet. Watching the interesting contrast of dirt marks on cream carpet. Who chooses cream carpet for a staircase anyway? But I guess that's why he made the rule to have no shoes on or up the stairs- oops!

"Hold the fuck on!" she shouts back at me.

"Come on!" Shouting louder back, I have to have the last word.

She ignores me and continues to rustle around, take her time and piss me off. She knows I don't like to wait so *why* the fuck am *I* waiting? To be honest, why the fuck am I even still here? And what the fuck am I still doing here? I 'came' now it's time to go.

From where I'm sitting, I can see the closed white wooden doors to the other rooms in the upstairs hallway, I didn't ever notice they were there. Shows you how much attention I pay to this place. I'm bored of waiting. So, might as well kill the time and explore the other rooms and add them to my list of places that *we* needed to fuck in or on.

Running my hands along the walls, as I walk down the hallway fingertips passing over the patterns of embossed feature wallpaper. Stopping in front of the first door, holding onto the golden door handle, which felt slightly warm from the heat of the house. Opening the door and peeking a little through the crack. Making sure there is nothing unpleasant waiting behind it. I don't know what's in here, could be anything? The bottom of the door drags along the thick carpet making this stupid noise.

Quickly, checking behind making sure she doesn't hear me messing around with shit that I have no business in. Swiftly and quickly, I push the door the rest of the way open, so it makes less noise and slide into the room like it's dm's on Instagram.

Ooouu fancy! Stepping into the room I instantly smell the aroma of *"man"* lurking in the air of this office. That spicy musky thick husk of his cologne in the room. His well-known presence fills the room, like shadows lingering over me. Plaques, medals and awards hung from the wall behind a large dark wooden desk. Brushing my hand lightly across the back of the chair that was tucked under, moves slightly to its side. Revealing his butt print firmly imbedded in the leather; from where he sits spending hours working hard to maintain his lifestyle. Maybe, *if* he spent less time working and leaving this house and more time with his wife, she wouldn't need to keep herself occupied with *working* on me.

Two large computer screens dominated the desk. Both placed at a diagonal slant. His stationary pot holds a selection of only one particular type of ink pen. Noticing how the desk has everything in its specific place, very tidy and clean. No watermark stains from cold glasses or hot coffee mugs or finger prints on the screens, none on the wood from where hands rest or tap, exceeding project timelines and overtime. A coaster positioned precisely to the right tilted at a slight angle. It all has a sense of excessive systematic order; like the stack of post-its beside the phone. Easily reachable if multi-tasking on the phone, when needing to take notes. But it's *the way* he's positioned them, close enough to the keyboard but far enough for the right amount of arm space to write a note, without having to readjust an arm on the desk if he had the phone to his ear. Pressing playback on his recorded voice message, I've never heard his voice before, now I want to place the voice that went along with this image of the man I see around the house and behind the small photo window inside Raee'ns purse.

"You've reached Wayne Stevens, I'm currently out of the country but I am contactable via email and personal mobile. Anything urgent, please contact Mrs. Raee'n Stevens. Anything else, please leave a message and your best form of contact. Thank you for calling." *BEEP!*

Sat in his chair, picking up his phone pretending to answer, mocking his voice and typing a whole lot of nothing on his keyboard. Messing with the things on his desk, angling them all an inch or so to the left and out of their original position. I can tell from the cleanliness of the room and the placement of objects that he has a moderate level of OCD. So, this should throw him a little off balance when he returns home. That's *if* he doesn't find my thong tucked into his bed.

Stepping out admiring my crafty handy work at the door. Raee'n is still not ready, she clearly isn't in any rush to pick up speed.

The door is completely shut at the second golden plated door handle, why? I never understood or liked the idea of closed and locked doors inside a house.

I just don't think that you should have to close doors in your own home. I mean, unless you don't want anyone up in there or to come out.

This room, feels different. Like it has a different use, I can't explain it but the rest of the house has this manly edge. This air of dominance you can only feel in a house occupied or co-habited by a man. I know they share this house and you can feel the split of feminine and masculine energy flowing through it but this room felt innocently emotional, warm? Unexpected and spare.

My fingers reflected off of the handle as my hand stretches out, getting closer to the shiny golden surface. Pulling down on the handle and opening the door a little, this gentle warm breeze crept out and blew past my face. More cautious than before, I push the door so slowly with my foot slightly over the door frame-

"You're so damn impatient! I'm done, let's go." Raee'n hopped down the hall with one shoe on and the other in her hand.

"You know what I'm like, you're lucky I didn't leave!"

"But you didn't, so come here and give me a hand- please?"

"Erm, no?" My hand still on the golden handle

"Girl!" She laughs nervously, "get over here!" She giggles, laughing at a joke that I didn't hear. Her eyes looking at my hand on the door, "…please." Struggling to put the shoe on her foot and balance at the same time. I let go of the handle and walk over, holding out a hand for her.

"You good?" She asks looking at me and past me at the door I just closed. I look back at the door then back at her.

"Yeah? I'm good, are you?"

"Nothing? I'm good." If she says so.

***

"So, dot, dot, dot where we going?"

Impatiently, feet up on the dash board of her car, smacking an irritated beat on my thighs with the palm of my hands. Annoyed and bored of her company, why did I offer to stay longer? *Why,* for fuck sake?

It's pitch black out here in the middle of nowhere, where she lives in. Way, way out of London, out here in 'moo-coo' land. You know where the cows 'moo' and the birds say 'coo' - Country! Nothing but fields and woodlands scattered everywhere. Greens and browns, grass and trees and mud and shit! Nothing at all like the city night lights in London. Nothing to look at out of the car window tonight but darkness covering the greens of fields and trees. The only thing I can see are the white reflectors on the open road flashing and outlining the lines as we drove past.

Raee'n eyes are set on the open darkness and her mouths closed accustom to the lack of conversation in between all of the fucking. I listen close to the speeding tyres, rolling on the road unaffected by the silence. The fact is, we have nothing in common aside from the sex. There's nothing to talk about; I mean, what do you say to someone you're having an affair with besides from:

"Hey let's fuck now." "Are we gonna fuck now or later?"
"Sooo... we fucking?" "Drop your trousers I want to fuck!"

Other than the sounds of sex; music or the television fill the lack of atmosphere and no vibe that I avoid. Miss me with the small talk, you know the whole trying to find something to talk about subjects are the worst because we both have absolutely no interest. I don't want to ever give her reasons to start asking questions and wanting to get to know me in *too* much detail.

"So... how's work?" Stop it! *"how's work?"*
I spoke too soon, next, she'll be fucking asking me how my day was.

"Fine, work is fine. Everything is fine...?" Addressing everything hoping she'd stop.

"You having a good day?"
I smile awkwardly, not wanting to entertain her. I might have to stop, drop and roll out of this car if she continues with this small talk!

"We never do this, you know, spend time together. I like it."
She holds onto my hand a little tighter, stroking the back of my hand with her thumb softly.

"Okaaaay." I decide to make use of my other hand that was free from her grasp and rub my finger along my bottom lip. A habit of mine when *shit really irritates* me or when my thoughts run deep and right now, I'm thinking I need to abandon the fuck out of this car!

"Our time... I like what we have umm, I was thinking that I could- or *we* - what? I just want to make every-what?" She laughs nervously whilst I'm shaking my head at the form of emotions attempting to exit her mouth in a scrambled jumble of words. I have no time for her to be catching feelings, this is the reason I don't hang around or chill with 'them'. Pulling away from her hand, I lean forward and turn the music on before she says some stupid shit that could lead to the end of us. The sex is too damn good to just stop this *thing* we have going on. I'll need to find someone who can take her place and train them to fuck how she can and I don't have that kind of patience. I know she isn't ready to see *me* walk away... so, I've done us both a favour by shutting her the hell up with the sound of music overpowering all this talking.

My phone vibrates in my pocket, texts coming in all at once, as she has driven into a place that can get reception. I don't know how people who live out here deal with this shit. Living next to corn fields or sheep, it's far too much of a 'horror movie scene' for me.

> *Tiana: "Oi wot u up2? I need to see you, Baby Girl misses u."*
> *Jai: "Oi Liyah where u @ B, come see me real quick. Call me."*
> *Blue Bird: "When u coming 2 see us?? ;)"*

Notifications coming through... Blue texts me, leading me into the thoughts of Mali-

"Who you texting?"

"Oh great, another question really Raee'n?"

She tries to peek at my phone and keep her eyes on the road at the same time. Ignoring her questioning I respond to the texts of my choice.

"You know we *are* allowed to pretend that we *can* talk and not just fuck all the god damn time!"

Slanting my head in the direction of her attitude and loud talk, looking around the car, trying to find who the fuck she thinks she's talking to, because it could never be me.

"First of all, I'm going to need you to bring it *all* the way in and take it down a few notches. *Who* the hell are you talking to?"

"You! I'm saying, can we fucking talk?!"

"I have nothing to say, what's the problem?"

"Soo, what Aaliyah? We just gon' pretend you didn't go psycho fucking crazy bitch this morning, all up my house, trashing the fucking place." She raised her voice, "You fucked up my kitchen, smashed frames and shit and go from hysterical to cool in three-point two fucking seconds! And I can't say *shit* about it, no?? Nu -uh. Nah, all that shit ain't happen? It's all in my fucking head huh? Okay say nothing."

"I said. I don't want to fucking talk about it!" Shouting over her.

"Well maybe you should fucking try!" She shouts over me. "Right now, you don't have a choice but to fucking talk! You can be whoever the fuck you are when you're not with me but when you bring the crazy bitch out in *my* house, we've- yes, you and I *WE* got something to fucking talk about, Aaliyah!"

"Oh, okay, so we can fuck all over your husband's house though, no? I lose my shit *one time*, mess up a few things and all of a sudden, I'm fucking crazy! Okay, really?? Now we need to talk?? Fuck you Raee'n!"

"No fuck you Aaliyah, don't try me! You don't think any of that warrants a conversation? A fucking explanation at least, like really Aali? The fuck happened? We just gon' sweep this all under the damn rug?"

"You sweep your marriage under the rug? What's the difference? Just add it to the pile of shit, you stay sweeping up under there." Petty, I know but I'm me.

"There's big difference Aaliyah! Huge!"

"How!"

"There just is, what the fuck? You can't tell me shit is the same!"

"I don't have to explain shit to you! There's no issue? For fuck sake Raee'n. Let it the fuck GO!" The car has gone from awkward silences to us screaming at each other, back and forth, louder and louder.

"Why! Why did you lose it? Why did you lose your shit?" She's not letting it go, I swear, this woman!

"I barely touched a *thing*, shit, relax! Acting like I went out on every room, like his office or the other fucking room! It was *only* the kitchen, some drawers, chill the fuck out!" I'm so bored of her noise. "Besides, I only messed up the spoons. Shit, a couple of seconds longer and your forks would've got *fucked* up." Shouting and laughing, not taking her seriously at all, mocking a fork in my hand and stabbing the air with it. Her face is far from impressed, her nostrils flaring. Eyes on me then back on the road. It's sexy when she gets mad. I'm turned on and shook at the same time.

"When did you go in his office?" She questions

"Earlier, when you took forever to get ready." Looking back out the window, as the nothingness outside turns into a little town out here in the middle of nowhere. The shouting match between us soothed down.

"I thought you didn't wanna know the rest of the house?" She spoke softer.

"I don't! But I decided to look for other rooms we could play *husband* and *wife* in. His office, by the way, is *now* on the list." My mind drifting off into playing secretary and getting spanked over his desk.

"Did you go in the other room...?" She turns to me asking slightly anxious, cautious... but I'm trapped in the scene in my head imagining the office scene. My mind has drifted to the left; by this point and Raee'n has thrown everything off of the desk and is dragging up my black pencil skirt, ripping the buttons of my shirt and-

"Did you go in any other room?"

"Urgh no, why?" she broke my dirty daydream. "You hiding something?"

"... no ..." she looks away "we're here now anyway."

Slowing down the car and perfectly parallel parking in front of a restaurant.

"Aali babe, I um, I got something, I want to." She struggles with whatever she is about to nervously say, looking in my eyes but over me not able to catch her words or maintain eye contact.

"Spit it out..." hurrying her up with my hands.

"I'm a- shit... I have," could she drag this out anymore? "I'm..."

My phone rang, holding my hand up and shutting up Raee'ns word conundrum up, I step out the car uninterested and answer my call. She can figure out what the hell she is trying to say another day on someone else's time.

***

I hate dinner dates! I fucking hate dates period! This is bullshit that couples do every month or whenever they feel like pretending to tolerate each-others company. Going out, getting dressed up all pretty and sitting together. Acting all civil, in a restaurant trying to rekindle the honeymoon period. Take Valentine's day for example; all that pressure and unnecessary expenses to do something nice and over the top to show your love for one damn day of the year because the calendar fucking told you to! When really, all you want to do is sit at home eat pizza and get some pussy. I don't know what was on Raee'ns mind, why she thought that *this* of all things is even an *idea - for - us* to do!? I mean, what exactly does she want me to say:

"Thanks for closing down half a restaurant so we can sit and eat
a plate of carbs in candle light. Alone."

There was no time to even say anything in between all of Raee'n not shutting the fuck up. She's been talking for the longest time and I'm not hearing what she has to say. I'm just going along and agreeing with her anyway.

I know as a fact, that when women talk to you, they're usually not participating in a real conversation where they want to *actually hear* what you have to say. No, no they are just getting you to side with their opinions and thoughts or simply getting you to agree with whatever it was they were going on and on and on about. Wouldn't you agree?

"You've been texting the whole time; your phone hasn't left your hands."

"Yeah, uh huh, my pasta was nice how was yours?" My face in my phone.

"You listening Aaliyah or you hearing me?"

Texting and talking to who I wanted to talk to and? She's not my woman; my phone is not her business!

"I'm listening, shit! What!"

"You don't say anything to me, you don't talk, It's all about sex with you"

"And *you* act like you don't know what I *cum* here for. And when did we turn into a married couple out on date night?"

"I thought it would be nice to take you out *especially* after your *episode* this morning."

"Can we get over it, or?" Rolling my eyes, my face back in my phone.

"Look, before you leave and I don't see your face for however fucking long. I wanted to have dinner- to *talk*! You tell me something, I tell you *something* you know how a general fucking conversation works!"

Now she has my attention with the word *'fucking'* just the way she's talking all dominant. I lean back in the chair staring at her and thinking of the ways I could shut her up nicely.

"So, what? What's your point, you have something you want to tell me beautiful? Come and tell me while you sit on my face!"

"Aaliyah!?" Her mouth drops open, her fork hit the plate and she folds her arms, waiting for an apology that she is *never* going to get.

"You *know* what this was about the moment *we* agreed to having *this* little affair. I'm your dirty little secret. If you want to sit down and have a heart to heart, candle lit dinners, you can do that with him. I'm simply here to please you... sexually, in ways he can't. Consider me marriage therapy; take several doses of me three times every two months or so and you'll be able to sustain your *fuckery* of a marriage, because I fuck the *woman* you once were back into you. Making you feel sexy enough to fuck your husband with at least one inch of passion." Smiling smugly, winking at my lover across the table, telling her some home truths that she is well aware of. Hmm, I'm beginning to like this whole conversation thing after all.

"Really Aaliyah, is that what you think about me?'"

She unfolds her arms, relaxing a little. I have a way with my words that turns her on. That and the fact that I signalled her mid rant to take her thong off, pull up her skirt and tuck herself under the table cloth.

"Did I stutter? You heard *every* word I said. You know you can't resist me." She stares at my phone in my hand. "Just say you want me and I'll put it down." Adjusting herself into the right position on her seat, rubbing my left leg with her foot softly letting me know she is ready.

"I - want - YOU. All to myself, no fucking phone!"

I toss the phone behind me, hearing it bump, bump across the restaurant hitting the floor. Probably fucked because you know how iPhone screens are. Every new model they create, they always add or take away some dumb shit! When all we want is a fucking phone screen that doesn't break when you drop the shit! But right now, I'm cool with a broken screen. I mean, who cares when pussy is on the menu.

Checking over my shoulder to see if any staff were looking or coming in this direction, the coast is completely clear.

"Excuse me while I get my dessert, I won't be needing a spoon." Slipping under the table no more words needed to be said. No words, no talking, no more fucking conversations, no more emotional bullshit. Just my tongue all up and against her clit, while she sits at the edge of her seat in the middle of the restaurant. I told you, I don't do dinner, I only do *dessert* and it's *always* my favourite.

6. *The Distant Gaze*

Looking up at the ceiling, I've been laying here for a while. Flat on my back trying to free my arms from Raee'n, without her waking her up. Her arms and the rest of her are wrapped over my waist and I'm calculating the quickest escape route out of this room, down the stairs and out this fucking house! But I have to be cautious during this transition because all women, yes, <u>ALL</u> women, including you; have this preinstalled alert system.

Preinstalled Alarm System *noun*

Definition An alarm triggered by movement

Women can be dead asleep. Knocked out, mouth wide open, right until the person they were laid up against, gets out of the bed and reaches for the door handle. Then you hear:

> *"Where you going, you okay, you alright, want anything, need anything?"*

Her head is off the pillow, asking five questions in one damn go! Girl, if you don't get your 'half asleep twenty-one questions' self out of my business! Lol, honestly.

Every so often, I move my body inch by inch, closer and closer to the edge of the bed. One leg hung off the bed, foot swinging waiting for another few inches to reach the floor. I *need* to take my naked self out of her bed, because I am not about to have her thinking she can get me sat around *another* table that I am *not* fucking on top of *ever* again!

In one fake yawn motion turning swiftly onto my right side finally freeing myself from her bodyweight, she turns outwards and moves closer towards the other side of the bed. Thank fuck!

Getting ready to leave but creeping around the room. Tip toeing silently like an assassin ninja on a mission. As slow as I can without trying to have anything make *any* kind of noise.

Putting my legs into my jeans – oh my God! This sounds so damn amplified, like someone rustling a packet of crisps in the cinema; loud in the dead silence, anticipating the murderer to dramatically pop up and kill someone in a horror movie. She's stirring a little- *aah shit*! Freeze! Fuck!

One leg in my jeans, the other foot floating in the air about to go in the other leg steady standing. Thankfully I've got my yoga standing tree pose on point! It's the only one I can execute, because the way these yoga bitches be bending, my body *cannot*.

Raee'n settles back into her deep sleep, *phew!* Honestly, it's moments like these, when I'm trying to sneak out of a *lovers'* house that make me happy that I refused ~~the forth glass~~ lies - the second bottle of wine last night and I've woken up sober enough to leave the building in an orderly quiet fashion. The hungover and partially drunk version of me is a whole different story; very loud, very clumsy with no fucking balance at all. By now the hungover me would've been flat on my back with a loud *'crash' 'bang' 'wallop'*. I would have tripped over my own feet or the air, waking her up and she'd be starting her *"please don't go"* campaign. I am *fucked* if she wakes up!

Slowly picking up my things from here and there, looking back at her before I left the room. Raee'n lay on her stomach, one leg in the covers the other over them. The breaking dusty daylight bounced off of her long smooth brown sugar body, looking like a snack with that sexy dip in her back. Reminding me of those artistic shots on Instagram that leave people wondering who the hell took the photo? I'm almost tempted to wake her up and fuck her back to sleep... but one, I am not Chris Brown and two, I fancy the attention and taste of someone else on my contact list. One of my *other* current situations. So instead I'll take a quick photo and admire her later and leave the room, closing the door gently behind me.

"Aaliyah? Where you going?" She calls me, just as I reach the final step down the stairs and my feet touched the floor downstairs "You still here?"

I didn't answer; I opened the front door quickly and ran out the house to my car. In other words, *"Bye Felicia."*

I'm slipping! Raee'n has seen *actual* emotions come out of me- fuck! Don't bother asking me any questions and sit there trying to read between the lines thinking you can suss me out- so don't. There are no lines. There aren't any dots to connect, what you see is what you get, yes!

She's had her dose of me so that should keep her quiet for a while; I'll stay away whilst I focus my attention elsewhere. Besides, I've been absent long enough from *Mali* Oh; you thought I forgot about all that? No, of course not! Intentional time away and avoiding contact is essential. The last time Mali saw me, I was inside of her and it's been about a week since my last form of contact- physical contact.

I've kept my distance at a good space for her thoughts to be randomly turning to me without her realising. I want her pussy to flutter at the sound of my name. I want her body to shudder with one thought of me. She'll be sitting wondering through cogs of her thoughts, asking herself questions she doesn't know the answer to over and over. Meanwhile, temptation has long taken over her mind.

I hope, no... *I know* she has been sitting there wet and frustrated, not wanting to think about me... but she can't seem to help but find me in the corners of her mind. I wonder if she's touched herself, even if only a few seconds; envisioning me controlling her hand rubbing gently against her clit. Perhaps she's closed her eyes fucking herself imagining how my pussy felt...?

Maybe she's feeling guilty for allowing herself to get 'got'. After all, she is in a *loving relationship* – that bullshit word. She wouldn't be paying me the slightest bit of attention if she was *so* in love. It's all too funny to me and all so cliché. Come on; it's all a myth - love doesn't exist! Why would it exist when 'lust' walks around so freely, fucking up the base and throwing things like sexual temptation into the equation so fluidly? Answer me that! Why does temptation feel so fucking incredible? It's like that taste on your bottom lip when you've had a bite of something so good to eat and all you want is one more bite... they always say *"one more little bite won't hurt…"*

Turning up the music in my car, the base vibrating off the speakers. Devious intentions filling my head, imaging myself all over and in between Mali.

Not giving a fuck swerving through traffic, bullying cars out of the fast lane with my foot down in a hurry to get to my destination.

"Hello."

My phone rang through my car speakers, cutting off my music and my focus, the phone automatically answers.

"Aaliyah, it's Mali? Where you been?"

It's as if I'm manifesting her towards me; like she could sense the thoughts of 'her' in my head - wait a minute, how did she get my number?

"I'm sorry, but my phone told me Blue is calling so *why* am I hearing your voice on my line? You're missing me huh?"

"I'm here…"

"So *why* are you telling me?"

"You gonna come over and chill?"

"Are you asking me or telling me?"

"Depends on which one gets you here."

"…where's Blue...?"

"Don't worry. She's about…"

Mali answers after a small pause then talks in a much quieter tone. That small pause would have been from her checking over her shoulder before she spoke. I know it all too well, I am accustomed to it. It's the same tone the women I fuck around with often use when they don't want their woman or man to hear what they are up to and this is always an indication that it's about to get real!

"I'm not worried. I want to *know* why you want me there? Your girl not enough, no?" Dark and suggestive, daring her to answer me

"Something like that." I can hear the deceitful smile in her expression

"I'm busy right now." Changing my voice quickly back to the light hearted 'I couldn't care less' kind of tone while my eyes are searching for the next exit off the motorway to head in the direction of Blue's place.

"See you later then?" she sounds hopeful.

"I don't know… tell *Blue* I'm not sure. But I might come over later."

Note: *Situation.*

The Test/ The Reminder

When stepping into any situation in which you could be potentially coming in between a couple, you need to test your targets strength. Just to make sure that they are ready for you and the risks that they are going to have to take on. The test is easy; all you have to do is throw their relationship at them in a few conversations. Then gage from their reaction *if* you should take steps forward in pursuing them. Because there is nothing more sexually frustrating then laying a female down, who you have dedicated calculated time in pursuing and just as you are about to give her the fuck she's wanting, for her to turn around and say:

"No, wait, stop I can't do this to my girlfriend/boyfriend,"

Bitch! Really?? You knew what we came here to do! She leaves all caught up in the morals of her conscious meanwhile you're so fucking frustrated you need to be banged like a Salvation Army drum! Urgh!!

So, that subtle reminder about her female is imperative. I cannot stress it enough! I stay quiet and give Mali the time to realise what she is about to put at stake.

"Course, I'll tell *Blue* you're coming over."

Test passed with flying rainbow colours! She answers swiftly, not thrown off. Saying Blue's name back to me confidently, letting me know that *she* knows *exactly* what she's doing.

Follow up Notes: *Situation.*

Signs to look out for in response to the Situation test are:

Guilt, doubt, mummering, uncertainty, a stutter or stammer in speech or deflection. Any kind of weakness and vulnerability.

"Do me a favour, when I hang up delete this call from her call log."

"Sure."

"I'll call back, answer. Say nothing and hang up after, say thirty-five or so seconds. Tell Blue I called, I had to go but will holler at her later and that I *might* pass by."

"Cool, got it."

Hanging up I wait, giving her enough seconds to delete the call she made to me from Blue's call log. I call Blue back and wait, saying nothing. No more to be spoken, after the thirty-eighth second Mali hung up.

Note: *Control.*

Okay now pay *very* close attention. Knowing *exactly* how this works is like a step by step manual process. To ensure ultimate control, you must first tap into every female fibre instinct of your being! As women, we have this unknown obligation to be in control of everything! You *have* to be in control of the various situations and outcomes that are going to take place *with* or *without* you being present.

So, with that in mind what's going to go down is this:

    -Mali has deleted the outgoing call she made to me *(in my control/demand)*

    -Mali will tell Blue that I called *(also in my control/demand)*

    -Blue's female control mentality will question *why* Mali didn't hand over the phone *(out of my control)*

    -Blue will look at her phone to check to see *who* called *who. (Her suspicions will be raised).*

    -Blue will then see that I *did* call her and that her girlfriend was simply *trying* to be helpful by answering the call and delivering a message from one friend onto the other.

And that boys and girls, is control at its finest.

Provided by Aaliyah CEO of Education in Temptation.

The idea of Mali *even* communicating with me, without her being in the room to know the context of the conversation will not sit well with her at all because being a woman, she also cannot help but have the same unknown obligation to be in control of everything! But I am three steps ahead and always will be! Because I do not need to become suspect to Blue's insecure suspicions.

I've done and continue to do some fucked up shit... but this... this one may very well be my finest, most ruthless zero fucks to give a shit, I've ever done! Mali is my friend's woman and I don't actually give a fuck! Blue doesn't love her, come on, she has no idea what love is let alone being in love with a woman is!? I mean, why should I give a fuck, when I have zero fucks to give. I mean, have you seen my behaviour? Look at my life; I have no behaviour at all!

And I enjoy it this way, who wants to behave?

Have I considered Blue for a split second? Yes... but I want what I want, regardless of *who* is in the way. Besides, how *I* rationalise the situation is this:

Am I doing anything wrong here? No, I am not in a relationship; I don't have a woman to explain my actions to. So, if anyone is doing anything wrong... it's Mali. Okay, wait, wait, hear me out. Think about it... *if* we get caught or Mali comes clean, which she won't, because they never do. All I have to do, is pull out my certified loyalty Friendship Card. That's been collecting points like Tesco and waiting to be used.

I've been a devoted friend longer than Mali has been a girlfriend and I've mended many of Blue's aching heartbreak breakups and will be here when Mali is long gone because... that's what friends are for.

'I didn't mean it, I didn't know what I was doing... it was all Mali's fault' – convincing right?

Besides, I have absolutely <u>no</u> intention of being the woman who breaks them apart, that would be cruel. I'm just going to make myself a part of Mali's everyday thoughts and movements. To be on her brain always, to fuck with her mind; I want her to close her eyes and see me imprinted on the back of her eyelids. To visualise me in *everything* she does... and later once I am cemented into her deep limbic system then and only then, I will lay her down and take off her clothes and fuck her the way she needs to be fucked!

There's going to be that one thing that will draw her close to me and I *will* find it. It could be her interests or disinterests, whatever it is it, when I find the *thing* that connects us, she's *never* going to let me go and will want to give me *all* of her, all of the time! But I don't want it all. I just want the majority and at my own disposal.

You're probably shaking your head and thinking I'm a bitch. But! At least I'm a bitch who is giving you some valuable lessons in life. Whether you're taking notes, highlighting and dropping post-it notes here and there, planning on using them effectively. Whether it's for a positive intention or for your personal pussy gain. Or perhaps, you've seen signs of this *very* same behaviour, my behaviour almost *too* close to home and need to make a phone call and call someone out there. Either way, you cannot deny that it's insightful, no?

Trust me, you will finish this book feeling some type of way. Having expanded your knowledge and not to mention, if I do say so myself, be thoroughly entertained. Besides, you knew *exactly* what I was about from the first chapter! Shit, you knew from the cover of the book what this was all about and here we are honey!

We all have a darker side to us.... think about it. There are things we wished we should, could and would have said, wanted to say and wanted to do. Thoughts and actions we wanted to translate and project from our minds to out of our mouths. But remain silent- for why? for who? Oh, because it's the right thing to do? Fuck off! Why remain silent and struggle in the thoughts of what you could have done or what could have been?

More than ever before, we are being encouraged to be ourselves, to love ourselves and put our needs first, above all others. Babe, you came into this world alone and will leave the same way.

Call it what you want but I am one of the very few people in this world, who choose to take part in the act of the darker side of my conscious thoughts and fucking own it! Too many people do fucked up shit and do not take accountability! I'm in this for *myself* and I'm living my best life, I ain't going back and forth with you bitches! Ha!

So, your own inability to not decide or judge how you feel about me just yet is because I challenge your mentality. I have you questioning yourself or things you've seen. It's okay that I'm making perfect sense even if it doesn't feel right, right now… it will, because here you are, *still* reading this book.

It's so easy! Anyone and everyone has the capabilities of breaking up a relationship, if they put their body and open their legs to it. Especially with this generation full of vanity and both men and women are more than happy aspiring to be the one on the 'side' like a helping of coleslaw.

Yes, it's as simple as that, after all, sex is just sex. It's not an emotion, it's not a feeling. It's a physical act that some people become attached to and mistake for something else, using it as a tool to win someone's affection. Making someone wait three to six months to get the pussy, so when you finally get it you become attached and emotionally connected to it.

But you're not *really* attached to it are you?! You were simply deprived for three to six months!! Told to wait, it's not the perfect time! I'm sure if you were starved for three months then given a meal, you would think that was the best meal you ever had! No Drake! Get out of your feelings and strip away your emotions just like every single layer of clothing you take off and always keep them separated. Sex is sex period!

However, the shit I do… oh, it's *so* different. It needs a level of articulate sexual intelligence and a female dominance that not every woman possesses. It requires certified time, effort, mindfulness, patients and above all power. The difference between 'side bitches' and a woman like me is that, I am not going to destroy a relationship or get in the way of what you have. I will not cause drama or call up your girl or man and tell them who I am to you, what we have been doing and how long we have been doing it for, begging you to leave and be with me.

What I do is this: I become the *main* attraction without attaining the details and fine print of a relationship agreement, status or label. I *am* the main attraction, the main focus! I am the reason why your girl fucks you right, because she's thinking about *me* and all the things that I do. I am The Ultimate Temptation!

Hate me all you want and call me what you want, that negativity you're feeling right now is not because you disagree with everything I've said- no it's because you couldn't agree more and agreeing with me doesn't sit well with your morals at all!

Deny it if it makes you feel better but I know you wish you had an ounce of what I have, let's face it. Whatever happens with any one of these females, I get to walk away unaffected, unbothered, uninterested and unattached! They serve their part-time purpose and then it's onto the next one.

Being me is so much fun because I know who the fuck I am and I am happy, I am powerful, I am selfish. I am a savage I. Am. Unfuckwithable!

Unfuckwitable (un-fuck-with-able) *noun*

To be at peace with who the fuck you are! When you are so secure within yourself, no one can affect or touch your level. Nothing anyone has to say or do ever bothers you, because you are the bad bitch, the boss bitch that gets the last the word in, that has all the comebacks and petty clap backs for days; that "ONE" who backs up their words with actions and dares anybody to try them. A woman who walks into a room, moment or situation and is noticed without effort.

Also, known as **Savage Mode** or *Beast Mode!*

***

Mali is already outside posted up against the wall, looking cute as fuck! She walks towards me with one arm out ready to hug me. Leaning into her neck, breathing in deeply the essence of her 'smell good' one more time. She smells so fucking good!

I cannot resist a woman who smells this fucking beautiful. It's so attractive but I'm not talking about the scent of their perfume, it's their natural personal skin scent that blends into their pores so fragrantly gorgeous. Making it something so original that can't be recreated by anyone else; that scent that belongs only to *that* person, no one else. Mali's is intriguing, profound, alluring and so fucking attractive.

"Where you been?" She asks me

"Concern yourself with where I am going…" folding my arms and tilting my hips, looking at her a type of way "How have you been?"
Her face lights up because up until now, I've never asked her that question before and here I am, stood a few feet away from her *appearing* pleased to see her with the intention of knowing the answer.

Note: (you getting used to my side notes yet?)
The small detail of asking how someone is doing is very important. We don't care to notice, however generic the words 'how are you?' may seem. They open a conversation and it lets the person who you're talking to know that you have an interest in listening about them and theirs. Everyone likes to talk but love it even more when someone is actually listening. And these days, people only ask you this question because they have something to say or have a reply waiting.

"I'm alright you know, trying to do my thing."
"Your *thing* huh? And what's that?"

Follow up question(s); proceed in asking another question and let the base focus of the conversation be about them and theirs. Don't detour the conversation onto yourself- listen.

"I'll show you one day." She said, sticking out her tongue playfully.
"We'll maybe, one day… I'll let you or maybe I won't."
"You will…" We pause for a moment taking in our playful option of words while her eyes follow down my silhouette then back up again. She stares at my lips, covered in a deep red matte lipstick.
"Where you been though?" Snapping herself away from my lips, eagerly asking me again.

"Busy! Come out of my business." She laughs with me "What are you doing down here unsupervised, without Blue's arm around your neck?"

"I saw you pull up and wanted to say hi… *separately* and away from the lady you know." Her eyes engaging mine.

"That's cute; you know your *lady's* watching us from the window, right?" I could see Blue is fiddling behind the white lace gauze curtains from the corner of my eye. Attempting to be discreet but failing to realize that her curtains are see-through as fuck. I spotted her up there the moment I pulled up.

Side Note: Always be observant. Vigilance is key

"It's cool, trust me…" Mali thinks I'm bluffing and doesn't look up.

"I trust no one…" I wink at her, pulling my shades down a little and laugh big and animated "HEY GIRL!" Shouting up at the window, waving at Blue. She reveals herself, with an awkward smile but waves back all the same.

"I knew she was there." She laughs

"Umm hmm. Step your game up. Pay attention and keep up!"

"You first" Mali steps to the side letting me pass

"Oh, I know!" I walk pass in front of her and glance over my shoulder at Mali watching my booty go up right, down and left.

***

"Yah Yah!!!"

Entering the bedroom, Blue threw her arms around me. She needs to drop that fucking name! Honestly, what is it with people and hugging me these days? Am I a teddy bear? Do I have *'cuddles'* written across my chest? Blue steps to the side and directed her hand across the room. My eyes set on Amelia giving me a little wave.

178

She sat on the floor, chilling against the wardrobe holding her knees to her chest. Her waist length hair is pulled behind her ears, smiling awkwardly...

"You've met Amelia, *right?*"

Amelia shyly looked away not feeling at ease with everyone's eyes set on her. Blue is all excited and enthusiastic because she's brought a 'fourth' person into the mix, to even out the one to one ratio in the room and keep me distracted and the hell away from Mali.

Aware of what she's doing, I sat comfortably and closely beside Amelia, I know Blue is examining me so if I act uninterested, she will question my behaviour. Besides, who in their right mind would turn down the probable set up with a pretty woman?

"We passed on the stairs the other night. You were in your towel, right?" I said light-heartedly, attempting to add some banter to make her feel at ease.

"I remember, I think I got you a little wet right? Sorry about that."

"It's nothing. It's not the first time a woman's got me wet!"

"Good one. You're funny."

"Drink?"

Amelia nods, accepting the offer and moves closer to me while holding out her glass. I can feel Blue and Mali looking over at Amelia and I getting closely acquainted. Oh, did I have a bottle of drink in my bag? I sure did! It helps the time pass quickly.

I got to know Amelia through sips of drink, sharing stories and long conversations. I found out Amelia has been with her boyfriend for many years *but* she's one of those girls who enjoys the attention of lesbians and plays up to the whole *'girl on girl'* thing. You know, your typical on trend Spaghetti bitch!

Spaghetti Bitch *noun*

definition

A fast girl/sometime-ish/them funny duddy girls there. A heterosexual woman, who once wet becomes curious about the same sex.

Familiarises with "spaghetti"- straight but once wet (I said what I said) or watered (drunk) becomes flexible (thirsty). Then she will participate in any sexual "lesbian" activities.

But when she's asked or retreats to a sober state; is straight as RuPaul's body without padding and more than likely blame it on a-a-a-a-a-alcohol. Because she was "sooo drunk" type of excuse.

Also known as the "I get filthy when that liquor get into me" type of girls.

Women like this are ridiculous and delirious! They deny their lesbian intentions, telling you all day they *don't* like women. But drop an ounce of alcohol into their system and they are forward, fast and flirting with you and wondering what your fingers and mouth can do.

"The whole girl on girl thing is so sexy to me!" Amelia's honesty is admirable. She didn't hold back telling me what she's about- once the liquid courage settled in her system. She talks with her hands following her words in movements and shapes. "And he doesn't see it as cheating. To him, cheating can only be through another man's penetration. He reckons, women can't do what he does for me, so he's not threatened by my desire at all."

"You'd be *very* fucking surprised at what we can do. I should show you and then you can tell him all about it."

Watching her is like watching a moving painting. She has these picturesque eyes, emphasising her stories. She could have been talking about polystyrene, bagpipes and dried kale- real random boring shit but people would listen as intently as I am now. Capturing my attention effortlessly while enunciating her words clearly, well-spoken but not posh. Her pretty little mouth formed her words perfectly with her very kissable lips.

"You're so funny! It's only an idea we discussed openly. He finds it a turn on as much as I do. Besides, I haven't met a woman I want yet. They're so odd with all these gender names these days. What does fluid even mean??" Scrunching up her face and shrugging her shoulders she pauses and takes another sips from her glass.

"You haven't been looking in the right places babe."

Let's be honest, finding lesbians who are in touch with their femininity are a dime a dozen. Honestly, not every day become a lesbian; shave your hair off and bench press

180

in the gym like your name is Michael. Some days, be a lesbian who embraces her femininity and the power of her pussy!

"She has to be a woman who I *really* want to *want*! A *real* woman, you know, nothing tomboyish. I have my boyfriend so, I don't need another him. I want a woman so feminine and stunning, I think it will heighten the attraction and make the climax so *delicious*." She says, describing my attributes, while her eyes are busy scanning all over me.

"I'm Aaliyah, have we met?" My hand held out for her to shake.

I noticed she didn't really laugh. Instead of flirtatious laughter, she would say:

"That's so funny!" or "You're so funny!"

"I'm being serious, let's do this!" Pretending to take my top off, she blushes a little.

"I'm Amelia, nice to meet you beautiful."

Covering her blush with her hand, she composes herself and holds onto my hand with the other.

Our laughter subsidies. Amelia uses my hand for balance and pulls herself up onto me. She sits on my lap with her legs around me, looking at me as she circles her finger along the bare skin of my revealed shoulder. Following the lines of my tattoo, lost for a few seconds. Looking back up at me she moves her face towards mine, placing both arms around my neck. Her lips pouted, our noses together, eyes closed and... she hiccups.

"I better take myself to bed." She diverts her pouted lips to my cheek and places her kiss there instead. Fuck sake! What an anti-climax! Getting her balance together, she gets up with my hands assisting her waist. I follow behind her to the bedroom door.

"Want me to follow you downstairs?" I ask.

Amelia looks behind me at Mali... then back at me. *Shit*! I *completely* forgot Mali was there, my bad! The plan was to make her a just a bit jealous not forget about her.

Then again, there is absolutely nothing wrong with a bit of healthy competition but by the look on her face, I've got her in her feelings.

"No, I shouldn't, I already can't keep my hands to myself. I won't be able to resist that look in your eyes for much longer. I'll probably jump on you the minute we step out this room. Then *you'd* have to carry *me* down each and every single step. Throw me on my bed and do whatever the fuck you want to do to me!"

"Damn!"

"Do you know Aaliyah, you are very, *very* intriguing? There's this *thing* about you that makes you... lustful, no... desirable. No, even better, tempting!"

Amelia sounds like one of those American movie stars from the sixties, where an overdramatic blue-eyed blonde actress throws herself at the dark and handsome stranger. However, she meant every word with this open air of honesty that only a small amount of people attain in this world.

"Thank you gorgeous." Feeling myself smile through heated cheeks. It's usually me who has a woman smiling from ear to ear, blushing uncontrollably?

"I was taught to *always* be honest and say exactly how it is. Goodnight sweetheart." Hugging me she whispers in my ear. "Another time, when no one's around and we can keep it between ourselves because no one needs to know."

"One hundred percent."

"You know where to find me." She sighs, unsatisfied with her decision to go to bed alone. Holding my chin gently, she leans in once more, kissing my lips quietly and discreetly. Her finger reaches for the waistband on my trousers. Saying nothing, tugging lightly like she's having a conversation with herself in her head, debating on what she should do next and questioning 'what if?' should she take me downstairs or stick to what she said. Letting go, she sighs one last time unhappy with her mindful self-controlled decision. Turning, Amelia waves at Mali then leaves the room, looking at me one more time over her shoulder subtly as she takes her slow-paced steps and her tempting thoughts to bed.

Closing the door quietly, walking on the balls of my feet across the rough, cheap carpet towards Mali. So I don't wake up little Miss Blue Sleep, who is completely out for the count, yet again?!

"First of all, she's not into girls! She's chatting a whole bag of bull shit!" Mali is *far* from happy about my attention being elsewhere all night.

"I know, but she doesn't have to be into girls for me to be *in* her. I just wanna fuck anyway! You heard everything she said, so does she!?"

"Whatever."

"Why do you care? You've got your babe, fix your face!" Laughing it off, I sat down facing Mali and lean on the bed in the same position she is resting. I mirror her comfortable slump.

"She's jus' gonna use you. Probably as an experiment." Her face completely uninterested in me reaching towards her and gently scratching on the bottom of her arm, watching goose bumps and hair raise on her skin.

"I want to be used. She can experiment with me or on top of me all she wants!"

Unimpressed with my laughter and the attention of my touch while my focus of conversation is on Amelia. Mali brushes my hand off and moves her body away from me, into a different direction.

Peering over at her woman, spread out in the middle of the bed- knocked out, fast asleep, mouth wide open leaving us two *all alone* yet again to entertain ourselves. I swear all this girl does is sleep? Either that or the narrative of this book has no need for her character over than a symbol of morality standing between Mali and me? Both Mali and I are sat on the floor with nothing else to do but look at each other. Well, I'm watching her trying not to look back at me. I wonder if she's thinking about me, thinking about her?

"What?" She snaps defensively, not sure how to take me ignoring her all night to now, all of a sudden being fixated on her face.

"Am I *not* allowed to look at you?"

"Seriously *stop*! You're all up on Amelia, now you're in my face- move man!"

"Listen, baby girl... when I'm with you, I'm *with* you. Don't worry about her."

Honestly, who do I think I am with these lines?

Mali doesn't know where to look, there's nothing in this room other than me, so she turned back in my direction. Studying her face, taking note of the smaller details I have noticed before. Like the small freckles scattered across the left side of her face and only just a few on the right. Her long lashes fanned out and curled without a drop of mascara on them. And her eyes; when you take a closer look and the way the lamp is shining on her face, she has these brown shades with streaks of dark green in her left eye. Those eyes though, what is she hiding behind those captivating eyes hiding?

"What's your story?" Head in my palm, waiting for her to answer me.

"What do you mean?" Screwing up her face, her dimples appear. She looks nervously around, not knowing how to answer.

"What's your story? Fill in the blanks, tell me about *you.*"

Mali laughed a little and shook her head then holds her attention at the ceiling, gathering her thoughts. She gazes up with those big beautiful eyes catch the light once more before turning to answer me.

"Miss Aaliyah really wants to know about me? Really?" She says sarcastically but I like the way she calls me 'Miss Aaliyah'.

"If I didn't want to know, I wouldn't have asked. And I don't ask *anyone* for *anything*. So, you better *answer!*"

Demanding, yes. But it's true I don't have to ask, I always get and I'm actually going to listen. Which is something I don't do but she *does* intrigue me. Plus, if I'm going to get deep into her mind, I'm going to need to know what's going on in there. Then I'll be able to adjust it for my personal advantage, of course!

She sits, silent. Observing the walls, as if she's hoping the words she wants to say would appear from hiding within the streaks of deep red matte emulsion and speak on her behalf.

Minutes pass and her thoughts are dancing around her head, no words spoken. Eyes lost in translation. Almost like she's left me sitting here to go find her story somewhere in the back of her mind. Only it's taking a while as she is unlocking blocked memories she's hidden away. It gave me enough time to roll her a perfect spliff from the stash of weed that Blue kept close by in a shoe box.

Breaking the distant gaze, she was caught up in away from the wall and onto my hand. Swaying the spliff and my gold lighter in front of her face.

"Start from the beginning…"

"Thought you didn't smoke this *shit!*" She mocks my words, imitating my boujie voice while placing the spliff between her lips.

"Yes, *but* I never said I didn't know how to *roll* this *shit*. So, spark up and start talking."

Giving her a little bit more time to put the right amount of weed into her system to relax her mind, her body and ease her thoughts into words. Her shoulders loosen; she slouches leaning her back against the side of the bed. Her arms rested on her knees, her head hung down. Inhaling deeply, she blows the smoke out into her lap slowly. Lifting her head up as the smoke descends from her face, Mali opens her mouth…

"Malikah Cherise Elise Davis." She laughs shyly, looking at me feeling placed on the spot with my request to get to know her. "What do you want to know?"

"Every-*thing* you want to tell me. Start from the beginning, what was home like?" Encouraging her, *I* want her thoughts to flow freely without any interruptions. She stalls, taking a deeper breath in and out before revealing what she wishes to share.

"Home was such a fucked-up place man! My mum's always been ghetto and loud for no real good reason at all and …" peering at me, unsure if she should, her eyes asking me *'you sure you wanna know?'*, I nod my head *'yes!'*

"Go on. I won't judge." Shooting a quick reassuring grin, Mali focuses her eyes back onto the wall.

"I left because of. To be honest, I had no choice, I… umm… my little sisters'- *their* dad! He's not *my* dad. He's a waste man! I told my mum he was a dickhead but she wasn't trying to hear me out. She *never* listened to a word I said, she still doesn't"

Inhaling and holding the smoke in a few seconds longer than before she exhales once more.

"He used to look at me *real* funny and throw these random side compliments my way, about how I'm turning into a woman. And how *nice* it was to watch me grow. The kind of shit a grown man should *not* be saying to no little girl! Mum used to laugh it off, thought he was funny she'd say, *'that's just the way he is, pay him no mind.'* She's so dumb I swear and he's – I fucking *hate* him!"

Mali drifted off into her own world, talking past me. Her face depicting every inch of disgust for this man.

"He kept coming in my room in the middle of the night. Telling me how beautiful and special I was and how much he loved me. At first, he never touched me… he used to jus' sit *there*… at the end of my bed, watching me sleep. Telling me he's going to protect me from the world saying and that *I* could trust *him*. He used to sit beside me, closer every night. Eventually, he was under the covers with me. Holding me in his arms and whispering in my ear, how he wanted to keep the bad dreams away."

Bracing myself but showing no reaction, I knew what she was going to say next and it kills me that we *all* know stories like this, don't we? And it's so disgusting that something like *this* isn't rare anymore in the world. It's so damn common and has become a statistic in this life; that one in five women experience rape or molestation in their childhood. Think about it. It means in every group of friends or sisters there is at least one or two of us who have been touched, inappropriately as a child or as a woman- fuck, it could be you who is that statistic, either way it's fucked up!

"The thing is, the nightmares didn't start until he came along. When he kissed me, his beard tickled but I got used to it. I got used to *everything*, imagine. The first time, he erm, he was… gentle. But he still tore me and I bled- a lot! He helped me hide and throw away everything: the bed sheets, my clothes and his too. He told me he would take away *all* the pain. That night he gave me my first spliff and I made my body feel numb when he touched me. It got to a point where I *actually* liked the shit!? Can you believe it? I used to actually wait up for this prick to come into my room excited and wet!? Waiting for him to fuck me, I wanted it because I thought he loved me. I was making the shit easy for him to slide right into me whenever he wanted to, because I *enjoyed* the feeling of him!? It was jus' me and him, no one else mattered. He made me feel so fucking beautiful, before him no one even looked at me. He got me into his bubble and I believed every – single – fucking - lie he ever told me! Like it was okay to do the things he was doing to me. I was only a kid but all the things we did felt natural. To be in love with a man, a grown man was normal to me?? I used to get so fucking jealous when mum went anywhere near him or when she touched him or kissed him in front of me. I remember standing outside their bedroom door, listening out, to see if they had sex. Pent up and vex that he didn't come into my room instead. I would throw these tantrums and pretend to be sick. Demanding he stayed home to look after me. We would always end up fucking in my mums' bed. It sounds so disgusting saying it out loud now I'm grown but back then it was different. There were nights he stayed till the morning. It was an accident the first time and he woke up panicking, thinking we got caught laying naked in bed together naked. So, I showed him how to lock the door in a way you couldn't get in unless you knew the trick. He called me his clever little lady. I didn't know any different, jus' a fucking kid and he twisted my head and fucked with my mind into believing his bullshit! Until this one time."

She shakes her head, breathing out her nose with a heavy puff and smiles, ashamed of her past. She takes a deep breath preparing herself for the next part

"He watched me walking home from high school. I was at the bottom of the road and he must have clocked me from the window or something. I don't know what happened but I had a few guys my age following me home. Kids being kids, jus' being dumb, laughing and joking around. Pushing each other and messing about. I was always cool with the boys, I didn't understand girls back then, not like I do now - I think I was scared of them or scared of feeling attracted towards them, either way, I kept my distance from girls. Anyway, he lost his shit! I think it was the hug or the kiss on my cheek Theo gave me that sent *him* over the edge. But Theo was only saying goodbye and *he* didn't give me a second explain. I stepped one patent school shoe into that front door and onto *that* horrible red carpet in the hallway… I always fucking hated the colour of that carpet! Who chooses red for a carpet colour anyway? But the *way* he snatched me up by my hair and dragged me down the hallway- fuck! At the time I had these single really long braids in my hair. My hair was so long, it fell right down my back and he fucking *dragged* it- like it was some kind of rope, wrapping it around his fist two or three times. I was kicking and screaming, holding the back of my head feeling and hearing my hair ripping from my scalp. It's crazy, I can still remember every sound and I've tried so hard to shut it all out and push it away. It doesn't matter how hard I try; I can remember *every* fucking sound *so* clearly. The look in his eyes, was like he was possessed or something? I couldn't see him anymore. It was not like him to hurt me like this. Punching me like I was some man the same size as him and not a little girl. He threw me at the end of the hallway and my body flopped and fell like a doll. I tried to get away, I tried to kick him off of me but he grabbed my ankle. My face was covered in my blood. My eyes were blurry as fuck, my head was dizzy, my chest was tight- I couldn't breathe or shout for help. It was like I forgot all my words. He held me tight by my throat with one hand and didn't let go. His hand was big enough to fit around my little neck. He didn't flinch at me trying to claw it off with my nails, he jus' pinned me to the floor, like it was nothing, like I was nothing! On top of me, dragging up my skirt, ripping my school tights and everything right off of me. I couldn't get him away, he locked his body between my legs holding them open and… rammed his dick into me so hard, my whole body moved. I couldn't scream through the grip he had around my throat, I couldn't make a sound. He tore me apart, blood dripping from my head, my face, my body was ripped apart. My blood was blending with the colour of that *fucking carpet*... wanna know how I knew?"

"How?" I asked her, listening to this raw story unfold. Mali turns to me, staring directly in my eyes. Her streaks of green in her eyes went away with the tears, as she wiped her face with the cuffs of her sleeves. But it didn't stop them from free-flowing like a wild waterfall down her face.

"Because my young pussy wasn't enough for him this time. Nah, he wasn't done! He wanted more and he wanted to take it all from me... he flipped me over, pushed my head into that fucking red carpet, put my body how he wanted it and held the back of my thighs open and shoved his dick into the back of me. And the way my face was pushed down on the floor, I could see my blood drip and disappear, blending into the carpet. I gave up trying to fight or scream, there was no point. I wasn't going to be saved. No one was coming to stop him. No super heroes, no prince charming, no fairies to wave their wand and make it all disappear. I thought I was dying, I thought he killed me, the amount of times I blacked out but came back... I wished I never came back! I wanted to die so fucking bad, wishing he would've fucking killed me! At least then everyone would know what he did because what would he do with my dead body? He couldn't stuff me in the wash basket, could he? Or throw it away like all the bloodstained sheets?!

I was just a fucking kid! I couldn't get him off of me! I tried so bad.... When he was done... he laid on top of me all out of breath and whispered in my ear that he loved me, that's why he did what he did. He told me to clean myself up, leaving me to pick myself up off the floor. Blood and shit all over me, I couldn't get up. I didn't move. For a second, I'm sure he thought he killed me. Looking at my body on the floor limp, not moving and completely broken. But he left me there all the same.

By the time my mum came home, I had showered and got rid of my bloodstained school clothes. Thrown away anything that had anything on it. I considered putting myself in the bin, because I couldn't get the feeling of him or my blood off of my skin.

I took my braids out and clumps of my hair fell out, some braids jus' dropped out.

189

I had these bloody bald patches at the back of my head but my hair was big enough and long enough to hide them. Washing the blood off my skin didn't make a difference, I still felt him all over me. Like this weight and it was breaking me to pieces.

I sat in the kitchen and waited for my mum to come home. Sitting there staring at the red carpet in the hallway dazed. Wondering if anyone could smell or see the blood that we *knew was* there. My little sisters were walking up and down the hall stepping all over *my* blood with their little feet. I kept imagining red blood spots covering the bottom of their tiny white school socks. He washed down the carpet but I knew my blood was there in the grains of the carpet somewhere, holding onto the strands because some stains you can't get rid of, like the ones in your memory… they stay. Mum had asked what happened, shocked at the state of her daughter looking like a fresh corpse. But before I could open my mouth, he placed a hand on my shoulder, squeezing me tight and answered for me. Telling her some bullshit about how I got jumped and beat up by girls from another school. He said he had 'it' under control… he had me under control. I *really* wanted to tell her but *he* made *sure* I kept my mouth shut! That night I sat up in bed scared as fuck! Watching the space between the floor and door as the shadows of people pass by my room. I pushed my desk in front of the door hoping it would keep him out and keep him away from me but he knew how to unlock my door because I fucking showed him! The minute I closed my eyes and started to drift off, I heard the sound of my desk scrape along the carpet slowly and him squeezing his self in the crack of the door that he opened. I pretended to sleep and didn't move, I wanted him to leave me the fuck alone. He came in with a bag of bullshit apologies and kisses all over me; kissed and sucked everything he hurt telling me he was going to kiss the pain away. He gave me a ketamine pill that night. I was gone for days, high and completely out of it.

I remember, this one time when I was fifteen and in my last year of school, my friends were talking about paedophiles and whatever else. I jus' sat there not saying *nothing*- silent and ashamed. I got brave one day and decided to tell my mum *everrry-thing*, I'm talking from beginning to end. I had *enough*! She needed to know what he was doing to me for years!!"

"What did she say?"

"Say?!" She scoffed "*Say*? she punched me in the fucking face! Telling me I was evil and tryna break up her happy family. And he sat there, saying nothing while she packed up *all* my shit and threw me out the house onto the streets... he jus' fucking smiled. He probably knew she would always choose him, I was so dumb! Of course, she wouldn't believe me, because women like her always chose dick over their kids! You know something, I didn't get to tell the dumb bitch that he made me get rid of a baby. More like he kicked it out of me! I think I was about four maybe five months but I could feel my baby girl moving around in my belly. Doing tumble turns, making me feel nauseous as fuck but I was never actually threw up. She gave me that sickly feeling you get right before a rollercoaster drop. She was never still for long and would keep me up all night.

I stole a pair of baby shoes from some expensive shop; these little cute cream things with diamantes'... I still have them too. I've lost so much stuff over the years, moving place to place but I'll *never* get rid of them." Her face lit up. She closed her eyes and smiled through the memory tight fighting back the on-coming breakdown. Holding her lips strong behind her teeth.

"I hid my bump under baggy jumpers. I always wore baggy clothes, so it made no difference to my usual. Besides, no one paid attention to me and she was a really small bump. Do not ask me what I was going to do with a baby? I had no fucking idea how I would hide her once she was born. I thought it would be beautiful to have someone love me, unconditionally. I hid her for as long as I could but he caught me, changing one day... asking me *'what the fuck is that?* I told him- why did I say it? I said, *'it's yours.'* He steps towards me, rubbing my belly slowly. For a split second, I thought things would be okay. But he punched me so *fucking hard* and I hit the floor. He kicked me over and over. I screamed, begging him to stop but he didn't stop."

Crying through the pain, her body shudders, unable to contain it. She took a few deep breathes and continued to speak with her eyes shut.

"He took her away from me and I couldn't fucking stop him. I tried to save her Aaliyah, I really did. But I couldn't stop the bleeding! I snuck out the house and took a night bus to the nearest hospital, holding my belly all the way. Telling her she's gonna okay but she wasn't moving. I used to tickle the left side of my belly and she would push her little body back on me. But she didn't move, she wasn't moving!" Calming herself down, she spoke quietly "I never knew for sure until they made me give birth to her lifeless, little body and I held her in my arms that she *was* a girl but I knew… I knew. She was so tiny, the smallest and most beautiful thing I have ever seen in my life. I wanted her to open her eyes and see me, even if it was for a split-second jus' so I could tell her I was sorry. I kissed her tiny forehead over and over, telling her I loved her. I thought if I hold her for long enough and kept her warm, against my skin that she would take her first tiny breath or squeeze onto my baby finger. Like those stories you see on the internet- those miracle babies that come back to life. It took about three nurses to take her out of my arms. I jus' didn't want her to be alone, I knew they were going to take her away and she would be lying there on some metal slab all alone, with some tag on her foot with no name, no time of birth and no time of death. It was my fault, I was supposed to protect her from *him*, I was supposed to keep her safe and I fucked up! She died before I got to the hospital… Imagine having to stay in the maternity ward with new babies crying and being born healthy, knowing yours died inside of you. I kept my curtains closed, looking at my flat stomach and the empty clear plastic cot the nurses forgot to remove from my cubicle and I kept closing my eyes and opening them, wishing she'd be laying in there sleeping peacefully, her little chest moving up and down… breathing and alive. I left the maternity ward without a baby in my arms, or in a car seat like the rest of the happy mums. I had to sneak out, I didn't give my details to the doctors and nurses asking me constant questions because I was a minor who jus' gave birth to a dead baby! I know I wouldn't have been able to give her much but she was *my baby* and she shouldn't have been taken away from me. He took everything from me. My home, my family and my baby and now I don't have nothing! Jus' another abused girl fucked up and dragged up. A reference number on some social workers paperwork, that hasn't been submitted because she finishes work at five and doesn't give a shit! Now you're ignored by the system that doesn't do anything but fuck you up even more, than they forget all about you once you're not an age of concern even though you're fucked up, damaged and broken."

She breaks down, burying her face on the edge of the bed, her body shuddering from her quietened weeping into the covers. I have always been unstable with people's emotions, especially with people crying, I never know what to do. I am literally don't know what to do in these situations. What do I say?

"You'll be ok." "there, there." "I'm sorry."

You can't say a thing. And I am a deer in headlights when it comes to any form of human emotion other than my own, which I don't deal with. So *how* in the hell am I going to help Mali with all of this emotion? But I can't sit here and do nothing? Mali needs a tissue, a shoulder, a hug, psychiatric support, counselling, something?! Reaching over her, I slowly put my hand on her shuddering back, rubbing in a circular motion.

She sat up, her face was soaked and her eyes are lost in the sea of falling tears. Flopping into my lap, she wraps her arms around me tightly. However, my arms don't know what to do, so I place my hand softly on her back- Am I doing it right? My eyes a little clouded, feeling a little choked up myself from thinking about everything she had openly told me. All of that pain, all of those years of hiding all that hurt and pain. People are sick! That man is trash and her mum is sick in the head and needs to be admitted to a mental institution! How the fuck can you choose a 'man' over your own child? How? How can you do that to a child that had no choice entering this world? But still women and mothers boldly choose to disregard them! I do not understand it, you are supposed to love, guide and nurture your child through this world? Women like that shouldn't have kids. They should be made sterile! Have them taken away from them or be put in prison and suffer along with the other 'vulnerable prisoners,' because women like that enable sick and twisted men to get away with the cruel shit they do to kids, for why? Because they don't want to be alone?!   What??

She better hope karma wears a muzzle the day it comes knocking at her door. Because she knows damn well her daughter was telling the fucking truth!

Feeling this *huge* knot in my throat growing and hurting, like I have swallowed barbed wires. Holding my emotions back but- Mali's flopped forward her arms and she's not letting go of me. Stroking my hands through her hair, trying to ease her pain somehow, what else could I do? Peering closely, seeing the scars on the back of her head. Patches of hair missing that refused to grow through the scars in her scalp where her hair was ripped out from what *he* did to her. Lifting her body from my lap into my chest, holding her tight, embracing her fragility and supporting her in my arms. I silently allowed my tears fall. Both of us here crying for the time needed for the moment to be what it is and pass on its own. Oh my God! I cannot imagine how it was for her to go through hell and all of that alone. Literally what the fuck?

"Okay come on, calm down girl."

Peeling her off of me slowly, she hung her head down not wanting me to see her face; embarrassed or ashamed. I quickly get rid of any evidence of tears and crying away from my face and compose back to my regular, chill, emotionless self. I can be empathetic to her but show no over emotions or be in my feelings like this, no tears and no time to be weak. The only useful advice my mum ever gave me whenever I needed some 'mum time' and support, she would put the kettle on and sit down with me and two cups of tea:

"We don't do tears; we have no time to be weak. You need to pick yourself up, fight it, figure it out and get on with it. If you can change it then do it if you can't move on and don't worry about it"

She would then place a tissue on the table

"Enough tears now, Aaliyah."

With that, she'd pick up her cup of tea and leave me in the kitchen to pull myself the fuck together- self-sooth I guess, who knows? Her parenting skills were not from 'maternal natural instincts' but more of the 'survival skills' kind but they worked. I should have asked Mali to tell me about herself in the kitchen. That way, I could have used my mums' technique; put the kettle on, said a few words of motivation and then bounced.

"Thank you." her head low, facing the floor unable to bring herself to look at me just yet.

"For what?" I rub her thigh gently.

"Listening, it's not like I can talk to…" She peers over her shoulder at Blue sleeping heavy and speaks quietly. "she talks about herself most days and I can't get a word in" Mali shrugs.

"It's cool, but don't get it twisted, I like to talk about myself too. However, I'm more of an interesting subject, right?" I cut her off with a little light hearted banter and unnecessary comment. It might not be the 'kettle technique,' but I need to stop us from going down a further emotional conversational path because I am not playing 'I've told you mine, now you tell me yours'. Nope! Nu-uh! Not that I have anything to say, I am NOT involved!

"You're alright you know Miss Aaliyah." She takes her eyes off of the floor and on me.

"Someone told me once, that the best people to listen are the ones that don't know shit… sooo go find someone," giggling a little, it may be too early for an extra sprinkle of my banter but I can't help it. She chuckles a little, at least she gets my sense of humour. Most people seem to think I'm rude- but I'm being honest, so if you think that's rude well then that is your problem babe, not mine.

"Well, thanks anyway." She hugs me again, my arms still not knowing what to do with themselves, patting her back lightly, don't ask, I have no idea.

"Seriously though," I pulled her off me again, "if this is your idea of getting me wet then I'm going to need you to try a lot harder girl! Because *this* is *not* what I had in mind at *all*!" Holding onto the bottom of my top, stretching it down and out showing her the big dark patches in places from her floods of tears.

"I'm sorry, my bad. It wasn't what I had in mind either." She cracks a slight smile.

"Don't worry about it;" looking over at Blue and her useless self, who is *officially* out for the night, "you want to go for a drive?"

"Erm, okay Miss Aaliyah but you've been drinking?" There she goes again with the way she says my name. I can get used to that shit. She sounds sexy, just the way she says it.

"*Please!* I only had like one or two, okay maybe three drinks. But relax, Miguel it takes a lot more to get with me. Besides, Amelia drunk most of it. You know *alcohol* tends to bring out people's truths. So, I pretended to be on her wave, to see how far she was willing to go." I stuck out my tongue.

"Aaliyah!?" Mali's a little shocked but she laughs with me anyway, shaking her head and removing the final traces of tears from her gorgeous face. She's so fucking beautiful!

"Sometimes you have to be a little deceitful and calculative to get what you want." I jingle my car keys in her face. "Are *you* down or what?"

"Is this you being calculative again?"

"Uh huh! You catch on quick." I wink, jingle my car keys again and like hypnosis, it works just like a charm.

"I'm down!" She grins at me and forgets her woes, she's about to be in for a good time.

"You know you won't be back until... I don't know when, so..." Letting her know the risk she is about to take, I point at her sleeping beauty.

"I can do what I want! I'm grown!" She *is* grown but she's in a relationship. She screws up her face but I can tell she's slightly worried about the '*anything*' that could and will happen once we leave this house. But it doesn't stop her from getting up, throwing on a different top, fixing her hair into her tied back over-the-shoulder ponytail and putting her shoes on. I watched her closely from where I sat, looking at the way she moves in the reflection of the mirror. I also watched Blue; making sure she didn't stir. How the hell does she sleeps so heavy? Honestly, it's making this so much easier for me to do the shit I shouldn't be doing. She is literally 'sleeping on her woman'. If Mali was *my* woman there would be no time for sleep, *ever*! Not even a nap!

"Alright, let's go." I snap myself out of my thoughts and nod at her. We leave the room, stepping quietly and keep our eyes on Blue. Closing the door behind us we kame our way down the stairs, quietly past Amelia's room then out the house.

***

"Where we going?"

I didn't answer; her I looked up at the night sky, enjoying the air and lights in the night sky. I love how they made the scenery change from the murky desolate grey city of hustle and bustle we know for the rush hour rat race and money makers turn to an almost peaceful, picturesque, pretty flawless depiction, full of lights of all types of colours sparkling on it's never ending black canvas.

"Seriously, where we going?"

"Mali, stop stressing, relax."

She keeps checking on her phone often, waiting for that, 'where are you?' phone call. And thinking about the explanation and reason or lie she doesn't know to give. So, she's tapping her fingers agitated from the idea of having to lie.

Parking up in Vauxhall at the back of a selection of gay clubs on the underpasses of tunnels.

"You're not serious!"

"I'm *very* serious; I want to dance so *we* are going in *that* club!"

"What if people see *us* together?"

"So, what! What can they say? We are two people going out to enjoy each other's company, without your woman," I giggle, knowing it's fucked up. "It's minor."

"I don't know if this is a good idea." She's shook, not so 'grown' now is she?

"That night when I met you in the club?"

"Yeah?" She says absorbed in my words

"You want to do that night all over again but better?" Taking her hand in mine and placing it on my lap, she stretches her fingers towards my inner thigh. We both observe her hand grip and settle on my body.

"Let's do it." She lit up intrigued by my offer of playful promiscuity.

"Kiss me…"

7. The Elapsed Everything…

My apartment has never been shy about letting sunlight right into it, shining bright as fuck and making me regret my choice of demanding big oversized windows with no blinds and no curtains. Especially now when the daylight is smacking me right in the fucking face and my head is banging! Fuck my life!! When did I get home and *how* did I get home? What day is it? My head feels like it is on fire! Like a marching band in drumline formation is trooping behind my eyes, reminding me that last nights' behaviour comes with repercussions by parading up and down my brain and beating on my temples like a mother fucking base drum!

Honestly, I'm getting too old for this shit! And it doesn't help that my phone hasn't. Stopped. Fucking. *RINGING*!!! Who the *hell* is calling me like this? Is my name Drake for my hot line to be blinging like this? I'm not answering! Fuck off!! Hiding under the duvet and throwing a pillow over my head, laying here on my back, I am not moving, I'm refusing to move, nope! Not today. Nu-uh! Maybe… if I lay *reeeeally* still for long enough, my phone will stop ringing? *Yes?* The kind of foolishness and fuckery of 'no logic' or sense that runs through your mind when you're obviously still coming down from whatever your dumb arse thought was a good idea to put into your system last night!

My phone clearly doesn't want to give up, set on vibrate and constantly buzzing. Sounding like it's trying to drill a hole right through my bedside table. Seriously, what is it with iPhone's and its violent vibrate anyway? Isn't the whole point of the 'vibrate function' to be discreet? To be alerted but not heard? So, I don't understand why this loud buzzing noise is coming from my phone and what time is it?

Peeking out of my covers, I turn my head that is still partly covered by my pillows. I watch the phone through the small breathing gap I created for myself, violently vibrating its way to the edge of the table. Sticking out my arm, opening out my palm waiting… it drops off of the edge right into my hand, closing my eyes again… reluctantly, I answer and pull the duvet back over my head again.

"What?!" Aggravated at the thought of even being awake.

"Aaliyah, is that you?" I can't deal with stupid questions in the morning. Why call my phone and ask? Who else is going to fucking answer? Your mum? The Cookie Monster? Cruella Deville??

"You called my phone so, who the fuck else is it going to be?!" My voice rough as fuck and croaky as hell, mouth and throat feeling as dry as your aunties' foot back.

"It's Blue, I want-"

"Blue, honey listen, if we are going to remain friends, you have got to *stop* calling my phone so fucking early!" I dug myself further under the covers. I mean it when I say that I am not surfacing today.

"It's twelve *honey*… what happened to you last night? You left out, where'd you go? Who did you go with?"

Her questions came at me one after the other with a whole lot of attitude, like *we* are fucking and *I* have to answer her or deal with her attitude? I'm sorry, who is she talking to? Because it could never be me? Besides, who fucking knows what happened last night? To be honest, everything is all over the place in my head and I can't remember. I know we were at a club; I know we were dancing and hands were where they shouldn't be. Laughing in my head amusing myself but I couldn't tell you *anything* else that happened, it's gone…

So… what happened?" She asked me again, demanding an answer, which snapped me away from searching through the flash backs of last night in my messy memory.

"Yeah, I didn't come over to watch you sleep honey."

"And Mali?

"What about her?"

"She went with you, right?"

"Yes?? I wanted a change of scenery and no one could wake you up, so we left."

"Then what?" I do not appreciate this interrogation, who is she to question me? So, what if I went out with her woman!

"What do you mean 'then what?'. We went to the club and that was it what do you want to know?"

"Why didn't you wake me up to go with you?" Did she not just hear me say 'no one could wake her up'? I *know* I didn't *actually* try but she doesn't know that, she was asleep! Who told her it was a good idea to close her eyes with me around her woman?

"Miss Blue, am I your woman to be playing 'rise and shine' with you?" Why would I want her to come anyway? The whole idea was to have some alone time, without her snoring the alphabet in the background.

"But you are *my* friend..." This must be a trick question because she knows our friendship is by force, her force! I may have known her for however long but most friendships stop and you become strangers who comment heart eyes and flame emojis on Insta. The friendship fades out, you both stops calling. No hard feelings and no love lost. You've out grown each other's need for a friendship and all you need to sustain the love, is to catch up over a coffee every few years.

"Why are you asking me these questions?"

"Would you not ask me if you were in my shoes and I went out with your woman!"

"First of all, your shoes are trash! Second of all, I wouldn't be asleep with anyone around my woman!" I would never put my feet is her 'use to be worn by an old woman' shoes, who died alone with a cup of tea in her hand and a soap opera omnibus on repeat, charity shop shoes.

"Well, you where the last one to see Mali. I don't know where she is? Have you seen her?"

"You're talking to me like you know something? Speak up because I don't have time for your attitude. Spit it out, regulate yourself and we can move the fuck on!" Putting her back in her place and slipping in a question. Once she starts to say more than the riddles she's talking in, I can gage where to go with my answers and not slip up on any information she doesn't *need* to know.

"Did you *leave* together?" She asks me with each word separate and clear like I'm five fucking years old. Look, I know I am in the wrong here but she has got one more chance to change her octave and take it down a few levels.

"Blue, we - went - to - the - club *to-geth-er*, why would we *not* leave *to - gether*? I drove us there. What, was I supposed to do leave your woman on the streets and drive off?!" Responding back with the same attitude she gave me. My brain is piecing the events of last night together.

"Did she go home with you?"
Bitch, that is a good fucking question!? Everything else is a blur, sooo I'm going to go with 'no'. No seems like the safest response at this point. I'll flip it and ask her a question, make her lose focus. Let's see how this goes- ready?

"No! Blue you know I don't let people in my house! You haven't come to my house so, why is your little girlfriend going to be here? Why are you having this conversation with me? You should be on the phone to your woman. You and I are not fucking or in any kind of relationship for you to be asking me a bag of questions. Mali is grown and she made her own decisions last night? So, question her on that?" Sitting up in bed, she's pissing me off and has me talking loud and flaying my arm about the place when my head is too banging for this level of energy this kind of attitude requires.

"I *have*! I've been trying to call her all morning, her phones off."

"Try harder and miss me with all of this!"

"I don't know where she is? Do you?"

"Blue please with the twenty-one questions."

Blue continues talking in my ear saying something along the lines of not being happy with me going out with her woman. That I wouldn't have done it if Mali was a man blah, blah bullshit blah, blah- girl bye!

I notice the other side of my bed is over turned. The pillows dented inwards looking like a head was laying there not too long ago. Reaching over and feeling the spot... it's still warm... who the *hell* is here? Blocking out Blue's noise, reaching under the pillow, I pull out a phone switched off- the fuck!!

Stretching my neck around the room, not seeing any sign of *her* at all but I know she's here. The armchair in my bedroom has a hoody, a pair of jeans and a top all folded over the arm of the chair, none of which belong to me. My ears instantly pick up the distant sound of *her* in my bathroom, flushing the toilet, washing her hands and finally... stepping her footsteps down my hall and back towards my bedroom.

"Hey." Mali says, stood in the open doorway, half naked and I can't take my eyes off of her.

Anticipating she would speak, I place my hand over the phones mouth piece and told her to 'sush'. She needs to keep her fucking mouth shut

"You *sure* you don't know where she is?" It's as if Blue can smell her here. As if she already knew the answer. I don't give a fuck what she knows. Mali's body though...

"I got to go... I've got to work." Define work... Mali could be 'work' so, technically, I could be going to 'work' and that isn't really lying?

"Aaliyah? Wait I-"

"Blue bye!"

The naked truth is in front of me and I can't focus! I have lost control of my eyes and they won't move off of Mali. Watching her naturally stroll through my apartment. Casually walking across my bedroom over to my bed and comfortably laying down... damn she looks fucking good in my bed!

"Morning Miss Aaliyah." Her face *beaming* happy as fuck! She wiggles down the bed, readjusting her comfort and places her arms behind her head, chilling happily. Mesmerised by her and way she's smiling to herself, gazing at my ceiling off into her day dream, ignoring the fuck out of my confused face.

"What the fuck are you smiling about?" Why is she so relaxed in *my* house? Like being in my bed, the night after 'who knows' what the fuck went down is some regular occurrence.

"Nothing happened…"

"Really?!" I lifted the covers dissatisfied with that answer. I'm naked, she's half naked, why did nothing happen?

"We fell asleep. Well you fell asleep, then I fell asleep…"
We both sigh, knowing what we both would have done. We didn't do anything at all? We must have done *something*? Why *else* would she be in my bed? I'm surprised at myself, it's not like me to be laying down in bed with a woman untouched and unfucked…

"You don't remember last night, do you?"

"Would I have this look on my face if I did? I swear you and your girl ask the dumbest questions! I'm starting to see why you're together!" Leaning back against the bedhead, pulling the covers up over my breast and tuck it by the sides of my arms. Mumbling and muttering to myself, talking shit about Mali and Blue- they are just as annoying as each other, I swear.

"Are you done?"

"Yeah!?" I roll my eyes in her direction. "Tell me because everything in my head is in low definition right now." Huffing and puffing, "We didn't do anything??" I had to ask again, to be sure.

"Every minute with you was amazing and we didn't do anything at all." She gazes at me.

"Can you come out of your daydream for a second and tell me, what happened rather then what *didn't happen*?"

"Oh, about what we did do… erm…" She pushes her mouth to the side, holding up her index finger to finalise her point.

"What happened?"

"Katrina, saw us leaving the club. You know, Blue's broke friend?"

"Yeah, I know her, the one that don't do shit but always *knows* shit and always up in other people's shit!"

"Yes her! Well... we were *all* over each other, probably kissing-"

"What do you mean 'probably'? Mali! I'm going to need you to be specific! No 'probablys' or 'maybes'!"

"Okay, yes! We were *specifically* kissing." She finds the time to joke around in the torment of my not knowing as much as she does. "Who knows what she saw, there was a *lot* going on!"

"Well whatever she saw, she told Blue! She asked me a whole bunch of questions, she fucking *knows* you're here - shit!"

Blue wouldn't dare attempt to talk to me like that on a regular day but I'm caught out here in the middle of a fucking lie, Shit! Fuck! Shit! Think, think, think! I'm good, don't worry I'll make it go away with a very good game of flipper

Flipper *noun*

definition

When a person(s) is the subject of negative attention within a situation, conversation or disagreement and they turn the subject/attention away from themselves by *flipping* it onto someone else. This is done by highlighting 'fault' that is not relevant to their own wrong doing of their own actions.

Flipper is often always played in relationships and friendships.

I'll flip it and reverse it like Missy Elliot and make her feel so stupid! Blue will end up apologising to me because I will make her believe that it's all in her pretty little head and that she has *absolutely* nothing to worry about; trust me (do not trust me I'm not to be trusted, I'll steal your girl) I am not about to let the little piece of info that Blue's little pot head homie Katrina gave her stress out my day, *please*. Blue can stay where she is, all angry and up in her feelings. I'll deal with her another day. Right now, I have a guest

"Why do you think my phones off!?" Mali shows me the black off screen of her phone then threw it to the end of the bed carelessly.

"It's off because you're a pussy that's too scared to tell your woman where you are!"

"Either way, I'm not trying to hear all her noise in my ear, talking about something *she* knows nothing about! You took me out to make me feel better, so? Maybe if she didn't smoke so much of *my* fucking weed, she'd stay awake long enough for me to let me tell her something about me! You're here making me feel better, what the fuck is she doing? Sleeping!? Literally!"

We pause, letting her relationship rant disappear into the air. She's cute but I wasn't trying to make her feel all of that. I didn't want to waste my night, so I thought fuck it! Let's do something, because anything was better than sitting in that room of sleep and emotions.

"You're just projecting your shit her way, because you're guilty. I see it all the time, in similar situations I'm in. You're not mad at her. You want to justify your actions and find a reason for being practically naked in another woman's bed- face it... *you* fucked up!"

My opinion on Mali's situation is absolutely true! My own thoughts and actions are deceitful and self-gaining. So, I don't see the point in sugar coating the situation. I won't let Mali sit here and think she isn't doing anything wrong, otherwise she won't consider there to be any risk. Then the excitement fades away and the nights we spend time together become mini counselling sessions, fuck that! She'll be wasting my time, talking my ear off and telling me what her woman isn't doing right, no thank you!

"You're right." Taking the phone from the end of the bed, her hand fiddles with the on button, toying with the idea if she should call her woman or not.

"I am waiting for you to tell me how we ended up here...? Clearly you remember more than me." Breaking her zone out, that smile appears on her face again. She turns to her side, resting half up on herself, facing me.

"We sat in the car for a little bit. You told me you wanted to have fun like the night we met. When it was you and me all night…"

7 ½ The Levitating Wave

Perspective *noun*

Her (Mali) perspective.

Definition
Perspective is to observe situations through your eyes.
To see, to view, to look, to watch, to experience. To formulate views and opinions regarding situations or topics.

"Kiss me." Aaliyah says so swiftly, how can I say no?

Leaning towards her I place the requested kiss on her lips and the tip of her tongue grazes across mine. She moves her tongue in this way that subtly takes the lead of the kiss. She's a natural leader, so I let her take the lead. Who knows where she'll lead me to? Wherever it is, I'm sure I'll follow anxiously.

I know I should *not* be here doing this but she makes it make sense, even though what we are doing doesn't make sense at all. I'm struggling and senseless and stupid, dismissing the consequences because, lately all I think about is Aaliyah. I *know* what I'm doing and what *she's* doing when she's doing it but for some reason, she dares me not to care and be careless, in spite of my relationship.

Our lips part ways as she lets go of my face. Stretching over the seat and across my lap, reaching for the glove compartment. I watch her body rested on my lap as she opens it and digs around it. She lifts this sort of hidden flap somewhere right at the back and sits up in her seat, pulling out a small purse size can of hairspray? What is she up to? She stretches above her head and pushes a button on the panel, turning the lights off and pressing another which sets a pink undertone of low lights that take over the car. Pleased with herself for setting the vibe, she unbuckles my seat belt with the sexy pout and jumps over and behind me onto the back seats.

"Come here." She calls me back to where she is.

"I thought we were going inside?" I look over my shoulder to see her sitting comfortably.

"We are *but* I'm going to need you to relax. You're checking your phone every ten seconds and we cannot go in *there* with *you* looking suspect and attracting unnecessary attention. So, hurry up and bring yourself back here!" She says things with such assertion and a raw essence of strength that you don't often get in women these days. Women tend to act coy or less of themselves to impress or cater to egos while making others comfortable but not Aaliyah, she's too real and it's so attractive to watch.

Joining her, I climb carefully over the car seat and sit next to her, ready to pay close attention to *everything* she does. She turns the small can upside down and twists of the bottom to reveal a fake can with a hollow centre for hidden contents as a large baggie of MDMA falls onto her lap- well okay!?

"Hold this one sec." She hands it to me and pulls out an old club flyer from the pocket on the back of the car seat and rips it in half. She keeps one half on her lap then tucks the other half back where she found it. Folding the flyer once more, running her fingers down the fold, she slowly unfolds it while holding out her hand in my direction, keeping her focus on her creation. I hand the stash back to her and she opens it carefully, staring closely at her fingers pinch the crystals, like fragile treasure.

"Pass me that, please." She points at a bottle of juice in her armrest. Knowing what she is about to do, I reach forward, open it and pass it to her.

She tilts the flyer at an angle resting it on the opening of the bottle, tapping softly, making sure her measurement went directly into it. Handing her the bottle cap, she twists the bottle closed tight and shakes it. Examining the bottle like a biochemist, patiently waiting for the crystals to dissolve into the juice and then places it between us on the seat.

Sucking the tip of her baby finger she dips it in the bag. Slowly drawing a good amount out on her finger and opens her mouth, sucking the crystal powder off of her finger. Repeating the same movement, she holds her finger to my lips.

"Keep it on your tongue for as long as you want. But it tastes like eight cans of shark shit… you don't have to if you don't want to…" She pauses, eyes wide, remembering my story about drugs and other things being forced into my body. But I'm grown and it's not the first time I popped Molly, so it's totally calm.

"I know." Reassuring her with a smile

"Tastes disgusting right?" She sounds mad funny, talking with it still on her tongue, wanting to get the best high but screwing up her face at the taste and trying not to laugh.

"Yeah." She's right, it does taste like eight cans of shark shit! Which always made me wonder; how can something that makes you feel a euphoric sense of intense energy that alters your mood and perception into pleasure and empathy that lasts for hours and hours, taste so damn foul?

Without hesitation I tilt my mouth towards her finger, allowing her to place the Molly on the tip of my tongue. I wait, trying to ignore the horrible taste.

She sits back, takes a gulp from the juice bottle then passes it over to me.

Resting back and chilling for a while, waiting for the buzz to begin which usually takes around thirty or so minutes. Listening to the music, we sit in silence. I wonder what she's thinking in her silence, I don't know what I'm thinking in mine? I should be with Blue but instead I'm *here* and Aaliyah is over there. But to be honest, I'd rather be here bopping my head to the beat of the music; her music is such a vibe. Her music taste in Slow Jams, Old School and New. Songs that have me agreeing with the lyrics and vocals that are drowning out my thoughts of Blue.

I can't stop myself from watching Aaliyah, fixated on her fixing her hair in the reflection of the blacked-out window and my mind is wandering off thinking about how she moves. Like the way she walks from one room to the other on the balls of her bare feet. Stepping, taking time, making sure the ground she's paved before her is solid ground. I can't describe it but I know what I'm trying to say- she's secure in

210

everything she does, in every way she moves- she makes perfect sense but *she* doesn't make sense! Let me stop and switch these thoughts off but it's so hard *she's* everything I want in a confident, in a friend and in a woman- it's sooo wrong.... what about Blue? Aaliyah is within the reach of my arms but I can sit back and admire her movements discreetly from over here.

Tingling sensations are rippling up, down and all over my body. Feeling like the thoughts that are running around and around my head. This high is hitting me nicely and I can feel it everywhere! My mind is doing a *madness*, thinking all these thoughts of her... Blue?

I need to stop checking my phone- I am gown! I'll jus' ignore the call and dismiss it; 'sorry I didn't see your call' or 'I meant to hit send'. I won't answer until I can figure out the right thing *to* say- *If* she calls- she's going to call? She's calling Shit! Wait, no she's not calling but what if she does call? What have I done? Shit! Relax! I definitely look crazy right now jus' sitting here distracted by my thoughts of guilt. I *know*, that Aaliyah *knows* she's got me caught up and wondering while I am here doing shit that I shouldn't be doing. Captivated and caught up in the idea of her and what we could be doing- oh boy!

Goosebumps and hair rise on my skin jus' thinking about the way she has my attention, questioning if she's looking in my direction because women like Aaliyah jus' don't go for women like me. She's got all her shit together and I'm trying to figure all mine out.

I *cannot* get her out of my head, I've tried to push the thoughts of her to the back of my mind. Jus' chilling with Blue and all of a sudden, out of nowhere Aaliyah crashes right into my mind and dominates my thoughts. I wish someone could explain, because I can't explain something I don't understand. I feel like my stomach is in knots; Ella Mai lyrics in my head boo'd up, boo'd up- when I should be 'Blued' up.

My hands are tingling and palms are itching to hold onto something. Fuck it! Grabbing her, she playfully screams out aloud giggling and landing her body right on top of mine. Feeling amazing with her body weight carelessly on top of me.

Closing my eyes letting my imagination take over- there is *nothing* sexier to me than sliding a woman's thong to the side, woah! *The fuck am I thinking!?* I am taken, I am with Blue but... I am not with her... I'm here and I am high as fuck!

"What are *you doing* to me?"

I ask her, she shrugs mischievously knowing *exactly* what she's doing to me. Closing her eyes, I close mine letting her kiss tenderly on my lips, enticing me while answering my thoughts with no words at all. Licking my lips with the tip of her tongue, she bites my bottom lip.

"I'm finding it really hard *not* to think about you..." I say, squeezing her body tighter. She arches her back and places more kisses up the side of my neck then she stops... with a final kiss and nibble of my earlobe.

"After tonight, you'll *never* stop thinking about me *ever* again!"

Holding my face, parting my lips with her tongue again. Intense and soft, she stops content with her tease. Laughing, she quickly climbs off of me and jumps out of the car.

Her arms up in the air, running her hands down the side of her face and through her hair with her eyes closed, dancing subtly moving on the balls of her feet moving left to right, to the music coming from out of the car, riding her own narcotic wave of solace and consolation.

"What are you doing?"

"Come here, I want to dance on you," Faded eyes open, reaching out to me. She turns, taking a few steps away from me. "Let's go." Peering over her shoulder, stretching her arm behind her, palm open ushering me to come on over. I take her hand and she takes the lead, walking together right past a *massive* queue of people who are waiting to get inside the club. Dressed to impress, in their best with side eyes wondering where we are going. Watching us closely as we casually stroll in front of them.

Aaliyah stops behind a bouncer at the closed club entrance, interrupting her stance and mid-shift conversations by lightly tapping her on the shoulder.

The woman turns around, with a face that was ready to start some shit but seeing it was Aaliyah and changes her expression. She's a short and stocky but well-built black woman; her hair shaved off with a gold ring in her nose and a gold tooth in her mouth. She smiles from ear to ear, chewing hard and smacking her teeth together loud as fuck on a piece of gum.

"Ali! Heya bubs, how ya doing? Long time! Ain't seen you about in a bit babes! You good, yeah?" Still grinning, gold tooth blinging, jaw swinging and smacking. She's an old school, cut from the ninety's laid back but crazy, cool type of lesbian.

"I'm good. *But* I'd be better if you got me and my company in the club..." Aaliyah, says with a charmingly sweet wink. The bouncer looks between Aaliyah and me by stretching her neck over us towards the queue of vexed faces watching and waiting. She checks over her shoulder and returns a just as charming wink to Aaliyah while still smacking on her gum.

"You know you don't even av' to ask me twice pretty lady." Unhooking the red roped barrier, she opens the club entrance door and the sound of music and vibes instantly drifts out of the doorway and into our ears.

"Thank you babe." Aaliyah gives her a polite platonic kiss on the cheek

"No problem babes. Av' a good time, yeah ladies." She addresses us both respectfully, not knowing my relation with Aaliyah and allows us to walk in. We step further in, hearing the bouncer faintly behind us shouting at the people in the queue, who are piping up about us getting in, telling them to get back and mind out or she'll dash them out the queue.

Stepping inside, Aaliyah nods at the woman sat at the entry cashier desk. The woman nods back at Aaliyah; letting us pass and continues collecting money from everyone else who are holding out their money and cards ready to pay for their entry.

213

Letting go of my hand didn't stop me from following her closely because tonight she's mine and claimed! No one needs to be checking for her, talking to her or looking in her direction.

We are fading and faded into the crowd unnoticed. Out of focus and way out of sight. Entertaining each other missing somewhere in the music but hearing *every single sound so fucking clearly*. Rushing and racing throughout my entire body! I can hear the music in my ears *and* I feel it all on my skin. Every single cord, banging beat, tapping acoustics and every other instrumental sound! My eyes closed, while my ears are busy separating all the sounds of the music then blending them back together again, like the perfect chorus to the perfect song you can't get out of your head. The vocals running through my feet, creep up my legs and along my spine like sudden surges of energy every time Aaliyah touches me or grazes her skin past mine as we exchange energy.

Popping more Molly to keep the levitating wave a drift. I can't hear or see the people around us, I'm focused only on the music and the sound of Aaliyah's breathing. Her arms up over me, holding the back of my neck, softly scratching me with her nails. Do *not* kiss her, not here. Do not touch too much of her, anyone could be watching. Aaliyah turns around and takes a step closer to me, cutting into my paranoia smelling sweet and destressing my distress.

Staring into the nothingness of each other's dilated pupils. My high, taking me higher, like a levitating tidal wave, high and strong. My feet can't feel *'my feet'* or the trainers on my feet. Lifted, faded, coasting, wave after wave we're slowly drifting to another destination, not giving a fuck about the risks we are taking!

"I have an idea…" Aaliyah shouts in my ear, snapping me back into the reality and flashing lights of the club. My eyes readjust but I can only see silhouettes and faceless bodies in the crowded congregation of this atmosphere.

"Yeah?" I'm intrigued

"Remember when we met in the club and you were introduced to me as Blue's woman?" Her hand dismisses Blue's name.

"…yeah?" I'm eagerly waiting to hear her 'idea'.

"I want to meet you again. Tonight, right now! Except, this time you're going to be a *single* and a very available woman. You're going to ask me to dance then you're going offer to buy me a drink, I might say yes, I might say no. *Then* you're going to ask if we can leave and go somewhere else…"

"You might say yes, you might say no!"

"Now you're getting it." She taps my nose with her fingertip.

Letting go of her, I walk away and push myself through the crowd, carelessly stepping on toes, new shoes and pissing people off.

Aaliyah stands across the way with her back against a wall, dancing. Pretending not to notice me, waiting for me to go back over there. Pacing, making sure I take my time in my steps, not wanting to come across eager.

"Hey…" I speak into her ear "I've seen you before, right?"

"You're going to have to try harder than that." She said looking over me, refusing my conversation starter but I've got this! I *can* get girls! Come on Mali man! You've got this! Taking a deep breath, I start again.

"Come here and dance on me instead of the wall."

Giving her no choice; pulling her softly towards me. She smirks enjoying my new-found confidence and places my hands on her hips while she dances on me.

"So, what's your name?" She says, gazing at me.

"Cherry." I've never done anything like this. I guess, I jus' go with it. I've been Malikah, Mali and Mika for so long now and this is out of my character, so why not be *another* character?

"Cherry…?" She questions "I like it."

"You going to tell me your name beautiful?" Will she choose to be another persona tonight? *Perhaps*, if we pretend to be other people, then *us* doing *this* will be okay. Because, if we aren't ourselves then *technically,* we aren't doing anything wrong?

Aaliyah pauses for thought, placing her fingertip on her chin and looking up, trying to find the name of a new persona or alter ego.

"…Logan." She decides on a different character.

"Can I get you a drink, *Logan*?"

"Depends on what it is, Cherry."

"Something sweet, warm and sexy with two ice cubes." I take her hand into mine and pull her towards the bar.

At the bar, staring, zoned out and admiring all the colours of the glass bottles displayed along shelves of the back wall. There's a massive mirror I keep catching glimpses of our reflections in because we complement one another so damn well. Stood together, looking great together and feeling better. Like an unstoppable cliché couple; Aaliyah and Mali, sorry more like; *Logan and Cherry.*

Positioning myself behind her with my arms either side of her. My hand is busy finding its way back at Aaliyah's waist again. Trailing, down her thighs and between her legs again. I place my hand on her and rest it just over her pussy. Locating her clit through her clothes, she tilts her head back, eyes closed enjoying the feeling of what I am doing.

"What kind of woman do you take me for?"

"The kind of woman who doesn't waste time. Who sees something she wants and takes it regardless if it's not up for the taking?" I speak directly in her ear and she gasps. Turned on by my tone of voice or my outspoken thoughts of her. But she takes her control back and removes my hand, placing it onto the bar countertop. She runs circles around the back of my hand and I observe her effect on me as the hairs on my arms rise with goose bumps instantly.

Discreetly, kissing on the side of her neck while we wait patiently at the crowded bar for our drinks to be made.

The barman moves swiftly, back and forth across the bar, grabbing the bottles he needs to make our drinks until finally, he places the glasses down beside us. Paying for them I keep one eye on Aaliyah, as she silently stares at the ice cubes floating about her glass. She brings the glass to her top lip and rests it under her nose for a brief moment smelling it before taking a sip. I've noticed she always does that; I take note of the things small things she does and the things she probably doesn't think I even pay attention to at all.

I wonder what she's like on a regular day, when no one's around and she's alone- Blue's alone. Blue... Yellow. Green. Red. Blue... Yellow. Green. Red. Blue...? The lights on the bar keep switching colours. Red lighting bright on the back of my closed eyes, making me feel like I am a red light special; in one of those old school R&B videos.

"What's next Logan?"

"Let's go Cherry. I'm over this place." Grabbing my hand in haste, I finish my drink as she pulls me away from the bar. Where she goes, I go. Leading me towards the exit of the club, down the low-lit unoccupied corridor. Forget what I said before; pushing her body against the wall, all over her. Her chest moving rapidly in, out, hot, heated and ready for me to make my next move. Hold her slim wrists in my hands, above her head and keep them there, so she can't move although she doesn't want to. My lips are over hers. Brushing my lips softly against hers, gently stroking my tongue over hers, heating the fire between us. But... I let go of her body... *completely* and turn away, walking down the corridor towards the exit with her behind me frozen for second or two thinking about what I jus' did. I'm not about to surrender and give her *everything* she wants, not yet.

She catches up to me and forces me to stop, pulling back on my arm and getting me caught up again. Holding her waist, my favourite dips on her body. She closes her eyes and pouts her lips, ready for another close encounter.

"Aaliyah...?! Malikah!!"

Hearing our names, we stop and turn our heads sharply at the same time, in the same direction to see Katrina. Ahhh shit! Dammit! She's one of Blue's people; I never liked her. Shit!

She's someone I'm jus' unable to vibe with and for whatever reason, our personalities clash. We're unable to find common ground but we stay humble and at a great a distance from each other.

She always wore a fitted hat over her shady, lying eyes. I've never seen her eyes long enough to know how she felt about me but it's obvious we share a mutual distrust for one another. Katrina uses Blue for money, weed and other things. I've always had a feeling that it's more than the friendship they claim to have only had in their history. But I can't throw stones, caught up and caught out here like Kelis in this compromising position with Blue's friend. Katrina has one up and over me and at the fault of my own hand *with* my hands where they shouldn't be.

"You two cool, yeah?" Katrina asks us but I can't answer, so I look away while onto anything else and Aaliyah cannot stop laughing to herself and hiding her face in her hands and burying herself into my chest but it's too late, we're fucked!

"Yeah, we're good man." Struggling to keep a straight face and the words that could make all of this seem like a normal situation while holding my laughter in.

"*Hi*... sorry, umm. I don't remember your name but we *have* to go!" Aaliyah takes my hand, dragging me and we run! Back in the car, buckled up, chilling and ready to drive to wherever Aaliyah is going to take me.

Unfazed by everything, she stares at my lips, taking a breath, she opens her mouth and she says

"Kiss me."

7 ¾. *The New Flowers...*

"Then what?" Mali finished telling me about last night but I have a few questions left.

"You never told me where we were headed next but I was like 'okay', fuck it! We came here, it was a vibe though." Pleased with her somewhat informativ version of events, which I can't fuckin remember at all! Who told me whiskey and Molly go together? Bad Combo!

"Define vibe?" I don't know why I asked but the bunch of questions I have left my mind without warning. My focus is something else, on point one minute and then gone the next. I'm a mess!

"You already know the answer, we didn't do anything. The combination, of all of that last night or... maybe it's jus' you?"

"Careful now. It's recommended only a little bit of Aaliyah at a time, don't overdose baby."

Getting up, leaving her in the room I walk to the bathroom looking over my shoulder peeking at her watch me and my body leave the room. She does look fucking good in my bed, though.

"What do we do now, Blue knows I'm here? Should I call her?" She shouts.

"Do absolutely nothing!" I shout back. "Wait till she calms the fuck down! Don't say shit, I'll talk to her, there is *nothing* to worry about."

Turning the shower on, she shouts something else back but I can't make out what she was saying over the sound of the running water on my skin.

Washing the night away; closing my eyes, putting my face into the water, tilting my head back, allowing the water to hit my neck, my throat and then run down my body. I love the feeling of the water running all over me, so soothing against my skin, I never have it too hot. There's something about an almost cool shower that soothes me. Water has always calmed me down and refreshes my mind and body.

The sound of it affects me like the sound of music; I can escape in the sound of the running water and leave the world of my wicked thoughts behind, the second the first drop of water touches my skin.

Feeling an energy of a person in the room, I pull away from the water opening my eyes. I wipe my hand along the fogged and steamed glass shower door and looking at me through the wet glass door, Mali stood. Saying nothing, she opens the door letting the cool draft rush in and linger at my back. Standing in the doorway of the shower, watching me move my hands across my skin, washing the soap bubbles of shower cream away.

"You missed a bit." She says instructing me to turn my back to her and the draft drifts in further along with her hand, reaching in and moving down my back. Feeling her hand removing the soap from my body; she places her hand under the shower and repeats the downward movement over my skin.

Turning back to face her, she steps in a little and reaches for my chin. Holding my wet face, she kisses me. Tugging her towards me, she closes the glass door and the draft leaves our bodies, together surrounded by water and steam. I lead her body under the water and kiss her collar bone. Watching the water run over her, reaching over her grabbing my shower cream. She watches me pour some into my palm leaning into her again, placing the bottle back on the shower shelf. Circling my hands together on her body. Washing her soft beautiful skin, as the water falls between our bodies.

A flashback of last night fills my mind and I close my eyes feeling the familiar feeling of her lips on my neck.

Her body feels perfect next to mine and at the end of my fingertips. I could get used to this- I stop edging her away from me and continue to wash her body down while she stares at me.

"Kiss me,"

She repeats the words, she says I spoke to her last night. While attempting to place her hand between my wet thighs; which are wet from two different things. Fighting to control that pulsing feeling of wanting to be touched but my legs stay firmly closed and I focus on rinsing the soap off of her body.

"Let me get you a towel."

Turning off the shower; I step out of her arms, away from her body and step out of the shower. Grabbing her a thick and fluffy long white towel, gesturing her to come out towards me. She steps out, body glistening with water drops and wet hair trailing down her back. She holds her arms up and I wrap her body in the towel pointing her towards the bedroom. Grabbing a towel for myself I follow, walking back to the bedroom and rest on the railings of my mezzanine bedroom.

"Are you planning on staying or-" Handing Mali a bottle of lotion, she sat on top of the covers wearing a matching C.K set, towel wrapped up and drying her hair. I have to admit her body is on point! Feminine athletic build, toned but curves in *all* right places; her stomach flat and packed tightly but not too much. Thighs thick as fuck, arms defined looking like they can lift me and flip me in any direction and anywhere she wants me to go.

"Why? You not enjoying the view?" She cuts into my thoughts, caught up realising how hard I'm watching her. "I'm thinking we should chill, seeing as though *we are* in trouble already. What's the rush, why not… jus' be?" She shrugs with the cheekiest grin.

"What the fuck do you mean *'we'*? You must be speaking French, because I am too grown and too single to be in *'trouble'*."

"Shut up! Climb on top of me and let me take your clothes off, *again*." This girl must be high still, she's getting brave… I like it though; the confidence is glowing on her. She almost made me take a step forward with the way she said that but I caught myself.

"How about you put your clothes on and Uber yourself home. Thank you!" Walking away, heading for the stairs with my hand pointing and directing her way out my apartment; she grabs my wrist and before I know it, the room flashes and flips by in a twirl and I'm flat on my back, on my bed hands above my head. Mali, holding me down firmly, sitting her sexy frame on mine with her face right above mine, looking down at our bodies together then back at me.

"You *really* want me to go...? She *thinks* we're fucking... *so*...let's fuck." Speechless, I *do not* know how the fuck I got here and how she got on top of me but, fuck! She's becoming hard to resist!

"You can't tell me last night didn't get you feeling some type of way. I know you jus' dried off and got dressed but, I *know* your wet and you want me- facts." She's not lying, I'm dripping! Her powerful, dominant voice and the force in her grip is making me melt.

"I don't remember last night... besides, I've had plenty of *other* good nights. What makes you think 'yours' was special enough to let -*you* -fuck?"
I whisper into her ear as her face buries into the side of my neck. I can feel her breathing me in, inhaling. My natural scent is that of an aphrodisiac and is known to drive women crazy! Her hand finding its way under my t-shirt and through the side of my high cut thongs. Holding back any excitement but my pussy keeps fluttering and dripping. As soon as she stepped into my room and I saw her body out of those baggy clothes for the first time.
On top me one leg between mine, rubbing her two fingers against my clit, slowly feeling me get wetter and wetter. Kissing me, holding me down with the weight of her body lying on top of mine *every-thing* I fucking love!! No, she can't have me like this! I want to run this! I need to be running these rendezvous.
Managing to move my leg an inch to the left, between hers to get her to rub herself against my thigh just enough... to distract her.

"Fuck, you smell so good!" She said between short soft kisses. Yes, I want to fuck but I don't want her to fuck me, no I just want her hands on me- all over me so I can move, get up and leave her thinking about this moment. Buts she's dominating and taking over me! I want her... I need to be in control of this, not her! But I don't know if I can resist. Arms back around her neck legs open and wrapped around her body and-

"Afternoon Aaliyah my love!"

Yes! Saved!! Eleni entering my apartment, stepping in she throws her keys in the bowl on the side table by the door. Rustling her way to the kitchen with her heavy 'flip flop' footsteps and my food shopping in her hands.

Mali's confused, not expecting to hear another voice or see another person in my apartment but me.

"Hey Eleni! I'll be right down!" Shouting back and standing at the top of the stairs, I made my way down them. "Like I said, get the fuck out my bed and put some clothes on. But first, go wipe yourself off because I *know* you're dripping," laughing I throw her top at her.

"Fine, but you *know* I *will* be getting naked again!" She lays back once more tasting me off of her fingertips. Keeping an eye on her as I walk to the kitchen, to join my Eleni amour.

Rummaging through the shopping bags grabbing the fruit; packets of strawberries and pineapple chunks. Eating pieces impatiently while rustling through the rest of the bags, seeing what else she's got for me to eat. Eleni stood in front of the sink arranging the new flowers, a big bunch that she bought. They were perfect pink peonies, dark pink oriental lilies', cerise germini and pink antirrhinum. Eleni has been getting me a fresh bunch of flowers every week or so… I think, for as long as I can remember. I don't remember much. She hands one steamed flower over to me, stretching her arm out, without glancing my way, while she arranges them. She knows I like to smell them just as she brings them home. Freshly cut, from a florist, none of those supermarket bouquets. I hold the single flower to my nose and look at the way the petals sit for a second or two, then hand it back to Eleni with her arm stretched out waiting for my little habit to be over and done with. She knows me better than I know myself, she's so much more than a cleaner on payroll, she's family. Like an aunt to a niece, that's how we are.

She's a warm comfort of energy that I love. Some days we sit out on my balcony sharing a bottle of wine and smoke away a pack of twenty while gossiping. She likes hearing all about the stories of me; trapped in a situation or hearing about the crazy ones that leave with a silent vendetta. Her favourite one that she always asks me to tell her again, was the one about the girl who stole my socks- I'm talking about all my socks! Don't you dare laugh! I'm being dead ass serious! Shit like *this* is exactly *why* I don't let people in my house, bitches are fucking crazy!

Okay, so let me tell you what happened right:

So, I was seeing this b-e-a-u-ti-ful girl right. I can't remember her name but anyway, we met somehow, somewhere I think I was shopping or she was- who knows but she would come by my place and stay from time to time. (I know right me allowing females up in my house) but there was this calming element of elegance that had me at 'hello beautiful'.

It actually took me a minute to realize all what was going on because the sex was so fucking intense. But one day, I noticed she had things all over my damn house! Little things you wouldn't really pay attention to until you really did. Like her own pillowcase that didn't match my sets but she placed it under my mountain of pillows. Her own mug in the back of the kitchen cupboard, a damn draw full of her clothes and her socks mixed in with mine! As if I was about this 'communal sock sharing' draw life! I mean is this what couples do? Just out here sharing socks and sock drawers?! She didn't ask me, she just did it? Like I would be okay with it all? Me? She was not okay. She thought she was actually living here or something? Either way, I wasn't down for it, she had to be stopped, she had to get out and be gone!

So, me being me and feeling far too fucking boujie to pack up her things and move them to the left. Am I Beyoncé to be moving everything you have in the box to the left? Who has time to do all of that? Not me! So, I asked her nicely, 'to get her shit together and go'- okay, well what I actually said to her via What's App was:

**"Baby girl, I'm going to need you to get you
and your shit the fuck out my house. Thank you."**

I left her to get her shit together and leave; later on, I get a text:

"I've left and I've left you a surprise. Xx"

I was speeding home, weaving in and out of traffic. I was anxious as fuck! All I knew was, I was not about to catch a case for a crazy bitch! Because if she had done any-thing to disrespect my apartment, my home, or my space, I'm killing her, she's dead! I was imagining all kinds of scenarios in my head of all the things she could have done like; write 'fucking bitch' on my walls with the red lipstick she always wore, or have completely trashed my apartment, smash up my things- who knows? Women are fucking nuts?

I step in the house. And. I. Am. Shook! Cautious as fuck, not knowing what to expect... but it was perfect, not a single thing out of place, it was so weird. Almost too perfect, if you know what I mean. I expected to come home to a madness. Who knows? She could have been on the floor of my bathroom, lifeless, blood gushing from her wrists all dramatic, broken and suicidal like 'why won't you love me?' bullshit. But the house was perfect, if anything, it felt cleaner... but unsettling. Something was different but I couldn't place it. I walked up my staircase, satisfied that downstairs was fine and there were no 'surprises' there.

My bedroom was also perfect, the bed made just the way I like; with all my cushions and blankets placed in a certain way. I pulled back the covers to make sure there was nothing hidden in the sheets or under the bed.

Imagine me walking around the house looking for this fucking thing, this 'surprise'. Then I walked towards my walk-in wardrobe, I saw the teddy bear I had bought for her.

(Don't come for me; it's all about your acts of intent. Some women like you to be straight up with your sexual intentions, while others who *blatantly* came to fuck will make you put in a little extra work to be and cute and romantic- she was one of them but the sex was worth it. Facts!)

Anyway, the teddy bear sat in the doorway but gutted from throat to crutch, stuffing spilling out of him. Sitting looking up at me like 'bruh, what did I do to her?'. I'm laughing now but then I was questioning this woman's' mental health because she had gone Jack the Ripper on a fucking teddy bear! And sat beside him was a small gift bag that I gave her something else in but inside was broken pieces, or what was left of a vase from this one time I sent her flowers to work.

(like I said women love that shit and sometimes you got to put in a little bit of light work for the pussy)

But the vase was smashed up and left in this bag without any broken piece on the floor! No shards of ceramic ruminants anywhere! By this point, I'm asking myself how? How?! Did she smash it, put the pieces in the bag and then vacuum it up? Or did she put the vase in the gift bag and hit it against the wall? Or drop it, so it smashed? Who knew? It was all a bit mad, imagining how angry and psychotic she would have to be to do some fucked up shit like that.
But I'm not done there no, no. Something told me to go check through my shit to make sure she had taken all her things. Because anything she had left, if she did, would be a reason for her to contact me to come back and get it. So, if I found anything else it was going in the fucking bin!
I checked through my clothes rails and her things were no longer hung with mine. I thought, let me check 'her draw' or the draw she 'claimed' was hers- crazy bitch! Her draw was empty, everything gone, good! But something told me to keep checking through my own shit, opening drawers and all was good... then I remembered the sock draw... wait for it... I opened the draw... and not only had her socks gone but ALL. The. Fucking. Socks. Were gone! Every last fucking one on them. Even the odd ones that I keep in a side box waiting on their pair to be found. She took them all!

What the actual fuck?! Do you know how crazy that is! Stop laughing, I'm being so serious! She took all my fucking socks!! Of all the expensive, name brands and designer things I have about the house like watches, clothes, bags and jewellery, this bitch thought 'nah imma fuck with her head and take all the fucking socks!' How mad does that even sound? What the hell would make you take all the socks? Someone who is nowhere near mentally stable, that's who! Was she sorting through them and thought 'fuck it let me take them all' or what?? To this day, I can't get my head around her level of crazy, because a normal crazy would have been to trash the apartment, go Lisa Left Eye Lopez and set the bathroom on fire or go 'Waiting to Exhale' on the walk-in wardrobe, throw my clothes in the car and blow it the fuck up! But to take my socks?? Bitch, my feet had never been so damn cold!

I managed to save one pair of Winnie the Pooh slipper grip socks found at the back of the unit after pulling the drawers out, because I could not believe she took all my socks, can you believe it?

I couldn't tell you why Eleni loves that story so much? Maybe it's the way I tell it, or the fact that she refers to her as 'Happy Feet'.

I adore my Eleni, I really do. She's the only one who I really trust and the only one I allow to walk in and out of my house freely whenever she pleases. It's comforting for me to see the new flowers, it's a nice feeling that a known warm presence and energy was in my house. I always look forward to seeing the flower arrangements and colours, she chose *every* week.

I've not always been a big fan of being gifted flowers, because they wilt and die. I never understood women who crave flowers on occasions or go all crazy when someone sends them a bouquet of *death* to work. That's really what they are no? I'd prefer you got a pizza delivered to my job or gave me a pair of *socks*- you know because my socks were STOLEN!?

But in all seriousness, I can't eat or wear flowers, I can only watch them die!? But Eleni takes care of the flowers, the apartment and me- she takes care of *everything*!

She's about older auntie slash nanna kind of age. I don't *actually* know how old she is because she always makes it up when I ask her. She has this smile but if I even attempt to guess an age that is anything over forty-seven, she frowns at me like I'm about to receive a Mediterranean olive tree branch beating. I know she's older from the deep-set lines in her skin but she has this gorgeous sun kissed glow that makes her look good for her age -whatever age that may be. Her natural glow gives Fenty Beauty highlighter a run for its money. Eleni is a gorgeous Greek woman with dark honey but soft golden features. She's short, round and plump with a cute big buddha belly that is tucked into her boot cut jeans, behind a random baggy t-shirt; with some sort of college logo, or cute kitten, or random island print you get on holiday or slogans she doesn't even understand. Even though they are baggy everywhere else, they are always tight around her middle. She's always happy and jolly, her accent is so strong and cute and her English at times isn't the best, she says:

"My English is not so happy!"

"How many times woman? It's my English isn't very good." Turning on the coffee machine, I pull mine and Eleni's mugs from the cupboard.

"Aaliyah amour, you gonna concern my English, or you gonna concern three cups?" She said, not even looking at me with a wide smirk on her face putting the finishing touches on the flowers, while I break down her broken English. She *knows* I have someone here, I can't get anything past her at all! She's too fast!!

"No, Fuck that! I'm not making her coffee. She's nobody special, she's going home in a bit anyway."

"You sure? In all the years I knew you, you never have, *neveeeeer* let someone here. Till' now! Today this afternoon. So, she *must* be special."

She stretched out the word 'never' with her finger going through the air at the same time as the word and giggles, "Happy Feet was the last one and you know how that end!"

"Hey! Happy Feet was fucking nuts and you know it! You should have stopped me, that bitch was clinically insane. I blame you." I poked her side laughing with her.

"Hey! You pick the lesbians, I pick the flowers!" Shaking her head, giggling to her own comedy, she shuffles herself into the other room putting the flowers in the centre of the dining table and wipes it down with a yellow jiff cloth that she always has stuffed in the back pocket of her jeans or clutched in her hand. She flips and flops with her gold sliders around the place, dusting here and there.

"Please Eleni, it's not like that" Not speaking too loudly, because this open plan apartment makes it damn near impossible to have a private conversation.

"Oh!" She points up, jiff cloth in her grasp. "She is someone who is on *your* bed, you tell her to strip the sheets. I don't know what you two been up to last night but I don't want to touch it." Giggling to herself. She thinks she's hilarious with all her commentary today.

"Eleni, we didn't do *any-thing*, I swear. At least... I don't remember if we did?"

"You forgot?!" She freezes, shooting me a look of concern. Waiting on my answer, eyes wide.

"No, not like that, I'm fine. Don't stress. We got drunk and done some dumb shit, I don't remember much is all I'm saying. You know I share my dirty laundry... literally, in this case but I don't have any to share because *we* didn't do *anything*?" She wipes up to the counter where I am standing, without lifting her head and not losing her circular cleaning 'wax on wax off' motion.

"You're not happy, you didn't do anything?" Moving me out her way, she continues to wipe the surfaces.

"I'm not! It's not like me to wake up naked beside a woman I haven't been inside of and vice verses. But this is different, I guess? I don't know, shit. Eleni stop with the third degree." Laughing at the faces she was pulling, she turns and opens one of the cupboards.

"Well, be nice. You dragged the poor girl to this middle of nowhere, place of yours. She probably thought she was getting some cookie." She slaps the side of my thigh playfully and loud with her heavy hand. "Make her coffee!"

Lifting her heavy hand, she pinches my cheek, pats my face then continues with the cleaning.

"The word is coochie."

"Same thing?"

Peering up at my room. Mai hasn't come down, good! The last thing I want is Eleni being all happy and extra friendly, fuck! I spoke to soon, here she comes. Nonchalantly walking down from the bedroom with her big hoody over her body smiling. walking towards us in the kitchen-

"Did I hear someone say coffee?" She thinks she's cute, she heard us talking.

"Sugar?" Eleni approached Mali and places a hot mug of coffee in her hand. Where the hell did she whip that mug out of?! Before I opened my mouth to answer, Eleni was already close beside her- this woman, I swear.

"Two please, thanks…"

"Eleni," Eleni Ignores Mali's confused face, whipping out two sachets of sugar from her back pocket and empties them into the mug.

"Cream?" Eleni offers her, cream while Mali and I are busy wondering where this little old woman is whipping out all the components for a perfect cup of coffee from. Her back pockets are like Mary Poppins carpet bag.

"Thank you, Eleni."

"No problem…" Eleni's eyes open wide, mouth open with a smile slapped across her face. Waiting for Mali to fill in her blank and tell her, her name.

"Malikah but people call me Mali."

"Pretty name, for such a beautiful girl." She places a teaspoon in Mali's mug. Miming and encouraging Mali to mix it, with a flick of her wrist in the air. She gently pats her back and guides Mali in the direction of the lounge.

Then sticks her thumb up at me with a big over the top, not so indiscreet wink and steps back over to me.

"Happy now? You've met her! Wait, where the hell did you get the sugar and cream from? With your Mary Poppins self!"

"A spoonful of sugar, no?" The yellow jiff cloth, out of her other back pocket and back in her hand "Yes, I like her. But! I'm not buying you anymore socks! So, don't fuck it up!" We both laugh at her very bad RuPaul impression, she's been watching way too much Netflix again.

I swear, she makes me so happy without even trying. Her presence in itself does that. I could be having a bad day, I get home see the new flowers and its' all over because I feel her energy relieve me. When I'm unwell, she pops over with a Greek dish to feed me and take care of me. There are days where I forget to cook and she has a pot of soup on the stove ready and things around the house are done without me asking. You know, small things that I forget to do. She has this sixth sense or care for me and knows exactly when I need her the most, she's always there. Sometimes I feel like she knows me better than I know myself.

I'm not a family person, I've not always seen, eye to eye with my own family. My mum's a snake to her own children and my sisters collect boyfriends and baby daddies like Pokémon cards. Believe me, when I say the only thing we have in common is blood. Eleni's family are back in Greece, she always says one day she'll go back but I know she will stay- who knows? But for now, she's my everything and my always. I know she's here- she's got me.

Singing away loud to a Greek song in her head with the yellow jiff cloth hanging out her back pocket swinging with her booty dance, that rag is never far from her side.

8. *The Twisted Connection*

Mali and I sat out on my wooden decked balcony. We *were* out here waiting for the wet mopped floors inside to dry, Eleni had long left my apartment and the floors were way past drying but we hadn't migrated back inside yet. I'm at ease with Mali being out here on the balcony instead of being in there and in the sanctuary of my space.

Head back watching as the sky gets darker, summer evenings are always my best. Sat out here, gazing at the sky and its' forever changing colours; from every single shade of blue to purples, oranges and pinks. Colours only the sky can conjure up. Colours that no paint palette can mix, remake or replicate but they naturally form. Right from where the sun is trying to hold onto the remaining shreds of the daylight as it slowly sets across the summer sky. And when the darkness finally falls on the night sky… there's still that last spectrum of light out there somewhere as the distant stars fight to be seen and reach your eyesight before the city lights. The clouds are somehow there moving and somewhat white, you barely see them floating in the sky at this time but they are there reminding you that the daylight will soon return… I swear, some things on this earth are just magical like that.

Sat comfortably chilling, tucked in the corner of a long chair with my huge fluffy faux fur blanket across my body. One leg hung out of the blanket and off the side of the chair. Extending my leg so that the ball of my foot is touching the balcony floor, circling it and feeling the never-ending grains in the wooden surface of the decked flooring. Running my foot backward and forwards past the small gaps between the slats of wood with each rotation my foot made.

Mali sat across from me but at a good distance on the other end of the big chair. Mali's energy has taken a shift; the confident, cocky and playful part of her personality has subsided and she has this quiet and peaceful element of calm which has taken over, in this zen kind of way.

Her big black oversized hoody falls over her, swallowing her body. Her legs stretched and her feet sharing the fluffy blanket. Head down preparing her second spliff, I watch her process and meticulous build up; the light brown raw paper held in her fingertips, carefully and tightly rolling. Not allowing the slight breeze to carry any of the weed away. Her eyes squinting focused with a sexy grimace on her face and lips held to the side. Catching me looking her way, she digs in her pockets, locating her lighter. Reaching over to me, having seen me open my packet of cigarettes and slide one out of the box of twenty. Leaning towards her hand to meet the flame, she lights me up then concentrates back on her own task of lighting her spliff against that gentle breeze.

Sitting back and blowing on the lit end of her spliff. She places it between her lips, staring at me. She inhales her narcotic and blows the smoke slowly out of her mouth and nose. Her hair is out of its regular slick back tied up ponytail and blowing away freely. With her hair down, her face and her features appear softer than her tomboyish stance and ways.

Music playing low through outdoor speakers in this mellow laid-back vibe that floated between us. The slow jams sound of my 'Aaliyah and Chill' playlist, weave around the comfortable quietness and tranquil silence. The conversation flow paused a long time ago, could have been an hour or so... Isn't it nice when you chill with someone and you are both so comfortable you can just shut- the- fuck- up-? Breathe and simply *be* with? There are not many people who can do that, trust me. Her silence could be from comfort or the not knowing what to really say. Perhaps she feels a type of way about telling me the very dark truths from her past. All that matters is, I *know* what's on her mind. I know her vulnerabilities and I can use this as my angle to get her right where I want her to be. *But* that in its self is *very* fucked up- even for me!? Because I know, in telling me all that she did, it has placed me in a much higher position of value than Blue.

Think about it, Blue doesn't have a clue about *all* that Mali really is; all her depths, her trauma, her flaws, insecurities and her dark past. She would have told me by now, because there are three things, I know for a fact that Blue *cannot* keep and they are: A relationship, her legs closed and a secret!

She would have told me in confidence- because what else are friends for but to keep the secrets you were told to keep secret?

With secrets this big comes the great responsibility of toying around with emotions. To be able to bring them to the surface individually. I just need to figure out how? Her heart is strong from her fight and suffering but her mind is tired, weak and easily susceptive to manipulation. Look, she's here, isn't she? When she knows damn well, she should be with her woman but it's clear I've got into her head a little already and got her to stay through very simple reverse psychology.

Everyone knows when a woman says "leave" she means "stay", right? And I have told her countless times to leave…

Put it this way; some women fall into the flames of the fire of pain and suffer the burns again and again while very few rise again. Hence, Mali's need for escape through drugs and other substances, which is something she's replicated from her abuse. But I'm here now and *I* can be that drug, that escape and that need to not want to waste a day, unless she's wasting it beside me. I already told you, I am very addictive, breathe just a little deeper, pause and inhale Aaliyah.

My thoughts cut by my phone ringing, picking it up I roll my eyes. I'm not interested. Do you ever ignore your phone completely, when it's blatantly ringing and in your hand? You just look at it, doesn't matter who's calling or what they have to say… you're just there watching it. Waiting for it to stop ringing, so you can go back to doing whatever it was that you were doing.

Blue has been calling me all damn day and I am not in the mood to entertain her and her bullshit conundrum of questions. She can continue to get a deadline, go to voicemail and leave a message after the 'beep' because it is not my problem where her woman is and what her woman does. Besides, all I have to do, when I eventually talk to her, is talk the biggest game of flipper. She will most definitely end up feeling stupid and apologising to me. I'll have her believing that it's all in her little confused head and that she has *absolutely* nothing to worry about;

"I mean Blue, come on why would I want your woman?
She's so far from my type and has absolutely nothing I need or want.
I need a woman who can bring something to the table that I have provided."

Then it's over to Mali to do all the kissing and make up fucking she needs to do to reinstall the security in their relationship and alleviate any doubt left in Blue's mind. Yes, we are all *very aware* that I'm in the wrong for encouraging Mali's 'fuck it' behaviour... *but* this is what I do and I do it so well, wouldn't you agree? However, ultimately the final decisions are within Mali's power. I *only* make suggestions, I'm not forceful and I am not demanding in the planting my seeds of deception. She's a grown woman, like she been saying over and over. She knows better! She *should* have control over herself and be at least, a little bit mindful of her woman and her relationship throughout her actions. But so far, all she's shown me, is that she doesn't have *any* respect for her relationship- at all! So why should I?

You'll sit there and think I'm a bitch for what I am doing but you know my points are not only valid... Hun! They are one hundred percent right! People are *so* fucking quick to blame the side chick, without looking at the full story, from all perspectives.

Everyone knows *exactly* what they are doing! We all know what we want to do and what we *should* and shouldn't do. You are in control of yourself and you know right from wrong; it's a fundamental lesson, installed in your system from childhood. So, to allow anyone else to gain the ability to access and corrupt your fundamentals or control your mind, in my eyes is just *weakness* that the predators of this world (like me), will seek out and end up encouraging you to do fucked up things you will later regret. So, don't be hunted, get hunting!

"Hello."

Answering my phone; a 'random' from my contact list is calling me, wanting me as they all do.

I'm completely uninterested but I'll make my words sound as though I am invested in this conversation and whoever the hell this girl is. I've got to start remembering when I've met females and exchange details.

Mali is busy looking as though she isn't listening. But you can always tell when someone is *'trying'* not to listen in on your phone conversation. They usually become slightly awkward and try to make themselves busy doing anything else. Either fidgeting or looking in any other direction but yours. Overthinking, that you think they aren't listening but what they don't realise is their eyes attain this glazed look of distance and un-focus from blocking out their surroundings and trying not to zone in to what you are saying. You come off the phone and you say something like:

"Did you hear that?" – invitation extension of the receiving conversation and they end up saying;

"Sorry? Oh, I wasn't listening,"- girl, you know damn well you were listening!

Sat back talking to the woman on my line with a load of flirtatious babbles of nonsense and charm. Her contact is logged in my phone as *'Chick from Starbucks'* with two tea cups emoji beside it, or as Siri says 'hot beverage'

Mali turns away from me unimpressed, giving me the exact reaction, I wanted. But she's observing me from the corner of her eye. I giggle at the nothing 'Miss. Starbucks Two Cups' had to say, I done it only to read Mali's body language and watch how she responds, detecting hints of jealousy all over her body.

"I'm getting off the phone now, okay cool. Bye lady." Calling her 'lady' because I do *not* know her name.

Hanging up the phone and concluding my act, I hold my phone in both hands looking, smiling away to myself pretending to text her but all I'm doing is tapping the locked black screen of my phone. Causing the continuing fuel to Mali's jealousy fire.

"That single life there boy." Mali turns her lips inwards finishing her sentence, her spliff and commenting on my conversation she *wasn't* listening to.

"Rather this life, than in a life with a situation like yours. Playing hide and seek, at *another* woman's house with your phone switched off, because *you* haven't come up with a good enough excuse, reason or lie to tell her where the fuck your arse really is and where you've been… all day."

Although she shrugs at her truth, it's been bothering her system. Overthinking about what she should say or what reason to give for her unexplainable absence.

Swirling my drink in my hand listening to the ice cubes clink and bounce around the edges of my glass, floating carelessly in my brandy and apple juice. I wait for Mali, to respond to me.

"I'm grown! I don't answer to no one." She's hilariously cute repeating her, *"I'm grown,"* mission statement, trying to convince herself that she's cool but her thoughts are bouncing around in her head like the ice on the sides of my glass, just floating about the place. Unable to come up with an excuse for her twenty hours of non-appearance.

"And I'm bored of you telling me 'your grown' and can do as you please! You know that freedom disappears. It becomes a myth when you're in a relationship. *And*, you *will* have to tell her where you're going, where you've been, who you're with what you're doing and when you're coming back! It's a written rule that comes in the guidelines of all relationship agreements- says it right here. Section 3b line 23; 'bae must share all locations and details of all those present when bae is not around'- see it's right there."

Pointing my finger up in the air at the imaginary contract, held firmly in my other hand. Ignoring me, she glances at her phone turned off face down on the table. She picks it up… looking at it, thinking about it… holding it briefly. Her finger hovering and hesitating about pushing down on the side button to turn it on. She doesn't want to hear the pinging sound of the endless *"where are you?"* notifications she's expecting the moment she turns it on… so she places it back as it was before… face down and turned off.

"I'm not trying to deal with that headache man," As expected. Shrugging her shoulders, she slumps back into the chair while preparing to roll another spliff hoping this one, will be the one that eases her mind and silences her thoughts of guilt.

"You want mamma to take care of it, baby?" Teasing her, prodding her with my foot.

"Whatever, you doughnut!" She shakes her head not wanting to laugh. But can't help but crack a smile. At this point what else can she really do?

"Don't stress. I already told you I'll deal with Blue; I've known her for as long as I can remember and I know how to handle her. I'll teach you one day, maybe"

"Who's stressing?" She laughs

"…Why are you with her Mali?"

I cut straight to the point; What? I want to know, why *is* she with her? I don't get it, at all?

Taken back by me and thrown off by my intriguing *honesty*. Didn't they tell you I was a savage? I'd rather say exactly how it is, then have it play on my mind and drive me insane. I don't need to be filling my head, thinking about it when I might as well come right out with it and say, ask or do it.

Adjusting herself in the chair once more; she pulls on both cuffs of her hoody hiding her fingers, peering down at them.

"I know, it's hard to believe we have anything in common right? …but," her high slowly affecting her speech and ability to get her point across with another pause, "she was there when I needed someone the most, you know? I haven't told her the shit I told you or what I've been through. I don't want to be someone's pity case. But she does these little things, she shows me that she cares and she's cute with it. She's been there for me, she pushes me. Keeps me in check and helps me to be better- I don't know." She said proudly, satisfied with her answer. I however, am far from satisfied or impressed.

"Sounds to me, like you're convincing yourself because she's the first person who's shown you any genuine interest since... well, your whole fucked-up situation."

"What?" She says uncomforted by what I said in return.

"First of all..." (you know it's about to be fire when a woman says 'first of all') "You're here Mali! When you should be respecting all 'those little things' she does for you. Second, you're so vacant when you're with her! I see it, you don't look at her with any kind of passion or lust or intensity. You told *me* your past, not her... why? You don't want to show her the real you, in case she's rejects who you are out of her perfect little bubble of glitter and gold. You're not comfortable enough to just 'be' without being forced to suppress yourself. Hoping that your slight *like* and tolerance for her will grow into love. You're scared of opening up and being rejected again. So, you'll stay, become complacent and wait while sacrificing your happiness for hers. I see it all the time with disjointed couples."

Attacked with the truth, she says nothing, staring into space like she's looking back at her own thoughts, wondering if I could hear them, because I'm right. I know I am right, you know I'm right and *she knows* I'm fucking right! It's all over her face, she would have had something to say by now. She would have cut me off or told me to shut the fuck up!

"Mali, *"I love her,"* would've been a believable answer. Those three little words."

"So, what about you *Miss Aaliyah*?" Mali deflects and changes the subject to me. Not responding to my statement because, that was the first time she's asked herself that question too. Accepting the truth is never easy, it hurts. But it's clear to see, now knowing what I know that her relationship with Blue is no more than a:

"Thanks for saving me babe; I'll love you one day- I hope."

What happened to writing people 'thank you' cards when they do something nice for you? Now it's, 'let's be together'? I don't know why do people do it? Why commit love to these things, because of conveniences? Why do it, why stay unhappy?

Holding onto the love they once had or the love they crave. People stay, unhappy, uncomfortable and settle for less. Honestly, people sit around asking for relationship advice on how to stay and be right when the first thing they need to do is leave baby girl and set yourself free. Throw all them and their shit away, because I do not understand the concept of allowing anyone to treat you in any type of way.

"I'm living my best life. I'm not going back and forth with drama and the women I fuck with understand they're not the only one. That nothing last forever. They get to escape their reality with me for a night or two, depending on my mood."

"Have you ever been attached?"

"Nope." No hesitation on *that* answer!

"Like, you've never caught feelings for any of them?"

"Nope, not at all." #catchflightsnotfeelings.

"What about your past, you ever been in love back then?"

"I see you're flipping the convo when we were talking about *you* and *your* situation." I laugh at her badgering and finish my glass in a final gulp, reaching forward towards the bottle on the table and pour another one.

"You *were* talking about my situation and *now* I'm talking about yours. I know that everyone has reasons to why they do certain shit... right?"

"What makes you think I have reasons? I'm a woman with a lack of commitment to morals."

"Nah! Not buying it! That's the shit you tell yourself, to make what you do easier. You recite it, like a mantra. Telling yourself over and over; if you're a bad person then nothing matters. You jus' keep on going and going but you keep going back to the *same* women. The ones that you say you're *not* attached to, because..."

"Because what?" Maintaining my cool while she pauses, looking out into the distance. Processing her thoughts in her current state of high; where logic becomes clear through realisation and explanation- like 'why is a chair called a chair' type of thoughts.

"Because, I don't think you actually realise how closely I've been watching you, Miss Aa-li-*yah*. I *know* what you're doing, what you've been doing... and to be honest..." she pauses again, then looks directly in my eyes, "I fucking like it! I suppose I'm used to people fucking with my mental. But you... you're on a *whole* different level, you're dangerous. You're forever on my mind and the people who tend to stay on *my mind* are people that are fucking with it and you're the only one in there! The only one that makes sense to me right now, it's so fucked up but I've let you do it. I know I act naïve and laid back but it's an act, jus' like what you're doing is an act. Except, I'm not like other women, I pay attention to *you*." She slouches back, not taking her eyes off of mine and for the first time... I don't know where to look.

"Seriously, what the fuck are you smoking?! You're on a next level of high!" Laughing off whatever the fuck she said to me but she sat up again, leaning forward, staring at me. Pointing with her spliff tightly between two fingers.

"You know... you're so fucking strong! It's sexy and powerful as fuck! It amazes me and has me in this kind of daze, thinking; 'how does she do it?'. 'How does she have me thinking about her at night while my woman is in *my* arms?'. It took me a second but I realised and I see past all of that now because I see past you! You're a fucking mess! You're scared to show anyone your broken truth. I've seen the scars on your body, underneath your tattoos. The burn marks on your back that you hide with your long hair. I've even felt that welted small line on your left hip, it's right beside your tattoo and it feels as if someone scored something deep into your skin. You've got a tiny scar by your left eye, you cover it all up really well with the make-up. Even the way you constantly drink the pain away, all makes sense. A basic bitch wouldn't see any of that, they don't see past this character and 'zero fucks given' shit you do so well. But I know abuse when I see it. You think I don't know a broken person when I see one?! I fucking lived that shit my whole childhood. Fuck... my whole life, I know!"

"You need to shut up!"

"Wait, listen. Hear me out real quick, what I mean is. What I am trying to say is. You... it amazes me that you are so fucking broken but you're okay. You're here; you're living life and smiling beautifully. Almost like a legacy to the statement 'things fall apart so that beautiful things can fall into place'- you know, I almost didn't see the signs but then it clicked. You don't want anyone close to you for too long because the last person you let in was the person who fucked you over differently! *So* bad, that you don't want to *ever* put yourself there again. So, you detached every emotion you can but you're addicted to the human touch. You stay distant but you see the same women, because you crave a familiar connection, I guess. You need it Aaliyah, you fuck around with them so much, because you want. No... you *need* to be wanted but you don't want anyone to stay- insatiable."

Silently adjusting my loose knit cardigan to cover up the skin I was revealing on my shoulders. Moving further back in my seat. Throwing back what I had left in my glass I held the alcohol at the back of my throat for a few seconds. Pressing the back of my hand on my mouth, not revealing the strong burn I can feel in the back of my throat and hit my chest, as I swallow. Ruffling with my hair, itching my scalp, aggravated at the thoughts of Mali thinking she *actually* knew *anything* about me. Pouting hard, grazing my tongue over and around my teeth. Taking in what the fuck she had to say. Thinking of what the fuck I want to say back to all that shit but I can't   think.
I don't know what to say or do. Fuck! I should've known she was watching me as close as I was watching her- but she's talking shit! She doesn't know shit! No one knows but me!

"So, what, you think you know me? You know what I've been through? Okay, if you say so." My pout turns, the anger in my voice starts to grow louder.

"Relax Aaliyah, I didn't say I know you! When you were sleeping, I saw all that shi-stuff on your body. I saw what you're hiding and you do it so well. I jus' wanted to let you know it's okay, I got you, I get it... I know."

"You think I'm some broken-hearted, defenceless woman calling out for attention?! Really??"

"No Aaliyah I-"

"What! Then!" My voice trembled.

"I was trying to tell you I see it and *I know* it. Trust me, I get it! And I'm here, I know what lonely feels like, I do." She remains calm, wanting me to listen to what she was saying.

Who does she think she is? Up in here likes she's a doctor? Or psychic Mystic Mali, to be guessing and predicting me? She *doesn't* know me, she doesn't know what I am capable of.

Placing my empty glass down on the table, I remove the blanket from my legs. On my knees, I crawl over to where Mali is sat, leaning over her and into her body. Already her hands are back around my waist. Holding her chin in my hand... pulling her face towards mine. I grab the back of her neck putting my hand down the back of her top making her moan by clawing my nails hard from the bottom of her back right up to her neck. Kissing up on her all slow, leaving her with the taste of my kiss and the traces of my lips on her neck. I whisper in her, holding the back of her hair in my grip, I pull it tight, making sure she hears me good.

"You don't fucking know *me*! This is who the fuck *Miss Aaliyah* is! So, get the fuck out!"

Shoving her hands away from my waist, I stand up and walk away from her. Opening the balcony door and stay stood beside it, pointing at the exit she needs to take. Reluctantly she gets up and walks slowly towards me.

"I really wasn't tryna upset you." She tried to regain eye contact.

"What were you trying to do, exactly!? Be abuse storytelling buddies, you told me your story, so now I've got to tell you mine!? I don't need to tell you SHIT besides, there's nothing to tell. So, go! Leave! Go on fucking go!"

"No, I-"

"Save it for your woman." I cut her off, I'm so done listening to her "You see that door... it opens."

She passes me calmly, brushing her hand across my waist with the front door in her sight, defeated. She attempts to get me to look in her face but my arms remained folded; waiting and ready for her to fucking leave! She fixes her hoody, tucks her phone and her things into the pockets on either side of her jeans, slips on her trainers and opens the front door.

"See you later Aaliyah." One foot out the door.

"I'll be calling Blue, to tell her *exactly* where you've been, seeing as though you're too much of a pussy to call her yourself." Oh, I *will* call Blue just to be petty, because I don't have shit to lose! I can't stand Blue *anyway* and It's about time I dropped her dead weight friendship and her out of my life.

"You know what! Fuck this!" Mali turns back towards me steps back into my apartment and slams the door shut, hard! Marching towards me. Shit! Fuck! Shit! "You don't get to fucking dismiss me like this! Fuck that!" I'm backing up in my own house and she's coming right at me! I am *not* ready for her to come at me and you know alcohol doesn't rate my ability to balance, this woman could be crazy?!

"Mali, just go, please!"

Turning in any direction my feet find to get away from her. Backed up into the corner by my dining table, hands up ready to fight back or surrender- you see *this* shit right here, *THIS* is why I don't let people in my house! My drunk arse was supposed to say my petty shit at the door and slam it shut, not say it when she's still in the fucking house!! Shit, who told me to drink so much? I'm not ready for this bitch!

"…I know you're never going to fucking admit it but I know you want me and every fucked-up detail because you're just as fucked up Aaliyah! You're a fucking head case! But all this point scoring is bullshit-"

"Just leave." I said quietly, my hands up by my face.

"No. Aaliyah! I'm not going anywhere and you're gonna fucking listen!"

Grabbing my hips aggressively pulling me towards her kissing me, my hands fall around her neck, her kiss just, it's… fuck! Rough and hot as hell, the way I like. I didn't expect this; I thought she was going to kill me! My body falling into hers she pushes me against my dining table.

"Get out Mali!" Trying to walk out of her grasp and away from the table but she holding me from the back, her arms not letting go of me. Kissing my neck. I want her to kiss me, be on me, I want her inside of me but I want her out of here at the same time!

"Stop… wait, Mali…" I can't concentrate; I can't speak through the tight heated broken breathlessness she is making me feel. I don't want her to stop, stop, don't stop, stop, don't stop.

"You know we both want this," loosening her grip, she delicately held my face in her hand. "We know what this shit is like. We know we're fucked up, Aaliyah no one else gets us- but *us*…"

Pushing her completely away from me- I couldn't, I can't… I can't stop myself, my hand opens and raises in the air, so quickly connecting with her face so hard, the palm of my hand stings instantly, throbbing.

"NO! I AM NOTHING LIKE YOU!"

Screaming at her, she stumbles back, her hand against the side of her face. Gasping out of breath, looking at me shocked but eager… Like… like she's turned on by what I did? Wait, what? Out of nowhere, before I saw her swing for me, I felt the back of her hand connect with my face! My feet move a small step back but I stand my ground. She hit me! She fucking hit me! The bitch hit me back!

We both stood gasping and angry right in the heat of whatever this is, chests moving up and down, so fast and heavy with long breaths trying to figure out what is happening and why we are elated by all of it?!

My desire for her has reached its dangerous peak. I knew it was there, I anticipated her showing me more of her but I never expected this. Messing with her head, forcing her to act a certain way, to show me more… and this aggression, this craving- let's do this!!

Grabbing up a pile of magazines off my coffee table I throw them at her, she puts her arms up blocking them and I swing for her again, she catches my wrist. Gripping me tight, squeezing and grabbing me she pushes me across the room away from her, my whole body moves with the force. In a split second, I charge back at her, diving into her, throwing my shoulder into her chest and now we are brawling, fighting, wrestling, tussling like two testosterone fuelled boys, scrapping on my apartment floor. Going blow for blow, punch for punch. Knocking shit over, punching, kicking, over and over again. Grabbing, kissing, beating, slapping, kissing, scratching, holding, hitting, kissing, kicking, punching, slapping and more kisses. Kissing more, pulling hair, scratches, kisses connecting lips and fist connecting punches.

Pinning me down again, I wriggle from underneath her after kicking her right in the stomach I get up, stood up. My heart is about to pound out of my chest, all I see is red. My fists still balled ready for her, waiting. She stood up, doubled over holding her belly, winded. She straightens up slowly standing tall above me across the other side of the room that we just tore to fucking pieces. Giving me this sexy side smile; in her eyes, I can see her next move coming but I'm not moving, she charges at me pushing me hard as fuck! I grab her not letting go and we stumble to the side tripping over her leg onto the sofa, I take her down with me. Landing on top of Mali and holding onto the back of her head, tugging on her hair, head back I slap her across the face, she lets out a sexy sigh.

Eyes completely locked, not even attempting to look anywhere else staring, trying to regulate her breathing. She sits up with me in her lap. Facing her with my legs wrapped over her body; pulling off what was left of my ripped clothes, she roughly undresses me tugging on my cardigan trying to get it off my shoulders quickly. She bites the side of my arm; it felt so fucking good- shit! Throwing the cardigan in some other direction across my apartment. My arms up, my t-shirt already up over my head and it lands elsewhere. My bra off next, following the rest of my clothes. Dragging her hoody off of her body, tugging and pulling off her top and sports bra up over her head, she hauls me towards her - tight. Our bodies touching, locked in this heat! This fire over every inch of our hunger and thirst for each other! Skin to skin, feeling some different type of way, I can't explain but this tingling thing across my skin, an energy, or power connecting between us, like we are intoxicated with each other, for each   other.

I feel like I'm high when she kisses me, the way she kisses me, it's like… a pause in time. Like everything stops but speeds up, fuzzy like little rushes of energy when she touches my skin.

Sat on her lap not letting go, both still panting and out of breath like we just fucked for hours and hours, going round after round. But we didn't touch, not like that anyway. Not in the way I wanted to, or thought, or imagined her touch. No, this way… so *aggressively*. This aggressive fucked up sexual tension release she wanted, that she built up and needed and it felt *sooo* fucking good! Too good!

This stinging on my skin, scorning and burning like hell! This is better than *anything*! It's what she wanted and what she needed. A release, an escape and a craving of being overpowered and beaten… whatever it is, I want more.

Her arms are wrapped over me, tightly, mirroring each other's grasp- holding her the same way she's holding me. Her face buried in my chest, my heart beating and pounding loud in her ear. She doesn't need sex; this is what she needed… what… *we* needed.

Sex is effortless; I can get that when I want, from who I want but I want more, I want this! *This*, it's more than anything I've ever felt… but it's so familiar. Have I felt it before? I can't explain it but my conscious is fighting something, I can't see it. I can only feel it when she pulls me against her skin, like I'm not close enough to her. She's satisfied, hearing it in her long deep breaths and feeling her chest move in and out slowly against my skin, soothed by it all… I've fucking found it. I've found that *thing!* The thing on her mind that's buried deep down in her limbic system. *This* is it! It's *so* much more than the abuse of her past and the story of her history that she holds onto. Mali has *actually* missed it! It makes sense now, she's missed *that* attention, the dark fucked up drama, abuse and aggression. It's all she knows, it's what she's come from. The thrill and the sick twisted, submissive perverse passion of wanting the attention and affection of someone toxic lusting over her. Damaging her, causing her discomfort and fucking with her head- she said it, I didn't take it in… that she welcomes the hurt and pain, physically or mentally. She wants it, she wants me to hurt her, at least then she has my complete attention, no matter how poisonous or corrupt. I've found that sick connective that had us before we even knew it did.

My skin throbbed from the sexual tension that came out of us in this violence. The aggression and anger pulsating *all* over my body. I've felt a familiar power over me, only this time, it's in my hands, under my control.

Running my flat palms over her back, feeling the scratches raise and set on her skin. My neck felt restricted and stiff from her hands choking me and forcing me down on the floor. Tilting my head back slightly, she gently kisses where her hands were and firmly embraces me once more; not letting me go.

Stillness surrounding us, skin to skin with nothing but the music on. The lyrics singing words into beautiful melodies of thoughts within this madness. As we listen intently, to the reliability of 'us' in the songs rhythm and acoustics all on repeat. Our hands attach to each other, holding bodies together. Her face pressed against my chest, ear listening to my heartbeat slow down and regulate back to eighty beats per minute. I get it; I understand what she wants- I *know* what she needs.

Giving in to this familiar exposed and the twisted connection, we lay on the sofa. Unmoved and wrapped over each other's bodies- not wanting to'let go.

Mali's body weight comforting and soothing me. Naked, bare, care free and trusting- she's exposed to me, in so many ways. Her energy calm again, she's at ease.

But am I at ease? I don't know? I think so. Looking down at her, she smiles through the darkness of dimmed warm lighting in the room, coming from the tall lamp that was knocked over in our battle. Listening to Mali's breathe change from fast and rapid to long and spaced out and soft as she drifts of to sleep.

Trailing the tips of my fingers along her back, revisiting the scratch lines, now completely raised. Short and broken in places and in other parts long and thick.

Passing down her smooth athletic but thick in the right places frame. Her small waist, curves, hips and thick thighs on top of me. Everything I admire in the body of a real woman, wrapped into this damaged package of a broken woman in my arms.

I need to remind myself to take - my - time. Remember the game, remember *my* gain. That's all I'm in this for, nothing more, no attachments, no promises. I get what I want from her, then I get the fuck out of this. But… I don't have to rush it… I can take my time with her, right? Time is of the essence, so this can go on for as long as I want.

I want control, I am in control of her and myself, I-*am* - in -control, for now. She's seen me exposed or so she says. I don't want her to see me or my scars but it's too late. She's closer to me than anyone has gotten. But as long as I stay in control, she'll never know… at least not the full story anyway. I need to slow down and take time but I can't slow it down now. Heartbeats beating heavy again, panicking but not panicked, catching myself.

Turning to my apartment taking a good look at the evidence of the struggle. It's a mess! The coffee table overturned, magazines scattered across the floor; pages open and torn all over the place. Things knocked over, kicked over, turned over and thrown over. Everything fucking *everywhere* in my perfect apartment… but the tranquil feeling I've always felt within the walls of my home is still here and has not faded in the clutter of chaos.

My eyes blinking starting to close, I'm exhausted, drained and relaxed. The humming hard vibrating sound of my phone opens my eyes to alert, search and locate it on the floor vibrating away with Blue's name flashing on my screen calling my line again, attempting to reach out to her 'friend'. Seeking friendly words of advice and comfort that will settle her unsettled mind, wondering where her woman is, when her woman is right here… with me, in *my* arms, in *my* home and in *our* mess.

Mali relaxes her weight, becoming heavier as she drifts off into a contented sleep. Leaving me with my thoughts running wild across my mind, so quick, I can't catch them.

Not wanting to wake her up, I carefully move my boy underneath hers. She stirs naturally, adapting herself in her sleep to my change of position and remains attached to me. Placing a kiss on her forehead, I'm confident she notices my caress in her sleep. Fighting with her unconscious dreams and nightmares, burying her face into me, she wakes up. Running her lips gently against my neck. Moving *so* slow, making me question if she's awake at all? Tracing her lips on my skin in the same spot. Tender kisses, so soft it's almost like she isn't awake at all. Her touch, has me wondering about *everything*. Creating more thoughts in my head, opening more tabs in my mind, all over again. Why I started this? Should I be doing this? What am I doing? What are we doing? Should we? Finding no answers, not a single one, because when she kisses me, it takes me way away… I lose my breath. I lose myself. Have I lost?

9. The Scattered Pages of Organisation

"Morning Aaliyah." The concierge greeted me as I entered through the rotating doors of the apartment building my boss lives in.

"Good morning." Nodding in his direction, clipping my heels past his desk and across the glittered marbled ivory toned, tiled reception floor towards the elevator. Every time I enter the building on his shifts, he's sneaking a peek and watching me pass by in my red-soled heels. I clock his reflection off of the inside of the building windows watching me. His eyes wishing, he could get a piece of me but *dick* isn't my type. He is a middle aged well-presented suited and booted man who has this cute little crush on me- aww bless him. He calls me downstairs every so often to come sign for a package of chocolates or coffee and pastries that a *"secret admirer"* had left   me.

It's obvious it's him! I play along, pretending like I don't know it's him and his old school ways of trying to get the girl. I try to catch him gazing at me but, every time I unexpectedly turn around, he regains his professional posture and does anything else but look in my direction- I'll catch him one day.

Pressing the numeric code in the elevator that takes me right into the penthouse apartment in the building. Gathering my files out of my bag, preparing them in order and tucking some under my arm. The elevator doors opens directly onto the ground floor of the apartment. The large ceiling to floor windows, stretches over the whole apartment and opens it up with an amazing view of the city from anyway you stand.

"Stevie, you home!" She usually greets me at the door with a large glass of wine and gossip. People with money have nothing better to do but drink themselves stupid, watch their money pile up and talk shit about other people. However, things have been far from its *"usual"* recently. The past couple of months situations in this house have risen and blown the fuck up! I'm talking backpack full of Semtex on a

TFL tube, blown up! Don't be all judgemental, I never *specified* the *ethnicity* of *who* was holding the backpack. It's just an expression- relax! Even though, we all know the *real* terrorist are white males who walk into a school, shoot up the place and get labelled as "mentally challenged" because he's come from a wealthy broken home. Oh, I *think we* most defiantly need to talk about Kevin!

Stevie Belling, the wife of Rick Belling, C.E.O of London City Airport, Rick is filthy fucking rich! He's making that A-rab, make it rain, rich sex kind of shmoney moves!! Successful and respected by all his peers of Caucasian 'privileged' business folk in the 'fly high, lavish city lifestyle society'. However, at home Rick was just another *regular* man, with the same *regular degular, shmegular* dumb dick like behaviour as any other man. In other words, he fucked up!

Mr Belling has been a *very* naughty boy! Caught with his trousers down and balls deep inside another *younger* woman!! Okay, slight exaggeration from me there. So, he wasn't *exactly* caught in the act of adultery but, he was caught cheating all the same.

It just sounds better when I tell the story like that.

Anyway, Mrs. Belling is a woman you do *not*, I repeat *'do not'* want to fuck with! She is not Dej Loaf, do not 'try' her, she will fuck up your shit! She's far from the defenceless, gentle and overly feminine woman she has made herself out to be. Oh, she knew what *all* Mr. Belling's spontaneous and unscheduled meetings, late nights and new airport project developments were really all about. She simply needed to catch him in his dirty little act, in order to start the court proceedings. She waited... very patiently, like a predator waiting for its prey to display vulnerability and weakness. Waiting for that one careless small slip or blind-sided moment. And it didn't take very long because men always choose to use their *"head,"* and not their intelligence.

All it took was a minor miss calculation in scheduled dates. Oh, and not forgetting a teeny tiny bit of help from the *'forgetful'* personal assistant. That's me by the way, hiyaaaa!

All I had to do is get *his two women* in the same place at the *same* time. Did I do that? Yes, I sure fucking did! It was worth every fucking hundred and thousands of my 'bonus bribery' pay cheque Stevie handed over to me. Sponsored by the bank of Rick. He couldn't really say anything about the large amount of money that went from his account to mine, because I'm keeping secrets for him too so, shut up and run me my money- lol! (I just wanted to sound gangster, you know, feel like Rhianna. Bitch better have my money and all that stuff, I lost myself for a second there)

The Belling residents has become a reckless battle ground. A cold world war has broken out between two people, who once upon a time were madly in love. And it's taking place right here within these luxurious feature walls, marbled floors and other unnecessary inanimate object of value it took to make this penthouse apartment a home of dreams. Which is *way* too fucking big for *only* two people but rich people have this materialistic attitude, to always go above and beyond their means when they attain a lavish (stupid) amount of money. Stevie is most certainly a woman living lavishly! Handling the divorce battle like a true 'fucking petty lady'; quietly, elegantly, strategically, connivingly and very vindictively. Rick doesn't know when he's going to step on tactically placed land-mine and get blown the fuck up by her scorned vengeance. She does not plan on letting go of a single penny and the cold war between them rages on!

Rick calculated their divorce will cost him half of his *entire* empire, so he has no plan on signing anything, anytime soon. Unlike Jeff Bezos the Amazon CEO whose divorce is going to cut his one hundred and seventy billion net worth in half- ouch! However, Stevie has *also* calculated that her life needs a constant financially funded cash flow and to settle on one large lump sum of money would never last! So why leave? What, so *he* can run off into the sunset with his new woman and take away *her* millions?! No fucking way! Stevie started with him from the bottom, now he's here stacking and she was with Rick when his empire was just an idea on a post-it note.

They are both going to stay miserable for the rest of their lives! Stuck in the misery of money together forever!

"For richer, for poorer, till death do us part"

Walking through the apartment looking for Stevie, her red lipstick print pressed against a *finished*, lonely glass of white wine. The empty bottle, close by and within arm's reach was placed on their oversized twenty-two seated dining table. Both were accompanied and left beside her open laptop. Leaning closer in and tapping any key, the bright screen opened up onto the most recent bank statements, revealing calculations of unknown and *new* expenditures; such as seventy-nine thousand pounds at a *much* younger branded designer female clothing store… oh shit!

"In the kitchen!" Stevie calls on me.
I step into the kitchen confused. Watching her run up and down preparing a full English breakfast for one. Erm, what the fuck is going on?

"You're in the kitchen? Cooking…? Don't you have staff for this?" I ask and she pauses, shooting me a quick look that I should know better. "Oooh, this is about his latest purchases, right?" Watching her not knowing what is in what cupboard, because the only thing she knew how to find in the kitchen in the cork screw for the pinot grigio.

"If he thinks it's okay to give that little bitch a fucking card to OUR account, he's got another thing coming! Did you get what I asked for?" Hot and flustered, she cuts off her rant and concentrated on scrabbling the eggs in the pan, with her palm stretched and open in my direction.

"I had to tell the pharmacist some bullshit to get hold of some so strong. What you got in mind this time?" Handing her a packet of very strong laxatives, she deviously taps her nose.

"If he wants her to run through our fucking money like that, then this *shit* can run through him and his expensive Italian tailored trousers." She cackles to herself like a witch over a cauldron. Stevie is about to hubble bubble up some fucking shitty trouble!

Emptying the pills into a pestle and mortar, she crushes them down to a fine powder and mixes it into the fluffy scrambled eggs. Serving up breakfast perfectly, onto the breakfast table set for one. Sprinkling her finishing touches like Salt Bae all over the plate, the food absorbs it instantly.

Filling two separate glasses of fresh orange juice from a pitcher, to a half full point. Tilting the glasses to an angle, to make them look as though they've been drunk from. Placing on in my hand and one bedside herself, she takes the remaining powder and tipped into the pitcher, stirring it wildly with a wooden spoon.

Shit! Looking left to right like a pair of meerkats, hearing Rick's leather soled shoes shuffling down the hallway towards the kitchen. She throws the pestle and mortar into the sink and throws the box of laxatives in my direction. Quickly hiding the box underneath my files, papers and notes on the kitchen side top, pretending to go through them. Flicking casually through the paper work talking shit about my work, whilst Stevie quickly busiest herself with other things in the kitchen.

"So, Stevie we have a few appointments to attend today, we have the Hayes meeting and- *Heeeey*, good morning Rick, how are you?" I stop talking as Rick steps into the room, he's dressed sharp and looking good in his suit, his *very expensive Italian tailored suit.* Greeting him with pleasantries and professional smile. After all, the man is paying me extra to keep my little big mouth shut about all that he gets up to. I know, I'm terrible but don't worry, Stevie is *also* paying me extra to tell her what he gets up to. Look, they can keep this war going forever. I don't give a fuck which side of the opposition I'm on, as long as my bank account stays as thick as my thighs!

Rick is somewhere between his late fifties and early sixties, who knows? He wears thin titanium glasses that always sit at the end of his nose, making him appear as though he was always in deep thought. And he should be, considering the fact that Stevie is trying to destroy his life, his bank accounts and now his arsehole! He's wrinkly and tired, but you would be too if you owned London's high-class prestigious airport *and* had to entertain *two* very demanding, high maintenance women at the same time. Not to mention a *very* forgetful personal assistant, who keeps getting things wrong but you can't fire hire because she knows waaaaay too much!

"Morning ladies…"

His neck cautiously pokes through the kitchen doorway while his feet wait anxiously. Guarded and insecure about what was taking place before his entrance. I turn back to my stack of papers, like I have a clue what they are? All I see is figures, dates and post-it notes along with an issue of this weeks' Vogue stashed in there too.

"Morning Rick, my darling! I've made you a full English breakfast sweetheart. You've been stressed recently, so I gave the kitchen staff the morning off and thought I'd do something nice for a change." She spoke softly, pointing out the well-presented table for one.

"That looks lovely!" Does it, Rick?

"Take a seat my love?" She prances about the kitchen like a devoted house wife, stopping in front of him with a soft sweet smile on her face and a questionable glare in her eyes.

Don't do it Rick! Don't eat that shit! His eyes dart from the plate of food and onto his wife's not so innocent face, as she waits for him to take a seat. Rick… don't do it.

Meanwhile, all I can hear in my head is ………….. *Bryson Tiller drop* … DON'T! But this is what happens when you've played with her and you've been dishonest- should have listened to Bryson, Rick.

"I'd love to Stevie but I've got to head off. Meetings are slightly earlier than anticipated. I'm sorry my dear." His vigilance at its peak.

"Oh, I put a lot of effort in this. Look I've made the eggs fluffy and a little runny, just the way you like them." And coated with enough laxatives to have him shitting bricks, houses and villages then colonising them.

She tugged his arm lightly closer to the table, poured him a glass of juice and forcefully handed it to him with fluttering eyelashes. I watch entertained by them both, patiently waiting for 'shit' to get real!

"Honestly honey, I don't have the time, really I don't. You've done a great job though sweetheart." You would think these two were still *madly* in love with all the *darlings' honeys, sweethearts* and smiles they were throwing into their communication.

Rick looks over at me, I raise my glass of 'laxative free' orange juice, eagerly taking a sip. If he's not going to eat the food, he at least a sip! The suspension is *killing* me!! Rick places the glass on the table and kisses Stevie lightly on the forehead- for fuck sake!

"Riiiiiick!" Stevie whines "All my effort will go to waste, come on at least eat your bacon, you love bacon." She tried to use the puppy dog eyes, that worked their charm during the sweeter days of the marriage.

"No! Of course not, I'm sure Aaliyah would *love* a hot cooked breakfast, with all the hard work she does running after us."

Come again, say what? Aaliyah would love to do what now? Rick! Don't come for me Rick! I am NOT involved! He nods, reaching out over at me! Don't look over here at me! There must be *another* Aaliyah up in this room, I am currently unavailable and breakfast for one is *not* on the schedule today!? What the hell was I thinking working for these Caucasians? This must be what the sunken place feels like, because I *need* to get the fuck out!!

"How about it Aaliyah, fancy a full English?"

No!? How about you take you and your three Homer Simpson hairs off to work and leave me the fuck alone and don't suggest dumb shit!! The fuck did I do to be involved in this game of shitty booty! They don't pay me enough for this shit-LITERALLY!!

Stevie watches the panic on my face as Rick walks behind me, ushering me to take a seat. I feel like I'm walking the green mile- Dead girl walking!! Eyes practically popping out my head, silently screaming for help- this is it!! I'm going to die at the hands of these Caucasians. What was I *thinking* working for them in this modern-day slavery they chose to call 'Personal Assistant'? Jesus, Mary, Joseph and all the cows and the sheep in the stable! Somebody! Take the wheel!!!

"How about you whip up one those quick smoothies to go and Aaliyah will have the hot plate? Deal, Ali? You need a big breakfast, you've got a lot on today. So, fuel up, eat up!"

"I ate already." The back of my neck is *sweating*!

"Ah, don't be silly there's always room for more." He's trying me! He's using me as the lab rat! He *knows* she's done something to his food. He didn't know *how* but he wasn't about to take the risk.

"Yeah… sure, I don't see any *reason not* to eat it." Awkwardly talking with a Disney Store Sales Associate fake smile on my face. Peering over 'the plate' while Stevie is flying around the kitchen, grabbing *any* fruit she could find and throwing it in the blender.

Rick waited for me to take my first bite but I keep on cutting and dividing the food. I'm telling you this now… if I have to bring this shit to my lips! I am gone! Goodbye everybody! Bye Stevie, bye Rick and bye Felica!

"Oh gosh! Stevie, this looks so good, I don't know where to start." Hoping she would give me a clue to part of the food that wasn't covered in laxative but she shrugs and silently mouths 'I'm sorry'. "It looks *sooo* delicious, you sure you don't want any Rick, I don't mind sharing, there's a *lot* here."

Cutting the food up with the knife and fork into smaller pieces twice over, stalling as best I can. How long does a damn smoothie take?! Fuck! Just give him an apple! Shit!

"No, no be my guest." Rick spoke to me but his eyes drift over to watch his wife closely.

"Okay! Done, now off to work! Go on, piss off! Enjoy your day!" Stevie handed him a flask and practically pushed him out the kitchen door in under three point five seconds.

I drop the cutlery and push the plate away from me. Stevie held a hand out for me to wait before I open my big mouth to tell her about herself! She stood waving Rick out the apartment. The front door shut and she huffed back into the kitchen, pulling her half flowery apron off and slamming it on the kitchen top.

"For fuck sake Stevie! ARE YOU TRYING TO FUCKING KILL ME!"

"Don't be so dramatic!" She grabs a wine glass and waves me off.

"Stevie!?"

"Did you die?! Look, I'm sorry and thank you for not blabbing." She laughs a little at me.

"Yeah, you laugh! If I had to lift that fork to my mouth, I would've snitched and taken you down with me woman!"

"Snitches don't get bonuses, unless it's info for me." She winks and sips her wine

"You do not pay me enough for this kind of shit! Now what? He didn't eat the shit!?"

"Aaliyah take note. In life, you must *always* have a plan b." Stevie is standing there, laughing to herself.

"What the fuck do you mean? The plan flopped, he didn't eat the food?"

"I had a feeling he wouldn't eat it and would want something that he could watch me make."

"Go on..." Holding out my palm, pretending to take notes with my imaginary pen in the other hand.

"What the old fool *does not* know, is earlier, I laced the blender with a fuck load of Viagra. So, when he gets up to give his presentation, his dick will be the only thing everyone will be paying attention to!" Walking towards her clapping; she takes a bow and thanks an imaginary crowd, holding up a spatula like an award.

"And for dinner..." She turns opening the cupboard under the sink and takes out a large tin of Pedigree Chunk dog food in jelly. She holds it with both hands, like a television commercial. "Meat pie! Just like my mum used to make my dad, when he didn't know how to behave! Because if he wants to act like a dog and chase after little bitches, well then, he's going to *eat* like a fucking dog!"

Note to self: Never eat at this house again! EVER!

"Enough about that bastard. What's going on today?" Stevie, turns to my direction, waiting for her itinerary on the day's events to be revealed...

"You've got a meeting at eleven then lunch with Cliff at twelve thirty." She rolled her eyes, "*Which* I will cancel. Oh, and here are your full flight details."
Handing her several sheets of paper from my pile. "First destination is Miami. I need to go over the hotel details shortly due."

"Aali, are you *sure* you don't want to come with? I could use the company and I'll send for you when I'm in Los Angles." She pleaded with me

"As tempting as that is, I can't..."
Send for who? Not for me, don't send for me! Because having eight weeks p-a-i-d holiday sounded a *whole lot* fucking better!!!

Stevie booked herself an around the world first class trip for one. She decided it 'was best' to go away whilst the lawyers and solicitors argued amongst themselves about the divorce settlement she would *never* agree to. Don't get me wrong, I like Stevie but I am not about to spend more time in *"the office"* than I have to!? Would *you* go on holiday with a fifty damn near sixty-something year-old woman, going through a heavy divorce slash midlife crisis?! The itinerary of this trip goes a little something this;

* listening to drunken stories all fucking night about how much of a cunt her husband is and how she can't believe he would do this to her

* How she hates to love him blah, fucking blah, after she's had one too many little bottles of gin from the mini bar?

* Introducing me to Dexter! The Jamaican pool boy with the swinging long ass dick. Because suddenly she's caught 'jungle fever'.

Nooooo thank you! I don't want to play the supporting actress in 'When Stevie Got Her Groove Back'. Having to watch her and Dexter playing kissy face whilst she throws Ricks money at him and his silky smooth one-line compliments like:

"No star coulda' shine bright like you, sweetness."

The same lines he tells *every* single middle-aged, wealthy Caucasian woman that stay at the hotel complex divorced, broken-hearted, lonely and hopeless. These women don't know anything Black and cultured at all! Now all of a sudden, she's getting that culture dick! Finding herself back home playing Bob Marley, cooking Jamie Oliver's Jerk Rice?! Hair braided, practically falling in love with the best sex she's ever had. Meanwhile Dexter is plotting how much money he can get out of her, because he spells 'love' with a 'p-a-s-s-p-o-r-t' practicing his signature on his indefinite- Jack arse!

Personal Assistant isn't exactly the title you imagine me having, right? But my job is not to run around and arrange her life. No, my job is to look good and be a familiar friendly face in her life. Bottom line is, she's lonely! Money alienates friendships and family ties, so I am paid to fill in their absence and accompany her on shopping trips,

263

meals and coffee dates. I also very regularly interrupt boring meetings and events like this:

"Sorry to interrupt. Mrs. Belling, you have a phone call. It's important."

"Excuse me." Stevie excuses herself with a ladylike head nod and adjusts her shift dress as she stands.

The hosts of the meeting return the head nod motion towards her as she leaves the room and heads towards me in the hallway. Taking her coat from my arm, she steps out of the building and straight into the car.

I complete her usual escape plan by walking back into the conference room:

"Mrs. Belling had to leave due to important circumstances. Please, take my contact and *we* can *arrange a date* to continue."

Leaving my contact details in the palm of the most powerful looking business woman sat around the conference table. Looking like she's in need of a stimulating release from her boring 'nine to five - plus over time', executive desk job. I walk back down the hall, heading towards the large rotating glass doors at the exit...

"Aaliyah? That's your name, right?" Hearing a French accent call on me.

I turn around, taking my flat palm off of the handle of the oversized door and set my eye on the head co-operate manager. Loving the way her accent falls off her foreign tongue and into my ears, sounding like pure sweet seduction. "My office now... please." She turns and walks ahead of me, leading the way. Texting Stevie, I let her know I'm tying up loose ends and I shouldn't be too long.

Stepping into the office of Miss Elise. She closes the door behind me and I hear the door lock.

"What have I told you about locked doors?" Crossing my arms, she presses her body against the door unbuttoning her perfect white blouse.

"I know but I-" interrupted by my hand tugging down on her red lace bra, circling my tongue over and around her nipple, waiting for her to finish her sentence, she couldn't concentrate on.

"But nothing! Unlock the door."

"What if someone walks- in- on- us?" Sentence broken again, my other hand up under her skirt.

"That's the whole fucking point!"

Her hands, falling over my shoulders and linking around my neck. Her legs wrapped over me, her back against the door. She reaches behind, searching the door for the lock. Unlocking it, she says something in French, so seductively. I'm guessing she said 'harder' or 'faster' or 'fuck me' who knows! Who cares! She could be saying 'red buses, midgets and a fillet of fish' or 'how much wood could a woodchuck, chuck, if a woodchuck could chuck wood?' and I'd still fuck!

Letting her go, walking towards her desk she follows closely and I take a seat. Without taking a second to think and caught up in the way I am sitting back watching her with my fingertip in my mouth. She throws her paperwork everywhere! The scattered pages of organisation and planning fly across the room and fall onto the floor. Sitting on the desk, right in front of me with her skirt bunched up to her hips and legs wide open. She lays her body back slowly, arching her back... wanting more. But before I get a taste and slide my fingers back inside of her. I stand up over her and run my hand up over her stomach, past her breasts then around her neck choking her, whilst her head tilts back on the desk telling me. Life is far too short to pretend you don't like being choked during sex- Elise fucking loves it! Her pussy tightens, refusing to let go of my fingers, wanting more and loving that rough sex.

High heels on and holding onto the desk looking back at me. Her body jerks forward, she keeps moaning and pushes back on me, the desk rocks with her body flow. I love watching her body move. I love hearing the sounds she made. The way she says my name, loud and not giving a fuck about her colleagues and employees in the other offices close by.

"Tell me what you want..." I can tell she's reaching her peak but not until she tells me. Hot and flustered that I stopped she speaks French "English bitch!"

"Taste me, baby."

Clutching her thighs, pulling her to the edge of the desk, she grabs on my hair pulling and kissing me. Her body shaking, wanting my tongue on her clit. She moves her waist in circles, while I lick all over her dripping pretty pussy. Her clit piercing between my lips, twirling my tongue around while her body shudders. She arches her back, one last time and gasps for air… easing my tongue to taste more of her but listening closely to her moaning louder. Her hand at her mouth, biting on her fist.

"Oh Aaliyah! Don't stop!"

I don't stop, I don't want to stop. What's the fun in that? I keep going, watching my fingers moving in and out of her.

Her face screwed up in a pleasure of agony, unable to take any more but not wanting me to stop. Watching me, watching her and watching me fuck her right, sucking her clit one last time. Her chest moving fast, in and out breathing heavy trying to catch her breath. Her body relaxes laying back on her desk. Wiping my chin, after feeling my little French cuisine burst onto me and drip down her desk. Taking my fingers out of her pussy slowly, her body not wanting to let me go just yet. Still tightly awaiting round two but I had to go, Stevie is waiting on me remember? Besides, there is nothing wrong with leaving them to want more.

Getting up and reaching for a scattered piece of paper to wipe my hand on while she is still out of breath and speechless. Fixing my clothes and hair, re-applying my lipstick in her mirror and removing any signs of sex off of my stance.

"You better clean this shit up, retype *all* these fucking documents and get what needs to be done for next weeks' meeting or I won't pay you a fucking penny!"

"Yes Madame… and my pay for this week?" She asks pulling up her thongs up her long legs.

"This should cover it." I pull six fifty-pound notes from my bra and walk towards her, counting them individually taking them from one hand to the other. Like most women, the sound of money excites her. Pressed up against her body, she opens her mouth wanting me to place the money between her teeth. But instead I let go of the money and it lands on the floor by her feet, as I walk towards her office door.

Walking confidently pass the faces peeking out of the surrounding offices as they whisper amongst themselves, pretending and acting like they didn't hear their manager screaming my name- I know, they know my name!

I stop and wink at the cute office temp by the printer, struggling with her stack of papers, looking in my direction, wishing she could take a copy of me to her desk instead of all those damn papers!

Elise loved to be roughed up, slapped about and have money thrown at her, as I play the role of an impossible client. No matter what she does, I had to stay committed to the role and continuously act displeased- each to their own fantasy. I guess, she needed to inject some fun into her time stuck in this office of characterless people and the grey walls they fade into, wasting away the days, weeks and months being controlled by annual salaries and paydays. Either way, I enjoyed the more dominant role, she insisted I provided to the experience of her fantasy. Sometimes all you want is a woman to lay back, allow you to do whatever the fuck you want to her and leave.

"How about lunch Aaliyah?"

Stevie suggested with her face in her phone, not bothered at all at the length of time it took me to exit. Back at the car, the driver stands, waiting to open my door. He's accustomed to my delayed departures from the 'meetings'. One hand on the open door the other hand out, discreetly with his palm facing me.

"No thanks. I just ate." I hold my hand out, palm facing him. We discreetly low-five and I hop in the car -he knows *all* about my deliberate delayed exits.

"I should've married a richer man. That way I wouldn't have to step in and do fuck all." Don't ask me what she did, because I don't pay attention to what I do. "Where were you?" She asked not caring for my answer, aggravated at her own bullshit.

"You've got a couple of hours spare until the next client you hate."

"I'd rather cancel and go shopping. Take a trip to the jewellers? What do you think?" Resting her head back, she sinks into her fur coat, calculating the money she is about to spend in her head. Her hand stretched out, admiring her rings while she played with them as they bling between her old wrinkly fingers and hands that don't match her young 'surgery' face.

My phone vibrated in my pocket, text from Elise, followed by a nude of the money in her bra:

French Boss Lady: "Same time next week… xxx"

Elise, legs wide open sat on her desk, leads me onto thoughts of Raee'n, laid out naked all over her husbands' desk with me… on top of her. Remind me to call Raee'n at some point, imagine how sexy that will be? Putting on one of those hideous ties that he leaves hanging around their house with a pair of high heels on. I'll make Raee'n wear one of his perfectly pressed pristine white shirts, buttoned right up to the top. So, she can unbutton them while I throw everything off of his desk. I'll take the tie from around my neck and tie her hands around me and-

"Look at the smile on your face! I need to meet your fiancé. A woman who can make you smile like that is good in my books."

"Fuck sake! Stevie, my sex dream was about to get to the juicy part! I was just about to sit on her face! Why did you have to open your mouth right then!? For fuck sake!" - *is* what I wanted to say…

Instead, I politely divert my attention away from the conversation. Hoping it stops her from dragging out the subject of my facial expression, because she's mistaken my minds sexual content for an emotional effect.

Do you ever get that, when you're looking at your phone? Someone has sent you a naughty text or a nude, telling you what *they* want you to do to them later and then *someone* interrupts your flow of thought with:

"Who's making you happy?"

That would be the wild, wild thoughts, generated by the nude on your phone screen, looking like a snack!

I should explain the whole fiancé thing. So, see, what happened was, I told Stevie I was in a long term committed relationship with all that extra emotional detailed bullshit that went along with that title. I lied- of course but I had to, I wanted the money and lack of responsibility this job brings. But now Stevie is under the impression that I'm *engaged*! Me? I'm even wearing a ring on my finger, to make my lie   seem   real.

My reason for the lie was this; in my opinion, employers like to see signs of long commitment and reliability. Be it professional or personal... so *naturally*, I lied. Thinking it would *never ever* come up again because I'd be far too busy managing her life for her to stop and ask me anything to do with me and mine. But with the current state of her marriage, her life is up in fucking air and she has become interested in mine. Giving me lectures and pep talks about the blunders she has made with her marriage so far. She goes on and on and on *and on* about what to do and not to do blah, blah bollocks and bull shit! Can you imagine *if* she knew who I *really* am, what I *really* get up to?

Just imagine the state of my application form if I answered the questions with *my* 'no filter, need to find my filter' and no behaviour self? My answers would have looked something like this:

Relationship Status: *Status! Bitch please, I am the status! Next question please.*

Hobbies and interest: *Cars, sex, money, having sex in the cars, having sex on money and women. Making them scream my name then leaving them mesmerized in the morning without saying goodbye.*

Employment Experience: *Previous experience terminated due to the 'husband' of former employer surprising his wife for a lunch date, to find*

she was already eating lunch, on the floor of her office... between her
assistants' legs. To clarify, I was the assistant.

Knowing all of the above, would you have hired me? Nope, didn't think so. Pretending to care about her is a whole lot easier than revealing my promiscuous and very insatiable lifestyle - not that it was any of *her* business! But I don't think Stevie would appreciate the details, including Raee'n, (the married one). When Stevie herself is on the other perspective of a cheating spouse dilemma. Feeling the torture, disappointment and stomach wrenching feeling of her husband fucking another woman. You would think I'd see the mirroring effects I'm causing in my own actions, right? Nope! I don't care! So, I continue to do what I do best – lie and *continue to* lie!

"So, when can I meet her?" Stevie pressed for an answer, I kept my attention out the window looking at the buildings surrounding the car.

"She has to fly out for work a lot so, I'm not sure." Shrugging off another lie about my imaginary spouse. I gave *her* an overpaid and overworked career. Moulding her on the girlfriends, boyfriends, wives and husbands who are never around. Stevie accepts my answer and moves on. At some point I'm going to have to get rid of this imaginary woman of mine in some miraculous, tragic and elaborate accident. I'll write her off dramatically like something out of a television soap opera.

Stepping out of the car, my phone rings in my hand, Tiana's name and pretty face on my screen. Answering and mouthing to Stevie to go ahead while I take the call. Waiting for to be out of hearing range, stepping into the brand name store, I continue.

"Talk to me baby girl."

"Right, so. I got hold of those hotels you asked me about." I hear her typing away, phone probably tucked between the side of her face and shoulder.

"What's happening?" Gradually, walking into the store brushing my hand along the clothes rails, uninterested in this 'old woman trying to hang onto my youth' brand.

"The deluxe suites have been booked."

"Okay cool what about the itinerary and schedule, baby girl?"

"Give me a bit and I'll get em' done, won't take me long. I'll call the hotels, see what's up and if they'll throw in any of that fancy bullshit in. The drivers are sorted in each destination, the cars are fucking nice! You should go!"

"Never! I need them as quick as you can. Everything you've done, email me now, okay. You got the details, right?"

"Course! I'll send them over."

"I'll transfer your money in five babes."

"Aight, no problem."

Stevie browsed her usual style of dresses and matching jackets. Bothering the sales assistant; expecting her to go above and beyond, when the poor girl is making eight-fifty an hour, finishes in fifteen minutes and doesn't give a *fuck* if there are any size tens in the back because she is not about to go *all* the way to the stockroom to check- fuck that! I'm sorry, it's out of stock!

Notifications pop up on my screen, Mali is no longer restricted to contact me through her woman's phone. I gave her my number, along with strict instructions; she can have my number *but* she *cannot* save my number. At the end of each text convo, call or face time, nudes or whatever. She has to delete it *all* off her phone-especially, with apps updating left right and centre! You need to make sure *everything* is erased and gone without a trace! No time for back up or evidence! Delete all that shit!

Mali: I can't stop thinking about u, wot have u done to me?

Nothing, she didn't want me to do. Responding in my head I place my phone in my back pocket.

"Is that your *fiancé* again!" Stevie said, holding a dress against herself in the mirror. Shaking her head, she hands it back to the sales assistant who discreetly rolls her eyes.

"No, I was finalising your hotel bookings and here *they* are." Right on time to stop her asking any more questions. Pulling out the iPad, hearing the sound of an email notification, drop in my inbox; Tiana is right on time.

I show Stevie the email confirmations with the hotel info all laid out and scheduled. She places her glasses on her face, doing what every older person does when handed a phone or smart device that is *way* out of their generation's league. Pulling it away from herself, pressing her chin to her chest trying to get her eyes and mind to figure out what the fuck she is supposed to be looking for. Once realising, she scrolls intently with one hand flicking through the digital pages in greater detail. A pinch of the screen of course, to zoom in and largen the font and...

"Nice Aaliyah! You always get things done to perfection. This is exactly why I love having you around."

"Exactly, *I* get shit done!"

If this was a nineties sitcom, like Fresh Prince of Bel Air; this would be the part where I pause out of the scene, smile deviously into the camera and say:

> *"What? Ooh, you actually thought I come to work, to work?*
> *Nah, I am a personal assistant who has a 'personal assistant'!*
> *She does the work and I get paid to look good."*
> ***queue audience laughter***

Tiana does *all* the work for me. I am far too forgetful to be able to remember anything on a regular day. Imagine when important things need to happen? No way! *Tiana* gets 'things done to perfection' and *that's* why *I* keep *her* around. Paying her to do my job leaves me plenty of time to fuck around, literally! And I did in one of their city mansions with *two* women at the *same* time- no not a threesome, I'm far too selfish for all of that! They didn't have a clue one another was there, because there is enough square footage to get lost in and play hide and seek the pussy. I'm talking east wing, west wing kind of shit! Oh, you think I'm joking? Let me tell you a story *real quick…*

This one time, I took this woman- what was her name now? I'm going to call her Miss Big Booty because that is what I remember. Anyway, we went to one of the mansions and we had a great fucking time! But she didn't take the hint and leave when we were done. Fascinated with the size of the house and the fancy things about the place- including me, obviously!

"This place is amazing. I don't want to leave!" She said laid out on the bed naked and annoying! Yeah, she was gorgeous and had a banging body. She was your typical Instafamous generic looking, big booty bikini modelling, jump in her dm's with a one liner 'not' about her appearance, because she's so used to swerving type of chick. I lost count of the times, I told Miss Big Booty to leave?! I wasn't like I was subtle about it either; how many times can you say:

"You need to leave. I've got things to do."

"Okay, how about I stay here while you do what needs to be done. And I'll be here, naked and waiting on you to get back?"

Welp! can't argue with that- sex on the return, why the fuck not? It's wasn't my house, so whatever!

Me being me, I took my time to return. Staying out the whole day… and night. She wanted to stay there and wait, so she can stay there… and wait! While I went out to the club with another lady, Miss Cute- we also had a great fucking time.

The night had come to an end, the club was finished, I was finished- I had way too much to drink. I jumped in a friend's Uber, because I could not remember where I parked my car!

So, everyone was being dropped off to their separate destinations- goodnights, goodbyes and see you laters, no worries. I know I'm the furthest destination so, I chill back, take a nap. Get myself some rest before Miss Big Booty Deejailee- Deejailee, that was her name!

Anyway, I hear:

"Last drop off ladies." Thinking to my half-asleep self, did he just say, ladies? As in more than one?

Opening my eyes in the Uber, expecting to be the last in there but no, no. Miss Cute from the club was in the front seat! Looking back at me like 'honey we're home' and I'm looking back like 'ooh shit!'

"Erm what do you mean last drop?" I asked the driver, adjusted my eyes to the daylight.

"Last drop, this is it!"

"No, you need to take her home!" I held up forty pounds on top of what he was already getting paid!

"I'm sorry ma'am, I'm done. Shift finished, I'm going home now."

So? Take her with you, shit!

"Oh, okay, I see you!" I took out another twenty-pound note, adding it to my already generous tip that Uber wasn't getting a cut of. I needed him to take this chick home! I couldn't take her in there! Miss Big Booty is waiting on me!

Meanwhile Miss Cute has her eyes fixated on me, giving me the 'I wanna fuck, so let's fuck' face and I needed to figure out how the fuck, I was going to play this one- or two out. I do not want or need these two women to see each other.

So, I sober up and I text Miss Big Booty inside, to make sure she was in the bedroom:

Me: "Go get in the bed NOW! I'm coming for you!"
Mss Big Booty: "I am already in it! Hurry up!"

"Hey! Listen! My cousin is here and she's sick. She's sleeping upstairs, so I'm going to need you to be quiet, okay?" I had to think of a lie really quickly, to make sure this all went smoothly but Miss Cute was drunk as fuck! I held her face, to get her to focus on what I was saying.

"Got it, keep quiet, yup. I can do that. Done. Cousin sleep, no problem." She formed a sentence of disconnected words. But she understood me. Leaning on my back, I took cautious steps into the house. Looking from my left, then to my right, making sure Miss Big Booty was out of fucking sight!

Dragging Miss Cute through the house and into one of the guest rooms downstairs, tucking her into the bed tight! Keeping them at a great distance from each other, making sure neither of them get out of the bed and go explore like Dora.

"Be quiet, okay." I reminded her.

"Why don't you come here and keep my mouth shut?" She took off her little black dress. Listen, if it meant her staying right where she was while our clits connected, grinding, moaning muffled with my hand over her mouth until she came and went the fuck to sleep then why not?

Hearing my name being called from the other side of the house- I needed to get to Miss Big Booty, before she got up to look for me.

Making sure Miss Cute was asleep, I shut the bedroom door, kicked off my heels in different directions and sprinted up the stairs, faster than Usain Bolt to the finish line. Fixed myself at the bedroom door and sure enough, Miss Big Booty was wide awake, naked, legs wide open waiting for me- as requested. I took off my clothes and jumped on her.

"Listen," I said, "we need to be quiet, okay."

"Why? Who's here?" Don't ask questions woman!

"My (pause for thought) my cousin's downstairs sleeping. She's a mess. (pause for effect) She had an argument with her woman and I don't want to be all loud and inconsiderate."

"Is she okay?" She asked concerned

"She's good. Anyway, seeing as though you have to be quiet... let me tie you up, so you can't move."

I pull out a silk dressing gown belt out of nowhere! I don't know where it came from, all I know is that I need these two to stay away from each other. So, if I tie her to the bed, she couldn't move. Trust me to end up with two women in the same house at the same damn time! Honestly!

"Aaliyah!" Just as we climax, I hear Miss Cute downstairs calling my name! For fuck sake! What is this?! I am not a machine, to be up and down this house like it was some cardio work out!

"Yes!" Before I stepped into the room and caught what little breath I had left, she dragged me down, threw me onto the bed and was between my legs,

"Remember, be quiet…"

"Fuck her?" – I just did! But this time it was my time to be quiet and that wasn't easy, I'm telling you Miss Cutes' head game was so fucking good!

"Aaliyah!" Hearing my name again from upstairs. You have got to be fucking kidding me! I thought that bitch was asleep! But she was calling on me for round two, when I was on round three or four. Who knows, I lost count- don't you dare count how many times!

Getting up, my legs are shaking like Bambi's first steps. Staggering out the room, trying to hurry my weak legs up this big for no damn reason, grand staircase! Holding onto the banister for dear life! Dying but laughing at myself for getting into this mess. I swear, shit like this would only happen to me! Me!?
By this point I am shattered! Back downstairs, pussy throbbing, body tired, legs weak like SWV. Head banging and caught in that weird place, where you are kind of drunk but kind of sober and kind of hanging all at the same damn time.

"What!" I have literally nothing left after the typhoon I just released downstairs, which was probably trailing behind me and dripping on the marble floors. Out of breath, out of everything and ready to tap the fuck out! Done! No more, leave me alone, I want to take a nap right here- goodnight!?

"I just want to cuddle. Come here." She pats the mattress beside her.

For the first time in my life, I was down to cuddle because I was worked by these women, these stairs and this bull shit assault course of a fucking mansion they had me running through was no joke!

"Aaliyah!"

My eyes shot open, trying to figure out what time of day it was. It was way into the afternoon and I had to get one of them out of this damn house!

I jumped out the bed and ran down the stairs, Miss Cute was already up awake and alert, no longer drunk and ready to leave.

"My Uber is here." She shows me Uber up and on its way on her phone. "I need

to get home to my lady before she starts her shit. I'm surprised she hasn't started."

"Alright, I'll call you." I escorted her out the house to her Uber, making sure she got in the car. Besides I like to watch her move with her elegant classy, 'fuck me but don't tell nobody' body, Kitagirl921 looking ass!

"No, you won't." She and gives me a kiss and just as she did, I saw Miss Big Booty at the door on her tiptoes, lurking and stretching herself to see who I am with... who 'my cousin' is.

"Okay bye!" I shoved Miss Cute into the Uber, waved her off and turned back to Miss Big Booty.

"Aaliyah?"

"Yeah?"

"Your cousin looks so familiar...?" She said looking like she was trying to place 'my cousins' familiar face in her mind.

"Does she?" I asked smirking to myself. "Hmm, you sure?"

"Yeah? I've seen her before, I'm sure. She looks soo familiar. I recognise her from somewhere? I don't know?" She shrugged it off, unable to find the familiarity and so did I.

"She gets that a lot. She's just got one of those faces, you know?"
"Yeah? Maybe?"

See the problem with The Scene being so small, is that you are bound to find yourself in a *scenario* where the women you are fucking with and are seeing separately, know of or *know* each other. And in this scenario, my scenario- these two women in particular... wait for it... wait for the tea, the milk and the cream! Kettle boiled yet? Are you ready to take a sip?

Maybe Miss Big Booty recognises *her* from *their* photos... together on Instagram all loved up and hash tagging statuses *ooor* maybe she recognises her, when she goes home later today, when she tells her the lie of how much *fun* she had on her girls' trip weekend because that's her woman!!!

Yes! The two of them, Miss Big Booty and Miss Cute are in a *relationship* and cheating on each other with *me*! And that, ladies and gentlemen is why I *needed* to keep them away from each other! Out of sight, out of mind.

You've got to admit it though; I'm *so* fucking good at being bad! I did say, women like that are generic. I saw them both one night at the club and they had heads turning in *every* direction. The two of them looked so damn stunning together! But together, they thought they were *too* nice. So, I thought... it would be a bit banter and fun to get them both and have them *both* keep me secret from each other. I didn't approach them that night, no. I went to the place where secrets are kept and it goes deep down in the dm's. All it took was some scrolling and hashtag searching to find their 'couple page' then I targeted them individually. I wanted them both and it's not as if what we get up to, would be a topic of their conversations during pillow talk, so why not? It was something new, something challenging and something I've never tried before and it was fucking worth it! #couplegoals

10. The Blackened Memories

"I mean Blue, *really?* Why would I want *your* woman? She's so far from *my* type and has absolutely *nothing* I want. I need a woman who can bring something to the table *I* have provided. It was just like I told you, nothing more than a spontaneous thoughtless moment *(Pause for effect, softer tone for delivery, hang head down slightly)* I wasn't thinking babe *(look up, slight sad side head tilt with a bottom lip drop but don't overdo it)* I didn't mean to hurt you in anyway." *(Sorry, not sorry bitch!)*

Watching her twiddle her thumbs, she bites the inside of her mouth looking like she's got it all wrong, like she should have *never* even come at me with *these* accusations at all... she opens her mouth

"No babe... *I'm* sorry" (Jackpot) "I should have *never* questioned you it's, see. I have this thing about trust and all that and I, erm. I didn't want to put it all on you but I had to ask, you know? To clear things up?"

That's right guys, dolls, bitches and hoes; we find ourselves, or more so *I* find *myself* back at the point where you came in... where the story began. Well, for you anyway.

I left it a few days until calling Blue back, which gave Mali enough time to be dedicated to her 'woman'. Have all the make-up sex necessary to fuck her body *and* mind right back into place. To place her on a pedestal, treat her like the queen she is and reinstall that stability into their relationship. However, Blue wanted to hear my version of events, to validate my loyalty in our state of friendship. What was there to tell? My actions don't need to have moral, they just are!

Blue's questioning me did not faze me because mind games are all the same. Trust me, you don't have to be fucking a woman to be able to fuck with her mind. All it takes is a few manipulative choices of words, along with a few compliments, apologies and maybe a gift to shut her, the fuck up.

How many times have you heard the sentences?

"I'm sorry baby, I never mean to hurt you."
"You're my everything, I'm not going anywhere."
"You're the most important person in my life right now, I'm not about to lose you.

You forgive and forget like nothing ever happened, happy as fuck to move on with no effort and no work done to reinstall what threw your relationship off balance. Unaware that you're now receptive for the same bullshit to happen again and again and *again*, because *you* my friend have just let acceptance take over and lower your expectations, allow me to explain.

Note: *Exceptions over Acceptances*
Women (or men of a *feminine* nature) in relationships accept shit on a daily basis; because of an easily pleased sense of ego. Don't get me wrong, I don't speak for *all* women out there- just… the majority, that make allowances for their other half to continue to behave a certain way. Women are the first to over analyse *everything* in a situation other than *themselves* when expectations are not met. Taking absolutely no accountability for what *they* accepted and allowed and continue to allow to happen.

This happens in both relationships and friendships but let me stop right there, I'm not here to help you, I'm here to help *myself*!! So, let me get back to Blue and this whole *'why were you out with my woman'* situation- and just like before. If you remember from chapter one, Blue was talking bullshit and going on and on about being friends forever, about trust, about loyalty and honesty and blah. Blah fucking blah!!
I stopped listening to Blue's speech a good while back, blocking out her irritating trying to be somebody she wasn't type of voice. Either way, I wasn't stressed about anything at all, as I have already pre-coached Mali on what to say but more importantly what *not* to say. It's all *fool* proof. Blue's suspicions will disappear in an instant.

Watching Mali, inside, chilling. Following the words Mali's beautiful lips form trying to figure out what song she is singing along to. Zoning out to the music lost in her own vibe. I wish I could leave this stupid balcony, this dry arse solo conversation, climb through the window and get lost inside Mali.

Looking up at me, as if she senses me day dreaming in her direction; I smile at her...she smiles back... coyly, swiftly then diverts the attention of her eyes onto anything else but me, before Blue could even notice our stolen moment...

"So that's cool?" Blue asked me.

"Yeah, one hundred percent." I have no idea what the fuck I agreed to do but whatever it was, it's shut her up. Thank fuck! "Are we done here, with this?" I got up stretching off this one-sided conversation.

She opens the window and climbs back into the room, diving straight on top of Mali. I step in after, pulling my sunglasses away from my eyes to the top of my head, having told all the lies I need to tell today.

"Okay ladies, I'm off."

"I thought you said you were gonna chill?" See *this* is the problem about zoning out. When you *decide* to zone back in, you could have agreed to sell your soul. "*Mali* said give one of your ladies a call and we can hit up a club."

"Oh, you did, did you Mali?"

"Yeah...I did," Mali spoke confidentially, she wants to play games? Obviously, she doesn't know *who* I am and the games *I* run. You know I will be more than happy to call one of my ladies over. If she thinks I'm jealous of *this* little 'honeymoon' faze they've got going on here, then she can think again. First of all; I was the one who fixed all of this. I told her what to do *and* what to say to get her fuckery of a relationship back right! That was me, all me, not her! I did this! I'm out here fixing relationships and building them back up like my name is Bob the mother fucking Builder! Urgh!

***

Mali thought she could handle seeing my attention elsewhere but I can see the green glimmer of jealousy in her eyes and that inflaming thirst for me getting stronger. She's full of frustration but acting nonchalant, watching my hands feel and grip Raee'ns body. Raee'n was my first choice, she wanted time away from all the fucking and anti-social bedroom behaviour. Having her over here with these two meant she didn't have to talk to me much because of all the free-flowing conversations between all of them. I kept my silence and observed the occupants of the room, interested in the comparison of the chemistry. Mali wasn't happy with Raeen's presence, however, Blue seemed to be rather intrigued by her and she might be able to get a taste, *if* I play this to *my* advantage.

"Show them Raee'n!"

I demanded Raee'n show them, or more so Blue her amazing sex face! No one can resist her daring eyes, her pouting lips and sexual intensity, making anyone anticipate her.

"Turns you on, doesn't she?" I encourage Blue with subtle banter.

"*Shit!*" Blue leant back against the wall, looking at Raee'n in a way that she knows she *shouldn't* be. Lusting and wanting what she can't have. Oh yes! Temptation has gotten a hold of Blue.

I have figured it all out during my time of playing around with a variety of women, that *all* people have weaknesses. Things that spark an interest and have them fall off their path of righteousness. Be it a cheat day on a diet or... a cheat day in a relationship, it's all the same thing. Okay, so it's a *very* wide field of comparison but let's face it; it's still a lack of commitment all the same. What usually sparks it is a compromising position, for example:

On a diet and someone comes your way with a chocolate or treat, telling you how good it tastes, tempting you to take a bite. Not to worry, no one's looking.

It's the same as say… a friend bringing a stunning chocolate skinned tone snack of a woman to your house. *Particularly* when your girlfriend has made you feel a type of way about trust and anything else you can think of that will make it okay for you to take just one bite. After all, one bite won't hurt… *especially,* when no one is looking?

"I think I'm actually wet." Blue said unintentionally, quickly slapping both her hands over her mouth. Her eyes darting around hoping no one heard what she was *supposed* to say in her head. But we *all* heard every word clearly. Raee'n and I turned to each other laughing.

"Relax boo. It's only for this sexy woman right here!" Raee'n laughed and turned to me. I wait for her lips to meet my kiss, slowly parting my lips inviting her tongue into my mouth and stroke over mine.

"And your husband? Right?" Mali interrupts our kiss with petty facts.

"It's shady over there." Raee'n accepts the statement of truth, "But what he doesn't know… won't hurt him, right," She directs her words to Blue then places her lips back on mine. Blue is still hung up on the sex face. Raee'n pulls me towards her, kissing and biting my neck. I can feel Blue and Mali watching us, like we're a series on Netflix. Raee'ns hands in places they couldn't see, acting up to it all. Kissing, grabbing, touching and feeling on each other. We turn to them slowly and they are captivated by us.

"Stop" I smack her thigh and point my finger in her face playfully.

"Shut up and kiss me!" Raee'n keeps her gaze on me and my body.

"There *are* people in the room Raee'n" I said, pretending to blush.

"Don't act like we ain't never had us an audience before girl."

"Shut up!" I look over at Mali, discreetly.

"I'm gonna get you another drink, you need to loosen up. Come show me where the kitchen is." She stood up mischievously, holding her tongue between her teeth.

"No, Blue can show you where it is" I wanted to see how Mali would react.

"It's downstairs; I'll show you where."

Blue happily leads Raee'n out of the room. Happy to get a minute or two to myself, pretending to like Raee'ns company is tiring as fuck! I do *not* know how people in relationships entertain each other for so damn long!? It's only been a couple of hours of having her here and I am done! I need a cigarette break, take five, a Kit Kat- something!

Out of nowhere, Mali is right by me. She smacked the cigarette right out of my hand. I'm confused, looking past her at the empty spot where she was sat trying to figure out *how* she got over here so damn quick and *why* she smacked my cigarette out of my hand?!

"What the hell are you doing?"

"Trying to smoke a fucking cigarette, the fuck does it look like I'm doing?"

I take another out of the packet.

"She's all over you, I can't-she," Mali stutters, frustrated, not getting words out.

"Can't what?? It was your *bright* idea- now she's here!" I relit my cigarette between my lips. Inhaling and blow the smoke out slowly in her face, "Deal with it, baby!"

"Fuck you Aaliyah!" She smacks me across the face. Glaring at me, pleased with herself. My hand immediately sprung up, because she's fucking crazy if she thinks she can just put her hands on me!! But she glowed, waiting for my retaliation. Bringing my hand slowly towards her face, I stroked her cheek softly, running my fingers under her chin and holding her gently. Hand on the back of her neck, dragging her towards me, I give her the attention she wanted with a kiss and her face quickly brightens.

"Come here beautiful."

"Blue's gonna be back in a sec?"

"Don't worry Raee'n is keeping her busy."

Pushing Mali down on the bed and onto her back, climbing on top of her. Sitting at her waist, running my hands up her body and her arms, holding her wrists above her head, her body locked between my thighs. I bite the side of her neck, she moans a little, not caring that her woman is *only* a few steps away from walking in on us in this *very* compromising position- love it!

"Aaliyah stop, someone's coming..." Her eyes darting back and forth from the door at the sound of footsteps edging closer and closer; my body not moving from on top of hers.

"What's your point? I only want to touch it." Tilting my head to the side, knowing there's now approximately three or four steps left for *whoever* it is returning to the bedroom and Mali has no control. Well, she wanted my attention and now she's got it... on top of her, enticing and encouraging her to open her legs, give in and let me slide my fingers around her clit.

"Nah, seriously," she struggles and whispers, enjoying my touch but scared as fuck "Come on, get off."

"You don't sound like you want me to stop." Mocking her, I take my hand out of her jeans, she watches me suck on my finger slowly. Her eyes go straight into panic, suddenly throwing me off of her- I hit the floor with a loud thud.

"Hey babe," Mali says suspiciously as Blue enters the room.
Blue looks over at me slumped on the floor, then back at Mali with that stupid stressed smile stretched across her face.

"What's going on?" Nervous and unsure of what she's walked in on. Sensing a shift of dynamics in the atmosphere.
The way Mali threw me off of her was fucking hilarious! I would have got off of her in time but I like to push the intensity. There's no harm in adding a higher level of dangerous rush of excitement to the element of getting caught. Otherwise, what's the fucking point?? Mali's heart is going to be excited and skipping beats like a white girl trying to dance.

"Mali was just telling me a dirty little secret." I laugh

"What!?" Blue's eyes bulge out of her head.

"Blue, relax! I'm Joking!"

285

"Okay, sure, no worries" Blue's panic left her body, she sounded a little flustered herself. Blue what have you been up to?

"Wait a minute! What did Raee'n do to you?" I point at her smiling and teasing- I'm terrible.

"Excuse me?" Mali did not appreciate the idea of her woman up to no good but is more than happy to let me taste her when I want- double standards these days.

"*Relax* Mali, nothing happened!" Blue's starting to sound like me- all confident. Do you see what temptation does to you, yes Blue! I am here for this!

"Oh, I know Raee'n. What did she do?" I point at her with my cigarette lit between my two fingers. The confidence lasted two point five seconds. She doesn't know where to look, so tucks her chin into her chest, blushing.

"What the fuck happened??" Mali asks, not liking this one bit

"Oh, ignore Mali. I'm sure she knows, looking is *just* looking. As long as your *looking* doesn't lead to touching or *fucking*... now that's a *hoe* different situation."
Blue doesn't answer, she stares off into a different direction trying to get out of the spotlight I'm putting on her. Mali is waiting on an answer; she's fucking *pissed*! I'm planting thoughts of another woman in Blue's *head*. I don't see why Mali gets to have all the fun?

***

The night's events thickened as we ended up in a bar. I'm entertained by Raee'n currently all over Blue. On the way over here, I pulled Raee'n aside and told her to have just the right amount of fun with Blue, in order to tease and mislead her further down the wandering path of my good old friend temptation.

Let's be real, Blue is affected by Mali and the feeling of distrust doesn't go away overnight. She is hurt and feeling vulnerable that her women chose to go out without her and had a great time with another woman. So why couldn't she do the same? Although, the fuel behind her current actions of possible deceit is Mali.

I have made sure it has nothing to do with me, I am in the all clear and back in the shining spectrum of *"friendships"* over *"relationships"*, bros before hoes or as us lesbians say:

Chicks before Clits!

This is all for the simple but yet *very* calculated and *very* well-planned purpose of leverage.

Leverage *verb*

Use of borrowed capital (Raee'n) for an investment (Mali), expecting profits made to be greater than the investment payable (Blue)

"A leveraged takeover bid." - I told you it was simple.

Raee'n would complete the task at hand, with ease and great pleasure. Mali might need the leverage of this whole situation to counteract the attack *if* Blue ever caught us.

Example:

"I can't believe you're sleeping with Aaliyah!"

Mali can get her with:

"Oh! So, you didn't do shit with Raee'n then, huh Blue!?"

Blue would be all like:

"That's different Mali! It's not the same, how could you? She's my friend!"

Mali will shout all emotional:

"Why the fuck do you think I did that?! I had to make you feel what you did to me!"

Then Blue would be apologetic like:

"I never mean to hurt you, it just happened."

Mali would come back with:

"Yeah, well, I meant to hurt you! You broke my heart, I fucking loved you!"

Blue would apologise, feeling it all slip away:

"I'm so sorry, please... let's talk about it"

Then Mali would be all sexy with the smoulder as she leaves:

"Nothing to talk about, it's too late- I'm done!"

Blue would be regretting what happened that 'one night in Heaven'- And, scene! As you can tell, I've pictured this all unravelling in my head and in the very vividly, word for word. Because once Raee'n gets Blue where *I* want her, she can do whatever she wants as long as I get every single detail! And by the looks of things, Blue is one more drink away from a conscious state of emotional weakness, where *anything* could happen. Once it's all over with; there will be a continuance of Raee'n texting inappropriate kinds of things, along with nudes encouraging Blue to text some filthy things back. I will be sent the screenshots, conversations and messages. Then all I have to do is forward Mali the evidence provided of what's really been going down in the DM's. See, that's the beauty of all this smart technology shit, it's 'smart' when you use it to your advantage. We *all* know that one friend or *we are* that one friend who has a backlog, stash and library of screenshots, conversations, messages, photos and nudes (send nudes) that the person on the receiving end doesn't know you have. But they are all kept, like receipts, evidence and exhibits from *A* all the way to *Z*. Because you *never* know when you'll need them in a courtroom full of your peers. So, I'll just sit back, sip on my drink and enjoy the show...

"That shit doesn't bother you?" Mali stands beside me, talking close enough for me to smell the alcohol on her breath. Unbothered to talk to her or give her any attention at all right now, I'm preoccupied.

"No."

"Really?"

"Raee'n can get close to *whoever* she wants and do whoever she wants."

"...So, you're okay with all of... *that*?" She points at them, making sure I can see the inappropriateness between them.

Swivelling my bar stool towards Mali, seductively running my hand up her thigh and grabbing the belt loop on her denim jeans, yanking on it. She stumbles a little step towards me, I continue to run my hand up her waist, brushing over her breast, trailing my fingers along her collar bone to the side of her neck. Giving her a gentle scratch, I open my mouth and she slowly leans into my lips, unable to resist. Turning my lips towards her ear;

"Raee'n and I are *just* fucking. It doesn't matter what she does or what I do" I kiss Mali's lips softly "but..." I grip the bottom of her jaw and chin, my nails pressing into her skin I turn her face, making sure she' s can *see* "*Blue is* your woman, so shouldn't '*all* of *that* shit' be bothering you? Look at them!" Letting go of her face, leaving my nail dents in her skin and her to gather her thoughts. I divert my attention to the cutie on my right-hand side that's been looking in my direction but too shy to come over. I walk over to her, talking directly in her ear and she giggles and blushes in an instant. Mali is torn; not knowing whether to drag her woman away from Raee'n or to tell the cutie I was talking to fuck off, drag *me* somewhere in this club and handle me. What would you do?

"Aaliyah, why are fucking with my head like this?" Making the choice I knew she would, Mali tugs on my arm.

"I thought you wanted me to *fuck* with your head? No? You know, Mali... green really *isn't* your colour babe." Burning from my words, her fists balled up.

"Nu-uh baby girl remember… it's still *my* turn to get you back. So, un-ball your fist, run along and go the fuck away!" Strong, dominant and dismissive as always. I smile all cute and scrunch up my shoulders followed by a nonchalant flick of my hair. Walking away, taking the hand of the cutie, who's name I have already forgotten and lead her to the dance floor. Mali is left with her corrupted thoughts of what to do next.

Silly rabbit, tricks are for kids.

***

Opening my eyes to the low lights of my apartment. How the fuck did I get home, what the fuck is going on?! Last thing I knew I was in the club. Now I'm here in my bed, where the fuck is everyone?

Sitting up, holding my head feeling the base drumming headache kick in. Fuck, not again! Jumping at the feel of someone in my bed who I cannot see in the darkness. Squinting, moving closer, Raee'n laying in my bed beside me.

"You okay?"

"Where's everyone?" Confused by the silence and stillness of being home "Downstairs."

"What!?!" I jump up at the thought of Mali and Blue in my apartment and alone. How did this happen!? They're *all* back at my apartment and I agreed to this? Urgh! I hate people over here in my space, for fuck sake! They're grown, they have two legs, an Oyster card and a phone full of all kinds of apps that can get them home, they don't need to be here!

"They're asleep. What's up Aaliyah?" She asks again, laying her head back down on the pillow half asleep, stroking my arm.

"Why are we here? When did we get here?"

"We all came here, you said it was okay, don't you remember?"

"No?! I don't remember a thing!"

Leaning over the balcony railing of my bedroom, I see them both snuggled up on my sofa. This was *not* part of the plan! The plan was, go to the club and get waved. Raee'n fuck with Blue, get her to do some incriminating shit, tell me then we leave and go our separate ways-done! I told you, zoning in and out of a conversation is a mother fucker. I swear, I need to take my own advice and pay *attention* but the things that go on in my head are *so* much more entertaining... what was I saying? Oh, okay, so I shouldn't have drunk as much as I did. At least, I think I did but I don't feel drunk. Just dizzy and disorientated. I don't remember agreeing to a "slumber party" at my place, there are way too many people up in here right now and my head is banging, fuck!

"You sure you're okay?" Raee'n peered over at me stood by the mezzanine railings of my bedroom. Holding my throbbing head, which is trying to fucking kill me!

"Take a wild fucking guess!? I *hate* people over here! I don't even want you here! This wasn't the plan, what the fuck happened Raee'n?"

"You told me to get Blue drunk?!"

"No, I told you to get Blue waved, not Amy Winehouse white girl paralytic!"

"Look! Your place was close, I haven't been sleeping, I've been up all night recently, because... of the-"

"First of all," I cut her off, one hand pressing my fingers on my left temple, the other pointing at her, "don't raise your voice. Second, if you're so damn tired, *why* are you awake and talking? Shut up and Sleep!"

I'm done listening to her, she's talking and not giving me any fucking answers. Like, *how* did we get here? *When* did we get here? She's comfortable in my bed and I'm lost...

Leaving her and cursing to myself. I walk away and carefully make my way down the stairs on the balls of my feet. Creeping quietly in my own fucking house, this is ridic-u-lous!

Feet firmly downstairs, walking slowly towards the sofa, unimpressed by the current two occupants taking up the whole damn thing with their bodies, without my permission. Blue is curled up in a ball with my blanket on top of her, face nestled into Mali's lap. Mali has fallen asleep sitting up with her hand resting on Blue's back. Probably soothing her as she found it hard to sleep with all the alcohol forced into her system by Raee'n. I should wake them up and tell them to get the fuck out my house but what's the point? They're already here and the image of them all snuggled up on each other, on *my* sofa is now imprinted in my mind, removing the memory of Mali and me on the sofa the other night.

I continue to search for the answers of how we all got here in the first place. I know I keep asking myself but maybe I can figure it out. I'm so lost and I can't think how? It's all a blur of bright lights, alcohol, drugs, music and laughter. But I *must* have let them in? Unless… wait, nope, nothing- blank! Maybe I should just drop the whole thing but I don't like to forget things and somethings just slip my mind, like the pinnacle point of the night of how we all got here.

There're glasses on the coffee table along with signs of social entertainment. But I do not remember a fucking thing! My mind has chosen to steal that memory and replace it with questions and confusion.

"You know Aaliyah… *green* really isn't your colour babe."

Mali opened her eyes to me pacing the room and my thoughts to myself and mistaking my misperception for jealousy over their intimacy and closeness on my sofa. Caught up in my confusion of events. Repeating me, mocking my words from the club- see, I remember that?

"What are you talking about?" I ask.

"Jealousy" She whispers.

"Please, I'm trying to figure out…" I watch her brazenly let go of Blue and stretch towards the coffee table and pick up a spliff. She cannot be fucking serious? Eyes on me, as she takes the lighter out of her pocket *"Don't you dare light that in here!?"*

Ignoring me, she sparks her lighter. Clearly, she wants to get dragged, she thinks I'm playing.

"Yo, wait, hold up. Stop, Aaliyah!" Before she could bring the spliff to the flame, I grab her up by the shoulder of her top and drag her through my apartment, open the balcony door, shove her outside and shut the door. She can stay out there! No one smokes weed in my fucking apartment! Is she crazy!?

Someone, please tell me I'm dreaming, this is a nightmare! I close my eyes and rest my head back against the glass door, breathing through blank spaces. Mali taps the window lightly, opening my eyes I turn to face her. She's waving at me to come and join her outside, I open the sliding balcony glass door.

"What do you want?"

"Come chill with me." She insists while I zip up my hoody but only to the bottom of my bra leaving enough breasts exposed for her prying eyes.

"I would but Raee'n, she… *wants* me." I point up at my room and made an attempt to leave. Not that I was going up to Raee'n anytime soon but she didn't need to know that.

"So, *I* want you now. You know they kissed, right?" Placing her hand on my waist.

"Excuse me?" I say, like it wasn't me that instigated the whole thing.

"Raee'n and Blue?"

Letting go of my waist, stepping away from me she takes a seat one of the chairs outside. Pleased with herself like she's giving me the 'tea' thinking she's telling me something I don't already know- how cute. She's waiting for my opposition to play, I wasn't going to tell her because now, I've decided I may just use it to my advantage more than hers. She puffs on her spliff, blowing circles into late air of the dark early morning. So sexy with it, sat back all bossy telling me to come and sit with her by patting her lap.

"What's your point?" I stand over her, not taking up the invitation of her lap just

yet.

"So, dot, dot, dot *you*...owe *me* a kiss." She remains cool, cocky and assured.

"How did you come to that conclusion? Raee'n was up on *your* woman, what does that have to do with me?" Sitting down on her lap, she wraps her arm around me and I place an arm over her shoulder, stroking the back of her neck with my fingertips, she closes her eyes enjoying my gentle touch.

"It's a basic mathematical equation, you know, quick maths. One plus some." She pulls on my zip, opening my hoody and holds my thigh. Her current state of high has her thinking out loud and making no sense at all, she wants to play but this is *my* game, always has been baby!

"Whatever Mali, I'm going to bed." Getting up, my body language was making her believe she was in control for a brief moment then. She threw her finished spliff over the balcony, and hurries after me. Sometimes, I enjoy a good old-fashioned chase.

"Hold up a sec Aaliyah." Stopping me from opening the door all the way, she holds onto my arm. Her eyes darting over me and to the sofa, checking the slumber of her woman. Mali's not on my level of risqué - my level of risqué is having 'zero fucks' to give.

"What do you want Mali?" I spoke louder, on purpose, laughing. While her eyes stressed and her head shook 'no'.

"Shut up Aaliyah! Jus' come." She pulls me away from the doors and back onto the balcony. Slowly closing the door shut, watching to see if Blue has stirred or made any movement.

Waiting for Mali to turn back to me knowing *exactly* what I'm about to do. My hand ready to swing on her face.

"What the fuck!" Mali held the side of her face, cupping it with both hands. I'm very satisfied with myself and the sound of the slap. Grabbing my arms in either hand squeezing me tight, I can already feel the bruises she's going to cause on my skin.

She kisses my lips slowly, her grip on me does not loosen. This contrast of pain and pleasure feels so good. We pause... letting me go, I stay, stood by her. My hands resting on her chest, her heartbeat matching mine. Why is my heart beating like this? Every time she touches me or looks in my direction. It's like I... I can't explain, it's like we, I mean she...? My eyes can't keep still, looking at her *everything*. Holding her face... she's... I don't know, I just... I.

"Come..."

Taking my hand gently, this time. She walks me over to the corner of the balcony that tucks away and out of sight of the big windows.

I watch her footsteps in front of mine, as they quietly step along the wooden decked balcony flooring. Leading my bare feet, stepping over where she wants me to go. Her footsteps stop, turn towards mine and step together. I watch her hand let go of mine as our fingertips gradually disconnect. She places her hands back on my waist comfortably. She pulls me in towards her and my feet step closer to hers. Caught in a trance of the way her body moves mine towards her, with the way she touches me. She lifts my chin gently; we stand facing each other in this second that I can't explain.

Her arms around me and mine around her. Closer, attracted and magnetic. I didn't notice the time pass us by... It seems to do that, to drift and escape me. These days, I blink and I don't know how I got from one place to the other. My mind drifts from one thing to another and all of a sudden, the days have changed and we're standing here together saying nothing at all, in our silence... in this *nothing* but something that we have started.

Does our silence mean we are both overthinking things, wondering, what we're doing? Or does it mean we are both okay with what *is* happening or *not* happening between us? Are we both trying to make sense of this chaotic beautiful mess we...? I made?

Is my silence waiting for her to put into words what I can't say, what I don't know how to say? Or is the silence because there is nothing left to say? Can she understand me through my silence and unspoken words?

Watching over her at the sky lightening up as it begins to change to the day ahead. Do you ever think, what if? What if the night doesn't want to leave the sky? It has no choice, time needs to change... days need to pass, you need to let go and move on. But what if the sky had a choice? Would it stay dark or light? Sometimes thoughts enter my mind and I let them take over, step out of them and let them be, even if they don't make sense, they're only thoughts after all.

Mali hands haven't moved away from me. You know, I never realised until standing beside her, how small I am compared to her and how much of her covers me in the morning breeze. My mouth subtly shoots a smile up at her. Her eyes on me, gazing all over me. Finding myself drawn to look at her even when I don't want to.

"You never told me... I want you to tell me..." She finally speaks, concerned, soft and thoughtful. Like she's been trapped in her own thoughts and wondering about   mine.

"Tell you what?" I preferred the silence of guessing what was on her mind and chasing my thoughts into the black hole of my wonders.

"Tell me..."

"There's nothing to tell..."

"Yes, there is..." lightly taking my chin in her hand, changing the direction of my face until my eyes set back on her face and her eyes locked into mine not looking away "Tell me why you're like this? Tell me why you don't give anyone the chance to get too close to you… the real you? Not the woman you have to be but the one you really are. What are you hiding?" Waiting for me to answer but I don't have the answers.

"Please stop." My head starting to beat louder than the palpitation in my chest, she's too close for comfort.

"Tell me *everything*. Give me the chance. I want to know about your scars…. all of them, not jus' the ones I've seen. You can tell me, you can trust me." Mali attempts to open up the Pandora's Box within me… how can I tell her? She looks down at my arm, where my hoody hangs loosely off my shoulder. Her eyes following the tattoos etched deep into the epidermis of my skin. Her hand moves, holding my shoulder and gently rubbing her thumb over the lines that form the top half of my traditional Japanese Koi Carp tattoo sleeve. I know she's isn't feeling the lines of the tattoo. No, her eyes and her fingers have found them, she can see *them*… she knows I have the answers and don't *want* to answer.

"I know they're there; most people don't see them. Most people look over you but I see you, jus' like you see me. I felt safe to tell everything. Holding nothing back. No one knows the things you do. I trust *you* Aaliyah and you can trust me. You can tell me."

She spoke with her focus on my skin. Fingertips trailing along the lines of my scars, I thought no one could see. No one notices them and I've never stayed in anyone's company long enough, to get close enough. It's easy to keep a distance and push people away and keep them hidden.

"There's nothing to tell…" I want to tell her everything but where do I start. There's so much to say but it's been kept away, along with the blackened memories and things I've locked away.

11. The Way She...

"So, what do you want?"

She asked me, I sat with my back to her; my head tilted back, looking up at *her* looking at me the way she does. That beautiful smile laced across her face, her dimples sinking into each cheek. I love the way she looks at me, I love the way she smiles, her eyes smile too.

"I see you thinking, c'mon tell me." That smile, so damn bright, look at it!

"I'm thinking about *you*" hiding my face, she points at my blushes I can never hide.

"What about me?" She's cute when she's pushy, it's annoying.

"Come on don't be cheesy, you can't ask me that."

"Seriously I want to know, tell me." How can I resist? I feel silly, I know I'm going to tell her anyway. But I still get shy and the butterflies that I thought were dormant go crazy when she looks at me the way she does. In this way that makes me feel like it's day one of falling for her all over again.

"...about me, seeing your beautiful smile for the rest of my life. Thinking about us and what we can have, together. When I was little, I watched a *lot* of television. These kids' programmes you know, like on Nickelodeon, Trouble and all that shit. Rushing home, so I didn't miss a single one. No record or Netflix back then, if you missed it you missed out." I laugh, thinking of the little tantrums I use to throw when I missed my shows back in the day.

"That was *way* back in the day," she chuckles with me and that smile I love, grew two sizes bigger.

"I know, I know. But I could always see myself in one of those shows. Not as a character but actually *living* in one of those big arse houses- like on Sister, Sister. With the two big staircases; one in the front of the house and one in the back. Everything set in its place, perfect. With an island right in the middle of the kitchen.

Upstairs three or four big bedrooms, three bathrooms, an upstairs a landing or like a balcony, I can stand and can see everything from, stood there just watching over what's mine."

"Who can you see with you?"

"Well, it has always been just me; I could always imagine myself in these perfect settings but they're empty... no one but me and the walls really." Feeling myself gazing off in a daze, thinking deeper into my thoughts.

"What about now?" Her soft voice, bringing me back to reality, out of my daydream and on the conversation.

"I see us... you and me laying together on this really big soft sofa, one that practically takes over the entire room, enjoying the comfort of our home..."

"Calm and peaceful, just us, right?" She asks, trying to see the vision of *'us'* that I can see when I close my eyes caught up in my daydream.

"No, not just us. A family... *our* family. Two kids, maybe three busy doing what kids do."

"Making a whole heap of noise!" She interrupted bluntly.

.   "No? Make you happy." Drifting off into the distance, seeing it all so clear, almost as clear as one of those shows on my television screen.

"You want that with me?" I nod at her blushing. I can never hide it even though I try. "Then I'll give you that, we can build that together"

"Put that on everything."

"Have I ever lied?" She answers me with another question.

I turn away from her and look down at myself. Sat with my knees to my chest and my arms wrapped around them, holding them tight, as if I'm stopping myself from falling apart. Trying not to tremble at the colour of the water running through the bathtub that I sat in; a watered down rose like red from the blood that is falling out of me and rippling through the water. Running down the white acrylic tub then trickle and disappear down the silver plug hole. But blood still seeped out from different places that felt like fire. My back throbbing, my hair wet, tangled and stringy falling onto it; soothing my skin from the burning.

It all happened so fast. One minute I was cooking us dinner, talking about work and other stuff and how much my manager liked the changes I had implemented.

I was boiling pasta… a big pot. Big enough for us to have pasta for at least for three days, twice a day. I liked to cook that way, it made things easier to measure as it was only the two of us. Saving us time and money, I like to count the pennies even though we never had to; it was just the way I was taught to cook- cost effective. Anyway, the pot was on the highest heat on our electric stove. I never liked cooking on those things, I've always preferred a gas cooker. There's just something about the sound of the ignition and puff of air when the blue flame comes on. I remember from science lessons in school that blue was the most dangerous colour of flames and watching it under my pots and pans let me know my food was cooking. Which is better than guessing and hovering your hand over the electric stove to see which hob is on and ready- it came with the house and I had no choice but to adjust.

I left work a little later today, later than normal. I was always home by the time the clock reaches six.

I decided to make her, her favourite meal to make up for my absence from the evening we always shared together, by making the meal her mother showed me how to make when we went to visit one festive or seasonal holiday.

I was busy telling her that my manager offered to take me out for a drink, to say thank you or to give me any kind of treat I wanted, all expenses paid. I must have been going on and on about it all. She always tells me I talk too much but I was so excited to tell her everything that happened today.

I went over to the fridge to get the vegetables. I heard her chair pull away from the kitchen table, I heard her get up but I didn't hear what she was doing, I wasn't really paying attention. I was talking and talking and talking all loud and all happy. Telling her what my manager said with my head in the fridge trying to juggle all the vegetables in my arms. The thing you do when you don't want to make another trip back to the fridge but end up going back to it anyway having forgotten one or two things.

But then she... then I... I felt it... *all*... *over...me*. Boiling... Boiling, hot, heat. Scolding, surging, scorching, burning sizzling fire like pain. Like lava running down my back and down the back of my legs.

I screamed so loud, shocked and petrified. I screamed out her name for her to help me. I wanted her to help me; I was in so much fucking pain and I wanted *her* to help... *me*.

It wasn't till I turned myself around and I saw her standing there... her face! I lightly stepped, screaming with every inch my body moved, gasping in between screams, fighting for breath, I couldn't catch my breath. My shoulders scrunched up, my arms out letting everything drop to the floor, holding out for her. But her face... her face. She wasn't smiling anymore. She was breathing heavy, her chest moving up and down so fast. The look in her eyes... *that* look in her eyes, like something I had never seen- wild!

In her hand, she was holding it! The pot was in her hand *empty* and steaming. The boiling hot water was soaking into my burning skin. My clothes hot, wet and sticking to me. Breaths in... but no breaths out. Nothing coming out, my lungs were too scared to breathe, too scared to move.

She threw the pot down and she *charged* at me, hitting me again and again and again. I kept screaming her name, screaming for her to stop. I don't know if it was, the sound of my body hitting the floor or her phone ringing in her back pocket that snapped her out of this possessed rage she was trapped in.

On the floor, on my back reaching out to her, tasting my own blood on my tongue, flowing thick, down the side of my face. Feeling more coming from my throat and out my mouth, coughing it up. She came back to me in a flash, the rage left her body, like an entity or daemon and she called out my name, shouting out *'No! no, no.'* over and over and *over*. Holding her head in panic, she fell to her knees, her hands shaking, realising what she had done.

Her face was a blur; pain was controlling my eyes, not letting me see much of anything. Blinking, trying to keep them open.

In one scoop she picked me up like the princess she always treated me as. I couldn't stop screaming, in her helping arms that pressed against my burning back. She stripped my clothes off me slowly, trying so hard to prevent my skin from coming off with each layer of clothing. Panicking in agony, her hands shaking she sat me in the middle of the bath. Turning the shower on cold, she kneeled on the floor running the water over my trembling body. Breathing heavy but deeply slowly, each breath getting shorter. Like the aching pain was taking over my ability to breath. Then, she started talking to me. Telling me how much she loved me that she was sorry, that she didn't mean it, what she did to me. She kept repeating how much she loves me, how much she needs me and how sorry she is. Trying to keep me awake, not wanting me to fade into unconsciousness. Telling me stories, she told me where she could see us then she asked me what I wanted, what could I see. She asked me, sat on the edge of the tub while showering me down. My head tilted back looking up at her, looking at me the way she does. That beautiful smile laced across her face her dimples sinking into each cheek- I love the way she looks at me, I love her smile…

"No… you, you've never lied…"

I answered her through chattering cold teeth, blue lips and through the panic attack trying to leave my system. She was right, she never lied- not once. She told the truth; Delilah has never lied to me once, not once, never! She loves me.

"C'mon get in baby."

Stood in our room, naked, shivering, freezing cold from the shower and the drops of water drops off of my hot skin. She pulls back the covers and laid down two large towels, one on top of the other. Taking my hand, letting me use her for balance I climb into the bed. Wincing, moaning and crying in pain with every single move as I lay down on my front. Resting my head onto my lumpy pillow that smells just like her.

So exhausted from all the pain, I wanted to shut down and close my eyes. Dying right now would be a great option, if it meant *all* the pain will go away and stop! All I have to do is hold my breath for too long and push my face deep into my lumpy pillow, until I couldn't feel anything at all. Maybe then I'd find peace. If I was dead, she couldn't keep hurting me the way she does. Maybe if I was dead, she wouldn't find me hiding, drag me across the floor the way she does and be able to take the frustrations of her day out on me. Maybe *if* I was dead, she wouldn't be able to lock me in the house the way she does. Maybe if I *was* dead maybe the way she hurts me just might have finally killed me!

Feeling her rub something on my back, I can tell she's trying to be careful but she cannot help the fact that she's naturally heavy handed and my skin was falling off my body like leaves on an autumn tree.

I wonder if this time I close my eyes, will they open in the morning? Does it make me weak to have these suicidal thoughts? Or does it make me a strong person who wants to be free? Free from it all, I can't figure it out.

***

"It's a good thing you brought her in twenty-four hours later, we can assess the current state of the burns, which I'm afraid are second degree," said the nurse bursting the blisters on my back and wiping the fluid inside of them away with the rest of my burned skin that she couldn't save, whilst I sat hunched over in a backless hospital gown, on a hospital bed in the urgent care burn unit.

The second we stepped into the accident and emergency room they took one look at my skin and they immediately rushed me over here to this ward with no questions asked. The look on their faces was enough for me to know how bad it was.

"That's what I thought, I wanted her to try and have a good sleep, try to keep things normal. I cold compressed it with a cold shower and wet towels on her back and changed them throughout the night." Delilah and the nurse spoke over me like I wasn't here. Like I'm a toddler who burned herself by reaching up on a kitchen counter for a hot cup of tea, rather than a grown woman who was getting skin taken off of her back and the back of her neck because her abusive woman poured a big pot of boiling hot water down her fucking back for no good reason! So, I left them to it... I had nothing to say, I haven't spoken in the past twenty-eight or something hours. Could have been less, could have been more but the concept of time no longer exists. The last thing I remember saying said was Delilah's name when she was showering me down for the fifth or sixth time that night, crying from all that pain, begging for help when she's the one that done this to me... she did *this* to me!

"I've brought the dressings, I wasn't sure which one but I brought them all in, once we get a good look I'll know, okay lovely."

A senior nurse pulled the dusty dim blue curtains back, after wheeling a cart of dressings into the curtained off cubicle we are all in. She slanted her head forward, looking at me over her glasses that sat at the end of her nose. Talking to me, at the same time as putting a pair of latex gloves on her hands. Her Scottish accent is soft and her face gentle. Reminding me of Mrs. Doubtfire,

"Right let's have a wee look and see how you're getting on, okay lovey."
The nurses spoke with each other about my back, Delilah stood back one arm folded over her and the other holding the back of her neck in aggravation that she has no control what so ever over me in this situation. She didn't want to bring me to the hospital at all; she didn't want to have to explain anything to anyone. She *hates* authority or anyone who challenges that. So, the fact that the two nurses spoke only to themselves about *her* woman, didn't sit well with her at all.

"Everything alright with her?" Stretching her neck trying to get a good angle to see what they were doing to me.

"It will be my love." The first nurse spoke to Delilah.

"We're going to wash your back off with fluids again, then dress the burns lightly with a petroleum jelly covered dressing, which will sooth the skin making it less uncomfortable for you to move. We want to save as much skin as possible. But you will have to come back every day to change the dressings, we don't want the skin to keloid." The nurse with the Scottish accent spoke to me, rubbing my shoulder gently. I shuddered, scowling in pain as they started to wash my back.

"It's okay baby." Delilah reached for my hand that was holding the edge of the bed and squeezing the thin black leather covered foam mattress. I instantly moved my hand away. I didn't mean to; I just... don't want her to touch me anymore, every time she touches me... she hurts me and being in the hands of these two nurturing strangers felt safer than what I have felt in a very long time. I know they are nurses and it's their job to care but still, I feel safer with them all the same.

"Do you mind if have a word with Aaliyah, *alone?*" The senior nurse asked, she caught me move away from Delilah or she could see from the state of me and the other scars on my skin that I was being battered by my woman!

"Why?" Delilah asked sharply, what she really wanted to say was, *'hell no'* and drag my arse home.

"I would like to speak to her *alone* regarding *her* injury." The nurse's authority, duty to care and age stepped up as she stood tall.

"Why? I was there, I *know* what happened! It was an *accident*!"

"Yes, I know but..." The senior nurse stepped towards Delilah calmly to try and reassure her but *my* Delilah is far from stupid. She knows that the nurse *knows* this wasn't no damn accident!

"But what? I already told the other nurse what happened!" She said pointing over to the other nurse who kept her head down and kept herself but attending to my skin.

"And what was that, exactly? Would you care to explain as I was not present?" The nurse narrowed her eyebrows looking down at Delilah through her glasses.

"…she fell." Delilah stalled.

"Oh? How so?" The nurse challenges her and Delilah doesn't know where to look or what to say to get the interrogation of my accident over with.

"I blacked out!" I spoke up, sick of the back and forth over me.

"Pardon dear?" The nurse turned to me, Delilah did too. Having not heard my voice for hours and hours. The nurses haven't heard me speak at all. All eyes are now on me. I could tell them everything and set myself free but what's the point? She'll find me, she always does. Or she'll make me come back with her words and the way she says things so sweetly. *If* they file a report and tell the police, what exactly will they do for domestic violence between two women? I know Delilah, she will use the small ounces of femininity she has left to get away with it. All she has to do is smile at them the way she does and fabricate a story she probably has in mind already, if we ever came to that conclusion. Then *I'm* the one who is *crazy* and I'm the one who has all the internal mental issues with my current state of mental health. No… I know her too well, telling them the truth will only cause me more pain so…

"I guess I had a long day. One minute I was standing over the stove, the next I felt lightheaded. I turned away from the stove, before I could tell Delilah that I was feeling funny. I guess I hit the ground. But when I opened my eyes, Delilah was over me screaming, hands all over me. This burning hot heat all over me. I was soaking wet and felt like I was on fire, begging for her to stop- to help."

"See! I told you she fainted!" Delilah added pointing at the first nurse, too heated to realise she said *'fell'* the first time and not *'faint'*- but whatever. I'm too tired and I'm far too weak for all of this.

"Maybe I'm just tired- of everything. Tired of it *all* and I just want it to stop." I spoke looking past the senior nurse and onto Delilah. Tears free falling from my eyes, while my throat tightens up, barely able to get my last words out. Wanting to let Delilah know I'm *soo* fucking tired of her bullshit! I want it to stop, I want her to stop.

Dropping my head to my chest, looking back down at the speckled vinyl hospital flooring under my feet that hung off the bed. Legs draped with the long-patterned hospital gown; It looks similar to one I've worn before with the patterns not making any sense, swirls or diamonds, or whatever these mints, off-whites and yellow patterns are. I let the nurses continue their job, that's all I am to them. Once they sign off their notes in my documents on the green papers in black biro pens then hand them over to the doctor, for he or she to write their notes on the white papers with colour coded triangles at the top of the page. It's things like the colour of the floor, backless gowns or how my notes are written down that I paid attention to in-between the hours of waiting for nurses and doctors, MRI's, neuroimaging examinations or blood tests that these hospital visits would bring. Along with a neurologist and diagnostics taking more notes then it's off to the next patient while I wait to get discharged. But by then Delilah would have had enough of all the waiting around and discharged me herself with no knowledge or clue towards my symptoms, diagnostics and aftercare- my head hurts so bad at times... still does.

It was such a small simple thing I was trying to tell Delilah. I wanted to tell her about work, that I was happy but because her rage took over her actions... I'm left with scars down my back and all over my beautiful skin. The scaring looks like paint; if you put a generous amount of paint on a piece of card and tilt it at an angle, then watch the paint dribble down it, yeah, like that.

The colour of my scars went from white, pinkish fleshy tones, to an irregular dotted like coloured patches. You could have played dot to dot on my back. The melanin is back on my skin but in a much darker tone. I would stand in front of the rococo golden vintage mirror in our room and angle my small vanity mirror so that I could see the process of the healing every other day, which surprisingly was quite quick.

The nurses themselves were surprised at how quickly my melanin came back considering how dense my pink flesh undertone was. But I've always been somewhat of a quick healer; if I cut my finger by accident, wrap it up for a night then check on it in the morning and the skin would already have started to fuse together, almost like it was not a serious accident at all or it could be a broken wrist or worse.

I would have preferred to have taken photos of the healing process on my skin. But Delilah had taken my phone away… and my house keys too. She would lock me inside the house so I couldn't leave, even if I wanted to, I couldn't get out. Locked away like protected property.

She kept me away from people during the times she hurt me really bad and I needed a lengthy recovery. A black eye was easy to cover, with all the spare time and hours spent learning how to contour flawlessly while having nothing else to do in my absence from the real world. I have perfected my makeup skills with a little help from tutorials on YouTube.

It's only a matter of time before I lost another job or had to leave the job because someone has noticed and questioned me about the marks on my body that I have no real explanation for. I could never predict when Delilah was about to have an 'episode'. I would need time away from work to heal from each blow and search my mind for a new excuse to take back to the office with me, I kept repeating the same explanation for a new bruise. I mean, how many times can *one* person keep falling down the stairs?

Delilah wouldn't let me leave if I had a big bruise or broken bones. She liked to keep me locked away from everything. So she could reinstall her love into me, in every kind of way; physically, emotionally, mentally and financially. Buying me gifts and showering me with attention, love and affection until I was all healed up, patched back up, had fallen in love with her all over again and ready to re-join the world.

She came home at the same time every day of her working week; all I did when it got to seven o'clock was stand and stare and wait at the door at end of the hallway. Listening closely to the many door locks of *our home* unlock one by one. And as each lock left its hinge, a breath of air of anxiety left my body. Once she was in, she'd shut the door behind her then lock each of the locks- one by one. I used to imagine myself pushing past her and *running*; I figured out the seconds I had to claim freedom when she opened the door but there was no one and nowhere to run to. I had nothing else but her and this place, she made sure I was isolated and the majority of my bridges with people burned a long time ago. So, I never ran, besides, when my imagination played out the visions of my 'escape', she'd always grab me the moment I got a foot over the threshold and choke slam me to the ground.

"Peek-a-boo baby." She said, every day she came home.

It was this joke when we first started dating. Laughing at some kind of something, I don't remember now. But then we used to say this to each other- 'peek-a-boo baby'. And it used to be so sweet, my heart would get excited or skip a beat when I heard it. Could be in a crowded room or behind me when I wasn't expecting to see her face… now it terrifies me.

I stood and watched as she would kick off her shoes and demand attention from me that I didn't want to give to her. But… even when I didn't want to, I couldn't help it, I hated myself. Because I couldn't stop myself from loving her the way I do. I'm hers, always will be.

I stopped cooking all together. It was microwave dinners and takeaways or food her friends brought over. Her people were always up in the house- uninvited and touching things, they had no business touching. Walking their dirty shoes all over my clean floors. Knocking things over and not considering the cost or the mess! The smell of weed filled the house constantly, I hated the smell! It always left this dirty hefty linger in the air, on Delilah's clothes, her lips and her mind. I always stayed out of the way and in the bedroom on the weekend nights they visited and wait for them all to leave. Delilah would pass out somewhere and I would take off her clothes and tuck her into bed. She's so harmless and peaceful in her sleep. Once she settled, I'd go clean up the mess they left behind in the house.

This one time, I thought everyone had gone home like they usually did. It was stupid o'clock in the morning and I just put Delilah in the bed. Cleaning up, I didn't even see Nicole- one of Delilah's stud man-ish looking friends. She was *so* big, broad and tall, she could have easily passed for a Tyrone or Jahiem. Big for no reason, built like a man kind of girl.

Anyway, I was bending over, emptying the second bucket of Delilah's vomit into the toilet; my Saturday mornings were almost *always* like this.

"I like what I see."

"Jeesuss!" Jumping out of my skin and dropping the empty bucket on the floor. Turning to see Nicole posted against the door frame. "Nicole, you scared the shit out of me! What are you still doing here?"

"I wanted to give you a hand." She smirked licking her lips.

"Oh no, I'm good but thanks?" I was confused; the cleaning has been done so no hands were needed to give.

"I see the way, see, I like how you move." Her sentence split in two still high, her eyes red raw barely open from whatever drugs she ingested tonight.

"Nicole, you should go lay on the sofa. I'll bring you a blanket. You're more than welcome to stay until you're sober." Ignoring her nonsense, I tried to move her arm which was blocking my way out of the bathroom but she didn't move it.

"You know I like you right? She doesn't deserve you. I do! You need to be *my* woman!" Nicole grabbed my wrist tightly and dragged me towards her. She spoke right into my ear and I felt her hot breath with every word she said.

"Nicole, get off me." I said quietly, if Delilah woke up and sees us like this, she's killing us both! No questions asked.

"I said, you need to be mine bitch!" Her big hand around my throat, dragging me by my neck back inside the bathroom. Shoving my body and my head up against the tiled wall. I felt the tile my head banged against crack with the force of her connection. Swinging on my tiptoes, desperate for the balls of my feet to find the floor, or anything to touch and feel. I needed to feel something under me but there was nothing there! My legs scrambling, feet searching for something! Any kind of surface!

"Nicole stop, please g-et of-ff m-e." Forcing herself so strong, up against me, I couldn't move. I didn't know whether to try and get her hand from around my neck or stop her other hand from going under my oversized night tee, pushing in between my struggling legs. I felt so lightheaded, the lights in the bathroom getting brighter and whiter ahead of my blinking blurry vision. Her hand getting closer and closer, telling me to:

"Open your fucking legs, bitch!" Through her gritted teeth.

"Ss-stop, p-please." Words so quiet, fighting to get out. She forced her fingers inside of me, I didn't want her there, I never wanted her there.

"Aaliyah where are you!" Delilah shouted out for me. Nicole instantly let go of me, she's shook of Delilah, everyone was! I dropped to the floor, trying to catch my breath so I could answer Delilah. Coughing, hurting and peering up at the blurred image of Nicole about a foot away from me, licking her fingers.

"Damn, tastes better than I ever thought girl." She stumbled drunkenly stumbled back to the doorway of the bathroom.

"Aali-YAH!!" Delilah hollered my name again; I can hear her aggravation growing.

"If you tell her, I'll kill you." Nicole laughed.

"If you kill me, she'll kill *you* bitch!" I rubbed my neck trying to get the feeling of her hands *off* of me.

"True, true but she'll never believe I touched you anyway. You're only some pretty little bitch, I've known her for years' baby. I'll be here when she's done with you and on to the next bitch!"

"Fuck you Nicole!" I spat at her feet.

"Whatever bitch, I *will* fuck you one day! I've just wanted to taste you. I Needed to see why she's still with you, she's not been with anyone this long. Now

I know, coz your pussy's way too good to let go. Delilah is crazy, she *will* kill *you,* Aaliyah. You should get away, run!" She left the bathroom swaying. Stupid fucking big for nothing, ugly can't get a woman because you look like a Tyrone looking *bitch*!

Wiping myself off with a wet wipe, it stings, a little bloody from Nicole clawing her way inside of me with her jagged sharp nails. Flushing the wipe down the toilet, I picked up the bucket and walked back to the bedroom. Shuffling cautiously pass the living room, where Nicole lay knocked out on the sofa snoring loud as fuck like she just wasn't bothering my system. I was so close to smothering her with a pillow. I never liked her! I always felt like she was looking at me some type of way, with something on her mind- now I know.

Delilah hung off the bed, fresh vomit hanging off of her bottom lip- *great*, just what I needed another pile of *bullshit* to clean up.

"Do you know how much I love you?"

"No?" I blushed as she looked at me with her hand on my cheek, holding it gently. She took my had and held onto me.

"You're mine!" I loved when her intoxication allowed her to show me her affection and open up to me with her truth. I know sometimes she gets aggressive but when she's like this, she's my baby, I know she needs me.

"I know..."

"If you ever try to leave me, I'll kill you."

***

"Then what? You told her what her friend did to you, right?"

Mali and I sat on the floor, tucked away in the corner of my balcony. No one could see us sat out here if they looked out of any of my windows. We were hidden and Mali's questions started to roll in, after listening to me tell her a *part* of my past. The part of me I hide and want to stay hidden. Being venerable is not an option for me and never had been. I keep it moving.

"Yeah, I told her. But I was so scared." I'm sat between her legs resting my back against her chest. Blanket on my legs and her arms wrapped around me. She held onto me tighter with each detail I told her.

"What did she say?" Her face resting on my left shoulder holding me tighter. Closer, so close I don't want her to let go.

"She laughed!?"

"What!?"

"She said, she knew Nicole was *curious* but didn't think she was brave enough to do anything."

"Yeah but, did she say anything to her?"

"I never saw Nicole again, *if* that's what you're asking. No one did."

"What did she do to her?"

"She probably killed her! People like that deserve to die!" I said coldly and it's the truth! I hope Delilah fucked her up or cut off the fingers she violated with me.

"What about Delilah?" Mali questioned curiously

"She ran me a beautiful bath with candles, bubbles, bath oils and my favourite music playing low from these speakers in the distance."

"That sounds nice."

"Does it?" I turned my head to Mali. "She said the water *wasn't* hot enough for me. I told her it was perfect but she didn't listen to me, she never did. She left the bathroom and I lay back in the bath. Eyes closed, relaxed and lost in the serenity." I don't do emotions at all! You would think I am sat here, remising and revealing but I stopped any emotions a long time ago. No point in crying, no uncontrolled feelings and emotions. I can't change the past. It is, what it is!

"Aaliyah?" Mali questioned me softly.

"I loved her, I really did." I felt my throat tightening- I'm not going to keep doing this crying shit! No more tears! "I opened my eyes and Delilah was stood over me. She had the kettle in her hand. The steam was coming out of the spout. I begged her not to do it. I got up so quickly, screaming and scrambling to get out. But she threw me down in the bath and poured the kettle on top of me. Luckily, it only got the left side of my body. The bottom of my stomach, top of my thigh and at the bottom inside of my left leg. I don't know what hurt more… my skin, or the look in her eyes. She didn't *fucking* care that she was causing me so much pain, she didn't care about me! She didn't care that she was hurting me! She turned away and left me screaming. I remembered to cold compress from the last time, so turned on the cold tap, grabbed a towel and sat back in the water. The burns weren't as bad as my back but they were still burns."

"Then what…"

"I waited a while and got out the bath, wrapping a towel around my body. My head was killing me. I'm sure I hit it, I think I knocked when she pushed me down but I don't remember much. I think I blacked out but I do remember calling out for her, she didn't answer. The front door was wide open, I looked around the house for her and she wasn't there. Expecting to see her past out with a bottle of Jack Daniels in her hand but she was gone! She left! Everything was gone! *She* fucking left!? She battered, burnt and scarred me and *she* left *me*? I put up with her and her *bull shit* for all those fucking *years!* Telling myself she would change, telling myself she fucking loved me and things would get better! This woman done the most to me and she walked out on me, just up and left. No goodbyes. No, I love you. No sorry. Nothing. Gone!"

Mali held me tighter, arms wrapped all over and around me. Why am I fucking crying!? I don't even care about Delilah anymore, fuck her! Mali continues to console me, pulling on the zip of my hoody; removing it off of my shoulders, off of my back and pushing it down my arms to my elbows. Her hands gently stroke the tops of my shoulders, running up and down my body, shuddering from the breeze but warming up from her touch.

She places her lips against my skin, holding them there so delicately, passed my skin, passed my tattoos and onto the scars on my body- saying nothing at all.

315

I watch her hands hold my body and lay me down on the wooden floor, allowing her to move my limbs where ever she wants to place them.

Endless running tears fall silently down the sides of my face, dripping past my ears as a lay, arms out of my hoody. She kneels over me kissing the rest of my body softly over the scars she found embedded under the ink of my tattoos. Opening my eyes, staring at the daylight and the white summer morning clouds hovering over me in the sky. There's no escaping, I know she's searching for every mark on me and connect her lips with my scars. Quick flashes of how Delilah put each one there, flicker deep in the back of my memories I locked away. Blocked away and forgotten. I forget things sometimes but my brain can never let's go of this trauma like stains on white fabric… they don't go away, you can still see them there and know they were there… that they happened.

Mali kisses up my legs, my left thigh, my stomach, my sides, under my breast, between my chest, my collar bone, my arms, my neck and finally my lips. Kissing me with *every-thing*, feeling caught in thoughts of my fall. Falling apart and putting myself back together again- her kiss, holding me together, what was missing.

"I'm right here. I'm not gonna go anywhere."

She turns, lying beside me with her legs wrapped over me like a blanket. Everything is on stand still, looking at each other intensely but softly. I watch her eyes wondering along my skin, taking it all in. My story, my body… me. She kisses, me over and over.

My thumb gently grazing her bottom lip slowly, she kisses my palm then moves towards my neck then back where her lips left traces of kisses all over my body. Stopping at my stomach, laying there not moving any further. The tips of her finger slightly on my skin, following the never-ending lines form the wing of my tribal phoenix tattoo on my stomach and side. I didn't need to look down to know that's what her fingertip is trailing. I know that pattern too well, because I know what it covers.

The phoenix bird is a representation of my new beginning and the power within me to rise through the pain.

I've always been fascinated with the idea of the mythical bird bursting into flames and through all that suffering, being born again. I was connected to this beautiful creature from the burns on my own skin, they were the ignition to start again.

Losing... I lost track of the hours and time spent here with her beside me. My hands not letting go, she's so soft. Her skin doesn't have a single visible mark but I know she is scarred, like me... broken, just like me... maybe. Her energy is too familiar, like something I've had before... wanted and waited on but I don't know if this is what I want to do? Caught up in her touching my body with no restrictions at all, terrified that she can actually see *me*.

Holding onto her wrist I follow her hand down my body, silently telling her where I want her to put it. To take it *slow*, take her time. She moves carefully, placing her body between my legs, letting her body weight lay on top of mine. My body pressed against the wooden floor, anticipating. I let go of her wrist but my pussy holds onto her fingers inside of me, tightly. My back arched, my leg over her, hands latched onto her back, palms hot and scratching at her back.

Eyes closed but I can see the shadows of the clouds imprinted on the inside of lids. Not making a sound as she fucks... no 'loves' my body slowly.

"Let me kiss it better, let me take it all away." Mali says between kisses. Moving away from my lips, her kisses reach my other lips. Softly, sucking my inner thigh right beside my pussy, placing her own mark on my skin. Her fingers easing slowly. Wet wanting her to keep playing with my clit; she licks lightly, teasing me. Head back not realising I'm still crying. Thinking about everything I told her and everything she's making me feel. More than I wanted. My heart pounding in my chest so loud I can hear it (let go) it won't stop, it can't stop... (let go) this feeling, it's...

Butterflies in my stomach, overactive and aggressive, wanting and needing her but how can I be feeling like this?

"Tell me you want me…" Kissing on me by my ear, she whispered

"I…" I can't tell her, I've told her too much already.

"Tell me, you need me." she waits for my answer.

Every stroke of her fingers inside of me felt like more than… I ever- oh shit! I don't want her to stop but I can't feel like this, I don't want to feel like this again. It's too much passion, too much affection. No? I can't feel like this… not again.

"Stop…" I can't do this, I can't. "Mali, stop!" My whisper in the noises of the morning starting to take over. Noises of birds, traffic and transporting people going about their day. "I said stop - please."

"What's wrong? Are you okay?" I stare at her- I'm not okay. "Did I hurt you?" No… but you might…

She sat up looking over me laying on the floor as stiff as the wooden planks underneath me. Arms by my side not looking at her at all, I can't look at her. Instead, I gaze at the clouds moving gently above me and across the sky. Crying, quietly? For fuck sake, I'm a mess!? I can't stop!

Breathing slowly, in and out I need to get a hold of myself and what the fuck is going on with me?!

Pull yourself the fuck together- we do not have time for this, Aaliyah no! You fucked up, I fucked up! You told her too much, I've told her- I've told her things, things no one needed to know!! What have I done? What the fuck was I even thinking? I wasn't even thinking; how could I have opened my mouth! I'm so stupid! FUCK!

"Leave me alone- *please.*" My hands over my face, hoping she would disappear, or I will wake up in my bed alone, forgetting everything like my other bad days. Like none of this shit ever happened.

"Aaliyah? You okay?" Her hand on my shuddering stomach, her touch like nothing I am used to- loving.

I can't focus, with her hands on me because it feels so right but it's so wrong. All of it! I can't do this again, she has to go! I can't get caught up in these feelings again. No, she's too close. This can never happen again!

Getting up off up of the floor quickly putting my clothes back onto my body. Fixing myself, running my hands through my hair, angry at my damn self! Don't fall in love you idiot!

"No!" Pointing down at her like a disobedient child. "No?" I question myself out loud. What if I do want to feel all that shit- *No, no, no, no you fucking don't!*

"Aaliyah-" She knows too much

"No…" She knows too much about me, fuck! "If you tell anyone I swear I'll fucking kill you! And I'll know it's you, because no one knows. No one!" I put my hands over my mouth, shutting myself up. She didn't need to know that either, fuck! Just stop talking and leave! I turn walking towards the balcony door.

"Aaliyah, let's just stay here…"

Wait? Where am I going, this is my fucking house!? Throwing my hands up, she steps towards me with a handout, I step back. Backing away from her, hands up to my side. I don't want her to touch me anymore, shaking my head.

Looking away from her, she's desperately trying to get me to look at her, attempting to calm down this erratic mess of a woman I am right now. But this is all too much. I need to get away from her, from *all* of this! She needs to stay away from me!

"What are you two doing out here?"

Blues voice coming from behind me, in the distance of the doorway, I didn't turn around- I froze! I stare at Mali, my eyes wide and my mouth open paralysed by Blue's sudden appearance. Where the *fuck* did she come from? And what the fuck did she hear? What the fuck did she see? Mali looks to and back from us both, she's panicking but keeping cool. "You two okay… everything okay? What's going on?" Blue asked us both.

"Yeah baby everything's cool," Mali's voice shaking "Aaliyah jus' pointed out the way to the station." Mali walks towards Blue but not too close, she still has traces of my body on the tips of her fingertips and tongue. Stopping Blue from stepping out into this and seeing me in the state I am in.

Get it the fuck together! Quickly erasing the emotions off my face. I shuffle my hair over my shoulder and scars-

Breathe Aaliyah, calm down; breathe in, come on, fix up! Do *not* let them see this side of you! Do not let 'anyone' see you like this ever again! No time for weakness or bullshit! Get it the fuck together and fix the fuck up! Breathe out, stretch, shake and let it the fuck go! You're okay, you're good! I'm good. Breathe, you're okay Aaliyah, come on, ready…

"But Raee'n said she's taking us home?" Blue adds.

"No, the fuck she's not!" Ladies and gentlemen, reintroducing Miss Aaliyah-back in full effect!! "You have two feet and an Oyster card so go! Use them!" I shooed them with both of my hands, dismissing them.

"Aaliyah?!" Blue looked between Mali and me, waiting for her *woman* to defend her honour but Mali knows not to open her mouth at all and leave it right there. Because she needs to be quiet with the taste of my pretty pussy sitting on her lips. "What? Transport for London is back up and running, so you can vamoose! You might not be able to hold your drink but you best believe you're about to hold down your Oyster card and tap yourself home! Everyone needs to go back to where they belong and leave *me* the fuck alone!" I said staring at Mali.

They are still standing there? Do they not understand me? Am I speaking a different language?

Mali said nothing, digging her phone out of her back pocket, discreetly wiping traces of me off of her hands onto her jeans. And holding out her hand for Blue with the other. They head towards the door and step out of my apartment. Watching them walk down the corridor towards the elevator. Waiting for it... three... two ... one... she did it. Mali looks back at me, over her shoulder with this look on her face and the second she did, I felt her lips on my body all over again like they never left.

Can someone please explain what the fuck is happening? This is not how this is supposed to be going. I should've stopped myself from talking; I shouldn't have let her get close to... me.

Sat back on the balcony floor, alone, in the spot I was earlier. Unable to make sense of any of this. Mind bleeding full of thoughts bouncing, from one side of my head to the over. Asking the same questions and finding new questions leaving the rest unanswered and open. It's getting dark and everything is going black. My head is hurting... closing my eyes, I feel her touch me. So gentle. I shouldn't have let her see, now everything is blurry and fuzzy and dark... this pain is getting worse and it fucking hurts...

...*Shit!*

12. The Black Sheep

"Family," a real funny fucked up word to me, actually makes me laugh at the whole idea and thought of it all, of them all!

My mum, (if you can even call her that) has never been a woman of words… or actions, or maternal instinct or anything if I think about it. To be honest *'woman,'* is also a very strong word to describe her; she acts more like a fucking child than a woman with all the excuses she's made and continues to make throughout her life. Which is a catalogue portfolio of very bad fucking decisions that *she* finds reason and time to blame everyone else and has absolutely no accountability over her damn self! Talking about her upbringing and the things she didn't have as a child. Like *love* and *attentiveness* and *nurturing,* or never having a mother care for her at all. So, you'd think she would go to infinity and beyond to not repeat the cycle and make sure her own children never faced the hardships and troubles she encountered in life. But oh no, (rolling my eyes right now, in case you're wondering). She didn't do anything and doesn't do *anything*… she's a lost cause and a woman who I want *nothing* to be like in this lifetime or the next!

If the choice was being my mum or being a parasite, I'd choose the parasite. Which funny enough is exactly what she is; seeing as though she fucks you up from the inside out, eating away at you.

She has done nothing to help or benefit the life of *any* of her children let alone her own damn existence! Leeching off of me, my money and the time I chose to give her. Which is why- you know what? Let me not even and stop myself right there. That's all a *whole* other story, no one has the time for right now. Because if I continue, I am going to be here for pages after pages trying to explain *what* kind of a *person* my *mother* is not.

So, moving forward, she has three grown-ish children there is nothing left for her to do anymore (but she's been saying this since we were like twelve!). Her only task is to continue to make the fucked-up choices which rather than grow tired of, I'm simply used to. Rather than be shocked or disappointed it's more of a *'oh okay, here we go again'* type of feeling.

My mother is nothing but a walking liability and hindrance to my life, rather than any form of help what so ever. Her idea of helping anyone is by boiling the kettle and leaving you in the kitchen after a firm shoulder pat to console your woes and tears, then shouting at you, telling you that you have absolutely *nothing* to cry about, so make yourself a cup of tea and get the fuck over it because there is no time for weakness! My bad, sorry- I said I wasn't going to continue but the woman gets to me... she, *Aaliyah... stop!*

Being the middle child has its advantages and disadvantages, as I take the term *'the black sheep'* literally, in every way, shape and form. I try to keep my presence a rarity. I am *nothing* like my sisters at all and I never fucking will be - thank fuck for that!

I am slap bang in the middle of two light skin siblings, I would have never noticed if my Jamaican Grandpops didn't adopt my family nickname and called me *"blacky"* throughout my childhood. So... it's safe to say, I noticed the difference. It has always been and will always be me vs. *them*!

You've seen Samantha's mentions, she is the first born. And all hope was lost right there as she has been solely exposed to my mothers' bull shit. She's your typical type of mixed-race girl; tall, skinny and with a head full of kinky curly hair. But now her head full of hair is currently being suppressed under a headscarf along with her common sense. Sam, having had three kids herself *just* like mummy dearest to three separate baby fathers. You know the London council house benefit street *dream*, if you will. I am not judging, I am just saying, how it is and that's a fact!

The only way to afford a good life in London in fact, in the U.K if you're not rich, is to live the Benefit Life:

1) Birth one to four children
2) Be handed the keys to a council property
3) Don't work no more than fifteen hours per week

Now looking at it, I see why people are not going to work and claiming disability funds for thirty years, with no medical diagnostics. *I see the benefits*; by their standards, the idea that going to work more than fifteen hours a week is stupid, right? I mean, why *would* anyone work when the country system will pay for your four hundred-pound shoes, three inclusive holidays a year, your rent, oh *and all* your bills?!

It doesn't make sense to me, that people who work forty plus hours a week are busy struggling and trying to figure out *why* they are paying so much fucking tax, when they can touch both sides of the box room they are renting for eight hundred pounds a month! Stressing about how the fuck they are going to stop the bailiffs from knocking because they are behind on a few bills??? Meanwhile, Tracy and Steven who haven't worked in fifteen years are on their second all-inclusive holiday of the year with their four kids and Magaluf!!!! Mad!

#thisislondon #finessethesystem #someonexplain #illwait

Sam and mum have this unspoken connection that I didn't need or want to understand. Like a code that no one could tap into because nothing the other person can do, is bad enough to divide the love between a mother and her first-born child. Not even one of mum's abusive ex-partners pushing Samantha to the ground whilst pregnant, trying to stop him from getting to mum and ending up in hospital, because the baby stopped moving? Mum promised to leave this man, which she did… *not* of course! Our mum chose her kids over dick?? Don't be silly!

And then… there's Thia (pronounced Fee-Ah), the youngest and the baby of 'The Fucked-Up Sister Crew' (trash tv series coming soon). Thia is the most impressionable of us all, just like any child *should* be. She's impressed with the presence and attention of anyone and when they leave, her interest leaves with them. She's almost Eastern European looking with her fair honey complexion, wavy jet-black hair that made her stunning blue eyes stand out and pop like crazy. Striking, beautiful little creature she is. My love for her is unreal but unfortunately, her morals also went out the window and she's just as *stupid* as the other two women in this *family*. So, naturally, I wasn't surprised at all when the seventeen-year-old *baby* of the family announced her pregnancy by her twenty-something-year-old, damn near thirty-year-old drug dealing, dick head of a crack coke head boyfriend who...

Wait for it... this is going to be good, I promise...

Wait, Ready...

She met in prison!

Yup! She met him in a high-security prison! You read that right H.M.P.!! Her Majesty's Prison. Let me spell it for you in case you missed it. Thia met him in p - r - i - s - o -n. Fuck knows what she was doing there? Visiting another criminal- so sorry, I mean *friend*. Apparently, he sent *my* sister a V.O (for those of you who don't speak *prison* that stands for 'visiting order'). The love story unravelled from there; prisoner catches eyes with young beautiful naive girl and prisoner wanted a *piece*. Young beautiful girl falls for *calculative* and manipulative much older prisoner, the end... sort of. *Appa-rently* there's an online social forum for this! According to Thia, *she* wasn't the only idiot who was subjected to this fatal attraction. It's common to meet your *man* behind walls, bars, barb wire, metal detectors, body searches, take your shoes off, empty your pockets, security gates, sniffer dogs, you sit on blue chairs, he sits on a red, reach over and get a feel up while the screws aren't looking kind of love.

I took the time out of *my* life to sit down with prisoner AF2129873 who has a *very* violent history of domestic violence, gross bodily harm, attempted murder after he got his *'get out of jail free card'*. Like this is Monopoly to be rolling the dice with convictions and letting people out to roam the streets to recommit and reoffend the crimes again because they haven't been rehabilitated back into society and never will.

Anyway, so, I do the big sister thing and attempted to get rid of him and his response was and I quote:

> *"Nah B, I ain't goin' nowhere you kno dat. I'm gonna breed 'er. She won't leave an' no one will want her wid nuff kids. Den ima put work on you-"*

By that point, I was done with the conversation and had to walk away before he could finish his king's speech. Because we would have ended up doing life! One of us in a prison block, the other in a box, in a hole in the ground, six feet under an unmarked gravestone!

I'm telling you if the McCann's can make a little white, blue-eyed, blonde girl go missing *and* no one questions them about their skills as parents *and* the two other children are *left* in their custody then I can definitely hide the body of a young reoffender that no one will be looking for.

I tried to tell Thia to keep her distance but let's face it- kids of today don't want to hear anything. She wasn't trying to hear me or anyone else because he had already painted a great picture in her head, about how life was going to be with his drug money. Buying her things here and there to keep her sweet, close and quiet. She expected marriage, kids, apartments scattered across the city, a night club life with bottles on deck and a different pair of designer heels on her feet daily. *Basically,* she wanted the life of an episode of Power, instead, she got a dream that lasted the first three episodes of season one.

Thia has this massive issue; of being unable to separate dreams from reality. Honestly what's wrong with the youth of *this* generation? They're so blinded, ignorant and don't fucking listen. Now look! Here she is, sat opposite me at this table with one hand over her baby bump attempting and failing to hide her hair over her latest black eye.

Well, like they say… those who don't *hear* feel.

Mum had her first child at sixteen, Samantha had hers at seventeen and little Thia will birth her first income tax, baby at eighteen. It's like they have this unspoken bond; a coven of women with no clue, no class and no self-appreciation to want better or do better. And they've got me sitting around this dinner table, for what? For who? Family dinner? Pretending to be some family that has regular weekly get togethers'. With mums' latest *boo thang* sat at the head of the table, like he won't be gone within six months. Then she's on to the next one so quick, the beds still warm as another man takes his temporary place in her life, cohabiting in this house of fucking *lies*! I lost count of how many different men I've seen come and go and sit in that tainted 'head of the table' chair. None of us sat in that chair it but *these* men.

Mum's type of man was *any* man who showed her any form of devoted loving attention. Typical life of an abused woman, chasing the love she never got from her father and idolising men, fighting the *"Daddy, why didn't you love me?"* daemons in her head. And then, when it wasn't all about *her* anymore, she would move on and very swiftly.

Her taste in men is like she's literally lined up a champions league football team and picked them out in a random rhythmic rhyme like:

"Ip- dip -fucking - do- this- one- will- do!"

You can see it in the product of her offspring. Congregated here today before her and looking like a fucking United Colours of Benetton advert or a Dulux colour chart for the many shades of brown available at your nearest 'do it yourself' store.

Samantha's dad; is an English Bill, mine is Jamaican Bob and Thia's is some Juan Spanish. (Get it? Some-Juan/one Spanish. English Bill, Jamaican Bob, like Marley? See what I did there?) Anyway…

The latest Caribbean receding dreadlocked fool is attempting to entertain us all with the delightful story of how he *met* my *mother* and got his indefinite stay. Is he Ted Mosby? Do I look like I want to sit here listening to this long-winded story? Mum sat beside him gleaming, moving her hands in an exaggerated delicate ladylike way so we could all admire her engagement ring. What the fuck ever, I'm not even asking or entertaining her, I'm not interested. From what my sisters have already told me about this guy… it's *not* going to last. But then again this might actually be 'the one' – who knows, lol?!

Thank *fuck* for Mother Nature's greatest most underrated human process of all time, *menopause*! Luckily for us, it has approached mums' life, body changes and hot flashes right in the nick of time, because the last thing *this* family needs is another love mistake child to mentally fuck up, neglect and ruin.

Mum ran to the clinic thinking she was pregnant, noticing unwanted changes in her body, to find out not only were her symptoms menopausal but… she also had a sexually transmitted disease- and at her big age! Come on! She got it from *this* man at the head of the table still talking shit about how much he *loves* her, when he's the one that gave her the fucking STD!! And she… *my mother* is going to marry him? HIM?! What grown arse woman do you know of, that has to take regular trips to the clinic, in fear of catching something unsolicited from her insatiable soon to be husband? Tell me, please!

Knowing my *Mother,* she'll probably stay with him even if… let's say, for example sake. She's followed him like a detective with that *'something doesn't feel right'* hunch. Climbed through the window of his apartment, to find him in bed with some blonde Eastern European escort who goes by the name of Cindy and *still* stay with him, because he's convinced her to, with his *'sorry I will never do it again'* speech. But we all know he'll keep fucking around with other women and she will keep taking him back because while she's in love but he's busy trying to divide and conquer the world, one woman at a time. Urgh! The thought of it all is so disgusting it's putting me off of my dinner before the food can reach my mouth. Nope!

"You not hungry Aaliyah? I can make you something else?" My mum asks, pretending to be interested in my dietary needs.

"I've lost my appetite, thanks." We both fake smile and shoulder scrunch.
Playing about with my Sunday roast dinner with my fork. Why did I say 'yes' to coming here? Letting go of my fork, it drops to the plate and I push it away from me towards the middle of the table. Sitting back, looking at them all, I can feel my face revealing me aversion for them all.

"You should try it. It's really nice." Sam is shovelling the food down her oesophagus.

"I'm glad *you're* enjoying it sis." Smirking with my elbow on the table, face in my hands watching her eat away and enjoy the meal. "How is it?" I asked, glowing sarcastically.

"It's lovely mum." She looks away from me, sensing my sarcasm and saluted the chef of our home cooked meal. Her best friend and mother who nods in approval at the commended compliment.

"Yeah, it's probably all that added *bloody* taste and texture of this non-halal, catch it, kill it, eat it meat feast of a meal." Scrunching up my face mockingly side smiling as Samantha freezes. Fork suspended in the air, wide eyed, looking devastated. I noticed the non-halal meat packaging in the see-through recycling bag slumped in the kitchen corner but I wasn't about to tell her. What? And ruin my entertainment? No way!

"Mum, it's halal, right?" The fork full of meat, dripping in gravy halted by Sam's mouth. Inches away from her taste buds that are tingling, smothered in meat and waiting for more.

"*Yeah,* I'm sure it is love." Mum said not sure herself, shrugging her shoulders looking left to right for approval.

"Mum!!" Samantha drops her fork and pushes her plate next to mine in the middle of the table. Grabbing her glass and drinking like a fish out of water, wanting her taste buds free of the meat.

"Well I don't know do I? Halal? Organic? Value? Vegan? It's all the same fucking thing, ain't it? Fuck sake!"

"No mum! It's not!" I don't know what's funnier; Sam panicking about the meat or the slip up of mum's cockney accent that she's been holding back from her lover. Who up until now didn't know my mother is common because she knows how to keep up appearances?

"It is NOT the same. It's..."

"Stop! Shut up! Sh! Please, not today! No one has time to hear the whole cut it right here, let it bleed out over there, wash it how many times bullshit! No one cares!" Cutting her off real quick, I don't need another lecture about good Muslim values.

Blue has been calling me none stop and I seriously cannot be fucked to answer. My phone vibrates on the table, a notification at the top of my screen pops up:

Blue Bird: "Call me asap it's important."

I don't know where she's going with that? She can wait. My phone vibrates again...

Blue Bird: "Call me!"

And again,

Blue Bird: "Need to talk. Call me or text me now."

Whoever told her she could be giving me demands and orders lied. Her and her problem can wait!

"I don't know where I went wrong? My oldest is converting to Islam that's why she's wearing that on er' head." Talking through pauses and sips of wine, my mum nods in our individual direction. "That one's my youngest. Er' fella is a drug dealer she met in prison. And that's Aaliyah, she's the one who likes other things but the same *thing*. If you catch my drift."

She gulps down what's left in her large wine glass and continues to eat her meal, happy about her overall analysis assessment of us all. We're all unfazed and used to her ways because she has this habit of pretending we don't exist and then presenting us to strangers and family at an event, like a proud parent, when in actuality she knows nothing about us and doesn't pick up the phone to call or check in on us.

Speaking of calls; Blue keeps calling my phone again. This girl needs to get the point. How many times is she going to call me?

"So, you like girls?" Who is this, three little bird's pitch by my doorstep, dreadlock wearing, praise Jah t-shirt wearing, Berres Hammond listening man sat at the end of the table talking to?

"You don't look like a lesbian to me. Pretty girl like you?"

"I'm sorry, are you talking to me?" I look behind me then back at him. Trying to figure out who he's talking to? I haven't even exchanged two words upon this man's arrival to the table. There wasn't any common courtesy of a 'hello', 'good evening' a 'hiya' or 'wa'um'. *Nothing*! So, he could never be talking to me? I don't even know his name and I couldn't give a fuck what he called himself!?

"Yes, I'm asking you!" He points at me with his fork holding a piece of food on the end of it, then shoves it in his mouth chewing mouth wide open.

"Don't start her off, for fuck sake." Thia muttered under her breath.

"I'm sorry Desmond!" I looked right at him.

"It's Royston." He corrected me.

"Okay Johnathan, I was close." I shrugged.

"Here she goes." Thia kept her head all the way down, chin tucked into her chest. She felt my side eye but I'll get back to her in a minute.

"See what happened Ziggy was, I left the vagina I have strapped to my tongue at home! What the fuck am I supposed to look like?"

Someone tell me why 'you don't look like a lesbian...' is an accepted statement of fact. My response is and you don't look like a fool but here we are!?

"Can we not please, I'm eating." Occasionally Thia spoke up, she pushes her plate into the middle of the table clanking loud against mine and Hijab Sam's plate.

"What is that supposed to mean little girl?" I snap at her little ignorant arse. Throwing a spoon full of peas along with the spoon in her direction. Childish, I know but if this little bitch wants to pipe up, she better look me in the face while she's talking to me and tell me her issue because I *know* I have too much to say about her and hers! So she better not try me!

"Real mature Aa-li-yah." Taking the peas out of her hair, she throws them back at me; for the first time this evening she's let go of her baby bump and I'm sat happily with my spoon full, ready to throw some more at her.

"Girls, girls! Enough!" Mum clapped at us, putting her parenting skills to use.

"Let the little bitch speak up!" Flinging more peas in her direction.

"Who you calling a bitch, bitch?" Fucking trashy lesbian!" Thia reaches for her

plate throwing more food my way. Back and forth we go, throwing food like two kids.

"Did I fucking stutter bitch!? Tramp? Look at your life!?" Throwing whatever is next on my plate at her. Might as well put the rest of this food that no one is eating to use.

"At least I'm not eating pussy, bitch!"

"Pussy is better than a crackhead, reoffending baby father you met in prison bitch! Clap for yourself, go on, you must be so proud! Sitting there trying to tell me about *myself*. Excuse the fuck out of me for not having a trail of kids behind me like the Muslim pied piper over here. All self-righteous and what not, leading her disrespectful kids to a road of poverty. You're all fucking clueless!"

"This is not my fight don't bring me into this Aaliyah." Samantha spoke between sips of water.

"Oh! You're fucking involved, you all are! Sitting here worshipping her!" Gesturing towards my mum, "Listening to this pathetic story of how she met *this* fool and *their* bullshit *'we're so in love story'* that's gonna end like the rest of them! He'll be out before the honeymoon period is up like every other fake Prince Charming, King Joffe and Prince Ali Baba that comes along offering to show her a whole new fucking world! News flash mum: it's not going to happen! Just be happy on your fucking own! With your fucked-up kids and their fucked-up kids! You're sitting there telling him you don't know where you went wrong? Really?! When *nothing* you've done for any of us has ever been right! You're not a mum, you're a fucking joke!"

Silence! All eyes on me and my mouth ready, Mum didn't know where to look. Thia placed both hands back on her belly and Sam done nothing while her kids ran around the table pulling on her clothes each time, they passed her- no respect at all.

My phone vibrating on the table again, breaking the silence, Blue is blowing up my line!

"Aaliyah, calm down."

First of all, when in the history of women, has a woman *ever* calmed down, when being told to calm down!! "Maybe your sister is trying to say that being with a man... could be a good thing?"

The sound of my mum's voice, I swear I'm going to lose my shit! Closing my eyes for a hot second, I'm going to count to ten. Breathe in... One... Breathe out... Two... Breathe in...

"It's not her fault she's stupid." I said quietly to myself, counting my deep breaths. Three... Breathe out... Four... Breathe in...

"...you know? Maybe she's saying a couple kids, would be nice? It's not a bad idea?"

"I'm sorry, when did she say that. I'm confused please tell me mother?" I almost got to five and she had to open her mouth *again*.

"For God sake Aaliyah! We were all enjoying the meal and you ruined it! You are so fucking selfish!" Mum rolls her eyes like *I* am annoying *her*? Calling me selfish when they invited me here on my good, good Sunday to listen to their shit- *that's selfish!*

"Are you serious? So what, we can all sit around this table gossiping bust lips, bruises and heartaches? You're all deluded?! Do you hear the shit that you say? How many times do I have to tell you all I'm a LES-BI-AN. Always starting shit!"

"Aaliyah." One of them said

"Why did I come here… I was having a good day before I came here- fuck!" Pushing myself back on my chair, I throw my napkin down and step away from the table and this joke family.

"Aaliyah?" Samantha called me.

"Let me leave!" Snapping back, I just want to get out of here.

"You used to be so lovely before that girl *beat* it out of you. What she did to you, that condition." Mum said looking at me lost and sad.

"Shut up mum- don't." Samantha silenced mum's nonsense.

"Whether you liked us or not, you tolerated us. But you were a nicer fucking person, not this little bitch you are now. I knew you should have stayed away from women."

"My sexuality and what women do for me is not a condition, mum!" What's she on about but I'm done with them all.

"That's not what I'm talking about…" A silence took over the room with this strange air of concern. Mum held her chin down to her chest and peered up at me with this weird look on her face.

"Mum! Shut up!!" Sam shouted, squinting her eyes at her and talking through her teeth.

"Yes mum, please shut up!" Mocking my sister, I encourage my mum to stop talking, no one knows what she's on about.

"No, she *needs* to know." Mum turns to me, "We do this all the time, you might have a problem but you are a *horrible* fucking person Aaliyah!"

"Mum?" Samantha said quieter, shaking her head.

"Problem? What are you on about?"

"My problem is you Aaliyah, you are the problem and everything that has happened to you is your fault! No one else! Stop blaming us for you isolating yourself."

"We do what all the time?? I'm so lost right now?"

"Aaliyah, she's had too much to drink, ignore her," Thia says

"No, I haven't! I know we shouldn't talk about it but you don't have to be a fucking cunt Aaliyah! We are your *family* and we love you! Not those fucking women you chase after! When are you going to stop and focus on you! You can't keep running away from this."

"Why do you keep bringing women into this?" I can't believe what she's saying, she's really against me seeing women right now?

"Listen to what I am saying!" Mum stood up "You have a fucking problem! You're sick, in the head!"

"I'm sick? In the head? Being a lesbian isn't an illness!"

"ENOUGH MUM!" Sam slams her hand down on the table and the unwanted plates of food rattle. Mum instantly stops. Everybody in the room looks in a different direction.

Mum is always on some bullshit; nothing she says makes any sense, she talks shit about everything and anything; something, or someone else.

They *all* get on my nerves!

13. The Boo Hoo's & Apologies

Here we go *again*- Blue, *a-gain*! Calling me *again*. Ringing off my line *a-gain*. Ignoring the call, sending her straight to voicemail, I don't know why she hasn't got the point? Who calls someone this much? Over and over and for what?! Why the hell hasn't she stopped ringing my line?

Do you ever reach a point in your day, when the only thing you want to do is, scroll through your contact list, hit the call button and go get you some of that good, good sex? This is what I am about to do and so should you... now! Regardless of the day you've had, do it because you can and nothing is stopping you. Go through your phone and tell her or him to come through and see you but be particular and selective with your choice of words. Don't be texting them:

> **'Hey stranger, haven't seen you in ages.**
> **Let's catch up,'**

Wrong!! You need to send them a text that tells them *exactly* what time it is, example: (now pay close attention to the context)

> **'Oi, you up?'**

(the national and international booty call question, usually followed with a bunch of inappropriate emoji's)

(they respond) **'Yeah, you okay? Why you up?'** (they know what time it is)

> **'I'm coming over, I want you to remind me how you like it.''**

(don't make it about you, make them *think* it's about them, when really, you're about to get yours)

> **'Hurry up and get here. See you in a bit.'**

Key points here are as follows: Keep it simple. Keep effective, Keep Straight to the point. Let them know as soon as you enter the threshold of their house it's clothes off, lay the fuck down, let me sit on your face real quick, fuck me, have a cigarette and let me be on my way. No small talk or chitter chatter and definitely no pillow talk. Get in. Fuck. Get out.

Now you've got the tips, go text whoever you need to text and meet me on the next paragraph.

***

"You think you can text me to fuck, any time you want?"

Tiana stands in the doorway wearing a black silk gown, tied loosely at her waist. Blowing, caught in the draft and up away from her skin. She pulls the gown open slightly. Stepping into *their* flat, brushing my hand past her waist. I could never decide which part of her body I preferred more watching her shut the door but not lock the door and walk up behind me, wrapping her hands over my hips and guiding me down the hallway to the where she wanted me to be.

"So, you *just* walk around the house like that, in lingerie for your woman? I know you put that on for me, now take it off!" Turning around, I let my trench coat fall off a little, sitting on my shoulders giving her a glimpse of my body.

"Maybe…"

"Nice place you two have by the way… let's fuck it up!" Straightening my arms to my sides, the coat drops to the floor revealing the tiny lace crotchless bodysuit I have on. Gently swaying my hips from left to right, her eyes follow my every movement.

"The first thing I thought about when she gave me keys, was you!"

"What about me?" Walking my red-soled heels down the hallway, slowly. I pressed my body against hers. Impatiently placing kisses on her body, her eyes closed with my fingers already inside of her, knowing exactly what she wanted to do…

"You inside of me and us fucking on every surface in here."

"We can make that happen."

I wouldn't be me, if I didn't accept the challenge. I want her to remember me in every room up in this house. Too bad the walls can't talk but don't worry, I'll tell you everything and I won't spare a single detail because I came here to fuck!

"We haven't got long, she's gonna be back soon." She pulls on the strings of the silk gown, letting it glide off of her skin and hit the floor in one swift movement. Absolutely *nothing* on underneath, that's my girl! Well not my girl, her girl but my girl too, only every now and then, I'm not SZA but I keep her satisfied only on the weekend.

"Come get it" Tiana steps towards me, her heels clipping along the laminate flooring, licking and biting her lip. Seduction all over her beautiful face, frame and waist. Moving her body down against mine, she kisses my pussy on the way down… she knows how to make my legs buckle. I swear, I felt the wall shake or was it my legs trying to stay standing and holding onto her tight? She listens to my body reacting to her. Mouth open, moaning quietly. I want her to put in work before I start calling out her name. Holding her back and digging my nails into her skin. I know her girl will be asking where they came from- fuck!

"For. Fuck. Sake! My phone." Vibrating loud as fuck, I can't concentrate with all that fucking buzzing.

"Fuck your phone!" Tiana says but all I can hear is my phone vibrating so loud against the damn laminate wood flooring, sounding like it's trying to drill a damn hole in it! How is this phone vibrating harder than an Ann Summers bullet?

"It won't stop, *especially* if it's who I *know* it is

"Whoever it is can wait!" Tiana is territorial with my body, it's cute. I love it. She keeps kissing and licking my clit, meanwhile, my phone has rung about seven times and my ears have picked up on the annoying sound of it vibrating along the floor.

"Let me answer and tell her to fuck off. Shit! Tiana, fuck!" I don't want her to stop but I had to push her fingers out of me with my pelvic floor muscles and get my phone. She hates when I push hard enough for her to come out but loved when I held onto her fingers tight and didn't let them leave my body.

"You're not fucking serious? Aaliyah!?" I step away from Tiana's naked body and bend over to pick up my phone.

"I didn't say you had to stop." Bent over, picking up my phone and looking back past the side of my thighs at Tiana. She crawls towards me, knowing what to do next.

Phone in my hand when I'd rather Tiana was in my hand instead.

Blue's name flashing on my phone, her assigned photo making me want to punch her in the throat- reluctantly, I answer. Rolling my eyes, the fuck does this chick want, all now!?

"FUCKING BITCH!"

Before I can open my mouth, Blue screams down my phone, howling at me, uncontrollably crying in mad pain

"Blue! What the fuck?" What the hell is going on with Blue making all this noise.

Tiana stood behind me, I don't know what to focus on right now. Trying to hold the phone against my ear and focus, when all Tiana is doing is making me want to throw the phone against the wall and smash it to pieces– oh fuck! Pushing back against her, hand flat on the wall.

"Cheating on me! Fucking bitch!" Blue shouting down my phone, what the fuck did she just say?

"What's going oo-on?" I ask Blue hoping she'd repeat what she said. I hold onto Tiana's hand tapping it, telling her to be still but keep her fingers inside of me on that same spot, so when I get off the phone, she can continue...

"Cheating on me! Fucking bitch! I can't believe this shit, this whole time, all this time! In my fucking face! Seriously? Really Aaliyah? This whole fucking time? I should've known like, come on!"

I froze. Shit. She knows! Shit, shit, *shit*. How? Fuck! *Fuck*! Mali must have told her or she saw us on the balcony? I won't say anything until she finishes.

People often if not always make the mistake of interrupting someone sentence thinking we know what they are going to say and interject with the incorrect words., rather than letting them talk, she could be talking about *anyone*!? I'm not the only side bitch the world has to offer.

"Don't act like you don't know what I'm on about! You two are always together!" I can hear the tightness of Blue's throat, she can barely speak through her emotions, screaming and shouting- Aaliyah be cool, do not give anything away.

"Blue, wha-what are you on about?" My words stammer from Tiana not caring that I am potentially in the middle of a crisis, pushing back on my spot, wanting me to scream!

"Mali has been cheating on me and *you* know!" Shit! She can't know but do I ask? I better ask? I need to ask? I should ask? It would be rude not to get to the bottom of this.

"With… who?" Waiting for her to get it together and answer me, "with who babes?" I ask again, in case she didn't hear me.

"You're really going to ask me that? Like really?"

"What do you mean Blue?" Freeing myself from Tiana's grasp, I shuffle down the hallway trying not to step on or trip up on my bodysuit around my ankle.

"Really?" Tiana threw her hands up in the air, frustrated that I pulled away at my peak but right now multi-tasking is out of the question!

"It doesn't matter who with! Because I, because…" Because what bitch? Spit it out, fuck! "Because, I don't know who, I just know she is!"

She sounds hopeless, crying hysterically down the phone but *thank fuck* she did *not* say my name! Phew! She's got me over here sweating, when the only part of my body I want to be producing any form of liquid right about now is my pussy. But no- I'm listening to Blue sounding defeated and she doesn't even know for sure, all alone and shit, wait… she's alone? She's by herself? Shit! Mali? Where's Mali?

"Where's Mali?"

"I don't know, she's never here." She continues to play the pity party soundtrack, like I have time to listen to this.

I need to think about this strategically. I'm not in the all clear, not just yet because if Blue gets hold of Mali in the state then it's a wrap. Mali is not as strong as she thinks she is. She empathetic and sweet and kind and sensitive and will fold with guilt and tell her everything!

"Who are you with?"

"I'm by myself, I'm always on my own. I don't know where she is or where she's gone, her phone is off. You're the first person I thought to call... so I kept calling you. I'm sorry, I don't know what to do."

"Blue, shut up a second!" Oh my god! I can't with her moaning and continuing with this pity party soundtrack!

Pulling the phone away from my ear. I need to think. Think. Think. THINK! I need to get to her before Mali opens her mouth. Think. Think. Think! I need to make sure none of her stupid little friends are around to influences her mind to the obvious. All it takes is one of them to point me out and its game over! Right Aaliyah, focus. Try your best to sound caring and gentle. Don't snap, do *not* lose your shit. Be cool, be empathetic, be thoughtful, be everything but yourself! Taking a deep breath out, putting the phone back to my ear- let's go.

"Blue. Breathe. Chill, listen to me, okay lady." Shutting her up the nicest I can but she's drowning deep in her feelings and won't stop fucking crying, it is not that deep to be crying rivers like this! "Blue! Fuck sake, shut up and listen!" So much for being empathetic and *not* losing my temper?? Let's try that again... Take two; on empathetic lifetime friend aaaaannnnd action!

"Okay..." She whimpers and stops. And, they said tuff love doesn't work?

"I'm sorr- I didn't mean to shout at you. But I *really* need you to listen to me, very carefully, okay babe." This is killing me, pretending to be *this* nice when you know all I want to do is tell her to come off my line with this bullshit, so I can go sit on Tiana's face after the day I've had.

"Okay," she sniffles, calming down.

"I'm coming to see you but I'm going to need you to do me a favour, okay babe. I'm going to need you to breathe okay, just breathe." This is ridiculous! I feel like I am talking to a child, not a grown woman! People are way too fucking sensitive!

"Okay." Hearing her struggling to take deep breaths with me.

"Good, keep breathing with me." I feel like I'm going to be sick, how do nurturing people do this?! "That's it, calm down... I'm going to need you to go lay down, shut the bedroom door and relax. Cry if you have to, I'm coming to lay down with you okay and you can tell me *everything* okay." I'd rather stay here and lay down with Tiana but Blue is a home mess. "When we hang up turn your phone off, don't talk to anyone. No one needs to know your business, I'll be right over- I got you."

"Okay" Sounding lifeless, she took the advice from her *'bestie'* trusting me and *my* advice. "You always know how to take care of me." Do I? "I'll see you soon, love you."

"Okay in a bit." I hang up and begin to untangle the bodysuit from my legs, pulling it back up onto the little bit of my body it was covering.

"What the fuck? Aaliyah?" Tiana is far from impressed, Blue's timing to have an emotional breakdown could not have come at a more compromising time.

"Baby girl, all I want to do is lick every drop of you up *but* I've got to go..." Looking down at her body, I'm so pissed off. "I'll call you later." Damn! Now I know how Trey Songz feels because I don't want to leave but I gotta go *right* now. Trench coat on and out the door, I wave at Tiana and leave. Calling Blues phone to check, she's turned it off- good. Now to go and fill her head with a bunch of shit, so she can drop these accusations and leave me the fuck alone!

***

Blue sat on the step in the doorway of her house, hands in her face, hopeless and helpless. I saw her as soon as I kicked open the rickety old, 'about to bust off the last hinges' it's been hanging from the gate.

Did I not tell this female to go lay the fuck down? Sat here, out in the open for someone to walk by, ask her 'what's wrong' and talk shit to her!? That's my job!! She stands up and her eyes set on me. Blue throws her arms around me, stumbling back a little about to lose balance but stopped myself from falling back. Her body trembling, uncontrollable tears, shuddering with all sorts of emotions.

"I got you, I'm here now. Let's go inside."

Holding onto her and giving her body support, we walked back into the house.

"I don't know what to do," her voice is a frail whisper.

"I'm so confused? Cheating? I just don't see it. Mali, she doesn't cross me as that type. You *know* I've seen disloyal people."

My job is to keep saying things that make her doubt go away. To be here for her and be on her side. Basically, to be an *'actual friend'*. To ask questions with concern, putting on my act perfectly. I need to know everything that she knows or *thinks* she knows. I will sit and be the friend who trash talks her woman, you know how all friends carry on. Quick to judge, when they only know one side of the story talking about:

"Leave her/his trash ass sis, you can do better!"

But that would be far too easy and the basic things to do. Instead, I'll convince her to stay. She has a 'good woman' and see's reading into things that aren't there. Blue doesn't know I have anything to do with any of this, so let's keep it that way.

343

Handing her a tissue and pouring her a shot of some whiskey that I found lurking in the back of a kitchen cupboard. We sat on the kitchen countertops, waiting for her to get it together and speak her mind.

"That's the thing, I don't know what's wrong with me, I'm a mess." I hand her another tissue while she keeps shaking her head, not knowing what to really say.

"Blue don't be ridiculous. Nothing is wrong with you!" Let's be real, if we make a list it will conclude that *everything* is wrong with her!

"Why am I feeling like this? There must be? I'm sorry, I don't know." I'm getting *really* tired of her talking in circles and repeating herself. Saying a lot of words and at the same time, not saying anything at all.

"Listen, I didn't drop my pussy plans to come all this way for *boo hoo's* and *apologies* and *I don't knows*! Talk to me, maybe I can give you some insight or help." What? Am I supposed to sit here and listen to this pity party *shit*! I can only act like I care for so long. I need to retain an essence of myself to be able to get her to say what she knows. So far, I've got nothing because the soft understanding approach isn't working.

"I can't explain." Bitch, you better! "But I can tell, like I *know* something is up. I can feel this change in her. Like this shift in her energy; she's slipping away from me. More and more every day. I know there's someone there. There has to be! I sense it."

"So, now you're physic all of a sudden?!" I screw up my face, she looks at me sideways. Fuck, I meant to say that in my head, I need to slow down on the drink. I say that but my glass is at my lips and I'm sipping on this sauce.

"Aaliyah, you're supposed to be on my side? Have my back?"

"I am, I do, of course I do." Rolling my eyes internally "But maybe, this shift of energy you're talking about and feeling, is the whole 'honeymoon period' coming to an end you know, the whole relationship order of shit."

"No!" She stares at me, her face serious. Is she staring me out?

"No?" She knows…

"No, I know, Aaliyah." SHHHHIT! I gulp my drink. "The way she kisses me," her face relaxes and her shoulders drop as her chin tucks into her chest.

"How so?" My heart is about to fail on me with all these damn palpitations she's causing to start and stop.

"It's different, it's *more*. Something like that doesn't *just* change, it doesn't *just* stop! It's usually a gradual thing you both feel. It's unspoken but you're both okay with the change. But she's definitely been kissing someone else, someone new? She dazes off, like she's caught up in someone else."

"I understand but you're going to need more than an assumption or a feeling. You can't just walk up to her and say '*soo, I think you're cheating on me*' where's the proof? Have you been through her phone, at least?" I already know she has and she's found absolutely nothing.

"Yeah, I've done all that and nothing's there. I've gone through all the messages, texts, photos, apps, call history. I've gone through emails, there is literally nothing." I *know*, *I* make sure Mali deletes it all. Everything, right down to the web browser history.

"Maybe you're overthinking, all the weed that you two smoke has led you to paranoid thoughts like these." Pushing another glass of whiskey towards her hands for her to sip on; she'll talk more, with a few more units of alcohol in her system. Waiting to see if her mind has made any connectives to me yet... so far nothing.

"Aaliyah, she's so distant, like she's somewhere else. Distracted and whoever she's thinking about- put it this way. It's always the small things that no one pays attention to in too much detail, like a kiss. It's a small change people don't usually notice but she grazes her tongue across the top of mine now, when she used to go under."

Time to do what I came to do. Finishing my drink, I reach over holding her hand in both of mine.

"Have you ever thought, maybe it's your own guilt playing on your mind?"

"What are you on about?" Blue looks up at me, confused and a little guilty.

"I know about Raee'n. She told me *every-thing*." Disappointment on my face, ready to use the leverage that *I* set up. Raee'n didn't tell me shit! Only that they kissed but I *knew* there was more, there's *always* more.

"Oh my god! Aaliyah I'm so sorry." She holds her hand to her mouth ashamed. She's vulnerable and it's a *perfect* time to use this leverage.

"Don't be silly, it's okay." I pause for effect. "When she told me, I didn't believe
her at first because I was so shocked. I expected more from you. Blue, what were you thinking, you're not the type to fuck around?" Keeping calm, I took both her hands in mine.

"I'm not, I wasn't thinking. It was out of character of me, I don't know what happened. One minute we were laughing the next she had her hand down my- and I didn't stop her I- I'm so sorry."

"Stop. You don't have to apologise to me. It's not about me, I don't care. It's about Mali, I thought about telling her because it's all *wrong-*"

"Did you tell her?!" She panics, cutting me off.

"No, *never*. Don't be silly! My loyalty lies with you. You're not going to do it again… right?"

"No! Never!" She shakes her head 'no' vigorously, side to side.

"Good! Then there's no need to say shit, ever! Mali can *never* know. It would rip her apart and you have to live with that pain you caused."

"I can't believe I did it, I'm disappointed with myself."

"Look, Blue. We all do dumb shit from time to time. Your secret is safe with me. I'm your friend and I know what you're like. You lose focus quickly. Anyone would be excited by Raee'n." I laugh a little to relax her into believing I'm on her side. "It's natural to dismiss what you did and point the fingers at Mali to alleviate your own guilt. But now you've started thinking irrational things that don't make any sense at all. Seeing things, you want to see, so you feel better about you. Rather than what it actually is… it's nothing."

"I didn't think of it like that" She wipes her tears away.

"I know you haven't. You're telling me about all these things, that she's changed but have you checked in to see if *she* okay? Is there something going on with her other than you? Have you asked her?" I'm throwing sentences, compliments and questions in like a psychiatrist- damn I'm good1

"I'm really disappointed in myself for not considering her feelings, at all." Positioning her thoughts easily, she follows my words.

"What I'm trying to say is, look at her situation. Of course, her focus is gone she's got a lot on... she's so distant... I can't say too much but she *has* spoken to me."

"Why didn't she come to me? What did she tell you?"

"You have to ask her that, talk to her."

"This whole thing has fucked up my thinking. Maybe it is me." Or maybe, it's me, twisting and manipulating your thoughts and words to my own advantage.

"Maybe, or maybe she just needs a little space sometimes." So, she can be with me. "You've got nothing to worry about Bluebird." Now it's time to reinstall her self-confidence "She's lucky to have you. Trust me, if you weren't my close friend. Girl, you know I would fuck you!"

"Stop!" She blushes, from the fake compliments. "Are you flirting with me?" She asks bashfully, wiping her tears away. Women are so easily pleased, honestly, all it takes is a few compliments and they are back on track. Feeling cute with their ego pleased and ready to take on the day.

"You messed up one time, it happens. We're human, we all fuck up sometimes. Don't beat yourself up." Reinstallation of confidence complete with a subtle reminder of her dirty laundry.

I set up the *"Raee'n situation"* intentionally for my own benefit and advantage. Yes, it's fucked up and now I have created this glimmer of guilt in Blue's mind, so she can stop watching Mali with suspicions and start to analyse her guilt affecting relationship. I don't need to know the full story of what happened with Raee'n. It could have been just a kiss, a quick rub of her clit, or it could have been a full-blown fuck but whatever happened, happened. It's enough for Blue to know she fucked up and now she knows she is responsible for seeing her guilt reflected in Mali's actions with a mixture of self-doubt and selfishness. Guilt is a much stronger feeling, one you cannot shake as it lays heavy on our shoulders. Not only has leverage been served but so has an *amazing* round of flipper. Manipulation at its finest, honestly, it's days like this when I amaze myself with how powerful my mind truly is. Then there's other days, where I'm looking for my phone and it's in my fucking hand and I don't even know what day it is.

"I feel so stupid, stressing myself out." Laughing, embarrassed about her erratic behaviour, I laughed with her, she's too damn naïve. Call me Geppetto because I am puppet master of manipulation at work.

"Don't feel stupid, it will be okay. She's lucky to have you."

"You always know what to say Aaliyah. You rationalise things and they all make sense." Yeah, I know because it's a very well thought out, calculated, manipulative, sly and clever process, if I do say so myself.

"I try." Hey, you either got it or you don't sis.

"I'm sorry you came all the way here for my nonsense. Where you coming from anyway, practically naked?" She laughs, lifting my trench coat.
I didn't get a chance to put clothes on, between running out of Tiana's and speeding, parking the car and running to Blue's house in my stilettos and trench coat.

"I am absolutely naked under here. Yes, I was *busy*." Pouring another glass. "I left her soaking wet, to come and dry your tears! You're welcome!"

"I'm sorry." She giggles back to her usual childish self.

"I gave up sex! Me!?" I add playfully but secretly I'm pissed. "I won't tell you about her though because the last one I told *you* about was Raee'n and your fingers got a little sticky." I raise my eyebrows at her and she looks away awkwardly. It's never too soon for a bit of shade. Most of my days are forecasted and predicted to be shady with showers of pettiness.

"How do you do it?" Peering down at the glass she held in both hands.

"How do I do what?"

"How do you not feel any guilt, for the people you hurt? Like, how do you shut the world out?" Now looking at me differently; with the same concerns I gave her earlier but unlike me, she is genuinely sincere. "How do you detach yourself from people like it's nothing? Not feeling anything? For as long as I've known you, I've never seen you in the state I'm in now. I've never seen you scared of losing someone or afraid of them walking away. Maybe I am a fool for believing in love or thinking I have it here with Mali. I know I fucked up but I need love, someone to hold me."

"I *do not* need that!" Snapping back! "Fuck a relationship! It's so much better to fuck and get it over with."

"Yeah, but don't you want to know what it's like for someone to look at you and only see you? Through everything, even in the dark, they see *you*."

"No, absolutely no attachments! Do you think I want to be sitting in the kitchen on the weekend crying to my friend, for what? Because I *think* I'm being cheated on, have no actual proof but have my own shameful secrets?? Blue, that's pretty fucked up."

"That was below the belt."

"No, that was the truth!" I look at her sideways

"Okay but it's nothing compared to all the good times we have."

"Really? Who are you trying to convince?" I take a gulp of my drink, bored of her speaking. My task was long done so why am I hear *listening* to her bullshit?

"Yes, really! Regardless of the bullshit, I will always favour how she holds me and I don't want her to let go. All I'm saying is, I don't know how you do it? How do you not want to fall asleep at night in the arms of a woman holding you tightly? You leave before any emotions can be exchanged! I love it when I move in my sleep and she holds onto me a little tighter. Snuggling her face into my neck, squeezing me and getting closer? What about mornings waking up beside someone and all you want to do is call into work sick and spend the day wrapped in the covers with her. You're missing out on connections- the small ones you never considered before, like her stroking your wrist. Running circles on your skin with her fingertips. Every time she touches you is like the first time and your skin is full of goose bumps again. There are times when she's annoying as fuck but you can't help admiring her because you *love* her." She blushes. "Even when you're feeling a type of way you smile because you know that with her is right where you're supposed to be. I know it's silly Aaliyah, but when Mali is with me, I feel *everything*. Most of it I can't explain- it's like butterflies and this static energy won't leave my stomach and I'm tongue tied, all at the same time. All my common sense goes out the window, not that I have much anyway. I'm *happy* and scared of losing her, who knows what's next for us. If there's a future? But I love her I *really* do. Every time she puts her arms around me, I feel protected and warm and everything makes sense, I make sense. With Mali, it's where I'm supposed to be-I love her, I *do*. This is *real* Aaliyah, soo real! It's her, it always has been. I want you to feel what I'm feeling, don't worry about the other bullshit you're running from, this feels amazing!"

Blue's face lit like a face full of Fenty Beauty highlighter. Her cheeks blushing, her eyes so bright, glowing in the thoughts of everything...

Everything she said... with Mali it's 'us'... I don't know what to say, I don't know where to look, how to respond, what to say back- I -

"I think I'm gonna be sick!"

Jumping down from the countertop, hand on my mouth, running to the bathroom. Standing with my back against the door, my head tilted back, eyes closed taking in everything she said. Catching my breath, slowing it down. Sweating; legs feel weak, struggling to stand, my head is heavy. Everything she feels, *everything* she said- all I could see when she was talking was Mali... but with me and the time that we have stolen together and shared. I know they're small and here and there but the *way* I feel right now... I can't get her face out of my mind- it's driving crazy that when-

"Bluurgh!!!" Head in the toilet feeling my stomach twisting and turning inside out. What is going on?

"You okay in there, Aaliyah?" Blue knocked on the door, whilst I hold my own hair back, getting the rest of this feeling up out of my stomach. Heaving so loud, my gut and throat are on fire! All I can smell is the alcohol along with mums' roast coming out of my stomach, making me heave again and again, fuck!

"Ye-ah, I'm fine." My voice shook, composing myself. Standing up and holding the sides of the cold ceramic sink.

Don't you dare be sick again, don't - you - dare. Breathe you stupid bitch! I don't know what's going on with you but you do not have time for this! Get your shit together and leave! Talking to myself in the mirror unable to figure out what is going on with me and these thoughts of Mali taking over my mind and my body.

Rinsing my mouth out, getting my shit together. I remove the running mascara trails from under my eyes. Whatever this is, I am not dealing with it right now- no time for weakness, control yourself! Enough now!

I have *never* considered the feelings of the partners of any of the women who I fucked with. I've never heard their side of emotions and feeling- maybe this is what this weird feeling is? It has to be guilt? Being here, talking to someone that I am doing this to? Fucking with her head and making her love insecure when love is supposed to be so secure.

Why did I think I could do this? That it was okay to do this? Why the fuck do I feel like this? Why is everything she's saying connecting with me? I can feel it all, in my belly, on my shoulders, on my skin and in my head- too close. I need to leave. My head hurts.

"What's wrong?" Blue handed me a glass of water as I step out the bathroom.

"Nothing, I'm okay." My stomach is on fire but I firm it and smile- no time for weakness! "See what happens when you talk to me about love?!" I force out a little painful laugh. "It's sickening!"

"Blue, I've been trying to call y- Aaliyah?" Mali charged into the house and her footsteps stop dead in her tracks. Eyes darting between the two women of her interest stood side by side. Wondering what the fuck is going on, struggling to maintain her cool. My eyes wide, signalling her to act normal, be cool, stay calm and relax, I got this. Do I though?

Blue tilted her head towards Mali, wanting me to deliver the recap of why we are all congregated here. I mean, yeah, sure I'll do all the talking? It's not like someone has set my body on fire and my mouth doesn't smell like eight cans of shark shit but okay??

"Blue and I have been talking, about *you*. She was all *worried* that *you* are *cheating* on her. But I told her it's all in her head, right? You know you've got a good one here and you're lucky to have her." Blue and I smile at each other, *'best friends 4eva'* I think I'm going to be sick again!? Fist to my mouth, holding back any vomit from projecting into this emotional bullshit. "Besides *if* you were *cheating,* which you're *not.* You'd have *me* to deal with." Which in my defence isn't a complete lie, if you change the order of words that is?

Mali knew I had it under control she has this level of attractive vigilance. She steps forward engaging Blue with a tender touch.

"Come here babe," Reaching for Blue, tugging her gently towards her, she embraces Blue in her arms. "Why would I cheat on you? Don't be silly, I've just been a little distracted lately." Holding her woman's head on her shoulder, she kept her eyes on me the entire time.

"I know, I'm sorry. I love you Mali." Blue's voice muffled in Mali's arms.

"Love you too…" Mali responds, without an *"I"* at the beginning.

Shrugging my shoulders as Mali stares at me all besotted and sad, like she has something to say to me. Like she's holding onto something? What does she want from me? I'm over here having to rectify her stupid errors because she's been distant with her woman, unable to fucking focus!

Feeling awkward and odd, wanting to leave and leave them to it but they're blocking the doorway with this sickening embrace of love and urgh, stuff!

"Let's go upstairs?" Blue asked, gazing at Mali. Well, at least someone gets to cum today! "We won't be long, wait here."

Who does Blue think I am? 'wait here'? No thanks, I'm good. She leads Mali by the hand upstairs and I lead myself to the kitchen to get my shit and leave!

Throwing my bag onto my shoulder, I pour myself another shot, more like a half a glass. *Do not judge me!* I've had a very fucking rough day!

Slamming the glass down onto the kitchen countertop, watching it wobble around on the surface then stop. Pissed at myself for putting *myself* into this mess, is this all even worth it?! I've got plenty of women lined up waiting but as much as I try and stop myself or occupy myself... I am stuck on Mali and I'm in a house while she is about to fuck her woman! Why am I here??

Leaning my elbows on the kitchen countertop, I feel her over me and on me. Mali holding me by my waist, roughly turning me around to face her. Grabbing my body with her hands under my trench coat, lifting me onto the countertop. Kissing me, so passionately, so deep, so hot and heavy. My arms wrapped over her neck. Her hands busy undoing my trench coat, wasting no time she opens my legs. I pull on her hair and bite her neck. She moans, loving the way we dominate each other. Wrapping my legs around her waist, her hand around my throat, holding it tight. Head back, her mouth on my breast her tongue all over me- fuck! Her fingers inside of me, my body moving to the edge of the countertop. Silently not making a single sound, fuck! Letting go of my throat, pulling me closer towards her staring right in my eyes- she kisses me, slowly.

She stops... out of breath, hearing Blue calling out her name from upstairs. She steps back, taking a good look at me. Trench coat open, legs open body on display.

"Are you fucking insane! I'm over here cleaning up your mess! What the fuck is wrong with you? Where the fuck have you been Mali?!" I whisper angry and aggressive but she's so… she does these things to me. Things I can't explain.

"Shut the fuck up and kiss me!" She whispers aggressively back, kissing me again biting on my bottom lip- just like what I do to her. Stepping back from me, she picks up two glasses with one hand and grabs what was left in the bottle with the other. One last glance at me, walking towards the kitchen door and smirks at me. She's fuelled and happy from our dangerous passion. Little bitch! Using me as some sort of sexual stimulant to go fuck her woman.

"You're actually sick in the head; stay the fuck away from me Mali!"

"Whatever, I'll be back in a minute." Does she *really* think I'm about to sit down here and listen to *them* fucking?

Honestly, people are taking me for a fool! I am done with this day! Taking my last gulp of drink, I grab my bag off of the floor and leave!
Stood outside, letting the breeze cool down my body before tying up my coat. Lighting a cigarette, taking a deep pull then exhale the day away while walking towards my car.
Fuck all of this!

14. The Night in Rome

Where the *fuck* is my car!! I could have *sworn* I parked it right here? Shit! Looking up at a big *'No Parking Sign'* fuck! How the *fuck* did I miss that? Fuckers towed my fucking car, the fucking pricks! They're lucky my handbag wasn't in there, you

"FUCKING ARSEHOLES! FOR FUCK SAKE!!!"

Screaming at the sign when no one is listening to me out here, alone on this empty street, throwing myself and a tantrum on the floor. I give up! I have had *enough* of today! Honestly, what the fuck else could go wrong?

"What the fuck are you looking at!?" Shouting at some guy pedalling past on his little bike watching me scream, shout, huff and puff and talk to myself. When it's totally *normal* for someone to do all of those things... practically naked and in a trench coat

"Go on! Peddle and fuck off!" Yup, he thinks I'm fucking nuts. Seriously though, what the hell do you mean *tow* my car? There should be some sort of sign telling you *not* to park here! Yes, I *know* there *is* a sign there but it should be a bigger one! One that you can see a mile off, before attempting to park saying something like:

"Don't you dare park here you little bitch!"

Or

"I wouldn't if I were you"

Painted on the street in fluorescent pink or posted up with flashing lights. I bet no one would park then! All these white, red and yellow damn lines? Park here and don't park there? Who can remember what means what? Or pay attention to, *especially* when you're in a hurry trying to save yourself, when you know you are guilty as fuck.

But innocent until proven otherwise, right? Every woman for her damn self! Come on, do you think I would be here if Blue called me with all that 'boo hoo' bullshit if I wasn't involved? Please, I am not the person you call and rely on in a time of need- leave me the hell alone! I don't care, call someone who does!

Look at the fucking time! I swear, today is *not* my day what the fuck else could go wrong now!? Not an Uber in sight, my battery is on two percent and I'm the idiot who doesn't leave the house with a portable charger because I forgot it on *charge*! I always leave it at home! Why do I even carry a bag, half the things in it I don't need? But all women carry useless and unnecessary bullshit weighing them down throughout the day... you know just in case?!

Now here I am standing on the street, in the middle of the night, looking like a prostitute who's lost her driver. Fresh from a one-hundred-and-fifty-pound outcall job for a fifteen-minute, cheap one-shot fuck!? Forget this shit!

Tapping my bank card on the wireless entry gates at the tube station, unfortunately, this is my only option. Black taxis don't and won't come down this way and if they did, I will end up screaming directions at the driver for taking forever. Because he's reading page to page of an A-Z of London instead of using Google maps- fuck that! Fuck my family, fuck Tiana for looking *so* damn good naked, fuck Blue and her jumping to damn conclusions self! (although she's right) Fuck Mali! Fuck the people who towed my car! Fuck TFL! Fuck the staff who refused to do night shifts on a Sunday that is resulting in me, running through the train station in these damn high heels that are not made for walking let alone running! Trying to hold down my coat and stop the cold breeze from finding its way up my coat, slapping the back of my thighs and breezing past my pussy.

Stupid damn last train home, can't get my car till the damn morning! Fuck! How could I forget the 'no parking' sign?!

I'll be handing Blue and Mali the penalty ticket fine for my car; for dealing with *their* damn drama! Do I look like Oprah to be sitting there handing her tissues listening to her pour her heart, feelings and emotions out to me?! No!!

The double doors open up to an empty tube. So pissed that I'm standing on the tube for however many stops. I refuse to sit on these dirty seats when I should be sitting comfortably and warm in my car, cruising through London not giving a fuck, because I am in MY CAR not on a dusty train!! Let me calm down, tubes aren't that bad, it could have been worse, it could've been a night bus situation. Urgh! The thought of it makes my skin crawl. Have you ever hit the seat cushion of a public transport seat really hard and watched the amount of dust, dirt and probable skin cells, come flying out of them?! It's disgusting! So, besides from being in a cesspool of germs and bacteria, a million mile underground with no natural light, unexplainable heat and no air con. I'm fine!

Who am I kidding?? I fucking hate it! Fuck this! Fuck this tube? And fuck this chick sat on the tube? Actually, hold on a sec… that's *not* a bad idea…

She's stunning; tucking her long braid behind her ear. Surprising me with her grey eyes darting around worried, fidgeting and nervous of her surroundings. Looking completely over me at the tube map above my head and back at the one held tightly in her grasp. Stretching her neck with each stop, looking out the window trying to find the names of each station as we pass on after the other. She runs her finger along the route of the map on her lap, locating her destination and how far she is from it. Her backpack making her hunch over, unable to sit back in the seat. She's awkward but gorgeous dark brown glowing skin, popping- I can't even guess how old she is. Flawless without a drop of makeup on.

She has on this oversized pale blue loose jumper covering what looked like denim short shorts that are barely touching the top of her thick thighs. She moves her hands so delicate and carefully calculating where she needs to go.

"Where you headed?" I ask her, loud enough for her to hear me over the clanking sounds of the metal tube wheels hitting the steel tracks, causing the tube to rock from side to side.

"Pardon?" I startled her concentration. I don't even think she realised another passenger entered the carriage, let alone one looking like a classy escort. Lol at my life. For a split second, I forgot about my lack of clothes until her eyes set on me in shock.

"Where you trying to get to?" I ask, intruding softly.

"Oh, I umm..." she looks down at her map. "Here." She points out her destination then sets her eyes back on me. She's so gorgeous!

"I hate to break it to you but you're headed in the complete *wrong* direction."

"Oh, for fuck sake!" She collapses her head in her hands, like she's about to have a breakdown. I <u>do not</u> *need another* dramatic female in my presence. I will leave her and go to the other end of the carriage, if her bottom lip even attempts to drop and quiver. "Which way do I need to go?" She composes herself while I invite myself over to where she is sat, standing over her and holding the pole. Leaning towards her; I point out the correct route with the changes and connections to get to where she needed to go. She smells sweet, like fresh cut flowers, like home.

"You've got to change, here to end up there."

"Where do I get off?"

"This is the last train, there's nothing heading back the other way."

"Really?" Defeated and devastated, "Honestly, it's my luck, or lack of. My first train was cancelled, second one, delayed. My phone is dead, I have the memory of a peanut, so I don't remember anyone's number. I mean who does? We all hit 'call' nowadays, no one remembers numbers anyway? I don't even know my own." She rambles on and I wait for her to take a breath or finish. But I don't think she's done. "I should have met up with a group of friends' *hours* ago, how am I going to get to them now? Am I even going to go the right way? Who knows, well you do and I don't but-."

"There's always a taxi?"

"Lost my card. Yup, I'm scatty too. I had the card in my back pocket. At least I think I did. Anyway, it's gone."

"There are night buses but I wouldn't recommend it for your first trip to London." Screwing up my face at the idea.

"That obvious it's my first time here, huh?"

"Yeah, a bit. That and the whole map pointing, weekend bag on your back and the *'where the fuck am I?'* look on your face." We both laugh at her situation.

"It's been a nightmare! I don't know where I'm going and if I get to wherever it is, where I am meant to be, I don't know where to go from there because the address is on my flipping phone! Do you know you're the first person who's helped me let alone spoke to me?"

"London can be cold at times. It's the city where no one gives a fuck!"

"Do you help every woman who looks as helpless as me?"

"Only the pretty ones." Forward? Yes, but I already know she's coming home with me. I'm about to give her control and make her completely comfortable with the idea.

"Well the last stop isn't too far from mine?"

"I really don't mean to be rude but… I don't know you and I've seen all the Taken movies."

She politely denies my offer and so she should! She's right, she doesn't know me. For all she knew I could be leading her to dangerous territory… that's only *if* you don't like being choked during sex- I'm joking! Come on, be serious, I'm not exactly about to take a *beautiful stranger* home and *fuck*… that would be ridiculous…

"Yeah, I've seen all those movies. You know she fights back in the second or third one, I think?" She stares at me with a blank expression, unimpressed with my kidnapping banter. "I'd be the same, London is a crazy place."

"I know, stranger danger and all of that." She looked back at her map attempting to find her way to her unknown destination- wait, what, no?

"I'm sorry; can we discuss the fact that you just said, *'stranger danger'*? Did you learn that in your *'how to survive London'* starter pack manual?" I laugh.

"Don't laugh, anything could happen?"

"Obviously, *but* only if you want it to." I pause, holding out my hand "I'm Aaliyah." She stares at me wide eyed, "this is the part where you shake my hand and tell me your name. You know, the usual 'meet and greet' context." I said with a cheeky grin on my face.

"Oh!" She laughs a little, still unsure but she relaxes with my friendly charm.

"I'm Rome." Her voice a little shook, not knowing where I am going with this whole introduction thing. But she doesn't need to worry about that just yet.

"Well Rome, *now* you know me!"

"I'm still not sure…"

"There are much more scarier people out there. You can charge your phone at mine, call your people, get the details and get a taxi, done. You never have to see ne another day in your life. I'd hate to leave a pretty woman like you stranded and alone. I'd offer to drive you but my car is-let me not, it's a long story babe. My night didn't go as planned."

"You to? It sounds okay but…" She peers down at what I'm wearing.

"This is not my every day and this is *not* the movie Taken. I was with someone, a bunch of drama happened blah blah." I point at my clothes, or lack of. "Hang on." Taking my purse out of my bag, pulling my driving license out of the window slip and I place it in Rome's palm softly.

"What's this?"

"My I.D; driving license hold on to it. It's got my name and address and now it's your security."

"Security?"

"An insurance slash assurance thing, just in case. I saw it in a movie once– not Taken! It's for you to feel safe, right? You can call your people when your phones up and running, tell them who I am and where you are. Give them my address, drop your location or whatever and let them know that you're good. The next stop is me, so…"

I shrug, knowing I'm the only option she has. She sat twiddling her thumbs, I turned to the doors waiting for the tube to slow down and pull up at my station. Looking over my shoulder encouraging her to get up.

"…come on."

"Okay, but no funny business!" She points at my I.D, following me and stuffs it into the back pocket of her shorts.

"Okay, but I am not making any promises"

***

"I'm beginning to think saying *yes* was the best decision I've made all day." Rome looks around my apartment; taking it all in while I continue my usual routine of throwing my house keys in the bowl on the side table, kicking off my heels and turning on my music; filling the house with the beautiful sound of soft chill acoustic vibes.

Following me, placing her shoes neatly beside mine at the end of the chaise- I like her *already*. Her backpack weight still on one shoulder, unsure of what to do with herself. Arms crossed over rubbing them, she shudders a little from the chill of the openness of my apartment; it takes a while to adjust to but I had long adjusted to that slight chill in the air. It's soothing to me.

"Want a hot chocolate to warm you up lady?" I ask, walking further into my apartment and away from her answer, knowing she's due to follow me.

"Sure." Pulling the cuffs of her jumper down over her hands.

"Is that your bedroom up there?" Looking up, she points a finger out of her sleeve, up at the mezzanine bedroom. "That's fucking dope!"

"Yeah it is! You can see the whole apartment from up there." Taking off my coat and swiftly switching it up with an oversized t-shirt that hung from the end of my banister. I'm not one to shy away from nudity, especially in my own home. I watched as she caught an intended glimpse of my body as I changed.

"Must be fun sleeping up there." Moving her stray braids behind her ear once more, she smiles a different smile at me. Looking at my face, she attempts not to look anywhere else. The way people do when they are trying not to look at someone, when there's nothing but skin, breast, thighs and body distracting them from the little input they have to give the conversation because all they can hear in your head is:

"Don't look, don't look"

"Who said anything about sleeping?" I tuck the extra-large t-shirt over my body. She doesn't know what to do with herself, awkward and wondering *why* she is here with a 'stranger' and not somewhere in the middle of London locating her final destination. "You can plug your phone up in the kitchen, taxi number is on the fridge." Walking and talking in front of her barefoot, I can hear her feet patting along the cold tiled floor following close behind my footsteps.

"Thank you." She finally peels the heavy bag strap from her shoulder, letting it drop heavily onto the floor with a thud. Rustling through it, she takes out her charger and stands in her continued awkwardness. Her charger in hand while her eyes search for an available plug socket.

"Over there…" Pointing at a vacant socket by the toaster with the milk and whip cream in my hand, I close the fridge door with the side of my body. "So… what's your story? What brings you to London Town lady?"

Taking two cups from my cupboard, watching her twirl one of her braids around and around her fingertip, searching for the answers for the two questions I asked.

"I haven't got much of a story; small-town girl lost in the city saved by a stranger. I'm here for a few days for a tattoo convention then back to the small-town sticks I go."

"Fair enough. Take a seat, I'll be done in a sec."

She looks around the 'seat-less' kitchen that has no seats to 'take' then back at me, not sure where to sit. I tap the black glittered marble countertop of the island. I always sit up on the countertops and saw no point in buying any stools or seating. She hoists herself up onto it and I continue to make the hot chocolate. Her vibe is intriguing; her energy feels real and something about her felt peaceful but complex at the same time.

My phone rings, cutting into my thoughts of Rome- with Raee'n calling. Rolling my eyes, letting the call ring out, I put my phone back down on the countertop close by where I stood and push it away from me.

"Boyfriend?"

"Nope, it's a woman." I laugh "I'm a lesbian or as the industry of acceptance calls it 'I'm a queer black woman'."

"Okay…" She pauses, not prepared to hear that. I don't dance around my sexuality, never have done. The last thing I want is someone thinking is that I take dick, boy bye! "Girlfriend then?"

"Not at all." I laugh harder. "No babe, it's someone I have *no* interest in talking to right now, especially when I have company."

Turning to check her reaction to that, she doesn't seem fazed at all. It's not always accepted; being this bold about your sexuality. I mean, I don't give a fuck, I am very proud of who I am. But you'd be surprised at how many heterosexual women '*say*' they're cool with it but are actually on the fence with it all. They have this thing, where you tell them you're a lesbian or part of the all those other letters community and they instantly act as if you told them you want to sit on their face! Come on, behave!

Not *every* lesbian is attracted to *every* woman out here, relax!! Just because we like women as a whole it does not mean we *like* them <u>all</u>. Everyone, regardless of sexuality has a type or personal preference of physical attraction. Can you imagine if everyone was attracted to everyone!? No one would get anything done and we would be an over-populating planet because everyone is going at it like fucking rabbits! I don't want every set of breasts I see in my mouth. So, don't act brand new, nobody wants you, sweetie. But in this case, I do want Rome because she's my type, facts.

"How? Like when did you know you were a lesbian?" She asks the mandatory follow up question as expected and I roll my eyes.

"How did you know you were straight?" I question back, placing her hot chocolate beside her.

"How do *you* know I am straight?"

"Every heterosexual person, male or female have the same follow up question, in conversation after a person tells them their sexual preference." Facts! (I am full of them today)

"Point taken." She nods in approval of my counter-response. "I guess you just knew then?"

"Cream?" I said holding up a can of whip cream, eye contact on lock.

"Yes please," Answering with confidence, her awkwardness had faded away. She doesn't take her eyes off of me as I move. "...I've been with a girl before." Another thing a heterosexual person may say in response to prove their acceptance of said sexuality. Either this or announcing they know of/know someone who is gay, to be able to ask the next question, which is always:

"Have you ever been with a man before?"

"Baby, men have their uses; sex with me will *never* be one of them. Careful, it's hot!"

Checking my phone again three missed calls. I place her mug of hot chocolate in her cold hands that were still covered by the cuffs of her jumper- this should warm them up… if not then I have something else in mind…

"No?" Blowing on her drink, cooling it before she takes a careful sip, "Damn that tastes good." Wiping the cream off of her top lip with her fingertip, she sucks off the cream.

"So, I've been told." Smirking at her, she quietly laughs and loosens her shoulders feeling at ease in my company. "What was it like being with a girl then?" I ask, spotlighting Rome in the conversation, having had enough of being questioned.

"To be honest, I don't remember much but I was a mess. *Sooo* fucking drunk!" She pulls a face and took another sip. I stood opposite her drinking mine.

"Oh okay, so it was one of those *'look at me, kissing a girl and like it'* drunk kind of moments?" Mocking her with a school girl giggle, flicking my hair over shoulder and an animated wide-eyed flutter of my lashes.

"What's that supposed to mean?" She's offended but I continue to validate my point.

"Most, if not *all* straight women have *lesbian experiences* somewhere between the fifth and seventh glass of double vodka and cranberry. They're a mess, kissing the face off their bestie and it's all *'giggle, giggle. What's that?'* Fiddle, oops!" I shrug, it's the truth- *they* all do it. "It's so fucking unattractive!"

"It was nothing like that!" She's not impressed with my theory, that is proven every Thursday to Saturday night in Central London nightlife, in a shitty bar like Yates- also, another fact!

"No?" I put down my cup and fold my arms, preparing to hear the most generic 'lesbian experience' story of all time.

"No. I never told anyone but I *actually* really liked her." She glows, flushed and flustered at her own thoughts.

"You did?" Unfolding my arms, unexpecting *that* response.

"She was fucking perfect! I remember her face in the morning. She was disgusted with what happened- I loved it. I knew *exactly* what I wanted. I had my eye on her for a little while. Anyway, she dismissed the whole thing, including me! And now she walks past me like I'm a stranger. I got over it because after all sex is *just sex,* right? So… fuck it."

"Exactly!" We clink mugs together in cheers and agreement and then slowly take cautious sips from our hot mugs "So, what was it like? I'm curious." I said, stood in front of her, my hands placed either side of her flat on the cold countertop.

"It was like..."

"Uh, uh." Cutting into her words, "I don't want you to tell me… I want you to show me."

She places her mug down and holds my face, her hands warm from the hot ceramic mug. Waiting on her, she peers down at me and back up again with a different look in her eyes this time. Seduction set deep in those big grey eyes, shifting her body closer to the edge of the counter, wrapping her legs around me. She opens her mouth…

"…take off your clothes and I'll show you *everything!*" She lets go of my face, picks up her phone and dials. "Hey, it's Rome… yeah, I know right? I'm okay. Yes, I'm sure. It's been an abso-lute nightmare!" Back to her happy go lucky small-town girl voice. "Luckily, I bumped into a *friend…* I know right, the chances?" She rolls her eyes and flaps her hand, imitating the person on her line talking too much. "Honestly, I'm okay… *yes,* I'm sure. I'm going to stay and start again in the morning I'm so fucking tired…yes, I'm sure… see you guys in the morning, okay, yeah, bye Hun, bye." She ends the call.

"Inviting yourself to sleep over, are you?" My hands already undoing the buttons on her shorts.

"Who said anything about sleep? I want to see what the ceiling of your bedroom looks like." Her voice back to the sexy seductive tone. "Now…where were we?"

"*We* were at the part where you show *me* how *you* like it."

"Yes, and I told *you* to take off your clothes. Hurry up so you can take of mine!" She lays back on the island counter top

"Say no more." Without hesitation, I took of my t-shirt, climbed up and joined her. Removing her jumper over her head and pull her shorts off; taking a moment to take in her sexy chocolate brown skin covered in tattoos. There is nothing better than stripping a woman down to her bare skin and her body is covered with tattoos- I love that shit!

***

"Hurry up tell me, tell me!"

"Relax! I'm getting to it." Chilling on the sofa, on the phone to Blue. She's squealing down the phone in excitement. I'm telling her about the night *in* Rome. Hearing the echo of the phone call on the loud speaker; I want Mali to hear *every* word!
I know she's somewhere there, she better be listening to this especially after her stunt yesterday.

"Come on tell me!" Blue impatiently wanting to hear another classic sexual story from yours sincerely...

"Okay so, I couldn't take my eyes off of her. She had this floral style tattoo up the whole side of her body, it was everything! Anyway, I'm on top of her. I wanted to watch her face while I was inside of her and she did *not* take her eyes off of me- it was so intense! The sounds she was making were un-fucking-real! Her leg was up on my shoulder. Our bodies were locked together and I was holding her down, she couldn't move her body away from me. All she could do was arch her back and tell me how to fuck her! I just met the girl and had her screaming my name!" Bragging about my ability to get a woman who I didn't even know to scream my name, it's a special power one possesses. Yes, I am that amazing!

"Oh wow!"

"My hand was drenched, she didn't want me to stop. My counter was soaked! There was whipped cream, strawberries and hot chocolate everywhere!"

"What the fuck? Were you cooking or fucking?!" She was cracking up down the phone.

"I couldn't tell you what we didn't lick off each other's bodies."

"No way! Your neighbours must hate you!"

"Fuck my neighbours!"

Laughing walking into the kitchen looking at the mess everywhere. All over the floor and the counter top with drip stains down the sides. Oh, Eleni is going to *kill* me. I should make a start cleaning it up but instead I swirl circles with my finger in the spilled cold hot chocolate that probably wasn't hot chocolate anymore.

"Where is she now?"

"I woke up and she was gone. Just the way I like my women in the morning- not here!"

"You're a savage! Wait till I tell Mali about this one!" Come again say what!? I thought Mali was there? All that energy and story-telling for what? For fuck sake- errrurrrgh!

"She's not there?" She better had fucking be!

"No?" Blue started to talk about her and hers. Zoning all the way out, I am not about to hear her babble. I didn't call to *actually* talk to Blue! I wanted Mali to –

"Knock, Knock, Knock!!!"

My front door knocked- odd? The buzzer didn't go off? Who the hell is here? I swear, if one of my neighbours have let my sister into the building again, I'm going to go mad! Who the fuck is here?

"Who's at the door?" Blue extended her ears, as if my door is her business to want to know 'who' is knocking it.

"Might be Rome. Maybe she left something?" Walking over to the door I opened it. "Or maybe she came for some more pussy."

"Blue... I've got to go." Hanging up before she could say goodbye, I stare at my uninvited guest stepping past me into my house.

"Miss Aaliyah, I got your coffee baby." She held out two take away paper cups, kissed me on the lips and walks in merely.

"What are you doing here Mali?"

"Drinking my coffee and you need to drink yours, before it gets cold and you start making your noise. And yes baby, before you ask yes, it's almond milk. Yes, it has three shots of coffee and an extra pump of caramel and just the way you like it, venti." She chuckles, handing me the larger cup out of the two she held.

"Yeah, I got the whole coffee thing, what the fuck are you doing *here* with it? That's what I am asking."

"What are you on?" Pressing the front of one foot onto the back of the other, she slips her trainers off of her feet and tucks the shoes beside mine. She walks over to the sofa and she sits comfortably. Picking up the remote, she turns on the television and I am still stuck wondering why the fuck is she here? Did I miss something or...?

"What do you think you're doing, leave. Please?" I pointed at the door.

"Again? One minute you want me, then you don't! Make up your fucking mind Aaliyah!"

"What do you mean *again*?"

"We need to talk about *us*, baby, I can't keep replaying this," she looks defeated. "I don't get what we are doing here, really I don't?"

"What do you mean *us*? There is no *we*?" Someone tell me what the hell is going on?

"That's exactly it, of course, there is an *us*! You know this but one minute you're all over me and the next you look right through me, as if you don't know me.

Fucking around with all these other women. This is not normal. *We* are not normal baby."

"What things? Mali, I'm really confused what are you on about?"

"This is what I mean! You're too hot and cold. All the times I come here and we chill together?"

"What do you mean all the times? You've been here like twice!"

"What?"   Her   face   is   as   lost   as   mine.
"You've   only   been   here   *twice*   Mali?   What   are   you   on   about!"

"What?! Aaliyah, don't do this. I'm here *all* the fucking time! I was here yesterday, I've been here! What fucking mind game or head fuck is this now?"

"No? I went to my family dinner. Then I went over to Tiana's. Blue kept calling me and I had to run over there to calm her down. I only saw you briefly yesterday."

"No…" Holding my hands tight, trying to get answers out of me. I have no idea why. "That's not what happened yesterday?" It's like she knows the answer. But I'm trying to remember "Aaliyah, where were you?" I can hear her talking, calling me *baby*? Too many voices going around that won't stop!

"I was… erm."

"With me. We were laying down chilling. You were with *me*…"

"What? I went, wait… no? What?"

"Aaliyah?" Catching contact with my dazed eyes "What day is it?"

"Thursday? Erm, Tuesday, I think?"

Mali didn't correct me or help me with the answer but by the look on her face, I can tell, I knew I was incorrect.

"Afternoon Aaliyah, my love." We both turn to Eleni, shuffling in with shopping bags and a fresh bunch of flowers tucked under her arm. Her speech muffled with the mail in her mouth. "Ah, hello Mali." She waves at Mali who walks towards her to help with the shopping bags. "I got the cookies you like Mali, I had to hunt them but I got them."

"Ask Eleni."

"Ask me what?" She looks over her shoulder not paying any attention to the situation and atmosphere she's walked into, distracted by her daily routine of activities.

"Ask her Aaliyah, go on!" Mali frustrated but I'm so confused as to what is happening, I don't have a clue what's going on.

"Eleni, how many times has Mali been over here?"

"Been here?" Eleni laughs out loud. "The amount of clothes I wash, she practically *lives* here." She shuffles off to the kitchen, singing away to herself.

"I don't understand any of this?"

"Go upstairs, go on! Go check your rails in the dressing room, check the drawers. Check everything, go on! Go!" Mali points irritated and loud, trying not to raise her voice. Stepping to the side and away, she throws herself on the sofa and places her hands in her face.

Slowly walking up the stairs taking cautious steps, not knowing what to expect. Wondering over time and feeling all over the place but in one place at the same time. Everything as if it was all moving in slow motion.

Up the stairs stepping into my closet room. Feeling overwhelmed and stunned; running my hand along a rail full of clothes that don't belong to me.

"I told you, see."

"… wait …?" Lost for words, I turn to Mali with worry on her face, stood behind me.

"Aaliyah?" Mali steps forward, waving her hand in front of my blank expressionless face.

"I thought this might happen." I hear Eleni's voice in the distance but none of this made sense. "It's been a long time." She held a yellow jiff cloth tight in her hand.

"What's going on?" Mali asked Eleni. "What's happening?"

"I'm going to put the kettle on and make some tea, she likes tea. Her mum makes her tea. I'll make her tea. You stay here… stay with her." Eleni spoke again, I started to drift back into my reality. "Sit with her and wait… she'll figure it out." Eleni patted Mali on the arm, looked down at me with a small smile and left the room. I can hear her flipflops getting further away as she went downstairs. I sat on the floor with one of Mali's t-shirts in my hand, peering down at myself realising that I'm wearing one of her t-shirts.

"Aaliyah?" She kneeled down to me. "You okay, baby?"

"Baby…?" Peeling up at her clothes on the rail then back at her and her oversized t-shirt on my body. "What moments? What times? Tell me…"

"You don't remember?"

"It doesn't make sense… I was *here* last night with Rome. So, you couldn't have been here… with me?"

"Aaliyah, who's Rome?"

"She was here… *we* were here last night? I met her on the tube? She had on- she was wearing. She's got these perfect braids she's a beautiful dark complexion. And, and she had a tattoo all over her and she had, she's got grey eyes. And she was here! I'm telling you, I know she was!" Frustrating myself and confusing myself because she *was* here!

"Are you joking?!" Mali looked at me sideways. Getting up and going over to one of my side tables in my room, shifting through a stack of my magazines one by one. She stopped looking at one and shaking her head. "You talking about her??"
She holds out the magazine to me and there she was… Rome, on the front of one my tattoo magazines. Her braids, her grey eyes *and* her tattoo. Taking the magazine from Mali's hands, my eyes darting from her head to her body. This is her but- wait? How? What?

"This *is* her but *we* were in the kitchen talking? It was her first time in London and she got lost, and, and her first lesbian experience. What the fuck is going on? It's her but she was *here*, I'm telling you she was!"

Mali snatches the magazine back and flicks through the pages and reads;

"Meet Rome, this weeks' cover girl as we talk with her about travelling, getting lost in London, tattoos and sex with women!" She shoves it back in my hand showing me the interview pages. With more photos of her scattered across the centre printed pages. My eyes pick up words I her interview, just like what she told me last night??

"Yes! That's her but she was *here*! I'm telling you!"

"Aaliyah, *WE* were here last night. No one was here but you and me!"

"No, look I'll show you."

Shooting up to my feet pushing Mali out of my way and bolting it down the stairs into the kitchen.

There was nothing. Nothing? Nothing!! No mess, no pieces of fruit or sign or any hot chocolate or footprints walking out of the kitchen and down the steps. It's clean- but it was a mess!!

"Eleni? Did you clean up in here?" I said with my hands rapidly tapping the spotless island countertop.

"No?" She said softly adding milk to the tea.

"But there was a mess!? You didn't clean anything? You must have?"

"It was perfect, like every day. Come on Aaliyah, come sit down." Eleni walked

beside me, her hand softly on my back, rubbing and guiding me to sit down on my sofa- My head hurts so fucking bad!

"… I gave her my drivers' license! I know I did. She put it in her back pocket. I saw her do it, she did it and she didn't give it back to me. She didn't, I swear she put it in the back pocket of her shorts and she didn't give it back to me… check my purse, I'm telling you it's not in there, she didn't give it back to me and she *was* here! Go on check it! I gave it to her on the tube and she put it in her back pocket. I SAW HER DO IT!" They think I am crazy- I think I'm losing my mind. Have I lost my mind? Mali made her way down the stairs, picking up my bag, she takes my purse out. Opening it roughly, she taps the little plastic window slip inside and… my driver's license is there?? What the fuck? I…?

Mali sat beside me, placing a hand on my lap and she places my purse down on the coffee table. Turning the purse to me, so I can see my driver's license is in there, clearly.

"But… she didn't give it back to me; she left it in her pocket. I don't understand…" I look up at Eleni with her lips inwards and that worried look on her face that I have seen before. I pause, thinking. Gathering everything… I… it's… no?

"Aaliyah… do you remember that day you told me everything that happened to you, that morning on the balcony?"

"Shut up!" I said softly not looking, trying to figure all this shit out.

"I came back as quick as I could and I haven't left you after that. I couldn't go after everything you told me. But we haven't been apart much at all. I go to Blue sometimes but other than that."

All I can hear is words that don't make sense at all. Going over things in my head that don't add up. What's happening, what's been happening, where I've been and who I've been with. It's all going around, overlapping and running over my mind. Like a season recap of a series, in case you have missed an episode or all the good parts- I've missed so much, how do I fill in the blanks?

"Maybe, to let her alone a little." The sound of Eleni's voice brought me out of my trapped thoughts. I look around my apartment, just the way I like it.

Open, spacious and full of things I love! Everything has a perfect place and a perfect position. It's a warehouse, split level apartment off of the Docklands Light Railway known to you fellow TFL underground users as DLR. Don't ask exactly where, because this is not WhatsApp to be sharing my location.

My ceilings are high and my walls are very tall, full of raw rust coloured brick or slightly bricked in places. It has this very urban un-established feeling to it. Big Georgian style windows allowing plenty of light in through them that bounces off of all corners of the apartment. There are *no* hidden spaces in my huge open plan living area, no hidden corners limiting me to see one room from the other.

"It's happened again, hasn't it?" Not taking my eyes off of Eleni.

"What's happened, are you okay? Is she okay?" Mali kept asking the same question, 'if I was okay?'.

My elbows on my lap, leaning over with both my palms against my face, running my fingers over my mouth.

"No... Mali, I'm not okay."

"Aaliyah? What can I do, tell me what you need me to do?"

I can't tell you how long, it took me to answer. It's all numb and through it all, I can hear the sounds of things surrounding me magnified so loud in my ears. Like the lump in Mali's throat, swallowing from the lack of understanding, while the concerns and confusions linger on her mind. The kettle boiling, bubbling and clicking off. The clock ticking the time by on the wall and the watch on my wrist joining the rhythmic ticking- tick, tock, tick, tock. Each breath as my heart beats slow and echoes in my ears. Not knowing what the fuck to do or say, to make myself or her feel okay. To make it all go away and start the day again.

One long deep breath in. Practice your breathing... One, breathe in. I turn to her and open my mouth...

"You need you to leave and *not* come back. I'm going to need you to stay far away from me. I have problems, this very *big* problem and I can't explain it. I don't want to explain it. You won't, get it. You won't understand."

"Make me understand? Make me get it. You've told me so much already why can't you tell me this?" She takes my hands into hers.

"Exactly, you know too much already."

"So, if I know too much, then what's the difference if you tell me the rest Aaliyah?" She pleads with me but I-

"I erm. I… forget things and I make them up, a lot of things… Because I fuck them up, they get all mixed up and I lose track of what's real and I erm. I…. I err… I need to go. Now."

Snatching my hands away from Mali's and grab my phone off the coffee table.

"Aaliyah tell her, it's okay? She's okay, believe me. Please tell her." Eleni pleaded with me. "Don't go, tell her. Please." Eleni's tears falling down her face, I can't deal with all of this, with any of this. It's way, way too much. I want to get out and away from them both. They're walking on egg shells around me, being so soft and delicate and fucking annoying!!

"FINE!! If you won't leave, I'll leave!"

"She has…" Eleni opens her mouth to tell Mali.

"Don't. You. Dare!" I shouted at Eleni for the first time ever! "Don't you fucking dare Eleni!" Holding in tears, my throat tightens, my words are caught there and it hurts so bad – No time for weakness.

"Aaliyah, please! Tell her, it's okay." Eleni clutches her yellow jiff cloth by her chest, letting enough tears fall for the both of us

"Eleni, I swear! You open your mouth and your fucking finished! SHUT YOUR MOUTH!!" I screeched at her and as I did, she jumps. My heart drops to my feet. I have never disrespected or raised my voice to Eleni. I love her too much. I want to hug her and tell her I am sorry but I have to go, I have to get out of this house. I need to get the fuck out and away from them!

"Aaliyah?!" Mali attempted to walk towards me, I hold up my arm my fist balled ready to knock her out of my way.

"Say my name another fucking time and I'm going to tell Blue *everything*! Stay away from me! Please!" I grabbed my purse, with the driver's license tucked behind the plastic window, threw it in my handbag, put on my heels and left the house - again, no trousers on, Fuck sake! I'm losing my mind! What the fuck?!

"No time for weakness." Mali hands me a pair of bottoms, reciting words I tell myself and have written around my place in quotes and useless places- to remind myself. She knows...

"Thank you." She knows something is wrong but if I say it out loud then it makes it all real. I've been fighting it for so long and I refuse to give in now. Her face in my palm, while I step with one foot out of my own door. I let go tracing her lips one last time.

"Stay away from me... please."

"Blank spaces clog my memory, blocked out from what you used to do to me. Beating me.

Holding onto me tightly, gripping and holding me...back from living, like your hands around my throat, haunting me. Wishing death on me. *'I'm going to kill you if you try to leave me'* ...Making me forget who I used to be. Faded with my loss of memory, clouded by my mystery being someone that can't let anyone get close to me. Pretending to be anything else than the shadows you left on me."

— To Who This May Concern.
Much love & light
Aaliyah

Traumatic brain injury (**TBI**), also known as **intracranial injury**, occurs when an external force traumatically injures the brain.

A cause of brain injury that has been under-reported is *domestic violence*. Often the victims do not seek medical care or attention. The nature of the attachment to the relationship may prevent the victim from calling for help from anyone with authority or healthcare professional. In the majority of cases, the victim absorbs the abuse to protect others from a reflection of said abuse; who are often under threat from the abuser. Used as an emotional tactic to keep the victim close.

Most cases of abuse will include: *emotional, mental* and most common ***physical***.

Fifty percent of domestic violence victims are held down, under gross pressure strangled at some point, in the course of their relationship- often repeatedly, over years. Those who receive strangulation to the point of losing consciousness are at high risk in the first forty-eight hours of strokes, blood clots and aspiration, which can go on to cause brain injury (*mild or traumatic*). Other causes are by blunt force/repeated force trauma to the head. Often these victims tend to have poor recollections of the incidents and not even aware they've lost consciousness. Which leaves them poorly diagnosed, leaving injuries downplayed as they don't know the extent of their injuries.

Symptoms of TBI: Unconsciousness and blackouts.

Inability to remember the cause of the injury or events that occurred up to twenty – four hours before and after. Confusion and disorientation. Difficulty remembering old and new information. Headaches. Dizziness. Blurry vision. Nausea. Memory loss/lapse. Poor attention/concentration. Irritability and emotional disturbances/irrationality. Mood changes. Confusion. Sensitivity to light. Overrun thoughts (slowness in thinking).

Do I make sense now?

Let us continue my story...

15. The Coldest End

Sat in the back of a taxi. Ignoring the countless and continuous missed calls from Mali, not opening or reading the messages. I'm not even going to open my WhatsApp, they can sit there and wait on my blue ticks and responses.

Voicemail: "You have fifteen messages!"

Skipping through all the *'hey boo where you at'* and *'come see me'* voice messages. Why am I listening? Everyone's voice is annoying as fuck! Every single one of them.

Destination unknown, I ask the driver to hit the motorway, maybe then I can focus on how many miles per hour the car is moving, instead of putting dates and places in order in my mind. Head back on the seat, the window open enough for the fast passing wind to hit my face as the driver picks up more speed. I close my eyes I want to gain focus so bad but my fucking brain won't let me. These non-stop thoughts and questions won't let me keep them free or to aside while I figure it out.

I know I've lost old memories but new ones? I've never forgotten something-someone so recent. Names, yes. Faces, it happens. But days, intimate moments… maybe she's too close. I thought I had control and the twisted connection was enough but another emotion or feeling has taken over. I've never been as bad as this… I'm trying to find where those memories with Mali are in my mind but it's gone and empty, just like the open motorway roads. The sounds of the wind whipping past my ears, blocking it all out of my head.

"Hey… I haven't seen you in a hot minute. I miss you; I miss the taste of you on my uurrm…?"

Opening my eyes to the sound of Raee'ns voice. Starting the message all over again, tilting my head with the phone lodged between my shoulder and ear. Trying to locate my cigarette box, listening intently.

"Hey... I haven't seen you in a hot minute. I miss you, how have you been?"

She giggles nervously, I can hear her smile. She clears her throat and continues talking quietly.

"Sorry I've been blowing up your line but I wanted to talk, to hear your voice, to tell you something. A lot is going on right now and I don't know how to tell you or what to say but I wanted to tell you about it all. Anyway, he found the last pair of sexy red thongs stuffed down the back of the bed." She sighs, *"...and it made me miss you. He knows I'm seeing a woman. Seeing you... 'was' seeing you. He hasn't left my side for a second. So, when you get this call me. I know your sexy ass is probably chilling with some other bitch but call me anyway- you heard me."*

Telling the driver, the change of destination, I sit back and think of all the things I'm going to do to her when I see Raee'n. Keeping Mali all the way out of my mind. I might as well, seeing as though I've forgotten so much of her already.

***

"Just here please."

Pulling up just before Raee'ns house, I step out of the taxi and walk up the cobbled footpath.

My eyes set on the door with her body on my body, on my mind. Maybe fucking around with her for a few hours will relax me and make me remember. I want to leave her breathless and wanting more and then... I'll leave.

Adjusting my hair at the door, I ring the doorbell and lean my body against the wall, waiting for her to come and get me. Somehow making this t-shirt and heels, I have on work. She's going to love every bit of me, especially when I – wait. Where the hell is she? Why is she taking so long to answer the door?

A minute or so has past and I can't hear *any* movement at all in the house or any footsteps towards the door... hold on. Ringing the doorbell again, standing back from the door looking at the driveway, not noticing her car wasn't there, fuck sake!! She could literally be *anywhere* and coming back at any time, let me call her and check.

"Are you fucking kidding me!" Great! my phone battery is *dead*! Again! She's not home and I am stood in the middle of *nowhere* with no phone and *no* female and no trousers on! Fuck!

Walking back down the front path, facing the house, stretching my neck to see if she has left a window open. If I can get in, I can at least charge my phone and be on my way. Spotting an open window on the ground floor of her house, I push my hand and arm inside to unclick the latch, allowing the window to open wide enough for me to hop on in. A quick look over my shoulder, checking if any neighbours in this predominately Caucasian neighbourhood are lurking through their curtains. Wondering what the fuck is a black woman with no trousers on, doing climbing through the window of this house. One hand on their receiver, ready to call the police on someone black, for no reason at all. Yes, okay, so I am basically breaking and entering but it's none of their business.

Opening the window wider, I heave ho my arse into the house and land heels first on the hard laminate wood floor of *their* living room.

Everything has that *manly* presence to it, as if this was the only other room he was allowed to put his taste into.

The main décor feature is a chunky dark brown leather sofa and the big boy recliner opposite it. That has a cup holder built in it for the days he gets to sit back and watch sports facing a ridiculously huge television. Maybe the size of his television is an overcompensation for the size of his little dick. That's got to be difficult for a man, right? Because when you think about it, that's all a man really has going for him. Women have it easier; for example, if her breasts are small, she might have a big booty, or long legs, thick thighs or are slim and slender, *or* have a small waist and sexy hips. You have a choice, there is always a multitude of things a woman can bring to the table because if she hasn't got one thing, she's probably got the other and if you're lucky enough, baby girl has got it all! But if you're a man that's got no junk in his trunk then really, you're just a man with an empty boot that better make sure his pussy eating game is strong as fuck!! Because just like the original Queen B Lil Kim, all we wanna know is

"How many licks does it take till you get the centre of the…?"
(ladies you know the rest of the song)

If you happen to be one of those men then there are definitely only four words *your* woman wants to hear you say to her and that's:

"Sit on my face!"

Running my hands along the banister, heading straight to the bedroom. I sat at the end of the bed looking at myself unimpressed with my clothes, which would not have been my first choice to come over here but I needed to get away from… well, I didn't want to hear the constant questions of confusion. Why do things I *want* to forget never leave me and the important things, small or basic shit I *should* remember run away from me like it never even existed or happened? It's as if my brain is playing tricks on my subconscious, whatever... anyway, this outfit isn't working it for me; a plain t-shirt and a random pair of high heels doesn't exactly say 'I'm here to fuck' now does it? No, I want to wear something more and less is always more so...

My eyes float around the room and along the dressing table, observing the separation and division of *'his'* and *'her'* side. I find it interesting that in an even space that spouses choose to share, there is always an obvious division of the two individuals tastes. Two people are never really *'one'* in the physical sense. Although they have *'ours'*, within that there are individual components and what both choose to share, in order to make it 'ours'. I can see that in the difference of the layout on either side of the dressing table.

On her side: are endless expensive and unopened bottles of perfume *he* purchased, thinking of her passing through duty-free. Before his flights to and away from home, keeping her *sweet* and she always does *smell* sweet. I get to enjoy the fragrances more than he does and be the opinion of which scents *we* like on her skin and *we* prefer the fruity soft ones over the rich and strong. Her hair brush is beside the bottles with long strands of hair caught in the bristles. She has her lipsticks sat in a holder with different shades of reds; from deep, to bright, to blood, to rouge- that always looked good on her beautiful lips.

His side; unorganised cologne bottles with missing tops. Tins stacked with his bits and bobs, like cufflinks and a gold Rolex watch engraved:

"Happy Anniversary. Love forever Raee'n xx."

Smelling his scent and holding his cologne to my nose. It smells okay, I guess. Dabbing it on my wrist, neck and a cheeky dab in between my breasts, of the most used bottle in the bunch. I wonder if it will turn her on, to recognise *his* scent on *my* skin?

There was this one time one of the women I was seeing... wait when was this again? Anyway, well, her woman caught a glimpse of a new perfume and scent on her skin- *my scent* to be clear. The amazing fragrance of me all over her beautifully blended with a perfume that I like to wear a lot. One that people know me by, a signature fragrance. One so noticeable that if I was in a room and you couldn't see me, you *knew* I had been there or was there, somewhere. So, anyway, when her woman asked her what that *'amazing'* scent was on her skin. She lied, saying that she had sprayed on this perfume at the shop and really liked it, thinking her woman would think nothing of her nonchalant answer. So, one day she comes home to her woman purchased the *same* fragrance that *I* wear and sprayed it all over her skin... *their* bed and *their* house as a surprise for her. When she told me, I could imagine the look on her face and the total mind fuck of it all! To walk into the house and smelling my perfume *all over* the place, expecting to see me somewhere and the perfume is all over her woman!! Imagine, closing her eyes, fucking her girl and smelling and seeing me in her mind-trippy right?

Catching a glimpse of his military jacket hung over the wardrobe; freshly ironed, without a single crease in sight. Rubbing my finger across my lip thinking about my next move. You know, I always *did* look good in camo print.
Both arms in his coat, feeling myself and admiring my reflection, kicking the clothes I had on under the bed and out of sight- ready to be found by him, at some point.
Now, this outfit right here says *'fuck me!'*. His military jacket on top of my skin with my thongs on and nothing else!
Laying back on the bed, heels on still waiting for Raee'n to make an appearance... waiting and waiting, still waiting, where is she? Rolling over to her bedside, I plug up my phone to charge and pick up a magazine. Flicking through the pages, bored of the electronic clock on the bedroom wall beeping away the minutes, reminding me I'm sat here, impatiently waiting. Not really looking at the pages of this thick magazine, leaning up against the headboard, legs crossed over with my high heels digging down

into the puffy bedding. Reading out loud *booooored* with nothing else to do but impatiently wait. So I read-

"Your pregnancy guide, week to week from morning sickness to preparing for the birth of your new baby to – WHAT THE FUCKING FUCK!!" Throwing the magazine across the room, it hits the wall and falls wide open pages full of *pregnancy care* bull shit! Stacks of them on her bedside table:

Practical Parenting, Mamma to Be, Mum's Rock.

They're all over the place! Pulling open her draws, I don't know what I am doing or what I'm looking for *but*, I'm going to fucking find it! *Something*, a dairy or a notebook somewhere in here under some more baby magazines and books pf baby bull shit! Turning pages of her Filofax and looking at the dates, waiting to see that circled date with stars or *'yay me'* or *'yay us'* or *'go team go,'* or anything thing like that. Here it is, circled with little pink love hearts all over it.

FUCKING BITCH!! Figuring out the dates in my head from the date circled, I don't even know what day it is today let alone fucking date. Makes sense now all her bullshit, about being tired and not drinking. Climbing over the bed and walking my heels right over to his side of the bed rummaging through his drawer, don't ask me what I'm looking for? Condoms? As if married people use them! Like *anyone* uses them these days. Tell me, who stops fucking because they need to slip on a condom? No   one!!

It's just… she said something about him using them. Why would I listen to anything she said?! She's a liar, she lies to the man she took ultimate vows, intending to spend forever and a fucking day with, every day! Why the actual fuck would she tell *me* the truth?! I'm such an idiot!

Walking around the house about to lose my shit! Noticing things that I never noticed were there before; baby bags, baby clothes and baby gates at the top of the staircase I *assumed* it came with the house! I've been so busy mocking *his* life, picking *him* apart, I never opened my eyes to all of this shit around me, like a bag full of dummies bottles and bullshit- shit, shit, shit!

Kicking one of the bags. the contents fall out onto the floor… I watch, as a baby bottle rolled down the hall slowly, it stops at the room with the golden door handle… *The* room, *that* room, I've never been in. She didn't let me go in that room, that day? She stopped me! Oh, my fucking- I remember. She stopped me from going in. She distracted me from going in with her shoe *and…* and she asked me in the car, if I went in. She was *definitely* distracting me, I remember now. I'm sure, I think I'm sure. *Well* I am about to fucking find out now! She's so sneaky, of course she is a sly little bitch!

My heels ripped the carpet the way I stomped down the hallway towards the room. Shall I go in? Should I go in? Can I go in? What would you do? – I'm going in. But I don't know if I want to… fuck it!

Deep breath in, reaching out slowly for the door, the anticipation building up inside of me differently. Deep breath out. Count to ten… One… Two… Three.

Holding the golden door handle down, pushing the door open. I stood in the hallway attempting to force my legs to take a step into the pastel pink painted room but they didn't move, I couldn't move- looking at it all. The cloudy sky mural covering the ceiling, the teddy bears and other animals piled into a corner of this baby girl's bedroom. A collection of pink artificial flowers hanging on clear wire hovering over a dark stained wooden cot sat in the centre. My hands holding onto the soft sides of the cot staring down at the soft shades of pinks, purples, yellows and cream blankets and muslin fabric cloths unfolded and slept in. The traces of a little person's body imprinted from laying there.

One hand inside the cot holding the tiny golden cross necklace clipped over the sidebar at the head. My legs failed to register my brain that I had stepped into the room. Shocked and dazed and confused and lost… just like I felt earlier, back at my place. But now here, alone looking at photographs on the far wall scattered in different sizes of white frames like a timeline of love and a journey. Starting with a sonogram, leading onto Raee'n resting her hands on a bump barely starting to show. The next few photos of the married couple. *Him,* standing behind her, arms wrapped over resting on her growing bump. Then both of them smiling, so happy. And then the baby's first moments of life in her mother's arms then her father's. Held with all that love it took to produce her, carry her and have her in their lives.

"I wanted to tell you... I tried to tell you..." Turning around slowly to the sound of Raee'ns voice, stood a few feet away from me with the baby girl in her arms. Cuddled, resting against her chest, sleeping soundly. "I didn't know how to. I didn't know what to say, so I didn't- I never said anything. I'm sorry Aaliyah." She spoke quietly, placing the baby in the cot and covered her gently with her choice of blankets. She admires her child and lightly rubbing her back. Looking up at me, stepping towards me- cautiously but my eyes stay on the small baby; she maybe a few months old. I'm trying to figure it out but... she... I don't know what day it is.

Feeling this anger build up in every fibre of my being, surging through my shaking legs to my clenched jaw, trying to make sense to all of this. How did I not *know* she was pregnant? Let alone had a fucking baby??

Aaliyah... count to ten, take a deep breath and leave, don't say anything just leave! You should leave and that's it, go! You. Don't. Need to say *anything*. There's nothing to say, take a deep breath. One. Two. Three. Four.

WHAT THE FUCK! Standing here in *her* kid's room wearing *her* husband's shirt, jacket, am I a dick head? My mouth wide open, trying to find the words that are jumping around my head.

"I was going to tell you but-"

"Fuck you Raee'n!" Blurted out of my mouth without me raising my voice. I didn't hear the words come out but I knew I said something.

"*Aaliyah?*" A whisper of shock, she glances over her shoulder at the baby then back at me. As if the baby can understand what the fuck I just said!

"Fuck you and your house, fuck your husband and your fake perfect fucked up world... a baby? Are you serious?!" My voice is shaking and starting to raise but I keep it together, telling myself not to lose my shit- not just yet. Telling myself to fucking breathe, to be cool.

"Aaliyah, please... look. I didn't want to lose you or him, or *her*. How was I supposed to tell you or, or, or mention it? What was I supposed to say? I tried but I couldn't do it. I wanted you, I needed you all. I don't know how it happened..."

"What do you mean 'how'? You fucked your husband! That's what happened. Wait, why am I? -I don't care, this is bullshit and you know it!"

"I didn't plan this?"

"Well you didn't plan on getting rid of *IT* either, did you!" Not taking my eyes off of Raee'n, I point down into the crib.

"Aaliyah??" Hand on her heart, she gasps.

"This doesn't make sense, how the fuck did you even hide this!?"

"I guess I'm good at hiding things... I hid you from him and her from you. Look, I know it's fucked up but... I've always liked girls. I got married young. We do everything together. I wanted to leave him but then I found out I was pregnant... I didn't know what to do. I met you and you reminded me how to be sexy and beautiful again. To have fun and not give a fuck about the consequences... but then, she happened and I needed to stay, I had to for her. I tried to tell you so many times, believe me I did but..."

"Tell me when! When did you 'try' telling me? When my clit was in your mouth? Or when my fingers were inside your preoccupied pussy?"

"Oh, fuck you Aaliyah!" She shouted at me, no one shouts at me. "I *could* see us together! I did, but every time I opened my mouth to tell you, I remembered who the fuck you are! You're a fucking selfish bitch!"

"Excuse me?!" She's lucky her baby is in the room.

"You only care about YOU! No one else matters in your *sick* games but you! You play with people's feelings and you get to walk away not giving a fuck. I go days, weeks, *months*! Without hearing from you! How the fuck did you think I could hide *her*? I hide you from my husband, why are you so shocked? You made it so damn easy Aaliyah!"

"How, did you not find the time to slip in 'I'm pregnant', how?"

"It happened! Okay! It just happened! And I wanted to keep her away from you. Your energy is so fucked up!"
Her child stirs in the crib and begins to whine, disturbed by our shouting.

"Wait a fucking minute! You're a married woman, having an affair with your husband's baby in your womb the whole time we've been fucking around and *my* energy is fucked up!! Really?!"

"I know it doesn't sound right but-"

"What we are not going to do is make me out to be the devil in this, so let me tell you what happened! *You* realized you're trapped by the mistake *you* married, so you hang onto *me*. A person who made you forget about your pathetic married life. While the *whole* time," I snatch the frame of the sonogram off of the wall holding it up to her face.

"Aaliyah, stop!"

"You had *THIS* inside of you, what the fuck?!"

"I NEVER ASKED YOU TO COME HERE!" She screams, the baby cries. She picks her up instantly and rocks her from side to side, calming her down and shushing her gently.

"Hey! YOU called me! You just left a voicemail on my phone!"

"Wait what messages? I haven't called you in months."

"What are you on about? You left a voicemail about missing me and your husband finding my thongs."

"I left those months ago. I just had the baby, I called you to- this is what I mean. You only pay attention to the shit you want to hear. You're so self-absorbed, it's unreal! You never noticed me, you only see yourself and always will! I never mattered, no one does. I only matter when you want to fuck me! That's the only reason why you're here, to *fuck*, right?"

"Of course, I came to fuck! That's what an affair is Raee'n!"

"You know what, you're right." Speaking quietly, looking at me in my high heels, thong and his coat, with her red lipstick on my lips.

Soothing the baby back to sleep, repeating her process of placing her back in the crib she continues talking "I used to dream about you and baby girl and raising her together without *him* having anything to do with us but you're poison! Look at the shit you made me do to your friend, you'll always be poison! A fantasy, an idea of a woman that isn't real, because no one is going to stay long enough to put up with your *bullshit*!! You'll always be a side piece. That's all it ever is and ever will be. Knowing you, over these years-"

"Years?"

"You've probably met the woman your supposed to be with but you're so caught up in yourself. You'll probably push her away, kill that relationship and you'll end up all alone like all the other poisonous people. Because that's what poison does. It kills everything and everyone around them until there is nothing left!" She stares at me sincere but smug; I felt my grip tighten on the photo frame and raise my arm. I want to smash it over her head so fucking bad. She stands back, one hand over her face the other over the crib she didn't know where it was going to land.

"No! Aaliyah the baby?"

I don't want to throw the frame at her, I want to drop it on the floor and step on it with my stiletto heel dug all the way through walk out and shout; 'fuck your baby'. But you know what? I'm not going to do that. It's too predictable, instead, I'll be exactly what she says I am. I'm *poison* right? And poison leaves traces on your lips then I'll leave. Oh, she'll be back they *always* come back.

Walking towards her one stiletto in front of the other, my eyes attempting empathy, my smile saying something else, something seductive and aggressive.

"Here." Holding out the frame, she snatches it from my palm quickly and places it on a side. Keeping her eyes on me, not knowing what I'll do next. I step to her side, peering over the crib at baby girl. Both my hands on the side of the crib. Reaching in one hand...

"Aaliyah?" Relax! I'm not going to do anything to the *baby* I'm not a monster. The baby is beautiful; tiny traces of tears on her round blushed pink cheeks from her crying.

"She's beautiful... perfect, like her mamma." I stroke her soft curly hair with the outside of my index finger. "I hope you enjoy her and the novelty a new baby brings because it's only a matter of time before he's back to flying around the world, leaving you to mother alone. You'll get bored and you will call my phone but I won't answer though... tell me something Raee'n?" I look up at her, hands out of the crib and ready to leave.

"Yeah...?"

"Where is your husband now?" One last sinister smirk on my lips, I head towards the door.

"Aaliyah wait, I'm sorry, don't go... please."
Not even letting seven seconds go by and she's tugging on my arm, not wanting me to leave. Damn, I'm good! I know I am, because I counted the seconds.
Grabbing her body, pushing her against the door she stumbles back. I hold her waist and move my kisses to her body. This feels so fucking hot, like the first time we met. Digging her nails into my back, anticipating and wanting to feel me inside of her. But I stall my fingertips waiting and wrapping her leg around me. She kisses me wanting me to

"Fuck me, baby." She said with a thirsty look on her face that I know.
Leaning forward she waits for me to kiss her again. Grazing my lips across her cheek, I move to her neck and bite her ear lobe then I whisper in her ear.

"Nah... I'm good. You don't want me baby; I'm poison remember?"

Stepping back from her naked body. She doesn't know what to do. Shaking my head at her standing there, her clothes at her ankles, still wanting me after everything she said- silly rabbit, tricks are for hoes!

Blowing her a kiss, I left, slamming the bedroom door so hard it probably rattled the baby.

Quickly running through the house, grabbing my phone off the charger and my bag from off her bed. At the front of the house laughing to myself, jingling the keys to the Range Rover in my hand. Time to take this bad boy out for a spin. I slipped the keys out her back pocket when I was feeling on her juicy booty. Damn I'm gonna miss her sex. Oh well, as they say, easy *cum* easy go!

***

Damn! They weren't lying when they said, 'the hottest love has the coldest end'! My nipples agreed, sat driving this car cold, in my bra and thongs. I have got to start taking better things with me when I'm doing these dramatic and impulsive exits, like fucking *clothes* maybe, shit!? Turning up the heat, thinking about it all. If I'm being honest. I should've known better; married people are the worst! They *never* leave each other, it doesn't matter how toxic it gets. They don't want all that time, effort and money invested into one person to be split down the middle and deal with court orders and paperwork. Look at Stevie, she tolerates her husband with motives and no love daily. Majority of married couples are miserable as fuck! Putting up and shutting up, talking a load of

'I love him, I need him, our baby blah, blah, blah!'

Please! Yeah, you need him as much as you need the taste of my pussy in your mouth! She was pregnant, really? Where the fuck was I? Where has my head been? I mean, I didn't see her- for a hot minute – but how? I thought I was slick but damn, she is one sneaky bitch! Who knew!

My phone continues to vibrate violently with the seventy-eighth missed call from Raee'n leaving the seventy-eighth voicemail. Probably panicking about her missing vehicle but it's not my problem. She not going to call anyone but me. That's right, who can she call? Her husband who's never at home? What can she tell him?

"So, the woman who I've been fucking with found out we had a baby, got me naked, stole our car and is currently driving around in it your clothes?"

All she can do is sit in her house, hope I come to my senses and return the car. But *apparently*, I lost my mind a long time ago! There are no senses for me to come to so, for now, I'll lean back and enjoy cruising in this car.

Warmed up and on a little liquid courage wave, provided by a small bottle of brandy I found tucked away in the side pocket of the car door.

Raee'n had given up on calling me and my car hijack wasn't fun anymore. I've been driving for a while and I'm bored of my own company. What else is there left to do? Do I want to go home, yes… no? A big part of me wants Mali to be there when I get back, if I decide to go back? And the rest of me is telling me she better be gone by the time I get back. It's the last place I want to be and don't want to be… I can't decide.

Standing by the river bank and letting the night breeze cool down the heat the brandy has given me, allowing my thoughts to dance around my head while I contemplate…

Jumping from one timeline to another like waves and ripples in my time. Closing my eyes, wondering if I'll wake up from another blackout to the next scene or the next moment in time.

Gazing at the night sky lit up from the office buildings with all their floors and windows shining bright... no one is there. How long can I overthink things over and over? There's so much I missed, how could I not know Raee'n was pregnant? She has a baby girl? Mali?

I missed Mali, I think I missed her. I've lost the time we had spent together? My answers aren't here but all these fucking lapses! Not able to put things together. This is when my head hurts the most. Can't let go of what's not there but I can't let go. It's so hard to remember the important things or things in general... the alcohol doesn't help but what can I say, I like to drink. But what can I say, I like a drink... okay I *just* said that? But I do like a drink or bottle or two. It drowns out the noise in my head... things I've tried to forget.

But out of all the things my brain let's go of, on a daily basis, *she* is the one thing and fucking memory I cannot erase Delilah. She did this to me, she hurt me and she left. Some days I forget the memory of her and I feel so warm but then it's like midnight hits and I feel her fists on me all over again. Her hands leaving marks all over me again. So, I *have* to drink and when I do her voice goes away, what she did to me goes away, how she made me feel goes away and then it all goes quiet and it's as if it never happened and no one needs to know that she still has this hold on me all these fucking years later!

They say statistically that a victim of physical abuse gets over it a lot quicker than a person who has been mentally abused. Don't get me wrong the healing process doesn't happen overnight... trust me, I know. According to all the doctors I've had, I am still in the 'healing process', fuck them! They don't know what goes on in my head; I don't *even* know what goes on in there half the time. I couldn't even tell you the date or day of the week, if it wasn't for the flowers- let me stop.

You know, I don't *actually* have a favourite drink, I like them *all*. The stronger the drink the better and if I blackout, at least then I get some sleep. I pretend to have a favourite drink and I pretend to be what people are fascinated by; to be Aaliyah.

Becoming her wasn't easy, oh no. Believe it or not, I wasn't always like this but I don't know who I was- I've forgotten- but they said that was another thing that would happen.

Do you know, there are girls and women who want to be me? They see what I am and what I have and they want it all! They want the expensive shoes, the name brand clothes, the big beautiful apartment, the car, the lifestyle, the likes and follows everything! They wouldn't want it if they knew what it took to get it and what it takes to maintain it, to be me, to be yours sincerely.

I'll tell you one thing though, it won't make you happy, you can't shop pain away with red-soled bloody shoes. Nope! If only they knew what I had to do to get here and to build the walls and foundation of protection around me.

I don't like people in my house because I don't want her to find me. I know she's there somewhere, waiting to take over my solitude and solace. Did you know, she used to lock me up like a fucking animal! I couldn't go anywhere. I've always hated locked doors, I don't want to be locked away- don't lock me away. She used to kick me so hard in the head, I forgot she even done it. Imagine?

Well, it's all true and everything I've become is because of her. I don't want to be with anyone ever again! I can't trust what they will do to me. I want to get close but then I forget, because I panic, I get the feeling. Then think and think and think and think and then the room goes dark my head hurts and the thoughts are gone. But then, they creep back, when someone walks into my life unexpectedly. Just like Mali, she hurts my head the most, more than anyone before.

16. The Damage

Opening my eyes, flat on my stomach face down on dusty the lilac fabric seat cushions of my sofa. Not knowing how I got here or when; my head pounding as usual.

The familiar feeling of my shaggy rug on the tip of my toes and fingers. Half of my body hung off the sofa; one leg and one arm. Drained, thinking about when or how I arrived home but I'm unable to figure it out like everything else. My body too heavy to move or get up, let alone stop myself from gradually sliding onto the floor – fuck it! Letting myself go, I slump to the floor.

"One day, I'm not gonna be here to cleans up your mess!" Not seeing her clearly, through the shaggy tassels of the rug smothering my face and blocking my vision. I know it's her from the light smell of disinfectant on the palm of her hands, misplaced English adding 's's' where they don't need to be and her Mediterranean tone of voice, Eleni struggled to lift me into a sitting position. Each of her hand tucked under my armpit, as she huffs and props me up against the sofa.

"Hey Eleni."

My voice croaky and little. My eyes refocusing on the things around me as my brain was busy sending messages to my neck and head to work together for me to lift my head up.

"Don't you 'hey me' you have worried me sick." Feeling her weight sit down beside me and move the seat cushion up against my back, I lift the hair away from my face and look at hers. Concerned and old but glowing with her olive skin. The worry lines in her forehead deepen as she frowns at me with sorrow in her eyes. "You don't call! Where have you been Aaliyah?"

"Eleni please, not today. My head is banging!"

"So, take the pills! You never your pills!"

"Fuck my medication, I keep taking them fuckers now and I'll need to take them for the rest of my life. I don't need an addiction"

"No? You're addicted to pussy and alcohol! That's better! Where were you!"

"Eleni please, I don't even know what day it is or how I got here, honestly."

"It's Monday! You've been gone a week!"

I look down at myself half naked again. When was the last time I was dressed? Pulling the fluffy blanket off the sofa to cover my cold boy.

"I am so fucking confused with this mess, my mess, fuck Eleni! I'm sick of all of this shit!"

"I know, sweetie, I know."

Not looking at me and my frustrations, she places her bottle of Ouzo on the table. She hates when I drink and keeps a bottle hidden in the back of the cleaning cupboard for our bad days we share. When she hears some bad news from home or when I have a memory lapse- now see, that shit I remember!!

Eleni taps two shot glasses against glass table and pours, letting the liquid overspill.

"Take it." She holds the shot glass in her hand, waiting for me to connect mine, nodding in my direction, saying cheers in Greek, she doesn't flinch at the forty-five percent liquid entering her system. But I twist my lips with the rough taste hitting the back of my throat and my taste buds. Making my mouth water and dribble a little.

"Jesus! Eleni, how do you drink this shit!?"

"Easy! Another!" She says, shrugging and pouring another shot.

"No thanks." I shake my head but she pours me another.

"No? You don't want your pills, so drink!" She nods with the shot glass in her hand once more waiting for me and again, she doesn't flinch. She throws the drink to the back of her throat and swallows. Slamming the glass back down on the table she leans forward, taking the yellow jiff cloth from her back pocket and wipes the water marks and spillage away. Folding the yellow cloth up evenly, she places it to the side of the table. I watch her movements closely; the weighty look in her eyes, the woe in the lines of her cheeks as her lips press together, thinking of the words she's translating in her mind or just finding hard to say but she isn't saying anything. Out of the same back pocket she pulls out a box of cigarettes, she taps the box upside down and pulls one out of the box. Eleni is the Greek Mary Poppins with a pair of jeans; the amount of things she pulls out those damn back pockets. Tapping the box again, she offers me the box, with her thumb at the opening so I can pull one out. Leaning back and digging her hand in her front pocket then back out rattling a small box of matches, she lights her cigarette then turns the lit match to light mine. Holding the almost burned out match to me, shielding the flame from blowing out. Once mine was lit, she shook her hand until the match was completely out and threw it down in the ash tray. Taking a big inhale, she presses her elbow to her knee and roughly rubs her hand on her temples then passes her fingers through her golden blonde short back and   side   hair-cut. She always ran her hands through her hair, it's so thick it would stay where ever she roughly put it. She's so old school with the way she does things but she has this knowledgeable elegance about her with a streak of *'don't give a fuck'*. Sat forward on the sofa legs apart in her straight cut jeans and bright orange vintage looking t-shirt that sat over her big round belly. I know she wants to speak, so I'll start.

"How many times have we done this Eleni?"

"Too, too many times. You come back, we sit, we drink, we smoke, we talk. You get better, for a little while. Then you go, you forget. Then we do it all over again."

"How many times?"

"Too many. I don't count them anymore, I stopped a long time ago."

"Me too." There wasn't anything left to count, how many times over and over, the same routine felt like the same thing. I know me and Eleni have sat on this sofa many times, sipping on this strong drink. Talking about what I've missed or where my mind has been. It's become the same thing to me with new information that I build up and place back together like a puzzle. But this time I don't want to go over anything. I just want to sit and enjoy the silence and let my mind get rid of the shit that I don't want to know.

"You need to tell her…" She turns to me revealing her woe.
Leaning forward grabbing the bottle pouring *myself* another shot, knowing where this conversation is going.

"Eleni, no? Please, I don't want to talk about it."

"What? And pretend you don't have this problem." Her eyes wide, looking at me sideways. "You *need* to tell someone, you think I'm going to be here for the rest of my days, picking you up from the sofa with my old ass and changing the flowers every Monday so you know what day it is? The flowers don't work anymore, you're getting worse! I'm getting too *old*!?"

"Stop playing, you're not old" I try to make light of the situation but the look on her face is telling me that my humorous ways of dealing with shit won't cut it this time.

"I'm too tired Aaliyah, I have my problems and my own family."

"Fuck your family!" Eleni does spoil me but I don't see why should share.

"No Aaliyah, fuck yours!" She snatches the bottle from me, "You *need* to tell the girl what it is. What's not going on in your big head!"

"But you're staying forever so, I don't *need* to tell Mali anything. So, we can stop talking about it now." Laughing it off, not taking in the seriousness of the situation- my situation, at all. Holding up my shot glass, I wait, she pours me another large over spilt shot and repeats the yellow jiff cloth cleaning method then folds and stuffs it into her back pocket.

"Tell her! Tell her everything!" She holds her hands up frustrated with my lack of empathy for myself. "Please…"

"What Eleni!? What!! What should I tell her, that I have fucking traumatic brain damage! That my ex beat the *fucking* shit out of me and my memory lapses over and over and over!? I don't even know what the fuck I'm doing half the time! That I lie, that I make things up and tell stories that have never happened, I mean they could have but who knows? Because I don't know! I know, how about I tell her that I'm scared as *fuck* that one day I'll wake up and forget who the fuck I am all over again! That I'll forget who she is, because I forget everything that I should remember. To lock the door behind me but I don't want to lock the door, I can't lock it! Eleni, I pay someone else to fucking do my job, because I don't remember the things I am paid to do!"

"Aaliyah you can try."

"How can I tell her that the things we have done... I don't fucking remember them! Anything! Fuck no! She'll leave me like just like Delilah... what if I tell Mali I love her but I forget-" I stop abruptly, taking in what I just said... 'love'.

"You won't forget that."

"...No Eleni. Mali is not mine to keep, none of them are. Mali will walk away just like Delilah did with everything I have left. No, I'd rather be alone and feel nothing than feel *any* of that *ever* again! No!"

"She's not *Delilah*; Mali is not her!"

"They're *all* like her! They're all the fucking same, they *all* leave! She'll get tired of me and leave! No one wants me because I'm poison!"

"No, she *will* stay, give her a chance to understand what's happening Aaliyah, please." Eleni heavy handily took my head to her lap, stroking her hands over the side of my face, soothing me while I hold onto her legs releasing the overspill of my emotions as the tears pour out of me like waterworks. Freeing everything I've been keeping bottled up and away, deep in the back of my mind trying to lose it in the mixture of memories and moments.

"I can't! I can't let anyone know. I'm so fucking scared of love. I don't want to wake up alone... again and lost. Mali will leave me, *Delilah* left me. Look at me, I gave her everything Eleni. I'm the one left with the damage. The burns and scars covered up in tattoos to remind myself. My pin number on the inside of my finger, my birth date hidden in my sleeve." I told you I'd tell you more about my tattoos and that's the truth- they keep me from forgetting things I can't hold on to. They're all like that, hidden messages to remind me of who I am.

"But you can get better, take your pills and tell her."

"Eleni, I don't remember what the lines on the fucking street mean, it's all patterns and bull shit! How many times is my car going to get towed before I learn?" Not holding back my tear stream down my face, neck and all over me, time for weakness.

"You have to, she loves you, I know she does. I see it. I see what you don't. I'm here more then what you know. I see it." She doesn't answer me because she knows she hasn't got the answers and neither do I.

"I am not hers to love and she's not mine... none of them are." I repeat myself often.

"Tell her." Eleni repeats her mantra but I haven't changed my mind.

"No, I'm not doing it." The tears begin to stop, no time for weakness "I don't need her to come into my life and I don't need to admit anything to anyone. It's fine. I'm fine. Honestly, I'm fine, it's okay, I don't need any of them Eleni, I have you." Wiping my tears away. Trying to prove to Eleni that I am okay under a slight smile and straightening my composure. I know she's not convinced, if there is one person that knows me inside out, it's her and I can never hide anything from her no matter how hard I try.

Taking my hand in hers, turning her lips inwards she closes her eyes for a few seconds, shaking her head, her bottom lip quivering, tears falling out of tear like her heart is shattered into pieces.

"No." She says softly

"Eleni, what? What is it? What's wrong?" Panicking, my eyes dart all over her, I have never seen her in this state. She's the one that's always holding me together.

"...Nooo!" She wails, "My Aaliyah, my love..." She holds my face, roughly in the other hands, she's always been heavy-handed. "You don't have me. Not anymore!"

"What are you talking about Eleni? Of course, I do."

"I can't be here, with you anymore. I quit my angel… I'm so sorry, I have to go and I can't take care of you anymore. Me staying here is not making you better and if I stay you won't get help."

She gets up from the chair, letting go of my hand, walking toward the door in an instant. Like she thought about leaving, like she was *really* going with her bag beside the door, ready for her to reach and pick up on her exit- no.

"Eleni… what? Are you joking? What do you mean?"

"You can keep my secret bottle for your bad days but I need to go." She tries to break a smile putting on her coat. "I have to go from you, because- you- I love you like my baby but you need love. If I stay here cleaning up and picking you up when you're down, you won't. You and Mali need each other."

"Eleni no! You can't leave. You can't quit on me! It's not even a real job you know that. You don't have to go; I'll look after myself more. I'll even do the dishes and make you coffee but you can't leave." She doesn't stop gathering her things to leave, "You can't leave me? I'll give you more money, I'll hire another cleaner and you can put your feet up, drink mojitos and tell her how to clean." She ignores my pleading and bargaining with her.

"I have to…" She doesn't turn to look at me, she means it… she's really going to go but she can't, I need her to stay- please stay.

"Please Eleni, don't leave me, please I'm sorry. I'll be good. I will, I won't shout at you ever again or leave a mess or come home drunk, please. Don't go, you can't go, please no. Eleni no, don't do this to me." Feeling like a child whose comfort blanket is being ripped from their hands and told they can never have it again. I am not ready, she can't go! Trying to get Eleni to take off her coat, pulling and tugging on her to stay.   "I'll pay you more please; please, don't. You can't leave me. Please, you can have more days off paid. Eleni please, no." Shuddering, screaming, balling my eyes out watching her getting closer to the door of my apartment. Pulling her coat off her arms holding onto it.

"Aaliyah let me go." She walks to the door, speaking quietly. Not looking at me, her head hung down crying.

"ELENI NOOOO!"

I scream at her and hold my hands over my mouth that are already drenched in my tears. She turns towards me, her little tote bag in her hand and throws one arm around my shoulder. Kissing my cheek over and over again. She kisses my ear by mistake, making the noises around me ring out hearing the sound of my blubbering voice and shattering heart. My chin in her hand she looks deep into my eyes.

"I love you! S*ooo* much! But you tell her. You tell her everything, take your pills and I promise, she will love every part of you," Eleni's tears fall on me. "Even the part that forgets my birthday and puts chocolates out to say sorry but eats it." She laughs a little. I always forgot her birthday and leave her expensive chocolates on the kitchen countertop along with an envelope of money as a *'Sorry I forgot your birthday but I forget everything'* present. But I would always end up eating the majority of the chocolates.

"Please... don't go, I'll die Eleni! I'll be alone and I'll die without you here... you're breaking my heart. I'm sorry, I'll be better. I'll get better, I'll take my pills, just stay, please stay."

Softly spoken holding onto her hand while she places her set of keys in my palm and says nothing else. She removes her coat softly from my tight grasp and turns away from me. All I can do is helplessly watch her walk out of my life. Everything is happening too fast and I can't stop it but it's happening slow enough for me to take in every single detail of this moment I never saw coming- Ever!

"Fine! You want to go so bad then FINE! FUCK OFF! Go on leave! Just like everyone else does! Get the fuck out! You're fired anyway! I'm sick your stupid yellow jiff cloth old arse anyway! You can't do anything right, go on, get out, fuck off!" Screaming, shaking forgetting to breathe in.

She opens the door...

"Goodbye Aaliyah," She digs into her back pocket one last time and takes out my medication bottles and places them on the side.

"Eleni, wait. No please, I'm sorry... please, no. I didn't mean any of that. Stay please stay." Don't forget to breathe- enough, no time for weakness.

This isn't happening, I'm dreaming. None if this is real, it can't be real. This is a lapse, a bad dream. I'll wake up in my bed and it will go away. If I just close my eyes tight and count to ten and I'll wake up and I'll see her putting fresh flowers in the middle of the dining room table- it's not real. It's just a dream. It's just a bad dream. Letting go of her, I stop, stand still and close my eyes-

"One..." My lungs not taking in air, my chest tight- wake up in your bed

"Two..." My legs feeling like jelly, like nothing- she's not leaving you.

"Three..." My legs are numb. Failing to recall that they are attached to any part of my body, giving up. Collapsing to the floor, face buried in my hand hearing the sound of the door click back on its hinge shut with Eleni walking out of my life on the other side. I don't need to open my eyes to know she's gone...

She's never coming back.

17. The Ruthless Reason

"Aaliyah... Aaliyah!"

Snapping out of my daze, daydreaming about something... I think, I don't know, do you? I don't know what I was saying or what happened. Sat in my car, parked up with Tiana in the passenger seat.

"You okay?" Her hand on my thigh, squeezing to get to the attention away from my daze and onto her.

Looking around, figuring out where we are. Parked up, down the road from Blue's place. How the hell did we get here? How long we've been here or how long Tiana has been calling out my name??

"I'm good baby girl, I'm okay." Unbuckling my seat belt, reassuring her with a glimpse of a slight smile.

"Where are we? I thought we were going out?"

"We were...? We are! But, erm... there's something I need to do first." Looking at myself in the mirror, putting on my sunglasses and roughly fixing my hands through my hair.

"Want me to come with you?" She says, about to get out the car.

"No, I'm good." My hand on hers, stopping her from unbuckling her belt, I lean over and kiss of her soft lips.

"Okay, imma wait here."

"Hold onto these." Handing her my car keys, she looks down at them and back at me. Her face asking me *'what the fuck?'* but she says nothing and does what's requested of her, she always did, I like that about her – but I think I've said that before.

"I'll be here." She assures me.

"I know."

Stepping out, leaning up against the side of my car, gathering my muddled thoughts that have been floating around my head for what feels like days, weeks even. Who knows? I couldn't tell you!?

But I know why I am here though…. but I don't know *why* I came? Something must have been telling me to come over here. I guess my mind has been fixated on coming over.

Head back staring at the bright blue sky, eyes squinting sensitive by the brightness coming through my sunglasses and giving everything in sight a tinted brown golden filter. Maybe I should get back in my car and forget coming here… should I go in? No, come on- you've come this far, keep going. Walking away from the car, my hand is the last thing to let go of the cool comforting metal- here I go, wish me luck.

The heat of the sun is beating down on me, dressed in an all-black I don't know what's making me sweat more, the sun or the nerves of my body, anxiety and palpitations. Palms sweating, twiddling my fingers taking baby steps towards the house. Gradually, breathing into a state of calm, without a clue of how to say what I want to say or *who* I want to say it to? Am I here to talk to Mali? Am I here to tell her everything or tell Blue? Someone needs to know, because I'm driving myself crazy! Frustrated with keeping all of this crammed in my fucked-up head! Causing me more blackouts then I've ever had. Losing shit, forgetting more, fading out. I'm dizzy and irritated to the fullest. Moving slow as fuck navigating myself through my thoughts and words that I want to say, should and shouldn't say.

Overthinking it all, but how do I tell her? All I have to do is open my mouth and speak, tell her how I feel and tell Blue the truth that I'm sorr… that I didn't mean to hurt anyone but I did mean what I did. I'm lost and selfish and going through changes and fazes, losing patients with myself…

But am I sorry? A genuine apologetic person does not find herself at the home of her lovers' house, about to reveal *all* to anyone who will listen, only to alleviate all her own, very fucked up guilt.

My heart is pounding out of my chest right now! I've never felt anything like *this*. My legs shaking with each hesitant step towards the old rickety gate at the entrance of *their* home, I feel sick, I'm going to be sick... no, I can't do this. You can do this, you can! No time for weakness, come on! Just go in and tell her everything! Tell her that all you want is... the front door opened, why is it open? Sweaty palms pushing it slowly, I step one foot in looking from my left to right at the empty spaces of their home.

"Blue? Mali...You guys home?"
Walking down the hallway to the staircase that turns with the direction of the upper floors, there's this unusual energy. Palm flat, slowly stepping up trailing along the cool surface of the walls.
"Aaliyah, I'm so glad you're here."
"Blue...?"
Blue's slumped in the middle of the staircase with her head buried in her arms and her knees tucked into her chest. She looks so small and helpless, sat there shuddering and crying. Reaching out for her I put my hand on her shoulder.

"Blue, I erm... I need to tell you something." Dismissing the obvious state she was in, she clearly wasn't okay but I came here with something I had to say. And, once I've said it, we can talk about her and hers. Deep breathe in, one- deep breathe out, two...

"She's leaving me." Her lip quivers, her eyes are burning red and vacant, practically choking on her words. Throwing me off, the words I wanted to say left my mind in an instant flash. What do I say now? Standing over her with nothing to say? No words of comfort that she's waiting for, hopelessly gazing at me.

"What?" The only thing I'm thinking and the question I wanted answered for myself.

"I have done *everything*. She said, she said has to go. We got into it, she was going out and I asked where." She wipes her tears away with the wet cuff of her sleeve, talking through tiny breaths in and out. "She said she's done and she has to go. She's packing up her things and I can't watch her leave. What did I do? She said, she told me she doesn't love me, she's in love with someone else! What went wrong, for her to fall in love with another woman? What did I do? She said that she needs her!"

"I…" I opened my mouth but nothing. No words, when I should be saying is *'it's me'*, I am *she*. I am *her* but I don't say a word. I stare at her. I wish I never came here, I want to take several steps back, walk out the house and never look back. How could I? I came here with the intentions to clear my conscious and confess. I am the reason for this emotional state Blue is in, why Mali treats her this way, look at the damage I've caused.

"Help me, what do I do? I don't know what to do to make her stay." She pleads with me and my assistance but-

"I can't, I came here to" I want to tell her "It's m-."

"I can't say goodbye, not yet… please."

Turning away from her, knowing all too well how it feels to be forced to say goodbye to someone when you're not ready for them to leave and you can't stomach the pain when they' re gone.

Closing my eyes trying to see how I wanted this to be. I came here for a whole different reason, for my own happy ending maybe. But how can I ever live with *this*, watching this girl fall apart because of a lost love? So fucking torn, I could try and save this 'love' but I want this 'love'. I want Mali to be my love.

"Stay there, okay…"

Stepping up over Blue's limp body, I follow the rest of the stairs up to the top floor where *their* room is. Gathering new thoughts and new words, ignoring the anxiety because now my plan has changed. The whole reason I am here has changed. Contemplating in the open doorway, watching as Mali places things in her bag. She hasn't noticed me standing here whilst she talks to herself, double checking to herself out loud that she's got this and that. Quietly stepping into the room, I lightly close the door behind me. Both arms behind me resting my sweating palms flat on the wooden door, fingers busy twitching. I clear my throat and Mali stops, setting her eyes on me, she smiles widely. That smile, I swear it does things to me but... I have to step away, I have to let it go... I have to do what is right

"Aaliyah? I was gonna call when I was packed up." Surprised and happy she rushes over to me, holding me tight- *everything* I want. She kisses me but my mouth tightens, not accepting the taste of her lips. One hand on her cheek, I smile at her then look away. All I want, is to run away with her, how am I supposed to put this? How do I do this? - do it gently, don't hurt her, you've hurt enough people in your life.

"What are you doing?" I ask softly

"I'm leaving. I should have done it time ago, I'm sorry. Eleni said I need to be there for you. And I've been thinking about the right thing to do... *we* are the right thing to do." Letting go of her, I walk over and sit on the bed; my eyes follow her movements as she walks over to me- I'm going to miss the way she moves. Closing my eyes, deep breath in

"Mali... I don't need you... you need to stay. Here... with Blue..."

"No." She turns to me "No, I'm not. I'm coming with you!"

"I'm not an option Mali! *We* are not an option! You can't do this, not like this."

"But I'm done pretending, I'm done with the games and the back a forth."

"This is going to kill her Mali, you can't do this to her."

"I won't say shit. I'll jus' leave, I won't tell her it's you, she never has to know. I'll never see her again. You can still be friends and I'll stay away. All I want is you!"

"Mali, it's not that simple." I wish it was "She's going to fall apart without you."

"And what about me? I don't want to stay. We can leave now, together. Jus' say you're dropping me off somewhere, I come to yours and we can jus' be." She sat down beside me, excited about her well thought out plan she thought was coming into action. And so it should… but it can't.

"No." I can't believe I'm about to say this to her- breathe "I don't want to be with you, I've never wanted to be with you." Fighting to say the words and mean it. She stares at me her mouth wide open. I can't do this and look at her.

"I don't mean anything to you?" She sounds so crushed, "But I want to be with *you*." She holds onto my hands, I pull them away from her grasp- I don't want to let go… I have to let go.

"…I don't want you… what makes you think I want you?" Head feeling heavy, telling hr lies with a straight face. The last thing I need right now is another *fucking* blackout! Get. It. The. Fuck. Together Aaliyah! My body feeling too heavy, my head feeling too light to get up and move at all, oh fuck staring at her… all I can see is the floor. I… she…

"Aaliyah, I love you." Hearing her voice in the darkness. Blinking a thousand times. My eyes focusing on Mali peering over me. Hearing crying in the faded distance, my senses struggling to revive from the conscious confusion of my surroundings. I don't know what's happening? How did I get here? What?

"Fuck…"

"Did you hear what I said?" Releasing her tight grip but still holding me up from tumbling over. The crying in the distance becomes louder. Blue? That's Blue? Is she okay?

"Let go of me, please. I don't want you." My head, thumping like crazy. Struggling, she restrains me effortlessly. Where the hell is Blue? I need to fix this and stop Mali speaking about 'us' and 'we' and 'love'- did she say she loves me? This is all too much, too sudden.

"Aaliyah, you don't mean that, I know you don't."

"I need to go, let me go." Managing to get her off of me successfully. Standing on my own, my hands on my head swaying; waiting for everything around me to stop fucking spinning so my body can take a step out the door and leave.

"No Aaliyah?" Holding onto me, again as I sway from side to side. She takes steps with me. "Wait a sec!?"

"Mali, move!" I attempt to push away from her.

"That's not what you want and you know it! Tell me…" Her hands wrapped around my waist. Closing my eyes remembering her touch, here on my body at another time. Another memory? What day is it? My lips want to move and tell her, I want her but my heart is pounding.

"Tell you what?" Giving up and flopping my arms to the side looking up at the fucking red ceiling. I hate this fucking place! "What! What! WHAT DO YOU WANT FROM ME!?"

"Tell me you love me too for fuck sake!" She screams back. "Tell me and I don't care

I'll tell her everything because I love you! Not her, jus' tell fucking tell me Aaliyah." Taken back by the look in her eyes. "I love you Aaliyah! Not her! I'm sick of hiding this and walking around like we are nothing! We have something! You know we do, no one has a connection like we do. The shit we've been through."

"Stop, no we don't!"

"Don't you dare walk out of here without telling me the truth? If you don't want me fine! But admit you love me and let me close this chapter. But I am not staying here!"

I knew what I wanted before I saw Blue, what am I supposed to do now? I'm a mess, my head, my heart, my everything! I'm the one to blame. Mali's arms are around me and I don't want her to let go. Our energy… she's not like anyone I've ever known but I have to save her from me… I have to save Blue. There is no other option. Holding her face once more, the effect she has on me is fucking unreal. Looking in her eyes, I can make it a habit to stare in them all day. How do I say, 'I'm sorry'? How do I say goodbye to her? How do I walk away? She can't love me…? I'm not ready for all of that information… love?

"Mali... I..." Struggling to speak. "I..." Say it! Tell her what you're feeling, say it.

She kisses me stopping any words from leaving my mouth; the way she kisses me, the way she holds me, the way she touches me. She's right, no one has a connection like this.

"If you're not going to say it, don't say anything." She knows I have to go and she doesn't want to hear it.

"What the *fuck* is going on!?" Blue appeared behind Mali. Looking at Mali's hands around me, holding me in a way she has never seen before. Caught staring into Mali's eyes, a way she has never seen me before. I look at Blue, then back at Mali... this feels like the last time. For a split second I forgot, I have to say goodbye, I have to end this.

"Nothing!" Removing Mali's hands from me, I push past the both of them.

"Aaliyah?" Blue stumbles back from my force "What the fuck?"

"You win." I say to Blue, she has no idea what I am talking about. But the game is over.

"Aaliyah, wait." Mali overlooking Blue, ready to get me and my attention again. Pointing in Mali's direction I stare at her for a few seconds before I say...

"... stay away from me!" Running down the stairs, I have to get the fuck out of this house! I have to get away from her! What was I thinking?!

Out the doorway and running down the street towards my car. I couldn't tell her. I can't... I have to go. Blue needs her, Blue loves her and I... it's too twisted to explain any logic from my brain. What if it isn't love, what if it's just all a game? It's not *real* and it's not love. *It's a game* that I started and it has to end. I have to get away- let me go.

"Aaliyah, hold up!" Feeling a tug on my arm, "Wait." Mali runs out in front of me, stopping me and standing with her arms out in surrender. "Hold on stop!"

"What now, just leave me alone!"

"Look at me Aaliyah, please." I'm unable to look, my chin is hovering over my shoulder. All I can do is listen to her broken voice, breaking me "Tell me you love me, I know you're scared but I won't do those things everyone else has done to you. What Delilah did to you, I would never."

"I… I don't love you, I never wanted you." I say not looking at her or in her direction.

"Look me in my fucking face and you tell me the truth! Tell me you never wanted me. Tell me to my face and don't you dare lie Aaliyah!" I can hear her agony, anger and strength in every word. "Don't you dare fucking lie to me! You lie to me and I. Am. Done! I won't chase you!"

"Why won't you just let me go!"

"No! You fucking tell me!"

I pause, lost in the honesty. My mind blinking through memories of 'us' and pausing, taking in a long deep breath- no time for weakness.

Deep breath in… one. Composing all the inner strength I have left… breathe out. Deep breath in… two. Applying my best *'I don't give a fuck face'* I look at her… breathe out.

Deep breath in… three. Ready. Taking steps towards her, filling the gap between our bodies… breathe out.

Holding her in my arms tight; standing tall in my heels over her in socks and no shoes on, running out the house in the panic of me leaving and never coming back. Just tell you're broken and you need her… no… no? You need to go away, let her go. She smells like a tropical fusion of cocoa butter, sweet mangos, diced pineapples and hot smooth chocolate. Fuck me, she smells so damn good!

I have always had this strong sense of smell, heightened by my desire, lust and attraction. I cannot resist a woman who smells amazing! Picking up each individual scent of Mali smelling too damn fucking good. I'm not talking about her perfume or cream. No, I'm talking about the warmth of her natural skin scent taking my thoughts to higher heights. I take in one last time

She shudders in tears, like the time she told me all about her broken past. I don't want to let go of her. I want to take her in my arms, carry her home, place her in the shower, wash away this awful day and never cause her any pain, ever again. Lay in bed beside her until she falls asleep and we could be just what she wants 'us'. How beautiful would that be? No one else would matter. Not me, the things I've done, not the things she's been though, not about choosing me or Blue. No, just Mali.

"I'm so fucking sorry. Sshh." Soft kisses on her neck, I let her go slowly, whispering in her ear clearly "I. Don't Want. You! It was all a game, to see if I could make you leave your woman and I can and now I know... I'm done, game over baby." Strong pout on my lips, arms folded, shoulders shrugged, eyebrow raised and her heart broken. Shattered to pieces as I keep up this pretence of who I am supposed to be- I told you, you don't want to be me.

"Wha-what?" Crushed, her whole body deflated, not expecting to hear me say that at all.

"I'm done with you Mali! You wanted the truth there you go." Shrugging my shoulders again, smiling without care.

"I don't believe you. You can't be this fucking fucked up!"

"Who I am is no longer your issue."

"Issue? You've got fucking issues! I fucking told you I love you. You're poison!"

"So I've been told."

"You heartless bitch!"

"Hey! You *don't* fucking know me! You don't get to judge me, you know nothing! A fraction of what I've been through? So, fuck you Malikah!" Walking away, hearing the fast pace of my heels clipping heavy along the concrete with every step.

"Why the game? Why are you fucking playing me?" Mali caught up to me, standing in front of me once more.

"Because I wanted to, okay! Because it's fucking funny. Because I can! I used you for the *fuck* of it. Look at you, packing bags?! You're so cute, like I would want *you*, come on. You're nothing! You've got nothing!"

I do want you but... you deserve to be loved and happy. I can't give you that. Blue loves you so much and she will give you everything- I have to let you go.

"You're lying!" She shook her head not wanting to believe in anything I'm saying.

"Watching you go back and forth leave her, don't leave, leave her. Oh Hun, I don't care where you go but you're not coming with me, I don't want you. It's not fun when the risk has gone."

"So, what? This is it, yeah? You don't want me, no?"

"Nope." Crossing my arms and tilting my head at her. I answer without hesitations as my heart rips in my chest. "I Never did!"

"After *everything*? You've been messing with my head? This can't be some game. I know you're fucked up... but fucking hell, what's wrong with you?!"

"You really want to know?"

"Yes! For fuck sake! TELL ME!" She shook.

"People walk around hurting each other every damn day! Lying, cheating pretending to love and be people they aren't, just to get the attention of someone they are interested in. Using people to get to where they want to be and not giving a fuck! I have scars *all over* my fucking body from being kicked in the head constantly fighting every day and being walked all over! Do you have any idea what it takes to survive a toxic love? To lose everything you were? To watch them walk away, leaving you with nothing! Beating and burning the shit out of you so bad that you lose your fucking mind!? There is no survival, you don't survive. It kills you. *She* left me!! I do fucked-up shit and it's okay because I can forget! Can't feel what you don't know? So, I told myself, no one will *ever* do that to me *again* and well... if you can't beat them, join them- right?"

"Aaliyah," she tries to hold me hearing my further truth,

"GET THE FUCK OFF ME!"

Feeling myself screaming through floods of tears drowning my face. I push her off of me "Go back inside; unpack your shit and stay! STAY! There is a woman in there that, for some fucking reason, regardless of what you've done, actually fucking loves you!" I look back up at the house, pointing at Blue peeking through the shitty gauze net curtains; window open and hearing every piece of drama down here. "And she will do anything for you, she understands what love is, she gets it and she gets to have you- not me. I don't get to have a happy ending. So, stay the fuck away from me Malikah, I mean it!"

"Aaliyah please. I won't do any of that, I want you."

"Nah, you want the idea of me. Go upstairs and tell her you're sorry. That you made a mistake, it's okay but she made a mistake too. She let Raee'n fuck but that's okay, you're even and it was all my fault, I made Raee'n do it. Tell her it was all me and I'm sorr- I meant it so I'll stay away from you both because the real me will fuck with your head so bad you won't even know who you are, lost in my bullshit. Up there..." I point at the window, Blue reveals herself past the netting, confirming she's listening "...is a woman who needs you much more than I ever will know. Not as a challenge or some sick game but actual *love*. So, go because whatever we had, I am done."

"Done what? You haven't even tried! Why can't we at least give us a go? I know you don't want to walk away. Let me know what it takes to be with you and I'll fucking do it."

"How many times Mali? Don't you get it? No, I don't want you!"

"Aaliyah..." Her face red, eyes clogged with tears while trying to remain emotionless but the tears are starting to fall. Turning away from her. You can do this, let her go and walk away... just give her another gentle push- deep breath in before you speak again.

"Go, tell her about your step daddy and the shit *you let him do to you*. Go on." I laugh, loud and fake, but it was very believable. "You're disgusting Mali!"

"No! I know what you're doing. Stop it! Stop trying to push me away!" Hand on the side of her head, covering her ears.

"Come on Mali, you wanted the man's baby and you thought I was fucked up?! Wow! Really?! I'm glad he kicked it out of you! What the fuck were you thinking wanting to keep it!?"

"Why are you trying to hurt me?" It's working! She's stepping away.

"Because *this* is who I am baby!"

Turning to step away for the last time, she tugs on my arm stopping me, again. I have had enough; she needs to stay away from me. My arm raises, extending out, punching her in the face- hard! My fist hurt instantly, fuck! I didn't mean to, I didn't know what else to do to get her off of me. I just want to get her to stay away from me but she's not listening or taking in anything I'm saying.

"I said stay the fuck away from me! Fuck Mali! Why don't you listen to me? I didn't want to do that, fuck!" I stood over her.

Blue is away from the window and standing close to us. She stares at me. One glimpse, that's all it took... that glimpse is telling me I've done enough and to back the fuck up. I know, she knows it's me, that I'm *the someone else*. The love that's been interfering with *her* love.

"Come on, come inside. I got you babe." Blue bends down to her woman on the ground frail, in the foetal position but keeps her eyes locked on me. Consoling Mali, gently and trying to calm her. Mali sobbed and Blue knows it was me, all this time; the ruthless reason why her woman would always choose to leave without telling her a destination. The texts that made her wonder who it is making Mali smile at her phone that she would tell her it was 'no one'. Tormenting her brain trying to remember Mali's passwords to her phone, waiting for the moment she could go through her phone but there was never a clue to what she had done or been doing. Those seconds she touched me for longer than what she needed to. The extra attention I would get that Blue thought was an understanding of each other's' personalities. Telling herself she's crazy, it's all in her head, nothing is going on. But it was right there in front of her face… a place far too obvious to consider.

"TIANA!" I scream, storming towards the car. Sunglasses back over my eyes, switching my hips with each step, walking like the boss bitch I *know* I am- fuck all this emotional shit!

"What was all that about?" Tiana asks stood by my car, pointing in the direction
of the drama that was taking place in the middle of the street.

"Stop asking questions, get the fuck in the car and drive!"

"What?" She asks another question, I open the passenger door and sat in the car. I am in no state to drive, my head is hurting. I can't see straight, this is all bullshit! I don't want to feel any of this, I want to forget it all.

"Drive! The *fucking* car!"

"Your car?"

"Do you see another car?!"

"Who the fuck is this?" Mali charging out of nowhere towards me, shoving me on my shoulder - shit!

"For fuck sake Mali, enough! What more can I say to make you believe me?"

"Who the fuck are you?!" Mali turns to Tiana.

"Me?" Tiana's attitude locked, loaded and ready, the last thing I need right now
is these two going blow for blow.

"Yes. you!" Mali steps closer to us.

"Don't worry about who I am. I'm the one woman who's getting in the car, that's
who the fuck I am!"

"Really Aaliyah? This kid, really?"

Mali could barely speak. Shaking her head at who she *thought* was my choice. Right now, all I want to do is go home. I'm too unable to keep this going or explain that Tiana is just another woman I use at my own disposal, disregarding her feelings and her relationship.

"Tiana! Get in the car." Tiana walks to the driver side, staring out at Mali each step of the way.

In the car, I throw my head back on my seat. Holding up my hand before Tiana could ask me another question, feeling her looking at me and wondering what the fuck is going on. But I have no answers, nothing to say, I don't want to speak, my thoughts stuck on if I doing the right thing? If you love someone, then you let them go and all that bullshit, right?

"Aaliyah! Aaliyah!" Mali keeps screaming my name over and over. Banging on the passenger side window. I can see her hurt and pain through the window but she can't see me through the heavy tint. "Don't do this, please." I don't want to do this but it's the right thing to do- it has to be.

"Aaliyah, look I don't know what's going on but… talk to her man. She looks pretty bad" Tiana turns to me, reluctant to start the car, feeling empathy for Mali.

"Just! Drive!" I spat coldly.

"You sure..."

"JUST FUCKING DRIVE TIANA, SHIT!!" I reach over and turn the keys to start the engine myself and sit back in my seat. My hand to the side of my head blocking Mali out but I can hear her pleading with me. Tiana nods, puts the car into gear, her foot down and we leave.

I stay watching the reflection of Mali in the mirror crying on the side of the road.

I think I did the right thing? I did the right thing, right? Tell me I did the right thing…Tell me, please.

I should have got out… I should have stayed.

I should have told her… it's too late now

18. The Clouded Blurred Vision

Feelings so deep, I could swim in them for miles and miles into my own abyss of nothing. I want to be numb and not *feel* a single thing inside of my mind or my heart- if I still have one. I mean, I must because this shit fucking hurts too much for me to not have one,

Shoes on my feet, unremoved. Sat sunken into the sofa like dead weight. My shoulders slumped, arms dropped lifelessly by my side, not moving. Depressed and drowning deep diving and riding these currents and waves of emotion. Don't want to move, unable to move, stuck. Trapped trying hard as *fuck* to stop the stupid tears from free falling but the more I stop myself the more the flow keeps on going. So, let them flow, let it go, I've got to let this go.

All I can see is her in everything I do and think and I can't let it go and it won't go away, it won't get out of my head. Up until this point I've never seen the face of a broken heart and it's killing me… the things she said she felt, the things she wanted. I should of just- I feel so stupid, why didn't I say yes, why didn't I tell her. It was the dumbest thing I have ever done, why did I leave her like that and let that be the last memory she has of me?

All I have is something so different prancing around the corridors of my mind… wondering and separating what's real within the thoughts inside of thoughts inside of what I *think* I'm feeling. Could this be love? I think it was? It felt like it but… I'm lost and frustrated because I don't have the answers to any of these fucking questions, I'm asking myself over and over. Is it over?

Why didn't I *just* let her come with me? Tell her to hold onto me and we leave, leading her the way home. Wasn't that the whole point of going over there, to go and get what I want? Which is her, I know it's… *her.*

I'm losing my sanity, slowly going crazy, further into my mental void because I can't decide if it was the right thing to do? Was it the right thing to do? She was never mine to begin with but she brought so much solace to my silent mood.

It wasn't the right thing to do? To leave her and walk away empty handed with nothing to hold onto, no one here. There's never anyone here with me. Just this pain and it hurts so fucking bad and it aches so much more than any scar or kick to the head that I have ever felt. I am in agony! I just want to breathe to close my eyes and wish it all disappears.

The way she looked at me, that torture in her eyes. I know *that look...* too fucking well; I used to stare past my own reflection in the mirror, lost in my eyes, taken away from reality when I lived all of that torture and discomfort and worry of being the one to blame over and over and over again.

Please, stop you're hurting me! I've made Mali feel the same way. That kind of feeling never goes away, trust me. You can try and you can pretend to be okay but you can't escape it. Not when the person you have given your *all* to has made you feel   that   way.

All you can do is keep going and hope that no one sees the poisonous cracks on your broken skin. Hide the pain in the joy and start again, smile and make-believe, tell yourself you're going to be okay... you're going to be fine Aaliyah. What have I *done*? What *did* I do?

Numb again, skin tingling but not really feeling anything; I don't deserve to feel a damn thing!

Time ticking the hours by and by again. Fucked up and confused and I'm somewhere between two hours after midnight again. Shifting, lost and time tumbling from ante meridian to post meridian. Tiresome of my own painful truth, unable to stop thinking about everything I've ever been through. And all the things I've done. About the past, about the present and about the parts I've missed- there's so much I've missed. The legs I've parted and the lips I've kissed. The people I've hurt; dragging them through

drama and chaos, I caused with no thought of care or concern. I didn't care about the women I've dismissed so easily and treated like nothing at all. For what? Because I wanted to but they all allow me to. So why am I acting like *this* is the first time I have done this shit to someone? Why the fuck am I feeling sorry for myself, sitting here playing the victim? Truth is, I am far from being the victim I was anymore. I know this, I am distantly gone from the target of abuse and violence through all of the fighting through these spare memories and placing things correctly that I've misplaced in my mind. What I can remember and what I don't want to remember. My sanity was lost a long time ago, at least I think it was? The trouble is… I know and then   I   don't   know.
To describe it to someone, it's like this; imagine falling down, tripping over but trying to stop yourself. So, you grab onto people and use them to hold you up, to keep you level. Like along the way I stumble but I keep going, not falling all the way but far enough to keep feeling the feeling of falling- catch me if you can.

Trapped, caught thinking of Delilah and that chapter of sweet love misery in my life. All I did was love her and it suffocated me, choked me and damn near fucking killed me.

Ever had someone break your mind, then my heart? Crazy, right? Traumatic Brain something or another they call it. I don't want to acknowledge it anymore, don't take my medication, don't want to see the doctors, don't want no more blood test, scans, shrinks and physiologist anymore! I don't want to see family, correcting me, confusing me and feeling sorry for me. I don't want friends around me, like I said I've known Blue for as long as I can remember- I don't remember when we met or how long I've known her.

This is all amusing to me, Delilah had once told me I would never feel *anything*. She said I refused to use my heart but she was so wrong about that. My heart was full, beating and loving just fine… until the day she left; that *was* the day it came to a halt, beating so low and irregularly, I couldn't feel it anymore, I'm sure it stopped.

I gave her *everything* and she walked out of my life and took my everything with her, leaving behind only fragmented pieces that didn't make any sense to me. Lost in my thoughts of trying to find who I used to be, before she was there. Something we all do when we love someone. We throw ourselves inside of the fire; so hot, so passionate, so zealous. Giving our 'love' one hundred percent of ourselves, not stopping to think, for a second about the effect when the fire dies out. Now, all you're left with is the painful memories of a love scorned, ashes, cinder and third-degree burns. *Literally* in my case, all because I gave too much and didn't know when to stop.

We are so careless with how we love, even though we were taught earlier on about the very thin line between love and hate. Love carefully, don't give them your 'all', save some of you for 'you'. Don't let them leave with your righteous love stuffed in their back pocket like change. keep it and hold onto it tight, protect it, you have to protect it. I didn't do that, I should of- but now *I* have to protect what I didn't then, because it's all I have now.

I had to put me together again and *no one* could have it. Defending it, I had to! I have no choice!

But it's like I had this need and want to prove at least one of the things she had beat into me right. That it's my fault why people walk away and leave, not realising it's *me* disconnecting, detaching, pushing and pulling away anyone who attempts to get close.

I refused to 'love'. No, not anymore or so I tell myself. I told myself I would *never* allow love in or out again. So, I kept pushing and I keep pushing from feeling anything! Destroying myself and wrapping myself securely in *this* person I believe it's okay to be; telling myself I never need to use my heart again. I tell myself a lot of shit...

I used to think my heart would never beat again; beating so low and irregularly, I'm sure it stopped- I forgot what it was like to *feel*. To get overactive butterflies in my stomach or the feeling of my heart skipping all those beats because I forgot the words I wanted to say when 'love' is right in front of me, from the moment I met- she had me.

I'm waiting for *her*, for Mali to arrive and take my hand and lead me to anywhere, where we can waste days together. Just flowing hopelessly in love, submissive and addicted. That's not what I feel, right now this ache in my chest is ripping inside me. I was so wrong and it hurts so much and I can't make it stop. How do I make it stop, someone make it stop. I'm losing- lost? What is this? Make it stop, please...

Punishing myself because I never wanted to use my heart again. It didn't even beat like it used to but now it's beating like it used to, sore, low and irregular. Do I even know what love is? I know what pain is, that's easy, I hurt the people I *force* to be around me? Disregarding so many relationships, murdering feelings, assassinating hearts and moving on swiftly like a savage.

So many fucking hearts and tears from *them* and *theirs* leaving them to face the music of admitting they have been taken over by temptation; deceitful, dishonest, lying and cheating. Hoping to work through it and stay together with the broken-hearted woman that can't be trusted again. Trying hopelessly to rebuild a relationship that will *never* be the same again, irritated by anything their partner does because the feeling of distrust won't leave their skin. No matter how many times they shower it off they can't help feeling sick when touched, because they know their partner touched   someone   else.

And through all pointless petty arguments about stupid small shit, meaning nothing at all but something like;

"Did you do the washing? See, I can't trust you at all?"
"What really, are you serious all of that from dirty clothes?"
"It's more than that, you know I can't trust you!"

But eventually, they'll let go doing what's for them.

Meanwhile, I am nothing but a bittersweet taste of regret. Already on to the next one because it, let's be real, it wasn't my problem.

Unfazed, walking away, saving only myself when *they all* needed saving from *me*.

I'm not playing 'woe is me' this is not a pity party but I don't deserve to love or be loved. If I did love Mali, love wouldn't have done all I have done. I fucked with her head and I wanted to. I knew what I was doing from the start and I didn't care. I don't care. No matter the cost, or the hurt I want what I want. But that's only the shit I do… it's *not* who I am. I know it's not who I want to be anymore but I have to keep going and be this person, I no longer want to be.

I am no different to Delilah and the things she done to me. It's too late for self-revelations now, it doesn't matter, too late. It's done now and it's over - I guess. Can't take it back anything I said. I knew exactly what I was doing. So what if I do love her, I'm a fucking monster! I am poison!

There are so many levels to this and I fucking *knew* what I was doing every step of the way. I did, didn't I?

This stupid head and brain of mine… I can't cope, I'm tired. With all of this, with myself, with what I feel, with what I'm supposed to feel, want to feel, don't know what to feel… leave me alone, go away, please!

***

It is way past stupid o'clock, the sympathy violin orchestrating the pity party has left the building!! And I am turnt up, just me! All alone! The way I *like* it! Am I drunk? Oh abso- fucking- lutely!! Eleni's good bottle of drink in my hand and something else in my cup, I have no idea what's in my cup?

A bitch is fabulous but a bitch is also constantly checking her phone for missed calls, blue ticks, apologies, emails, snaps, dm's, instant messages- anything honey!

Waiting, for Mali to call me, message me, text me, direct message me, private message me, what's app me, slack me, ping me, tweet me, snap me, email me, iMessage me, surprise message me bitch, just call me dammit! So, I can tell you what I wanted to tell you and that I didn't mean any of the shit I said. I was *talking* shit, I always   talk   shit. I was trying to protect you from me, I was trying to do the right thing for once because, well because Blue loves you and I … I'm sorry. I want to tell her I'm sorry… but it's too late, she's gone. And I'm doing the right thing for once!! And letting her go because *that* is the *right* thing to do- right? Right?

I should call, should I call?? No! I am not going to call… no I *refuse* to call her. Maybe I should call. No, I won't. Man, I feel like K. Michelle right now. Let me stop I'm supposed to be focused, I ain't just sitting around, waiting around for her to see my worth. I love her, maybe? Maybe I should call but I'll never call! Aaliyah does not chase people! Aaliyah gets chased!

Hiccupping through my drunk, drinking going around and round and round and round in circled thoughts. Oh, you know I am *not* sober but, it's the only way to stop the voices going over and over and over and over and over-

"It's your fucking fault!"

No, it's not!

"It's always been your fault!"

Shut up! Who's talking? Anyway, where am I chasing her in these sexy heels of mine? Psssh! *Please!* Me? Never! Right now, I can barely walk and you want me to run? Nu-uh! Nope!

…I should go see if she's okay though. I fucked up this time. I hope she's okay. No! Fuck her, does she know *who* I am out here? Fuck her! Fuck all of her! They are lining up to be with me; everyone wants me! They all want this!! They all love ME!

You know what, I am sick of checking if she's gonna call, I'm turning my phone off. No, that's not good enough. Now, how do you get the fucking battery out this fucking bastard phone! Oh yeah… iPhones can't do that, can they? I forgot. I always forget. Sorry, I appear to be… I am waved! Lost in my own damn sauce.

If I throw the phone away from me, I can't check it?

Tossing the phone across my coffee table it tumbles and lands face up. Great, fucking typical! Another gulp from the bottle, another sip from my cup. Ignoring the burning at the back of my throat as the layers of internal lining strip away from the non-stop alcohol. Oh, you know I am *not* sober, it's the only way to stop the voices going over and over and over, wait, I said this already- shit!

This drink wasn't my first choice. No, no, I have managed to finish what was left of three very high percentile drinks and a bottle of red from two thousand and five tasting, sweet like juice over the- I don't know how many days. I lost count, I wasn't counting and I couldn't tell you what day it was. What day is it? I can't tell you? I don't know.

Phone back in my hand- how did it get back in my hand?

Sat down staring at my phone, not going to lie I want it to ring. I want her name flashing across my screen. I wonder if she feels the same? She might be waiting on me to call-

It's funny, that instead of picking up the device we hold in hour hands ninety percent of the day and use it to *communicate*, we would rather *wonder*

"What are they doing…?"

How are they feeling? Hoping they feel some type of way or are doing the same as us. Stuck thinking about what they are going to do, hoping they are hurting just a bit, so that you can feel a little bit better and you don't have to snoop on their social media to see what's up. Asking friends to prey on their Instagram or checking WhatsApp, reading between the lines of riddled sentences, captions and statuses like:

"I should have known." "need some space." "endings are beginnings." "not everything is a loss." "I need me a me." "the distance between dreams and reality is called action." "put yourself on." "focus."

And any other bullshit quotations they have found online mimicking things they've found on their timeline- screenshot, copy and save because *'this me is meee!'*.

Don't you dare act like you haven't got at least *fifty* white images with black centred text, storing them like collectible cards, waiting for the right emotional or motivational moment to arise and upload that bitch online or to use as a caption?? Don't make me check your phone!? Gone are the days you used to write in your diary

"Dear Aaliyah, today was a bad day dot dot dot"

Now it's, let me caption this with emoji's and tell the world… Sh! No-body cares! I cannot focus, what was I saying. I'm never going to find my peace of mind, only pieces. Man fuck my pride, I take it all back! There's no way I can take it back. Call her, no don't call her, you better call her, you know I can't call her. She's probably terrified of me and of taking a chance on me. I mean, would you call me, would you want to be with me? Nah, I'm a liability; I need to come with a warning disclosure:

"Warning! Fucking with Aaliyah leads to severe side effects:
Will shatter your heart, fuck with your mental and leave you broken,
abandoned, confused and destroyed.
Approach with caution.
Very addictive take three times a day"

Look at me, checking my phone *a-gain*, like some fool who didn't just break someone's heart and shatter her emotionally. She isn't going to call! What is wrong with me? Everything! Standing up, letting the phone fall to the floor, stomping on it over and over and over. There!! Problem solved, now the screen is smashed to fuck and I can't see anything at all. But I'm not satisfied. When have I been satisfied? Am I insatiable? Can I *ever* feel content? Will I ever be happy?

Do I want Mali, like *actually* want her, or do I *want* the idea of her? What if I get what I want... maybe I won't want her anymore? Does that make sense? Something always looks good when it's someone else's and there's a level of risqué. But when they become yours it's all meh, okay, I guess. But *now,* I want her and I really can't have her, maybe that's making me want her more. Maybe this isn't even love because... because... I haven't figured it all out yet.

I do that a lot; I take things and I fuck them up and put them back expecting them to be okay. What I am trying to say is, what if I get her and then I don't want her anymore?

Please stop!

Unable to rest these thoughts dancing around my head, so I dance with them. Slowly swaying my hips from left to right. Then right to left, practically naked as usual with my heels and one of *her* t-shirts falling big and baggy against my body offering me some kind of something.... comfort?

She had a white fitted tee on the day I laid my eyes on her and that smile, not knowing I'd feel like this.

My Mali... but she's not mine, she's never been and never will belong to me. Not now, not after how I handled her. I want her to be all over me giving me love, loving me again, holding me again.

Closing my eyes, I can feel her arms right here holding my waist, dancing with me- oh Mali, what have you done to me...

...I couldn't even tell you how many days past since Eleni left me; all I can tell you is that the flowers on my dining room table have wilted from the brightness they once were to a dead dank dying dark brown. Petals have fallen off the stems onto the dining table and the smell coming from the water was far from pleasant. It didn't bother me though; nothing matters and it's never going to be the same.

They look funny though, dying slowly, probably dead. The whole apartment looks funny, it's so empty but when you really think about it, it always has been. All this stuff and things of no value, have no real value because it's empty, like me, there's nothing in here with any purpose at all.

I mean, why is my sofa so big when it's only me who sits on it? Why does the table have placement plates laid out when I don't entertain people here and why have I spent so much fucking money on art? Paintings with big blobs of abstract bullshit that a child could have painted for less. I could have painted them, I could have done them all and showed them to one of my old therapists and head doctors and asked them what the fuck *they* see when they look at it.

Always asking me "so how does that make you feel?" it makes me feel like I've wasted my money for an hour appointment each week, being asked 'how I feel' when they are the ones with a degree or qualification and are *supposed* to tell *me* what I am feeling. Asking me what I see with blobs of paint on white laminate cardboard. Want to know what I see? I'll tell you what I see. I see rare beauty of a love lost, internally fighting defensive daemons in her head telling her it's her fault when it's not. All she wants is love but won't let anyone get close, except this one time- almost, but everybody knows almost doesn't count.

On the floor, head back going through phases and stages, looking for someone to find me here alone, in this empty space I created. Vacant, only memories and moments dancing in the clouded overpowering puffs of cigarette smoke above my head. I haven't even seen Mali since, since the day I ruined our lives. I don't know when it was but there was a time? There was a time when everything was okay and it all made sense.

I haven't left the apartment or answered my phone or taken my medication. I'm not okay, I am out of my mind or having a prolonged outer body experience, looking back on who I am.

My house phone wouldn't stop ringing. So, I dragged the phone the fuck out the wall and now it's laying in pieces on the floor but now, at least it's stopped ringing. Forgetting how to silence it, my brain failed to coordinate my hands to locate reason and deal with it calmly and my drunk inner voice was telling me to:

"Fuck. It. Up Sis!"

So, I did. And it smashed. And when it hit the floor and stomped on it. Well then, the drunk me thought,

"Go on! Smash something else girl!"

And then I was like,

"Alright! Maybe smashing something else up in here will make me feel better."

And for that split one second, I felt myself smiling. That sound of things hitting the wall was so fucking satisfying! But once the noise ended and my smile faded, this need to smash something else came over me, then another thing and another after that.

Now, I have broken pieces worth thousands scattered across what used to be my apartment floor. I wanted to throw them so, I did! They're mine and so is the phone. However, as dramatic as my life is, it is *not* a movie, I am *not* an actress and there is *not* a film crew to come and clean this shit up! No, no, just me and let's *not* overlook the fact that I tried to murder my iPhone a few days ago, which is now sat plugged in, on the charger, falling apart and taped together. I am unable to answer to everyone's and anyone's calls and texts anyway but I wanted it on. I guess I want to know *if* someone out there actually cares about me or is trying to call or get through but the phone wasn't making a sound, only lit up through a cracked black ink screen and brown tape.

My phone going off again, no sound; a fucked up off-beat dying vibrate kind of like my heart. Barely beating but beating so low and irregularly, I'm sure it stopped- I forgot. Ignoring my phone and my heart laying on my back, sprawled out across the floor of broken pieces, I light another cigarette. Lost count of how many I've had but my chest is tight and weighty, trying to deal with my constant inhaling of nicotine and tobacco.

Blood-stained hands and cut palms. See, I attempted to be my own 'clean-up committee' crew. Picking up glass and pieces of what used to be my *most* expensive sculpture with my bare hands. And well, shards of glass cutt my hands, struggling to put it back together. Maybe… I should've started with putting myself back together and none of this would have happened.

Looking at my palms, feeling the glass splinters linger in my skin, like an unwanted ex-girlfriend. You can't see them but you can feel them and you know they're there, somewhere; you can't get them out. So, you scratch and dig and pick at the surface hoping they'll go away but some remnants stay embedded in your skin, reminding you every now and then when something is too sensitive to touch.

Throwing another empty cigarette packet into the pile of boxes building up. Music blasting, a 'heartbreak hotel' playlist. Playing the best break up ballads and slow love-sick, love songs on repeat. The apartment rattled from the bass and it feels so good surging through my body, feeling this soothing sensation on my back through the floor. Secluded and disconnected from the world, lost in my own world, not wanting *any*one *any*where near me. Well, apart from *her* but it's all too complicated to comprehend and she's never going to be where I want her to be so… I have to let her go. There's no other choice, it doesn't matter '*if*'. Can't submerge in love, can't immerse myself in her love, so I've got to save myself, protect myself, let go and get out of love.

Sinking in my thoughts, easily drinking away my problems, floating in my own clouds of smoke and desolation. Inhaling my emptiness, laying here clutching Eleni's bottle in my hand and drinking from it with her yellow jiff cloth wrapped around my bloodiest palm. Trying to find the scent of Eleni hidden within the yellow fibres of the soft cloth concealed with disinfectant and other cleaning products. I can almost find her scent but she's hard to seek her out over the smell of tobacco on my lips, drink on my taste buds and the constant echoes of voices running through my head exhausted by them all. Unable to silence them, undecided but I can hear them all… everyone is talking all at once:

Raee'n telling me how poisonous I am. Eleni telling me she loves me but has to leave me. Blue constantly crying- everyone is so loud, shh a *minute*! I need to hear what Mali is saying. Speaking in circles, saying the same shit she was trying to say… I didn't listen. Why didn't I listen? I don't want to listen; she doesn't have to speak or say a word. There's nothing left to say but the circles keep turning, voices and thoughts keep going and going. The only way I can block the voices out of my head is by grabbing the neckline of her t-shirt on my body, holding it up to my face, right under my nose and breathe deep breaths in and out.

Her tropical deep dreamy fusion of cocoa butter, violets and sweetness along with the warmth of her natural skin scent. All the fragrances reminding me of her when she holds me. Eyes shut as tight as possible, trying to clutch onto the clouded visions of what we were but her face is distorted. I want to see her. I need to see her, I need to tell her everything! She needs to know; she has a right to know.

Where do I start; how do I start? I am going out of my mind. I am a recovering, undercover over lover, recovering from a love I haven't gotten over. Maybe I should be on my own but I don't want to be alone.

Repeated emotions bouncing from one thought onto the other, insanity reasoning with anxiety and overthinking bargaining with my emotional instability. I am the visual representation of 'a mess'.

"FUUUUUUUUUUCK!!!" Make it stop, please.

My temples pulsating, beating and banging, holding the side of my head. Another painful sip, the drink scolding my thoughts, my throat and setting me free from the voices- relieving in the silence, for now.

I can remember *some* little things, not much. This one-time Mali overslept, we woke up in the morning beside each other, she held me close. She should have jumped up and left out in a hurry but she stayed with me in her arms, I was wrapped in the essence of her. Who needs her? Not me I'm fine! On my own... *I love her... maybe.* I think, I do not need her, *I need her.*

Laying here looking like the *ultimate* 'side chick'. Let's be honest that's all I've ever been to anyone, some side snack. I'm just very good at convincing myself and them that I was way more than that. Decorating it with excitement, promiscuity and heated intimacy. All I'm good at, is fucking people then fucking off. Fuck it! She needs to be with me.

Where's Eleni? I need her to help me up so I can go get *my* Mali. But I don't know where she's been, a week or so has gone but my flowers need changing and the place needs a clean! Look at the mess! Where is she, what does she think I pay her for? She knows the flowers need to be changed, she knows she has to help me, I can't keep track without them.

"Eleni!" Calling on her...waiting for her to come. "ELENI!"

She's not coming, she's gone away. No one's coming, I've done this! Played too many fucking games. I *am* the product of my own actions; my own doing and I deserve to be on my own. Alone.

Pretending that I love my solitude when I hate it, I hate being alone. I don't want to be all alone here, I can't bear the emptiness of it all but here in these walls, I've convinced myself I'm okay. Struggling to fill the emptiness with my love of things… like this and that in an attempt to feel whole on my own. No one wants to be on their own but, if no one is here then no one can leave and leave you behind, or let you go. You can't be content with solitude and being alone if you're lonely- it's not the same thing.

Clouded visions, wanting to hear whispers of someone calling out my name through the open spaces, someone to take care of me.

Needing to see all corners of the rooms of my home. Scared and hidden from the darkness of my memory of what Delilah did to me. I have to see the light, no blinds, big windows. Open spaces and *no* locked doors, please don't lock the door, I want to leave. I want my mum, let me go, please Delilah.

"Eleniiiii! Pleeeease!"

Weeping like a child without any tears left, howling and frail with my hands over my face. Tears mix with my bloody palms, leaving blood stains on my face. Waiting desperately for Eleni to place her hand on my back and to tell me that I am going to be okay. To feel that warmth and comfort of a human touch on my skin. To know that she's there, I need her here, I can't do this alone. Who's going to help me on bad days like this, when I can't function, can't move and can't get make my heart work?

She's gone away… She's not coming. Tell her to come back- *please*. Tell her I'm sorry and I didn't mean to shout at her or hit her. I have no control over this emotional roller coaster that I can't get off. All I know is all I've got and it's… I fucked up! I fucked up!

It's so hard not to think of anything to do with Mali, she's *only* one person and she's staying on my mind, I didn't say goodbye and we didn't close the chapter, so there's no closure in anything we ever were. Maybe she's done with me. No stop, stop, stop, STOP! I cannot be this broken. Stop thinking about her just stop! Pull yourself the fuck together, you do not have time for this! I need to tell myself, I am *not* going to think about her.

I am *not* going to think about her calling my phone, ringing over and over again waiting for me to pick up. To tell me she's coming over, she can't stop thinking about me too and she needed to hear my voice, like I need to hear hers in my ear; causing my skin to rise in tight goose bumps, running over every inch of my body. I am not going to think about her in an Uber on her way over, watching the buildings pass by through the dark window waiting for the driver to pull up to my building.

I am *not* going to think about her arriving, looking up at my building then back at her phone as she tries to get through to me again but she doesn't give up. I am *not* going to think about her buzzing the buzzer *not* being able to get in, calling my phone again and anxiously waiting for someone to exit the building so she can slip past the closing doors.

I am *not* going to think about her making her way up the stairs two at a time in a rush to see me.

I am *not* going to think about her walking down the hall, standing outside my door hesitating to knock, gathering her words.

I am *not* going to think about her raising arm, knuckles close to my door getting ready to...

"KNOCK KNOCK!!"

Mali! She's here! She came! She's here? She's come for me, she's here. Knocking over the remains of the bottle onto the floor, not caring that it's pouring onto my shaggy grey rug. Struggling to jump up and find my feet, stumbling trying to run towards the door, fixing my hair, myself and my face. Wiping away the dried spots of blood and wet tears with the back of my hands. I think I forgot to take a breath, so excited. Grabbing the door handle, swinging it open so fast and forceful, it hit the wall and bounces back a little but I stop it by bumping it with my body.

"Can you keep the music down *please*?"

Wait, what? Where is she and what the fuck is my old arse fuck neighbour doing at my doorstep? Looking at me like I'm crazy when she has a bright grass green fluffy dressing gown wrapped around her old, short and stumpy body. The fuck does she want? I didn't even hear what she said. She's old, white, miserable and lonely. So, she probably said something about turning my music down.

Yes, it's loud... so!? You try drowning out fifteen voices and flashbacks in your head.

I look her up and down, while leaning against my doorframe. My 'no balance' self is trying hard not to slide my dumb arse down it. Holding myself up with the very little energy I have left in me from scrambling to the damn door excited, for no reason. Thinking for a second that the law of attraction actually worked in my favour.

I visualised my door knocking and it's this old bitch, not my woman! The fuck?!

"What do you want?" My words slurred, scowling at her.

"Will you turn it down!" She huffed and puffed, making me giggle.

"Do you know what time it is?" Squinting at my watch, holding it so close to my face, barely able to make out the hour or minutes. Pointing at my watch, my wrist still held close to my face. She has no right to bother me before eleven p.m.

"Well, it's been going on for days now. I cannot hear my television, I'm missing my programs." She attempts to state her case, holding onto the opening of her ugly dressing gown. Stepping back, regretting she *ever* came to my door. All wound uptight because she can't hear her stupid soap dramas and sip her tenth cuppa tea in peace- Oh, boo hoo Ethel!

"Well I, Well I," mocking her voice and pulling her faces. "Get. The. Fuck away from my door, before YOU end up *missing*!" Shoving a bloody palm in front of her face, her eyes open wide peering over my shoulder at what probably looked like a murder scene. But the only thing dead in there, is my heart.

She waddled her fat arse away, quickly down the building corridor. Slamming my door shut, marching back into my apartment and my spot of misery and self-pity, turning my music *all* the way up! You thought it was loud before, well hold onto your dressing gown Ethel because the volume of this music is about to get real!

Dancing with myself *by* myself. Unable to keep my eyes open, drifting back off to the interrupted vision of Mali on the back of my eyelids. Smiling, I can feel her here, her hands on my body.
Oh Mali, are you okay? Do you miss me? I miss you. Do you want me? Do you love me?

"I'm not supposed to love. I don't know how to tell you... I think, I think I just might have fallen in love you with you. But I'm so fucking scared of you... I'm terrified you'll hurt me and I can't feel all of that again.... I'll die."
Visualising her on me, close behind me. Arms over me, feeling her breathing gently on the back of my neck. Moving with me to the rhythm of the music, lost again. Causing my skin to rise again in tight goose bumps again; running over every inch of my body. Starting from my ankles, working their way up my legs, like her hands stroking me, tickling the inside of my thighs.

"That feels nice." I wish she was here, touching me, dancing with me.

"Knock, Knock, Knock!!!"

Opening my eyes, back to the reality of my surroundings that I have destroyed. The image of Mali faded again, floating away with my mind's deception and alcohol intake, drunk as fuck lost in too much sauce. For. Fuck. Sake! Urgh! I am not opening the door to that old bitch, she can kiss my pussy and the bass vibrating through her apartment, which the council is *probably* paying for with her old pension scheme self. I paid for this!! All of this! This is mine! Ain't no old BITCH telling me what to do! No!

"KNOCK, KNOCK, KNOCK!!!"

I swear, I'll kill her! If she keeps fucking disturbing me! She *will* end up missing, for real and no one will find her. Stamping towards the door slowly, concentrating on placing one foot in front of the other; lightheaded trying to keep myself up. I. Am. About. To. Lose. My. Shit! *Who* does she think she is? Banging on the door loud, like *I* owe *her* something!
I can't concentrate, I can't see straight.

"What? What! WHAT!!!" Eyes closed, body feeling fragile, I am about to break into a thousand pieces with a single tap. The annoyance of being disturbed making me shake, I want to be left alone but I don't want to be all on my own. Neck stretched forward, hands out, fists balled up. Frustrated and irritated as fuck! Because I had her, even if it was only for a split second. She was mine and she wanted to come with me but I didn't know then what I know now. I want to take it all back, I don't want Blue to have her, I don't want anyone to have her, I want to choose her and now I'm falling into nothing- with nothing and no one to have and to hold. Tears forcing past closed eyes, uncontrollable shaking from *every-thing*! My throat tight, barely able to speak- delicate. From the lack of sleep, the lack of food, the constant confusion of my life and my mind; full of voices that won't stop! Thoughts racing up and down my mind, they won't go away. Lost in *who* I am, who I was and who I want to be. It hurts *sooo* much. My lungs tired, my chest tight, like I can't breathe. I can't breathe. Wishing that every breath that I take she was here taking it with me. Knowing that I've done the wrong thing, this pain in my chest from what I feel. This *is* a love and loss all at the same time, torturing myself because I'm so scared... what have I done?

"What do you want from me…?" My lips quivering, my head hung low.

"*You*, Aaliyah…"

"*Wh-what…?*" Words barely spoken, soft, frail.

Tightening my eyes at the voice I'm hearing entering my system, ringing through my ears. Lifting my head, opening my eyes, confused by the bright light and the distorted double vague vision of the person stood inches away from me. Blurred blinking through my clogged imagination, tears and hopes of who I want it to be here saving me. Is this reality, I could be day dreaming again, imagining things I want again. Asking myself if I'm sleeping or awake? Please let it be in this time I want to be saved from myself.

Trying to get a clear sight of *who* it is in front of me. Her arms held wide open; my knees buckle and decline, what the fuck? Catch me!

"I got you…"

Is this all a fabrication or is she really here? Is *this* really Mali? She calls out my name again asking me if I'm okay. As her silhouette blurs into the darkness, I see right before a blackout- not now, please. Feeling myself falling forward, I hear the voice again.

"I got you…" The voice isn't recognised in the faded darkness surrounding me. Feeling her against my fallen limb body. Catch your breath, breathe! She wraps her arms around me, my arms flop around her neck; effortlessly she lifts me up, like a tiny broken princess. She feels different… I inhale her deeply, wanting that tropical deep dreamy fusion of cocoa butter, violets and sweetness. Along with the warmth of her natural skin scent but something is different… something is not the same.

"Mali…?"

"Whose Mali"

I know *that* voice, no? It can't be. No, how did she?

"…Delilah?"

"Peek-a-boo baby."

For the people we used to be... and for the people we are becoming

- Growth

www.lmleoni.com
Tsunami Ink Publishing's TM
Published in 2019 Copyright. Liyah Mai Leoni.

Printed in Poland
by Amazon Fulfillment
Poland Sp. z o.o., Wrocław